The Winter Agent

GARETH RUBIN

PENGUIN BOOKS

PENGUIN BOOKS

UK | USA | Canada | Ireland | Australia
India | New Zealand | South Africa

Penguin Books is part of the Penguin Random House group of companies
whose addresses can be found at global.penguinrandomhouse.com.

First published by Michael Joseph 2020
This edition published by Penguin Books 2020

001

Printed and bound in Great Britain by Clays Ltd, Elcograf S.p.A.

A CIP catalogue record for this book is available from the British Library

ISBN: 978–1–405–93063–5

www.greenpenguin.co.uk

MIX
Paper from
responsible sources
FSC® C018179

Penguin Random House is committed to a
sustainable future for our business, our readers
and our planet. This book is made from Forest
Stewardship Council® certified paper.

The item should be returned or renewed by the last date stamped below.

Dylid dychwelyd neu adnewyddu'r eitem erbyn y dyddiad olaf sydd wedi'i stampio isod.

BETTWS

Newport
CITY COUNCIL
CYNGOR DINAS
Casnewydd

To renew visit / Adnewyddwch ar
www.newport.gov.uk/libraries

By the same author

Liberation Square

To Hannah, for adding the colour. And to my grandfathers, Bert Rubin and Charles Barr, who landed on the beaches of Normandy on 6 June 1944.

'In wartime, the truth is so precious that she should always be attended by a bodyguard of lies.'

– Winston Churchill

This book is inspired by real events

PART ONE

CHAPTER I

Individual security
The agent, unlike the soldier, who has many friends, is surrounded by enemies, seen and unseen. He cannot even be certain of the people of his own nationality who are apparently friendly. The agent must, therefore, remember that, like primitive men in the jungle, he has only his alertness, initiative, and observation to help him.

– Special Operations Executive manual for new recruits: 'How to be an Agent in Occupied Europe', 1943

8 February 1944

Marc Reece straightened the black woollen jacket that lay on the counter like something abandoned to the bitter winter outside. He traced his finger over the four Bakelite buttons, up the machine-made seam that strained as if the wearer had put on weight since it had first been fitted, past the stiff, finely turned lapels, and on to the wide collar where two silver lightning bolts formed a pair of letter 'S's, like slashes in the fabric.

'I could have it cleaned by Friday. Will that be sufficient?' he asked. His accent was not his own. And yet he had cast off so much of himself in the past few years, leaving it all in the dark, that there was no one around him who knew his true voice.

'You are slow,' the soldier in front of him replied irritably, his lips protruding as if in spite. 'Make sure you press it well.'

'Of course. Thank you,' Reece said. 'And how is the Obersturmbannführer?' He did his best to smile.

'The Obersturmbannführer is fine. As am I.'

'Of course.' Reece hesitated slightly and dropped his gaze. He focused on the jacket. 'Herr Scharführer, I have a friend. He was an antiques dealer before . . . and often still comes across fine things – beautiful clocks, paintings – that their owners are unable to keep. Perhaps the Obersturmbannführer would like to meet him sometime?' He raised his palms to indicate the new world, one that had its opportunities as well as its costs. This opportunity was to possess items that, until the inversions of the previous years, only the great aristocrats and industrialists of the age could have dreamed of possessing. The cost was dealing with black marketeers.

The sergeant smirked. 'I imagine some of these items are lacking in provenance.' Reece nodded. They understood each other now and he was glad to have gained the soldier's confidence. It could prove invaluable in future. 'It might be possible. I will speak to the Obersturmbannführer and see if he is interested. He does have an eye for fine items.'

'Then he won't be disappointed. I'm sure there would be a market back in Germany if he ever gets bored with the items and wants to dispose of them.'

'Yes, perhaps. Does your friend have anything in particular at the moment?'

'I believe he has an especially fine set of silver cutlery – eighteenth-century Italian, he told me.'

'Eighteenth?'

'Indeed, Herr Scharführer.'

The German sergeant seemed intrigued. As he spoke, something outside caught Reece's attention. A wailing sound. It was a human voice, although there was something inhuman about it. The soldier ignored the noise, no doubt having heard it many times.

'Well, perhaps. But if your grubby little friend is even thinking of passing off a fake . . .'

Reece pushed the sound from his head and concentrated on his words. 'Oh, he wouldn't be that stupid!'

'No. I should hope not. If anything is less than a hundred per cent genuine, he will be very sorry indeed.' The sergeant rapped his knuckles on the counter.

'He knows that. It's my reputation too,' Reece replied. Through the ice-fringed window, in the five o'clock twilight he saw the source of the sound: a young woman being dragged barefoot along the frost-covered pavement by a pair of men in leather trench coats.

'That's right, it is,' the soldier said sternly. 'And I will require a fee for this introduction,' he added.

'Of course, it is the normal business practice.'

'My fee will be fifteen per cent of the sale price.'

'A fair amount, Herr Scharführer.'

The men threw the young woman into a waiting car, one on either side of her. The engine gunned and they rolled through the sparse snowflakes whipping along the rue du Haut Pavé. Bare trees seemed to sag under the weight of the season.

'What are you looking at?' The sergeant glanced over his shoulder, to see where Reece was staring. But the car had gone and there was only a view across the ice-bearing Seine to Notre-Dame. It was skeletal grey through the snow, hunched on its island in the river like a dying animal. Red-and-black swastika flags rippled from lamp posts all around it as if they had snared a beast, and below the banners, an anti-aircraft gun pointed over the cathedral's Gothic towers. In a moment, the snow seemed to gather and swirl, blotting out the vision, as if the cathedral stones themselves had taken fright at the world that had gathered around them and had retreated into the white, blind weather.

Reece recovered himself. He had to, he knew. 'I will speak to my friend and send you a note to arrange the introduction,' he said, folding the jacket and placing it at the end of the counter.

'Good.' The sergeant looked at his wristwatch. 'Damn it, I'm late. You have kept me talking.'

'I apologize.'

'And do take better care of your appearance. It's slovenly.'

'I apologize.'

According to Reece's identity card, he was a hundred and eighty-four centimetres tall, with brown eyes, black hair, a slim face and clear complexion. Thirty years old. It didn't mention the layer of stubble on his cheeks, the product of the shortage of razor blades.

The soldier turned and strode out into the snow. Reece looked around the shop. It was stacked with the cheap household goods of a tabac-laundrette, one of the everyday edifices of French society. Every draught-enticing gap had been plugged and it was still freezing – it was years since there had been wood or charcoal for the stove, and the gas was available for only an hour during lunch and supper times.

He went back to the jacket. Black – not just for the darkness but for the practical reason that it hid the oil stains that Waffen-SS panzer regiments inevitably attracted. A little red piping to add a flash of energy, and those two unmistakable silver lightning flashes on the collar. Like boys playing. Boys with a game that had become a churn of wanton, nihilistic destruction. Reece had had two years of people like the

6

arrogant Waffen-SS sergeant. Every day he had had to fight harder to keep himself under control.

He went to the window and wiped away a film of condensation with his sleeve, only to see the tiny beads of water on the fabric turn into ice crystals. The Seine had frozen over this winter, the harshest anyone could remember. To the human eye, Paris's great artery had ceased to flow, although below the sheen there was unseen movement. Reece recalled setting his feet on the surface weeks earlier and calculating if the impenetrable ice were a sign or a warning for the city.

The city, itself frozen in ice, had been waiting for four years for a sign; ever since the young German troops had fanned across it in two hours in a textbook example of efficiency and with no more resistance than harsh looks. The faces Reece saw on the street and the buses now were haggard with waiting for the ice to melt. Reddened flesh sagged under every eye, and foreheads were permanently tipped towards the ground, unable to face the visions in front of them. He felt for these people. His purpose set him apart from them.

He stamped his feet and turned the shop sign to 'closed' before stepping into the back room. Dusty boxes of pencils and children's colouring books sat on the shelves and at the rear a narrow wooden staircase led to the attic above. He hauled himself up with the aid of a rope that served as a bannister, into the little room that was his bedroom.

A radio propped up on a stool was playing folk songs about country lives while, at a wooden dressing table squeezed under the eaves, a woman sat with her narrow back towards him, slowly brushing her dark hair. In a small, cracked mirror he saw her lips making tiny movements, silently singing along.

'You know the song,' Reece said.

She stopped but didn't turn to him. 'It's very old,' she said, placing the hairbrush on the dressing table. Her voice was low, speaking to herself more than him. 'My mother sang it. Sometimes she had friends over to play music.'

'Did you sing with her?' he asked.

'Sometimes.'

'Your first public performances.'

'Yes.'

Still she kept her back to him; he watched her lips and cheek moving in the mirror.

'Tell me about the songs you wrote.'

She put her chin in her hands. There was something immensely sad about the action. 'Some of them were good. Some were bad. Most of them were bad, I think.'

He sat on the bed. The mattress was made of horsehair, which made it rough to sleep on but warm in the winter.

'That's usually the way.'

She turned to face him and smoothed back her hair to reveal a pale oval face with a slim, aquiline nose and dark, hooded eyes. The top button of her blouse was open, over the top of a cotton cardigan. She reached for a wooden case, took out a thin cigarette and lit it, letting blue smoke curl up to the ceiling like a Chinese creature.

'Well, Maxime?' she said. She put the case back on the table between her wireless transmitter and a .32 Colt 1903 hammerless: the semi-automatic that Reece had taken when they left London, slipping it into a shoulder holster underneath his parachute suit.

'I want to kill three men I've seen in the last ten minutes,' he said. He glanced at the Colt. He could take it right then and go in search of the two in leather greatcoats who had dragged the girl into a car. He wanted to raise the gun and squeeze the trigger and see their lives ebb in the place of hers.

He knew he couldn't. Times would change, but for now he had to remain in the city's formless background.

'You and half Paris.' She turned back to the mirror and began dusting powder on to her skin.

He lifted a novel from his bedside table: Proust's *À la Recherche du temps perdu*, then went to his shaving kit and took out a phial of perfectly clear liquid, which he used to fill a pen. He noted down, on one of the book's blank pages at the back, the date, and then the rank and insignia on the Waffen-SS uniform he had been given. The invisible ink made no mark on the page; it would require a re-agent to do that.

The transparent note formed the latest in a record of insignia and ranks. A few past entries had an additional piece of information: the forwarding addresses of where to send the uniform when an officer was being posted elsewhere and the cleaning would not be ready in time. In that way, the book constituted a clandestine record of German troop locations and movements.

Reece flicked to the next page and ran his finger down. It was a special section devoted to units heading to the Pas de Calais. He had been ordered to pay particular attention to any regiments posted there and to probe for any additional information that he could glean. The number of panzer divisions heading to that stretch of coastline indicated that the Allied invasion was expected there. And Reece knew how his superiors in London would pore over that information.

He, the Wehrmacht, the French – everyone was tense, waiting for D-Day, believing it must come soon, desperate to know when and where. Time and again, Reece had calculated what he needed to prepare for it, for the time when he and the circuit would co-ordinate a Resistance uprising, sabotage train and telephone lines and ambush German troops on the roads. He needed more men. He needed more ammunition, more money, more chocolate and coffee to hand out as favours. He needed a lot.

He shut the book.

'Can you close up the shop?' he asked.

'All right. Then what?'

'Stay at your safe house this evening.'

She turned to face him. There was a shadow of dark rouge on the bones of her cheeks. 'Where are you going?'

'To collect some photos from Luc.' The raw weather dropped gravel into his voice, roughing it as if he had been drinking cheap spirits.

'Is it the SS document?'

He hesitated. 'I'll take it to London tomorrow.'

'It must be urgent.'

He would have liked to tell her how important it was: that he had been ordered to drop everything else and take it himself to the Cabinet War Rooms beneath Whitehall to place the photographs – more precisely, a film developed into negatives and any prints Luc had been able to make from them – in the hands of his Officer Commanding. But even within the circuit, security had to be maintained. 'I'll be gone a week,' he said. He should have been going for longer, really. He needed the rest. But he was needed in Paris. 'I'll see you when I get back.'

The tip of her cigarette glowed pale, threatening to fade into grey ash. 'Will you bring some coffee back? I would like some real coffee. It's been so long I hardly remember it at all.'

'You prefer it to roast acorns? I'll try, Charlotte.'

Charlotte. It wasn't her real name, but it was the one he knew her by: her service name, the one by which she was known to other agents. Like Reece, she also had a series of cover identities with identification documents in those names.

He pulled on woollen gloves. 'Be careful while I'm gone. The Gestapo are stepping up patrols.'

'All right.'

He glanced at the pistol beside her transmitter. 'Take the safety off.' She stubbed her cigarette out in an empty ashtray, lifted the grey-handled gun, flicked down the safety lever and replaced it softly on the table.

CHAPTER 2

He descended the stairs. Behind the shop, he unchained his bicycle and pushed it out on to the road before stuffing some newspaper pages down his coat as a guard against the frost. One of the pages, he saw, was for a new invention to conserve what little heat people had in their homes. It was a sort of miniature apartment, made of wood, that homeowners would construct entirely within their largest room and live in, turning the rest of the house into an abandoned frozen hinterland. For a moment, Reece pictured life within this shrunken, claustrophobic world. Strange, but then the people of France had felt their lives constricted day by day for the past four years, so perhaps some would barely notice if they were living in a giant coffin.

He climbed on to his bike and pushed away. The rendezvous would be in Montmartre, the hill north-east of the city centre, but he wanted to avoid the checkpoints on the closer bridges, so he decided to take the long way round, via the place de la Concorde, which was sandwiched between the Champs-Élysées and the Louvre. It was so cold that his muscles rebelled as he attempted to turn the pedals.

Reaching the quai d'Orsay, he remembered the times when the riverside had been lined with pavement artists at cheap easels. The frost, and the shortages of everything now, from paper to paint to money pure and simple, had since driven them all away. In their place, a line of German armoured cars rumbled along the road. After four years of occupation, the gun-topped vehicles were still a sight to stop small boys in awe and leave their parents staring at the ground. Two blankets had fallen softly and deftly on the city: one of snow and one of shame.

If there was something of Paris that he had once loved more than anything else, it was the Seine. Yes, the guide books would always talk of the city's art, and the postcards would show the Eiffel Tower – now an abandoned iron tomb – but it was the Seine that he felt below his feet wherever he was. He had felt it rise and ebb away a thousand times in the two years since he and Charlotte had dropped from a Hudson into a northern French field.

Two years. It felt like more. He had been sent to take over Beggar, one of the Paris networks of Britain's Special Operations Executive. The man he was replacing had been taken by the Gestapo, Reece had been told, sobering the moment.

He had set about rebuilding the circuit and there were now four other agents with him, tasked with aiding the local Resistance groups, directly sabotaging German movements and – more than most SOE networks – gathering, through bribery, theft or tapping lines, intelligence about German operations. Reece had been selected, he was informed, due to his three previous years in naval intelligence, giving him an understanding of how information could so often overcome the force of arms.

The circuit had known successes: Operation Beggar Five had gleaned vital information about the building of the Germans' Atlantic Wall, which was designed to repel any amphibious Allied invasion on the western French coast. And they had known failures: Beggar Twelve had resulted in two brave railwaymen being arrested and executed for sabotaging locomotive axles. That failure came painfully to Reece's mind far more often than the successes.

The place de la Concorde was full of women strolling about in *feldgrau* uniforms, the 'grey mice', brought over by the Germans to administer the occupation and support the troops. Those who had just arrived stared around and pointed out landmarks to their friends. Those who had been here a few days carried handbags stuffed with jewellery and clothes snatched from the shops of the Champs-Élysées. And above them, the signposts were now in French and Gothic-scripted German as the occupiers sought to control the very geography of Paris.

Some of those occupying forces were milling about in front of the heavenly Louvre when Reece reached it a minute later. More than a palace, it was a sweeping statement of all that France had once aspired to be: majestic, elegant, serene. Its art gallery was the finest in the world, Reece's father had once happily informed him as they stared at its curving harmony. It now gave Reece a grim sort of satisfaction that those men standing outside would be disappointed when they went in – little of the collection was left. Most, including the world's most famous portrait, had been hidden away years ago to protect it from prying occupying fingers.

Also in the Louvre's fine courtyard was a group of people, a hundred or more. Most of them, dressed in neat but inexpensive clothes, were ranged before a platform upon which a man dressed in a blue uniform, with a band on his arm displaying a symbol reminiscent of a curved swastika, was shouting to make himself heard. Some members of the audience wore the same uniform and blue berets. He was lit by arc lights.

'France is stronger than ever before!' he cried, his fists striking down towards a lectern. 'We of the Aryan race have purged our nation of its foreign Jewish influences and corrupt Freemasons.' He stood back for a moment, to allow a few shouts of approval. 'France is a nation once more, once more with the holy mother Church at our centre. Once more with our children ready to live honourable lives.'

Such honour, Reece thought to himself as he rode past the man ranting in the snow, surrounded by foreign officers stealing his nation's past, piece by piece. *Barely even pride.*

Thirty minutes later, he finally made it to the hilltop cobbled stones of Montmartre. Degas, Matisse and Renoir had lived and worked here. Toulouse-Lautrec had painted the girls in the nightclubs that sprang up clinging to these steep streets and the area retained a subdued air of artistic revolution. He walked his bike towards the most famous club of all. It was 6 p.m., dark, and if he didn't hurry he would be questioned. Although the Paris curfew was from midnight until five in the morning – and then only loosely imposed – if he ran into a militia patrol they might be bored enough to start investigating him.

He turned into the rue des Saules, a lively street full of wide boys who had somehow avoided being sent to Germany for the Obligatory Work Service, older men and women who had been in the street since the time of Toulouse-Lautrec and would stay there until they dropped down dead, and stern-faced militiamen who couldn't wait until the streets were cleansed of these filth under the tutelage of Pétain and the Pope. And there was one building the militia hated with particular venom: a salmon-pink cottage that had been a centre for all the artistic vices. Reece dawdled as he passed it, wheeling his bike, its rear wheel squeaking once on every turn, and glanced up at the sign, which showed a boisterous rabbit leaping out of a cooking pot. The cabaret within had come to be named after this sign: Au Lapin Agile. The moniker had replaced the former name for the bar: Cabaret des Assassins.

Reece stopped, propped his bicycle against a wall and crouched down to examine the chain. He adjusted it, taking the time to look around. Nothing out of the ordinary. He checked each direction again, stood up and chained the bike to a tree. He didn't like doing that, in case he needed to leave quickly, but bicycles now cost a month's salary for a working man. At least the snow had stopped – it would have been biting cold on the hilltop.

Entering, he found a handful of old men lined along wooden benches with glasses of piquette – the thin and unsatisfying ersatz wine made from adding water to already pressed grapes and fermenting the mush – set in front of them on rough tables. They were all smoking thin roll-up cigarettes or long, narrow pipes. A couple of them had grandsons by their mute sides – the fathers must have been forced labour in Germany. A few young women were giggling together in the corner while, on a tiny stage area, a white-whiskered accordionist was packing up his instrument, to be replaced by a pretty young singer with gamine hair. The lights were low and she began to sing a light-hearted song about arriving in Paris as an ingénue and being corrupted by the locals. The young women began to chant cheerily along, giggling at the occasional raunchy line.

'Yes, sir?' the waitress, carrying a tray of glasses and a near-empty purse, asked expectantly.

'A glass of red piquette. Whatever's the cheapest,' he said, glancing casually around the bar as he placed a couple of francs in her hand. He received a glass in return. He knew the bar well enough for an RV; not so well as to be recognized by the regulars. There were three exits: the main street door, a side door and one rear passageway that led to the back room and toilets.

He thanked the waitress and ambled over to a table in the corner, close to the rear passage. No matter how many meets he had been through safely, they still touched his nerves because the environments were unpredictable – civilians, public transport, the weather: any or all of them could scupper it. So he would be on edge until Luc arrived and gave the safe signal.

Reece had recruited Luc himself. A local printer and photographer, he had been useful in producing false travel permits sooner than they could be sent from Britain. Unlike the rest of the circuit, he therefore had no cover story, instead living under his own identity, Luc Carte.

Reece unrolled a copy of *Le Matin* from his pocket and set about reading it: the safety code to say that all was well. But as he glanced at the articles, he noticed the barmaid's gaze reflected in his glass. She was staring straight at him. Then she looked away and glanced along the corridor that was out of his sight, and subtly shook her head at someone. He heard the creak of floorboards and she stared at him once more before returning to collecting glasses. Informants and collaborators were a greater danger than the Germans and he fought to control a twist of worry.

Reece watched, alert to any further sound, and when she turned her back on him he quickly stood and moved to the mouth of the corridor to check. His fingers slipped towards the knife in a sheath hidden under his jacket lapel, a slim steel blade about the length of a finger. It wasn't the way he wanted the RV to turn out – much was riding on it – but he might not be given the choice.

'I wouldn't, my friend.' Reece wheeled around. The man to his left had looked up from his book and was speaking just loudly enough for Reece to hear. The man, who was wrapped in a thick scarf, gestured for Reece to come closer. 'Black market.' He waited for recognition to steal across

Reece's face. 'They're no better than the Boche – getting rich off our empty bellies. No better at all, if you ask me.'

Reece glanced towards the corridor. Perhaps that was it: petty criminals, rather than men set to watch him. He relaxed a little and his fingers pulled back from his lapel.

'I see, thanks,' he said. Yes, it was easy to read too much into a situation, he told himself, to be over-cautious. He moved back to his seat and tried to concentrate instead on the singer, who was now on to a song of lost love. As she reached the end of the chorus, the main street door opened and a small, neat man with a trim goatee walked in. He had a book poking from his coat pocket, his own safety sign. Reece settled back in relief.

He lifted his hand, as if greeting a friend whom he had arranged to meet for an evening in the relative warmth of their local bar. Luc returned the casual, complacent greeting.

'How are you?' Reece asked as Luc pulled out a wooden chair.

The man who had spoken to Reece got up to go to the bar.

'Fine, fine. Frozen, but fine,' Luc said as he sat and unbuttoned his jacket. Reece wondered if the film and prints were held within its lining. 'You just can't get warm these days, can you?'

'You can't. Not at all,' he said. In order to seem natural, they would have to spend an hour or so chatting, chewing the fat before they could part. The secret, Reece had found, was to forget all about the RV and just chat to a friend – after all, it could be a lonely life, unable to talk to people who knew who you really were. Even if it hadn't been poor security to make friends with civilians, there was always the barrier that you couldn't even tell them your real name.

'Were the paintings good?' Reece asked. Something flitted across Luc's face. A grave look, before it was wiped away.

'Yes. They showed the anniversary.'

Reece's grip tightened on the edge of the table. So the photographed files concerned D-Day. That was why they were needed so urgently in London. Luc dropped his voice to a mutter inaudible to anyone but Reece. 'Defence operation.' Reece lifted his finger to stay Luc from saying anything else. He would see the pictures himself soon.

The man to their side came back with a glass of grenadine. 'Can I get you a drink?' Reece asked Luc.

'A beer, please. Whatever they have.'

Reece stood and moved to the small bar in the corner of the room. An old woman was taking her time choosing from the sparse offerings. She dropped her purse and Reece bent down to help her pick her few dirty coins from the floor. Her gnarled fingers scrabbled impotently on the floorboards. 'Please, madam, allow me,' Reece said, placing his hand on her elbow. She smiled in gratitude and creaked herself upright.

He managed to recover the last of the money but just as he was about to drop it back into a hand-embroidered purse the street door burst open and two men, one middle-aged and heavy-set, one young and athletic, both wearing brown leather trench coats and dark hats, came charging in. The young singer's mouth fell open and she cowered into the corner of the room.

Luc stared at the men, then at Reece. They knew – the whole bar knew – who these men were. It was just a case of whom the Gestapo were looking for. All conversation, all movement, ceased, as if the hands of the clock had been halted. Reece stood up slowly and glanced surreptitiously at Luc. He saw the fear in the other man's eyes. The next few moments, he knew, would decide whether they would be alive a week from then.

And yet, as the Gestapo men stared around, checking faces for their quarry, Reece noticed that he felt strangely calm. He had imagined this moment so often that now it had come its potency was almost drained. And they wouldn't take him. He had long ago decided that. His fingers touched the third button on his jacket. Hidden within its split rubber was the L-pill, a glass capsule of potassium cyanide that would take five seconds to work. He knew that if he couldn't talk or fight his way out he would cheat his captors of his life. But for now: wait and watch.

The younger Gestapo officer's eyeline fell on Luc. 'You,' he said, pointing a leather-clad finger.

Luc's face fell.

And then, madly, he ran.

His chair crashed to the floor as he attempted to bolt to the side door. Reece willed him to make it but knew that it was a forlorn hope. Before he could even get his hands to the exit, the Gestapo man had leaped forward, crossing the room in two bounds, and grabbed hold of Luc to drag him down. Reece started for them both – driven not by decision but by instinct, muscle memory. But a hand took hold of his jacket.

'Don't you dare!' Reece looked around and saw the heavier German pointing a pistol at him. A Radom, he saw, copied from the American automatics. 'Don't move.' As he did so, the far door opened and a splinter of light fell on a man in the uniform of an SS major.

'Please,' Luc gasped. The major stepped calmly inside. For a second Reece felt for his Colt, but it was back in his room. Charlotte would have transmitted with it beside her then hidden it behind the skirting board, wrapped in rags. And a voice at the back of his head said that was probably for the good – he would have little hope in a firefight against three men.

The heavy man, who had a rough tattoo of a knife on his hand, pushed Reece aside and spun around to address the whole bar in German-accented French. 'Any of you move and I'll take you all in!' He brandished the pistol.

'I surrender!' Luc cried, putting his open hands in front of his face and wincing as if already feeling the blows. 'Gentlemen, I surrender. I won't fight.' Everyone in the bar stood still and silent. So much of France, these days, did the same. So many men lived on their knees. The athletic man pulled a pair of handcuffs from his trench coat and bound Luc's wrists with a grin.

The SS major came further into the room, scanning it efficiently. His gaze fell on Reece. 'Do you know that man?' he asked Reece, calmly, in good French.

'No, sir,' Reece replied. 'No.' He did his best to sound meek.

'Not at all?' Reece shook his head. He hoped no one in the bar would contradict him.

The major turned to the heavy-set Gestapo officer. 'Where was he sitting?'

'Over there, sir,' he replied, pointing to Luc's overturned seat.

The SS officer looked to the customer who had sat next to Reece. 'Did they speak to each other?' he asked.

Reece looked into the man's eyes. The man was nervously fiddling with his scarf.

'Sir?' he said.

'I asked you if these two men' – he waved at Reece and Luc – 'spoke to each other. Look at me!' he barked as the man glanced at Luc. 'Tell me now, or you will be joining them.'

'I . . .' Reece heard the man's voice failing him. 'I . . . didn't see them do so, sir.'

'I will give you another attempt. And if you are lying, it will go hard on you. Did these two men speak to each other or greet each other at all?'

Reece forced the thought of what the Gestapo did to SOE agents from his mind. He had to remember that he was an innocent and frightened passer-by caught up in something he didn't understand and wanted no part of. And he prayed none of the other patrons would speak up from fear or the hope of payment.

The man with the scarf looked at the glass of piquette Reece had bought. His fingers slipped towards it and drew it in front of himself. 'No, sir,' he said.

The major gazed around the bar, seemingly challenging anyone to dispute what the man had said. The waitress dropped her head. 'Is that true?' he asked her.

'I think so, sir.'

Reece silently thanked her. Paris was full of barmaids who would happily inform to the Germans. She was not among them.

'Herr Sturmbannführer?' said the Gestapo man who still held the gun on Reece.

The major's eyes met Reece's and stayed there for a while, as if searching for something. 'Check his papers.'

Reece reached into his jacket and handed them over, including a deliberately dog-eared identity card in the name of Marc LeFevre, a man who ran a tabac, and his ration book.

The Gestapo officer checked them. 'Why haven't you used your tobacco ration?' Reece looked at the full set of coupons. He couldn't tell why on earth the man would care. Then he realized. The full book had come in from London with the last drop – a gift to keep the circuit's spirits up – and the man must have suspected something like that. It was a trick Reece would remember next time.

'I have bronchial problems. I worked in a forge for years. If I smoke cigarettes, I cough up blood in my sputum.'

The man looked disgusted and thrust the book back at Reece. 'Now, what –'

'Wait,' interrupted the younger officer who held Luc. They all looked at him. 'Where was this forge?' His accent was French. So he wasn't Gestapo, like the others, but probably Carlingue, the Gestapo's French auxiliaries, used for sniffing out resistants.

Reece had the story pat and rehearsed, but still it was nerve-wracking to repeat it. 'A village near Reims.'

'Which one?'

'Dortin.' He looked over at Luc. How had they found him? How much did they know? His mind was working on two tracks: to deflect the questions put to him, and to work out what, if anything, lay behind them.

'Dortin? My aunt lives there. Colette Bernard, she runs the post office. Do you know her?'

Reece thought for a second and shook his head. 'The post office is run by a gentleman named Édouard. I'm afraid I don't know anyone called Colette Bernard.'

'Where . . .'

The SS major was becoming impatient. 'We don't have all night,' he said.

'Sir, if . . .'

'Send the prisoner to Amiens and be done with it.'

'Yes, Sturmbannführer Klaussmann.' The officer glared at Reece as if slighted. 'Get out,' he barked.

'Yes, sir.' Reece walked rapidly out of the bar, with every step fearing that he would hear an order to stop or feel the grab of a hand. But then he was outside in the freezing cold with the streetlights, painted blue to ward against air raids, leaking a dim glow to the snowy pavements below them. Luc had been taken, and the photographs were gone. He had no idea how much the Germans knew about the circuit or were about to find out. And he had to get back to Charlotte. He unlocked his bike with a shaking key and rode away at speed.

CHAPTER 3

German counter-espionage

Special gangs are being used for the more unsavoury types of CE work,
e.g. as thugs seizing suspects for the Gestapo, contacts for hotels, brothels,
etc., as well as general spying for the SD. They are mobile, subsist largely
on the proceeds of private property they have raided and are recruited from
amongst the lowest social types and criminals.

A grey Mercedes slid along the darkened road. The sound of
the tyres spraying through puddles was drowned out by the
air raid sirens. A slim man in the back of the car, aged somewhere between mid-fifties and mid-sixties, gazed up at the
sky and at the searchlight beams that were producing a score
of false moons. The raids, those that Göring had promised
would never touch Berlin, had become almost mundane
now. A nightly falling of buildings and rising numbers of the
dead. An oaf, Göring. The very definition of a man promoted
beyond his abilities.

'Admiral?'

'A little further on, thank you,' the man replied. He kept
his eyes on the purple sky with those milky beams rolling
back and forth on clouds, searching for Allied aircraft.
Four years ago the RAF had been on the verge of total
collapse. Now they came soaring over, night after night,
like crows. 'Just there, by the gate.' His voice was quiet and
contained. Perhaps the obvious lisp necessitated a considered enunciation. More likely it was just the character of
the man.

The car came to a smooth halt and the driver applied a creaking handbrake. Admiral Canaris waited for a minute, watching the drizzle on his window. Then he opened the door and hauled himself out. The weather did nothing good for his joints.

Brooding a little, his eyes cast down so that the rain collected in his white eyebrows, he walked slowly through the gateway into the Tiergarten.

He didn't pause for the weather and he certainly didn't pause when an authoritative and angry voice called over from the road demanding to know who he was. Some policeman. The driver would intercept the man and show him an identification card to make him instantly shut up.

The Tiergarten was bare these days. Occasional blades of grass, a few bushes with leaves, mostly just the skeletons of trees. His shoes sank a little into the earth as he made his way across the lawn towards a path that led deeper into it. In the dark, he knew the way by touch. The slightest glow of light came only from the searchlights overhead, bouncing off the bottom of clouds.

He found the path and turned along it, between banks of trees, wooden huts, an abandoned food kiosk. There was movement here and there among the branches — even the birds had been accustomed to the sirens — and he strode thoughtfully on until he came to the first of a set of huge and ornate buildings built decades earlier. Officially, the zoological gardens were still open for the children of Berlin to gawp at the exotic creatures and throw grit and stones to gain their attention; indeed, the large-scale destruction of the exterior wall had made it free for any who wanted to pick their way through the rubble. But an air raid of 1943 had broken apart most of the buildings, either killing their residents or setting them free to charge along the streets until trapped or killed by police. It had been a moment that threatened blood-madness in a city built on the promise of order.

He passed the alligator house, now just a shell surrounding a stagnant concrete pool, the reptiles having died under those Allied bombs. For a moment he stopped to appreciate what was left of the nearby elephant enclosure, once elegantly designed to look like a golden Siamese temple, with four bulging towers at its corners. Within was a pen formed of thick iron bars, built to withstand a charge from the largest beast. A hulking silhouette shuffling from one side to another showed Canaris that one solitary animal would be waiting out the war here, so long as it didn't starve first.

He moved on through the desolate lanes of the zoo, occasionally catching sight of a lonely nocturnal creature, until he found another structure, this one built for humans, its doorways empty. The genteel Yellow Veranda, enclosed by expanses of iron-framed windows, was where he had once dined in the Sunday sun with his wife when they were first courting. But time had changed the veranda as much as it had changed him and there were no cloths or flowers on the tables now. Indeed, there was only one table upright. It had been set in the middle of the stone floor and dusted roughly clean. A man sat at it, the tip of his cigarette shimmering red.

'Admiral.'

Admiral Wilhelm Canaris, chief of the Abwehr, the military's intelligence service, sat down in a heavy wooden seat and looked out through the line of windows. The glass was filthy. No one had looked through it for years. He cleared his throat. 'The SS. The SS have something,' he said.

'What do they have?'

'A man.' He adjusted his jacket.

'I take it he's important.'

'He does appear so,' Canaris replied, peering up to the roof. Birds were nesting in the rafters. The whole of man's built environment was returning to the wild. 'For what is coming. The invasion. For how we prepare.' The young man waited for him to continue. 'D-Day will happen this year. And I would put our chances of repelling it at sixty–forty.'

'No better?'

'Our entrenched positions against their speed and numbers. No Blitzkrieg this time. Hand to hand.' The sirens seemed distant now, muffled by the dirty glass. 'If it fails, I doubt they will try again for years, possibly never.'

'I see.'

'Earlier today I had a meeting with the Führer. Himmler was there. It turns out the SS has a source in London. He's well placed. Within the British intelligence apparatus.' He didn't bother to cover his contempt for Himmler's name. After all, Himmler hadn't attempted to hide his smirk when Hitler had revealed how effective the SS's intelligence-gathering wing, the SD, had been in placing and cultivating their new agent. The venerable Abwehr, which had existed long before National Socialism and retained its independence from the Party, looked down on their SS rivals as upstart street thugs. What made the rivalry more pointed was that the SS's numerous recent successes had shown up the Abwehr's lack of them. Himmler had personally passed the SD's information to Hitler, keeping much of it from Canaris. Indeed, the admiral found himself increasingly shut out from the most critical decisions.

'How well placed?'

Canaris considered. 'I can't say precisely, but with the kind of access that could reset the scales.' Himmler had enjoyed dangling it in front of Canaris, knowing that the little glimpse would infuriate the spy chief. The trait that Hitler and

Himmler most closely shared was their puerile joy in demonstrating themselves to be more successful in military matters than the Prussian aristocrats bred for the mess room.

'Has his information been tested?' the younger man asked, blowing a plume of smoke from his nose.

'Of course. It tallies with what our existing agents in Britain have told us, although their information was far thinner.'

'And do we have this man's name?'

'Only his service name: Parade.' Canaris knew no more, and that irked him.

'What material has he sent?'

'So far, primarily intelligence about British troop and naval movements; some about their agents in France. But he has promised' – he hesitated – 'more.' The young man looked intrigued. Canaris ignored him and stared at a monstrous building a hundred metres away, lifting high above the tallest trees. A six-storey castle made of concrete and iron, complete with octagonal towers at each corner, the Flak Tower rose from within the zoo. Its four huge twenty-five-tonne guns pointed at the sky ready to blast whole armadas to the earth. A military defence, for sure, but also a psychological one to tell the people of Berlin that the enemy would never populate their sky.

'So this . . .'

'Rommel is going out of his mind with frustration. His troops are too thinly stretched along the Atlantic Wall – the panzer divisions could take days to arrive if the Allies attack in the right place.' He paused for a moment. 'It seems Parade has gained a few fragments of the Allied planning for D-Day, important information about their command and communications structure, and their naval Order of Battle. Not yet the date – that won't be decided until nearer the time anyway, dependent as it is on the weather – but planning for the formation of their bridgehead. There seems to be a chink in their defences and Parade himself has suggested how we could exploit it with a highly specialized operation. Himmler is quite taken with the idea.' He removed his spectacles and cleaned them with a handkerchief from his pocket. 'Operation Parade One does, however, require two pieces of intelligence in order to execute it. We need to know certain details of their army Order of Battle and whether the landings are coming in Normandy or Calais.'

'He thinks he can obtain that?'

Canaris replaced his spectacles. 'The Allies have gone to great lengths to compartmentalize access to such knowledge. It's released only as and when strictly necessary. Parade will be able to see the Order of Battle as soon as the invasion force leaves port and he promises to transmit it to us immediately. For once, I don't think the importance of this man is idle boasting on the part of the Reichsführer.' Himmler had asserted that Parade would be the fulcrum upon which the Allied invasion would turn: a claim transparently intended to support his bid to become heir to the Führer himself, whose health was beginning to fail – but Canaris had to admit that if this man fulfilled his promise, the weight of the battle would be with Germany. Canaris had long ago suppressed any professional arrogance, and yet he felt slighted that the fool Himmler had gained such a golden prize.

'Impressive.'

Canaris made a non-committal gesture. 'Regarding the landing locations, however, he is not confident of securing that information. We will have to look elsewhere for it – and we will need it well in advance of the Allied flotilla departing in order to execute Parade One.' He lost himself for a moment, brooding on where they could obtain such intelligence. There were other agents, of course, but none had much hope of gaining the information. On current indications, at very best, the German high command would be making an educated guess based on scraps of information. No, they needed something concrete. And despite all the resources of the Reich poured into it, they were no closer to finding such a source of that information.

'Do we know any more about Parade?' the young man asked as his cigarette burned down. 'How he gathers his information?'

'Indirectly, it seems. Himmler was quite inordinately pleased to inform me that Parade has developed a handful of sub-agents in useful places: one in the Admiralty, one in SOE, I believe. There may be others elsewhere, although, personally, I wouldn't count on it.'

'Quite a feat.'

'Yes, but a plausible one for a man with talent. The Abwehr has had some success infiltrating our own agents in the same places. Not as much as I would have hoped, but some.' He watched a dark bird flit through the trees. 'The Reich has been on the back foot for the past year, despite what Goebbels would have us believe, but the access that Parade has could turn that around and give us momentum again. I want this man working for us, not Himmler.'

'I see. And what is Parade One?'

Canaris rubbed his hands slowly together, as if attempting to rub the stain of Himmler's sweat from his hands. 'A deception operation. Himmler has made all sorts of promises about its ability to destroy the invasion from within. He's an arrogant child. But this operation – ambitious as it is – could be . . . effective.' He thought for a moment, mulling the strange draw that the Reichsführer had for Hitler.

'My job will be easier if I know about the op.'

'In time. I don't have all the details myself yet, and I'm a cautious man.' He pictured Parade One in action: a form of warfare ready to cut through the Allies, as the Blitzkrieg had. The Allied troops in disarray, a rout drowning in a red-soaked tide.

The young man blew a line of smoke into the dark before stubbing his cigarette out on the tabletop. 'I take it, Admiral, there is a reason for you telling me this at this precise juncture?'

'There is. Parade is what the SD have *gained*.'

'Is there also something they have lost?'

'Yes, there is.'

'Careless of them.'

Canaris watched the final, tarry smoke from the cigarette drift away. 'Quite. The SS had a Hauptsturmführer working on the operational details for Parade One. He went on a binge with some French girl two days ago and now suspects his notes were examined – photographed or otherwise copied, presumably.'

'A hell of a hangover.'

'Indeed. The document is based on information from Parade, and it is possible that there are details that could help us identify him. Either way, if the document gets to London, the information in it would make the British aware the Reich has a source among them. And that will change things. We need to acquire the document before our British or American friends do.'

'I understand. What about the girl?'

'No trace so far,' Canaris informed him.

'And the Hauptsturmführer?'

'On his way to a less comfortable war on the Eastern Front.'

'He got off lightly.'

'That is probably true.'

The silhouettes of men atop the Flak Tower could be seen scurrying between the immense guns. Canaris could hear the rumbling of aircraft engines overhead now. He waited.

'How does Parade communicate with Berlin?'

'Wireless set.'

'Anything of his age or background?'

'Nothing more.'

A massed formation of fighter-bombers appeared over the rooftops and, within moments, the Flak Tower opened up, its guns drowning out the approaching aircraft. 'How is the Führer?' the young man asked.

Canaris checked the time on his wristwatch. 'The Führer is as the Führer always is.'

'That is reassuring.'

One of the planes spun away and fell into the distant darkness, but the loss did nothing to prevent a score of flashes on the horizon and thudding explosions that shook the flagstones of the Yellow Veranda. The bombs fell closer and human voices cried out as the side of a nearby building crumbled to the ground. 'The Reich has had its summer,' said Canaris. 'Parade will be our agent for the winter.'

CHAPTER 4

As he rode away from the bar, Reece replayed the encounter with the Gestapo. Could the French collaborator who had grabbed Luc have detected a foreign tone in Reece's accent? He trusted not. It was quite natural anyway, the product of his itinerant childhood.

Reece's New Yorker father had moved to Paris before the Great War, as an art dealer in love with the belle époque and an Englishwoman who had run away to escape her stifling family. Reece had been born a week before the first time the Germans had rolled across the French border – well, the first time for a generation – and had been immediately plucked up and taken to Manhattan to spend the first eleven years of his life there. He had spent his childhood on Broadway, watching the theatres brighten the night sky and frightening his mother on the most hair-raising rides at Coney Island.

They had all returned to Paris when his parents proved unable to resist it in the twenties. Five years later he had been sent to his father's old school in New Hampshire, where science bored and languages engrossed him. While there, he had developed a fondness for sailing, a pastime he kept up during a degree in the history of art in London, and a few subsequent years writing for art magazines with minimal readerships. When war broke out he had volunteered for the Royal Navy, his knowledge of France and the French and German languages assigning him to the Intelligence section.

There he had seen the weakness of the German navy compared to that of seagoing Britain, but he hadn't shared the confidence of his brother naval officers that this meant the Germans had lost before the fighting had even begun. He had heard of the size of the Luftwaffe and Wehrmacht mechanized forces and realized that this war, unlike the last, would be built on speed in the air and on the ground. To his enduring anger, he had witnessed his expectation become a searing reality first-hand at Dunkirk, as thousands had drowned or been shot to pieces in the saltwater.

'The beginning of the end,' one of his comrades had said.

'We'll find another way,' he had replied.

Back in London, he had decided to fight for Paris, the city where he had first kissed a girl, first had his face slapped by another, first put on a suit. And so, in the summer of 1942 he had put his name forward for MI6. But when the call came, it wasn't from them but from a new service, one that Churchill had personally instructed to 'set Europe ablaze'. Reece had joined the Special Operations Executive without a second thought. In those days, hardly anyone harboured second thoughts.

It was during training that he had met Charlotte.

'Are you here for the course?'

She had been walking, a peach-coloured suitcase in her hand, up the lane from a station in rural Hampshire. He was in a small sports car that a friend had lent him and he recognized her immediately as someone touched by the Parisian artistic demi-monde. She wasn't one of the Surrealist artists railing against the dead ways of the older generation, though; she had the air of one who stood aside at parties and watched. He saw it in the way she turned her whole body to face him and the black pillbox hat with a half-veil she wore, as if she were in mourning.

Also, she answered him in French.

'If this is to test my discretion, you are not subtle,' she said.

'No test. A lift?'

She placed her case on the rear shelf, climbed into the front and said nothing more, watching the countryside as it passed, not looking at him for the ten minutes it took to arrive at Beaulieu, the large country house officially known as station STS31 but known sardonically to the agents as the Finishing School.

At the gates, an army guard checked their documents. 'Why have you arrived together?' he asked.

'He picked me up on the road,' Charlotte replied in heavily accented English. The soldier raised his eyebrows. She shrugged.

It was such a Gallic response Reece had to smile to himself. He saluted the guard and drove in. In front of the wide house itself, they were met by another, older soldier. Although he wore civvies, Reece could tell by the keen way he studied them on their approach that he was one of the conducting officers. 'Maxime, Charlotte, nice to see you both here. And you have met, I see.' Reece hadn't asked her name, but it seemed to suit her somehow. Usually service names started with the same letter as the agent's real name, to make them easier to remember. So what was her real name? Camille? Clarice? Cécile?

'Come on in, we'll get you settled.'

She went on ahead, not looking at him. He watched her calves as she ascended the stone steps and wondered about the cool, sad air that seemed to envelop her. Of course, many of her compatriots had arrived surrounded more by grief than by anger, and yet there was something that said her sadness was deeper even than theirs.

36

The first day was dedicated only to outlining what they would learn on the course. There would be detailed instruction on the German intelligence services they would encounter: the Gestapo; the Abwehr and the SS's intelligence division, the Sicherheitsdienst, or SD. Of the three, the SD were the most dangerous for Allied agents, the Gestapo the worst for the occupied people. Both were drawn from fanatical supporters of National Socialism. Most Gestapo men were former police officers, with a substantial number of convicted criminals recruited especially as auxiliaries for the more brutal duties. Many SD had been brought up under the Nazi system and were now ready to dedicate their talents to maintaining the racial superiority of the German people.

In contrast to those bodies, the SOE recruits were told, the Abwehr, the armed forces' intelligence service, paid some respect to laws of arms. They had existed long before the Party's appearance and intended to exist long afterwards.

As often happened with overlapping intelligence services, those three bodies were often locked in rivalry and mutual loathing. And that meant a circuit could slip between the cracks.

'Who is in the ascendency?' Reece had asked the conducting officer.

'Without doubt, the SD. Himmler's wolves,' the officer replied. 'As brutal as the rest of the SS, but with some brains to them. The Gestapo are holding their own but they're overstretched in terms of manpower and we predict they're going to come under direct SS control sooner or later. The Abwehr are running out of steam. They're too old-fashioned.'

After that there would be instruction in use of codes for scheduled – sked – transmissions, rendez-vous patterns, explosives and infiltration into enemy locations. There would be specialist training at other centres after this one, they were told, to teach them the skills for their specific roles within their networks.

In the evening they congregated in the school's bar. Reece sat next to Charlotte and pushed a glass of brandy across the table. She took it and drank.

'It's to see how we behave when we're drunk,' he told her.

'Yes, I thought so.' When she spoke English, it was with all the tip-of-the-tongue delicacy of her own language.

'They'll keep plying us with it until we're legless.'

'Let them.'

'Fine by me.' He tried to identify and understand her. Yes, she would have been at parties, never giving herself away. Perhaps she had once given too much away and had learned her lesson. He swapped to French. 'Which arrondissement?'

She looked at him without blinking. 'The eighteenth.'

'Ah.' So she was from a modest background. 'Your family?'

She screwed a cigarette into a wooden holder, lit it and blew a line of blue smoke to the ceiling. 'My mother's in Geneva.'

'I'm glad. Your father?'

'He died three days before the Germans arrived in Paris.'

'Maybe it was a blessing he missed it.'

'Maybe it was. His grave overlooks the Eiffel Tower.'

'Was he a soldier?'

'An engraver. Too ill to fight.' She tapped ash into a tin ashtray on the table. 'Do you think I am telling the truth?' she asked.

'Good question. I have been wondering. But yes, I think you are.'

'Then, from now on, I will lie,' she said quietly.

'But I will know the truth by a process of elimination.'

'That doesn't always work.'

He sipped the beer he had poured for himself. 'You don't want to know about me?'

'No. I choose not to.'

'Yes, that is your prerogative. How did they find you?' he said, lighting a Gold Flake.

'They just did.'

He shook the flame from his match and tossed it on to the table. 'I would have thought you would be hard to find.'

'I thought that too.'

They sat for a while, watching the other recruits. Some bore excited expressions; others looked serious and dour. A few were already drunk. 'All so ready for it,' Reece said. He felt more determined than ready. He had a strategy, but not yet the plan and the tools.

'All to fall to earth.'

'With a bump.' She was perceptive, of course, but those who never joined in were always perceptive. What else were they to do while they stood on the sidelines but watch the players in the game and try to discern the patterns in their movements? It was hard to say how much of her now was a product of the war and how much was a product of her parentage, her upbringing and all the other influences benign and malign that shape one's character. Reece himself had often felt peripheral to others. He put it down to his childhood, split between the bold enterprise of Manhattan and the pleasure-stews of Paris. He rested his cigarette on the edge of the ashtray. 'I need some fresh air. Shall we go for a walk?' She stared into the corner of the room, allowed a line of smoke to drift from her mouth and pressed the cigarette into the ashtray with force. She turned her eyes on him. Dark green, freckled with brown.

Outside, dusk was coming down like muslin cloth. An autumnal dampness was in the air and she took his arm.

There was a cool breeze that smelled of slowly rotting leaves. She came closer to him and he felt the heat radiating from her. She wore a thin wool jumper.

'How honest do you think they'll be?' he asked. 'I mean, will they tell us what the Gestapo will do to us if we're caught? Or will they leave that to our imagination?'

'I've heard things that I would not have imagined.' The timbre of her words told him that her thoughts were still across the English Channel.

'Yes,' he said. He had too. Some of it had happened to his parents' friends. He often wondered about the Jewish artists he had known. He had been named after Marc Chagall, a friend of his father's. Chagall and Max Ernst had got out in time. Others hadn't. 'Do you have Jewish friends?'

'Yes.'

'What's happened to them?' She shrugged, and gazed at the ground. They walked through the woods in which the six large houses and numerous smaller buildings of the Beaulieu estate sat. The trees were still mostly clothed in leaves, although there was a moist mush below their feet that cushioned them and prevented any sound. 'Your shoes will get damp,' he said.

'They will get a lot worse when we parachute into farmers' fields.'

'Or into the arms of the Gestapo.' The joke fell a little flat.

Her voice was soft now. 'Why are you prepared to do it?'

He stopped and turned to her. Mottled shadows were falling across the delicate pale oval of her face. She would have been a muse for one of the painters whom she found interesting. 'You're not actually French, are you?' she asked. 'Your language is perfect, of course, you know that. But there's something . . .' She drifted off, looking into his face.

'I was born there.'

'Where did you grow up?'

'Some there. Some in New York.'

'Then you have a choice. About where you're from.'

'It doesn't feel like it.' He leaned back against a tree. The rippled bark of the trunk had a film of evening dew. 'I hate them,' he said. There was no malice in his voice. It was a simple statement of fact. 'For what they've done. What they're going to do. I would shoot every one I could. Officers, other ranks. Not one is innocent. I would enjoy seeing them suffer. Which arrondissement are you really from?'

She gazed up into the sky. It was overcast and there were no stars to see. 'The seventh.' There were dots moving in the sky. 'Yours or theirs?' she asked.

He narrowed his eyes, although it didn't help much. 'Ours, I think. Could be Hurricanes. Intercepting.'

'I hope they come back.'

'So do I.'

'What are they training you for?' she asked, tracing the movement of the planes across the sky.

'Circuit organizer. You?'

The fighters disappeared and she dropped her gaze. 'Wireless operator.'

'A pianist,' he said.

'I really was one once.' Through the haze of a slight mist coming down he could just make out a thin, rueful smile. It was the first he had seen break on her. 'I played in bars full of arrogant Sorbonne students.' Then the lips relaxed into the shapeless semi-pout that had occupied them before. She walked a few steps deeper into the woods. He followed her. 'It seemed to matter then.'

'It will matter again.'

She looked at him in the same unblinking way. 'Do you really think so?'

'I do,' he said.

She paused, considering. 'I hope you are right.' Then she walked into the forest.

Reece looked up at the sky over Paris now. It was heavy with clouds. As he pushed open the back door to the tabac he saw Charlotte making ersatz coffee on a tiny stove fuelled by sawdust. The thin brew was strained from roast acorns – it would be barely drinkable even in these days when hot drinks were vital to stave off the bleak weather. In the corner of the room a radio was whispering a broadcast from the BBC's French service, Radio Londres. A man with a nasal voice was calling on Frenchmen to oppose their occupiers and make any collaborators pay.

She saw the look on his face. 'What happened?'

He closed the door and without a word went into the shop to check through the windows, looking for any sign he had been followed. He returned heavily. 'Luc's been taken.'

She removed the pot from the stove. 'When?'

'Just now.' Reece thumped the wood of the staircase.

'Gestapo?'

'And their French friends.'

'The Carlingue? How much do they know?'

'I can't say,' he replied, sitting on a pile of sacks, his muscles exhausted. 'They didn't arrest me too, so they can't know everything. Maybe they don't know much at all. But we might have to leave this place.'

'Do we go now?'

'No. We should have a day at least before he breaks – if he breaks. They're taking him to prison in Amiens.'

'Why Amiens?'

'They've done it before – to spread prisoners around the country, or something. I don't know.'

'So what now?'

'We set a watch on their transports. We need to know exactly when they're leaving. And I need to contact the others right away,' he said. 'We can't give him up.'

Her glance told him she knew what he was planning. 'You're going to hit the convoy?'

'I'm not going to abandon him. I need you to transmit to-night. Priority channel. Tell them Luc has been taken with the photographs. We'll intercept the convoy tomorrow night.'

'Do you want me in the op?'

'I can't risk you.' There was a pause. 'You're harder to re-place than the rest of us. There's a shortage of wireless operators.'

'I understand,' she said. She probably did understand. There was a shortage of pianists, sure enough, but that was not the true reason he wanted her to stay away from an assault that had, at best, a fifty–fifty chance of coming right.

'Tell the others to be here at nine. Then get to your safe house, stay alert and don't come back until I send word. If the op is successful, I'll go with Luc to recover the film – if it's safe – and then straight to London.'

'And if it's not a success?'

'Then those who are left disperse and try to get home independently by any means possible,' he told her. 'You too.'

She gazed at him with her dark eyes. 'Is this the kiss goodbye?' The air seemed to slip around them. It whistled through the bricks like breath through a flute.

'You need to get to your safe house.'

She lifted a pink woollen coat and pillbox hat from a brass hook beside the rear window. 'Goodbye, Maxime,' she said as she opened the door, letting a cold gust of wind enter.

CHAPTER 5

Emergency action
If an agent has been arrested, find out the reason for his arrest and whether he has talked. Help the arrested agent to escape if it can be done without prejudicing the security of the organization.

9 February 1944

At half past one the following afternoon, a few kilometres north of the village of Chambly, two hours' cycle ride from Paris, the chain of Reece's bike rattled and clanked in a country road that was more mud than tarmac. He had passed a hamlet and a few farmhouses with horses leaning over broken fences. From the lining of his jacket he took a map, printed on silk in order to go undetected if he were to be patted down, and a compass hardly bigger than a large postage stamp. He traced his route and confirmed his position by checking the bearing to a church spire in the distance. The bend he had just come around was the right one. He was on the main road, with a forest on one side and open fields on the other.

Two hundred metres from where he stood, a slim lane branched away into the woods. He took that turning and hid his bike in some bushes. It would be there if he had to get away through the forest – if they had dogs, it would at least give him a chance. His last lines of defence would be the Colt, hidden under the bicycle seat with his leather shoulder holster, and a stiletto knife in a sheath strapped to his forearm. He took the gun, checked there was a .32 hollow-point round in the chamber and covered the bike with branches and scrub. Then he climbed down into a frost-glazed ditch beside the main road, wrapped his arms around himself and tried to picture another life.

After an hour of dreaming of the easy days he had left far behind, a low hum seemed to sweep through the landscape. He crouched lower, straining to see around the bend in the road. It could be the truck. It must be by now.

First there was a rumble on the road, then an old factory delivery vehicle caked in debris, fit for little more than scrap, chugged into sight, its engine creaking noisily – with petrol so scarce the van had been converted to burn woodchips, sending it back fifty years in engineering development. Behind it was a civilian car, a Peugeot with a metal charcoal-gas tank attached to the roof. The two vehicles turned up the side road where Reece had stashed his bike, but he didn't move, instead carefully watching both directions on the main road to see that neither he nor they had been followed.

Satisfied that there was nothing else in the vicinity, he took the Colt in his hand, pushed himself to his feet and cut through the woods to where the vehicles sat silently in the lane.

Still among the trees, he called over. 'Are you having problems?'

'Trouble with the wheels,' a man's voice returned.

Reece emerged from the treeline and walked quickly over. The door of the van opened and a slim man in his twenties with a neat black beard emerged.

'Why are you late?' Reece asked, sliding the pistol back into the holster.

'Checkpoint. Have you started without us?' Thomas, the circuit saboteur, who wrecked train axles and poured ball bearings into tank fuel lines, often seemed to enjoy these occasions. Some agents had joined up for the excitement, and Reece suspected Thomas was one of them.

Another face appeared from the passenger side: Hélène, the network courier, who carried messages. 'Hello, Maxime,' she said. Her voice, usually warm, was stern now. 'We're ready.'

From the small green car, Richard, the final member of Beggar, emerged. The weapons instructor, who showed the local resistants how to use firearms and explosives, stretched and shook out his long, powerful limbs. Clearly, cramp had been his enemy on the journey.

As circuit organizer, Reece's role was to recruit and culti-vate sources of information on German troop movements and operations. He also directed the Resistance groups as much as he could, leveraging munitions supplies from Britain for influence over their use. The major *réseaux* were far better these days than they had been at co-ordinating their actions – nominally now having a united overall council – but still the Communist Francs-Tireurs, the apolitical Libération Nord, de Gaulle's Free French and the smaller non-aligned forces viewed each other with suspicion, impeding their effectiveness. At least it meant that when one group was infil-trated by the Gestapo the disease didn't immediately spread to the others.

For a moment Reece watched the backs of his agents as they unloaded their weapons and equipment from the van, praying that they would all be there at the end to load it back in again. Ops like this – face to face, small-arms fire – were rare, especially for Beggar. It was like being on the front line. To quell the worry, he focused on what Luc had had in his possession: a set of photographs that could prevent another ocean of sinking bodies, worse than the carnage he had seen at Dunkirk.

'This way,' he said.

He took them quietly through the woods to the spot where he had been watching the road and pointed out the terrain and vantage points. A heavy sound high above made them all look up. The trees' bare branches became damp. 'It's good,' Reece said. 'The rain will slow them down, distract them too.'

'Poor lambs,' Thomas agreed loudly. 'Wet in the rain.'

As Richard and Thomas returned to the van to collect a three-metre string of caltrops – brutal barbed spikes that would burst the tyres of anything driving over them – Hélène spoke to Reece under her breath: 'Are you certain they'll come this way?'

'No, but they're short of fuel and this is the direct road. So long as they stick to their normal schedules, they should be here within an hour or two.'

'You think we can take them on?'

Reece didn't want to answer the question – he hated lying to his comrades – and yet the truth was that he knew the op was as likely to fail as to succeed. And if it failed, then they were probably destined for the same cells as Luc. So he helped Richard carry the caltrops towards the road. 'We'll have to get in place soon,' he said. 'Let's start building the firing positions.'

On the second floor of a dull building on the rue des Saussaies, close to the Élysée Palace, where ageing and venal French presidents had enjoyed near-mediaeval trappings of power until a few years earlier, Sturmbannführer-SS Siegfried Klaussmann was reading a letter from his wife. An ornate clock from the last century melodically chimed half past two as he placed the final pink page on the desk before him and smoothed his palm over it. Over the course of six sheets, her tight handwriting had described life at her cousin's country estate. They had much better food than they had had in Bonn – as much mutton or pork as they could eat – and she prayed every night that Siegfried would soon be able to kiss his second child goodnight.

He too wanted to tuck his children into bed. He picked up his pen and held the nib above a sheet of notepaper. It hovered there for a while as he decided on the reply – how best to assure her that all would be well, that it was less than two months before he would have a week's leave, and that, ultimately, he could do more for their safety and well-being from his small office in Paris than sitting alongside them in the Rhineland countryside drinking Riesling.

There was a light rapping on the door. He screwed the top back on his pen and placed the letter in the drawer of his desk.

'Come in,' he called.

A bright-faced Gestapo officer in shirtsleeves entered. Kriminalassistent Karl Schmidt saluted and addressed Klaussmann by the SS rank that he held and preferred to his Gestapo title. 'Something has come in, Herr Sturmbann-führer,' he said, standing stock still on the threshold. 'Urgent, from Berlin.'

'All right, give it here.' The younger officer strode in and handed over a yellow-brown sheet of paper. A message typed on to strips of white paper had been glued to it: *An English cell will hit your prison transport today.*

Klaussmann was instantly alert. A previous message that had arrived in the same fashion had informed them about the SOE spy they had arrested in a bar in Montmartre the previous night – Luc Carte, that was his name – and it had been a good pull. The message had given no more than his name and location, but the interrogators would draw a torrent of information out of him.

Klaussmann was used to receiving anonymous notes from the public – usually informing him of the presence of Jews or Resistance safe houses, even one or two suggesting the location of downed Allied airmen. Half of them turned out to be false reports, the settling of petty scores of the type that wartime threw up by the hundred each day. The French, he was more than aware, had an image of the Gestapo as an all-seeing, all-pervading clandestine organization cleverly and ruthlessly pursuing fragments of information. The reality was that it was frustratingly understaffed for the job it had been given and virtually all its information came from local informants pursuing their own agendas. But notes such as this one and its precursor, apparently from a highly secret source in contact with Berlin headquarters, were something he had not previously encountered.

When the first one had arrived, Klaussmann had enquired where this information was coming from. 'Don't ask,' his superior had informed him. 'I've also been told not to ask.' That had been an interesting response – certainly, the Reich was full of secrets, but few of them were kept from senior Gestapo officers.

He opened the window. Spots of rain entered, but he appreciated the promise of frost. He was Prussian, despite his Saxon fair hair – light grey now – and a Prussian winter was something to behold. The chilly air helped him think. So one of their prison transports was a target. Why? He considered: the note was from the same source that had informed on the man taken in Montmartre. 'The prisoner we brought in after the last message. Luc Carte. What's happening to him?'

'He's one of those you wanted sent to Amiens.'

Klaussmann grunted. 'So I did.' As the Second Front edged closer, his colleagues had been doubling their efforts, filling up the prisons of Paris to stave off the danger of an internal revolt. But too full, and there was danger of the prisoners rising up, which could be very dangerous indeed. So some had been sent outside Paris. 'It must be that transport. When does it leave?'

Schmidt checked his wristwatch. 'It already has, sir. Half an hour ago.'

It was a frustrating answer. 'Are we in radio contact?'

'It would depend, sir. They might have a field radio.'

'Find out.' Schmidt departed to find a transport officer, leaving Klaussmann to wonder about the message, and its sender, again.

He returned to his soft leather chair and drummed his fingers on the desk's polished teak. The SOE networks and the French terrorists were a personal grievance for Siegfried Klaussmann. He had seen what they could do to his brother officers when their guards were down and he knew well the effect they were having, draining Germany's resources by diverting men and vehicles from the encroaching Eastern Front and preparing the ground for the Allied invasion.

He had lived through the catastrophe and hunger of Weimar's dying days and he never wanted his nation to go through that again. He didn't want his sons to go through it. So here he was on the ground, using what ability and experience he had to prevent it happening, and that meant tearing the spies apart before they could reduce Germany to chaos once more.

Schmidt returned after a few minutes with a Wehrmacht sergeant. 'Feldwebel Krepp, Herr Sturmbannführer,' Schmidt announced.

The man saluted.

'The prisoner transport to Amiens this evening,' Klaussmann said. 'Can we contact them?'

'I'm sorry, Herr Sturmbannführer. They don't have a radio.'

Klaussmann silently cursed in irritation. 'What vehicles are they in? How many men?'

'A motorcycle with sidecar in front; the van with the prisoners and two guards . . .'

'What sort of van?'

'An actual prison van. Enclosed, metal.'

'Good.'

'And another motorcycle with sidecar behind.'

'How far will they have got?'

'They'll be outside Paris by now.'

'They're about to be attacked by British spies. What troops can you send after them?'

The soldier looked flustered. 'Fastest would be motorcyclists, sir. Outside the city, they could run at perhaps eighty kilometres per hour. Twice the speed of the transport.'

'How many could you despatch?'

'Four with sidecars. Eight men in total.'

Klaussmann calculated the odds. The spies would probably number fewer than half a dozen men and their weapons would be light – but they would have the element of surprise and would be in good hidden firing positions. They might even have called on a *réseau* to add to their numbers. No, he didn't want to risk failure. 'We need more force.'

'We have a 222 Leichter Panzerspähwagen on standby,' the man volunteered. 'It's armed with a heavy machine gun and cannon. We can send a full platoon after it in another vehicle.'

'How fast is the Panzerspähwagen?'

'It's a four-wheeler, so sixty kilometres per hour. Seventy, perhaps, if the road is good. It should catch the transport in an hour. We can send a motorcycle with it.'

'Where would that put them?'

The sergeant went to a map on the wall and moved his finger along the road crawling north from Paris. 'Before Beauvais. The countryside or one of the villages on the way.'

Klaussmann considered. Yes, it sounded like the right move. 'Good. Send your men. Tell them to order the transport to turn around. Then your men go on to look for an ambush.' The edges of his mouth twitched up. 'The spies will be expecting a van and a few guards. They'll get a full platoon with armoured support. Now, we want them alive if possible, but don't let them scuttle away back under their rocks. When you have them, bring them straight to the cells here. Is that understood?'

'Yes, sir.'

'Then go now.' The sergeant saluted and rushed away.

The only concern would be that the spies might see the troops coming and melt away like cowards. But so long as the 222 was fast, Klaussmann was confident of success. This could be a big deal, he thought. Previously, when just one member of a spy network had been arrested, it had often led to the capture of the full circuit within forty-eight hours – when the right physical pressure had been applied to the man. If the troops could capture three or four of them, the outcome would be assured.

Reece and Thomas each took a heavy axe from the van. They selected a couple of mature elms in the side road and swung their axes, the heads cutting deep into the moist trunks. Behind them, Hélène and Richard set about building screens for the firing positions from branches and mud-encrusted farm detritus gleaned from the field opposite. Blocks of wood should provide some defence against bullets.

It was after 3 p.m. by the time the two trees had been felled. The van – which proved more powerful than it looked – dragged them into place across the narrow lane, blocking it. There they were bound together, and to other trees, with three strong iron chains. Nothing short of a panzer could now turn down that road. The van was left on the forest side of the tree-trunk barrier, ready to drive away into the woods; and the green car, which had been left at the entrance to the lane, was backed out on to the main road.

Reece and Thomas assembled a Bren light machine gun and three Sten sub-machine guns, with five thirty-round magazines to slot into them. The Sten was a gun prized by agents for its light weight and for the fact that it could be easily broken into three parts for concealment or disguise. In the middle of the night, unable even to see their hands in front of their faces, Reece and his fellow SOE recruits had learned to identify, strip, reassemble and fire Stens, German Walther pistols, the British Vickers and the German Schmeisser MG 34/38 machine guns as well as a host of other guns. For some it had been something of an adventure. Reece had seen the reality of what these weapons did to men and for him it was no cheap thrill. He gave Richard and Thomas two magazines each. He took the fifth. Hélène would operate the Bren from the treeline.

As well as the guns, Richard had a pair of heavy bolt-cutters and there was a Mills grenade apiece. 'Pineapple, my friend?' Thomas asked as he handed them out. 'They can be very bad for one's health.'

Reece examined the road surface and selected a small pot-hole. Inside it, he carefully placed a metal tin with wires running out through a hole bored into the side then covered it all with grit. He hoped to God this would work. Then he retreated to the side of the road and watched his comrades, their earnest preparations for a fight that they might not survive but were committed to for the sake of their fellow agent. How many of them would live beyond the day, he couldn't tell. They all deserved to.

Thomas was twenty-nine and had been brought up in Aberdeen by a French mother. He had a talent for getting on with people and had introduced Reece to some useful sources. The Canadians had sent over twenty-five-year-old Hélène, a Québécoise. The rest of them laughed at her accent, saying she would blend in perfectly so long as they found a community of sixteenth-century peasants to hide her in. In idle moments she spoke of her husband and son. Her boy was the reason she had volunteered for this, she explained, so he would never grow up in a world where the Nazis ruled half the Earth.

Then there was Richard – a cheery, strikingly handsome English boy in his early twenties with rosy cheeks. He had a degree in French and Spanish, and that was more than enough for SOE. Unlike the others, he actually seemed happy in France. He enjoyed French culture, books and frequent trips to the local cinema to see those films chosen to stir French nationalist sentiment: biopics of Napoleon or creaking old stories of the Three Musketeers. He had once revealed to Reece, with the extra pink of embarrassment in his cheeks, that after the war he wanted to be an actor. He had caught the bug at university and was sure he could make a go of it. Reece had assured him that if he could survive living in France under a false identity, appearing in a Wilde farce would be a walk in the park.

Thomas handed the last of the grenades to Reece. 'I'm sure I don't need to tell you that these are as likely to kill Luc as our enemies,' Reece said. The others silently concurred. 'Use them only if you have to and you are sure – *sure* – that the only casualty will be the Boche.' He looked at them, shivering and rag-tag in the winter wind. If something happened to one of them, it would be on him for life. He accepted that responsibility because he had no choice. 'It will be hard going. We're all at risk, but it's worth that risk – not just for Luc, but also for our friends and our families at home. You all know what's coming. It's the liberation.' He waited for a breath of hope to breeze around them. 'We're trained, we're ready, the weapons are good and they don't know we're coming. So we'll hit them hard and fast and we're going to win. Are you with me?'

'We're with you.' It was Hélène's voice, barely audible as dusk and rain began to fall. Despite the danger to their lives, he was glad it was these people he was with. What they had already been through meant that he knew them and trusted them more than his oldest friends.

'Good. Then good luck. Let's get into position. Richard, we'll wait for your signal.' Silently and quickly they wiped their faces on their sleeves and filtered to their firing points.

'See you all soon,' Richard told them as he took up his Sten, the bolt-cutters and a pair of binoculars and walked briskly to the front position to act as look-out.

Ditches ran along both edges of the road, separating it from the fields on one side and the forest on the other. The agents were distributed at three positions on the forest side, each hidden from the road by the rough screens.

Richard was in the first position in the forest-side ditch. Twenty metres along the road, Hélène manned the Bren, hidden at the edge of the treeline. The third position, in the same ditch, contained Thomas and Reece. In Reece's hands was a metal box about the size of a football, with wires running from it to the other tin buried in the road. A few metres beyond them was the supposedly abandoned car, left in the road at a crazy angle with its doors open, as if it had skidded. The full line stretched around sixty metres.

As soon as the entire prison transport had passed Richard, he would pull the caltrops, hidden on the other side of the road, across by means of an attached rope, so the vehicles couldn't reverse. The abandoned car would block their way forward. The Germans would therefore have to halt in a short stretch of road, leaving them exposed. The gunners would simultaneously fire on the army escort: Thomas and Reece would take out the driver of the van and anyone sitting beside him while Richard and Hélène would focus on any outriders. They would then outflank and kill any survivors. There was a high chance the Germans would outnumber them at the beginning, but the agents' momentum, surprise and superior firing positions should triumph, Reece calculated.

Once the men were down, Reece and Richard would cautiously approach the van and free the captives, using the bolt-cutters if necessary.

Thomas tried to settle himself beside Reece, attempting to hide from the wind. 'It's freezing,' he said.

'You don't need to tell me.'

'I'm unable to feel a vital part of myself. Much more of this and I'm in severe danger of a very quiet social life when I get back to England.' A farm truck passed them.

Reece crouched lower in the ditch. The pin-pricking rain was running down his face in cold rivulets and his limbs were so stiff he couldn't be certain they would move when the moment came. For half an hour he listened to Thomas attempt to make conversation and jokes. At least it took their minds off what was to come.

He was beginning to wonder if he had got it all wrong – if the transport had taken another road after all – when he saw Richard's arm lift up. 'Get ready,' he said.

'I'm ready,' Thomas replied under his breath. Within moments Reece heard something closing in. One, or perhaps two engines. Light buzzing like mosquitoes muffled by the drizzle. Motorcycles. It had to be the transport. He wanted it to be the transport. 'Don't wish it too soon,' Thomas said quietly. Reece met his eye then turned back to the road.

A second later, something burst around the bend further up. A motorbike with sidecar, ridden by a gust of grey.

Reece pressed himself down. The rider would have the standard-issue rifle slung across his back and the sidecar passenger would be armed with a sub-machine gun. Sweat mixed with the rainwater coursing down Reece's back.

Behind the motorbike something bigger – the square, grey-painted van – loomed. There could be up to thirty men and women crammed inside, shackled, beaten, part of the Gestapo's lethally successful hollowing out of the Resistance and SOE networks. And after it, a second bike and sidecar appeared. Good – it was what Reece had been expecting. He glanced at the Sten at his feet. The bronze bolt was back, the selector switch set to automatic firing and the safety on. But what he held in his hands was far more vital at that moment: the wire in his right hand and the metal box in his left that would detonate a measure of plastic explosive in the tin buried in the road surface. He had spent an hour checking and rechecking his calculations for the right amount and angle for the plastic: enough to disable the vehicles without killing the men imprisoned inside. But: chance. Chance was always the unwanted element.

The transport was two hundred metres away now and the ground vibrated with its approach. Reece looked up the line to the others. All were pressing down as low as they could.

A hundred metres from Richard's position. The first bike and the van were within range. Reece's breath became shallower and his fingers twitched, feeling the copper wire hot and sharp between them.

He could just make out two shifting figures behind the windscreen of the van, its wipers going as the rain came down harder, like a sheer wall. Those men would be the first to fall when Thomas, who was a fine shot, fired from his position.

The front motorcycle passed Richard. Reece moved the wire to within a hair's breadth of the contact. He tensed as he prepared to bring them together to make a circuit. Then he froze. Something had entered into the rain-soaked hinterland of his vision: more movement in the distance, far behind the second motorcycle. A straggler from the transport, perhaps. If it were a civilian vehicle, they would be caught up in the battle. He snatched his fingers back, leaving a gap of air and rain between the wet wires.

It was coming at great speed: a third German motorcycle, no sidecar. Reece caught his breath as he saw the rider lift his arm and a pair of sharp reports rang out. The rider was firing a pistol into the air. He was signalling to those in front of him. The motorcyclist at the front of the convoy looked over his shoulder. Reece's carefully mapped-out plan was about to burn.

The lead motorcyclist steered to the side of the road and slammed on the brakes, skidding to a halt. The van did the same, but its weight meant it couldn't stop on a whim and it sped past its escort. The second motorcycle was right after it.

Behind its rear wheels, the caltrops glinted as Richard hauled them across the road. Reece couldn't tell what the new rider was doing there, why he was attempting to signal to the others, but he knew that the plan was in danger and he had only seconds to execute it.

With a silent prayer, he pressed the electric wire to its contact. He saw them unite with a blue spark that instantly disappeared, washed away, and his heart skipped. The calculations on how much plastic explosive would disable but not destroy – had he got it right? He doubted himself. He doubted the figures and the manufacturing process that could have made the mixture too rich. He himself might be the author of Luc's death, he knew.

Then there was the sound: the noise of fireworks – a sharp explosion that rent the air. And in the same moment the ground beneath the van's front axle turned into liquid bursting upwards, lifting the front of the vehicle into the air and tossing it like a ship on high waves.

'Go!' Reece screamed through the rain.

The first reply was the hidden Bren. Reece felt the air shiver as its rounds sliced through, aiming at the closer of the two stationary motorcycles behind the van. Its rider and passenger, already alert to danger, jumped from the vehicle and used the sidecar as shielding, firing back as best they could towards the sound of the gun.

The rider and passenger from the second bike were low in the opposite ditch, less ready for a firefight than their colleagues. Richard sprang up, his Sten ready, and dashed across to flank them.

At the same time Thomas fired a volley into the front of the van, smashing holes in the windscreen. The driver and his mate ducked down, threw open the doors and leaped out, the driver flattening himself to the soaking ground, a pistol in his hand, while the other, armed with a Schmeisser, dropped into the ditch on the fields side of the road.

The third motorcyclist arrived at speed, but he hadn't seen the caltrops and they tore his tyres apart, sending him crashing into a tree, where he lay, unmoving.

Reece aimed his gun, set to automatic, and fired at the van driver. The bullets sprayed out, the empty cartridges spitting from the side of the stock, but the man's prone position made it a difficult shot. They went too high, thudding into the van's wheel. The driver, sensing rather than seeing where the fire was coming from, shot back. Six, seven bullets went over Reece's head, before the seventh grazed his ear.

The scene was confusion and chaos now. Although Beggar had the upper hand, trapping and outgunning the Germans, within seconds the initial impact of the assault had worn off and the six surviving soldiers had gained good defensive positions. The shock of fear flowed through Reece. Defeat and death seemed to hover above them.

The two Germans from the van cab had mistakenly identified the abandoned car as a firing position and their error gave Thomas time to hit the driver's mate. At the same time, the two men from the first motorcycle spread out and began shooting back at whoever they could see. But Beggar's fortunes took a boost the next moment as the Bren took down the second motorcycle passenger. That made the numbers even: four soldiers, four agents. In an instant Richard was on top of the second rider. The two men struggled hand to hand, their weapons discarded, water spraying from their limbs and the fetid pools on the road.

Reece knew they had to press home their advantage before the Germans could retreat to better positions where they might have a chance to defend themselves.

He emptied his Sten magazine in the direction of the first motorcyclists, hitting one, he thought, then dropped the gun and drew his Colt. He broke cover, jumped out of the ditch and went for the van driver lying on the ground. The soldier saw him coming and shot in Reece's direction, but his laid-out defensive position now worked against him, making it hard to hit a target moving at speed. Reece saw his angular face and pulled the trigger. His arm tensed for the recoil, but there was only a dull click: his round had jammed in the barrel. In a flicker, the face of the German changed from terror to the amazement of a man spared. He twisted on to his side and scrambled for Reece's legs, heaving and tipping him to the ground.

The back of Reece's head slammed through the flood on the road, into the crumbling, potholed tarmac. Grit and wet stones broke through the skin, into his flesh, scraping on the bone. The impact knocked all thought from him except the instinct to take hold of the body that was now crawling like an insect over his torso, pinning his arms so that he couldn't reach his gun.

It was then that muscle memory took over. The toughest part of his SOE training had been a two-week stint on a Highland estate, Arisaig, where two former British officers from the Shanghai Municipal Police had instructed recruits in the dirty fighting they had seen win battles on the docks. By instinct, Reece's hands grabbed and found a close-cropped head. He brought his knee up sharply, feeling it connect with a curving jaw.

The man grunted and rolled to the side, spraying brown water across them both. Above, bullets were cracking the air in every direction and the van's horn was blasting a continuous note over the cries. Reece skewed on to his side, twisting and sliding away in an attempt to get to his feet, but the other man had a firm grip on his jacket and dragged him back. Reece looked now at his adversary – a sergeant in the Feldgendarmerie, the army police who kept the civilian population subservient to the occupying force. He looked to be in his early twenties, but those years of training had given him the muscular physique of an older man. Wet filth covered half his face and had soaked into his fair hair.

Now that the shock of the assault was over, the German seemed to relish the fight. Perhaps he had looked on at his infantry comrades with jealousy – the Feldgendarmerie would assist the SS rounding up and killing civilians but mostly their duties were to control the population through bullying and intimidation. Now, finally, he was in a real battle. Reece kicked hard, his heel thudding into the man's armpit to break the grip, allowing him to pull himself away.

The German dived for his pistol, sending a flurry of sopping dirt across the ground. In the same moment Reece grabbed his Colt, but the magazine had come away when he was knocked down. He turned to see the German, his face running with mud and oily water, drop an empty magazine from his gun and rapidly pull a full one from his belt. Reece raced him, recovering his own magazine and slotting it back into the body of his Colt, his limbs weighed down by the saturated cloth around them. The German levelled the gun. Seeing the barrel pointing straight towards him, Reece made a blink-of-an-eye calculation that its bullet would hit him on his right side, and collapsed his left knee, dropping to that side. One, two bullets went past him. But the Colt was still jammed and Reece had no time to eject the round and re-cock it. He only had time to throw the weapon straight at the sergeant's face, forcing him to lift his hands up in protection.

It gave Reece a second's grace. He drew the stiletto knife from the sheath strapped to his arm and sprang forward. The German loosed two more shots. One went wide, but the other, Reece knew from the feeling of being punched, had found its mark in his left shoulder. It spun him so that his right hand, which grasped the knife, pitched forward towards the German's chest. But the sergeant, whose reflexes were fast, caught Reece's wrist before it found its mark and raised it up above both their heads. There was a struggle of strength, and the bullet wound in his shoulder meant Reece's was ebbing away. There was nothing else for it. He opened up his hand and let the blade fall. At the same second he lifted his left hand, trusting only to instinct, and snatched into the air. His fingers closed on the steel hilt. And his momentum carried it slick into the stomach of the German, slipping under the ribs.

Reece heaved with his weight and then the full blade was buried in the man and arterial blood was pulsing down the narrow hilt to cover Reece's hand. The German looked down in amazement and sagged at the knees. For a second, both men stopped still.

Reece knew what he had to do. He twisted the weapon, opening up the wound. The German screamed out in pain and Reece turned it back to its previous position before lifting it with all his strength to find a lung. He withdrew the knife and the sergeant gasped. It was as if he believed it was over. Reece whirled around behind him, grabbed his chin and stabbed the tip of the knife through the man's windpipe.

On his bloody hands, Reece felt the air escaping from the hole in the soldier's throat. It lasted for two breaths before the muscles fell lifeless and he slumped to the ground. Reece let him drop. It was the first time he had killed anyone he could see and touch. Rain washed the blood from his fingertips in thin streams.

Coming to himself, his body and clothes soaking with dirty water, he knew that the bullets were still flying. Two more slammed into the side of the truck beside him and he felt a burning in his shoulder. Looking down, he saw it was a shaking mass of red and tattered cloth that looked as if it had exploded outwards and the arm below it was becoming numb, falling to his side.

He checked around. The momentum of battle was back with the circuit. One of the soldiers from the first bike was shooting at Thomas in the ditch, but Hélène was keeping him pinned down and the other soldier, the one Reece had hit, was lying on the ground, half his head missing. Richard and the other surviving German, who had ridden the second bike, had broken apart and were exchanging fire. As Reece watched, Thomas drew the pin from a Mills and lobbed it towards the soldier opposite him. It went wide and dropped on to the road. The German fired another volley and ducked down. Then the grenade exploded and the whole world became a silent film.

No noise, no sound, no desperation. Everything seemed to blur. Through the smoke, Reece saw Richard crawling up the road, one leg trailing uselessly behind him. And something terrible, something inhuman, had happened to his face. His lower jaw had been shot away, and it now hung, held only by muscles and ligaments. He held his hands upwards in supplication, begging for aid, unable to ask for it.

Instinctively, Reece started for him. He didn't even know if his plan was to cover him or to pull him to safety but, first, he had to get there.

Almost immediately, Richard stopped and pointed at something further up the road that Reece couldn't make out. He began to crawl faster, as fast as he could, but he stopped and his body shook seven times, each one for a round fired from a German sub-machine gun behind him. And his body fell in the road. Reece knew then, with a hollow pain, that he had failed him.

Yet there was no time to mourn. Reece flattened himself to the side of the van and watched the two remaining Germans holding out in covered positions. He had to force them into the open. He scanned the ground and grabbed his Colt, ejecting the jammed round and chambering another before spinning around the corner of the van to see one of the Germans stare at him with an expression of surprise. But Reece froze before he pulled the trigger as another sight stopped him in his tracks.

Further up the road, coming around the bend, was a bulbous vehicle topped with two heavy weapons: a machine gun and an autocannon that spat explosive armour-piercing shells. 'Panzerspähwagen!' Reece screamed at Hélène, rainwater spraying from his skin. It would be upon them in twenty seconds. If it got among them, the battle was lost. The remaining soldiers would regroup behind it and use it as a mobile fortress. She looked where he was pointing and turned the Bren in that direction, although its armour and distance meant there was little point wasting ammunition on its body. 'Grenades. Go for its wheels.'

They had to change tactics: now they had to attempt to free the prisoners before they had wiped out the German soldiers, and run.

Reece fired at the soldier on the ground, who was trying to crawl into a safer position. The bullets went into his back, causing him to shake violently before falling motionless. Reece ran to the rear of the van and tried the handle, praying that the explosion had somehow broken the lock. But he had no such luck.

He dashed back to the man he had cut apart just moments ago. He was lying on his front, still leaking blood, and Reece turned him over to expose the ragged throat before hunting through his pockets. There it was: a metal ring of keys in the man's hip pocket.

The Panzerspähwagen, a four-wheel version built for speed and agility, was a hundred metres away now and bearing down fast. Thomas was shooting at it, although Reece knew he was wasting his time unless he hit the tyres multiple times, and those would be lucky shots. He ran to the lock and tried a key. It didn't fit. Neither did another and, worse, when he tried to pull it out he found he had pushed it in too hard, his muscles working at their maximum preservation-of-life level, and it was jammed in. He had to patiently work it out, gently twisting and shuffling it until it came away. There was banging from inside, pleading cries to let them out. 'Wait,' he whispered under his breath. The third key went in. He paused to hope that it would turn. It did.

Bullets hit the ground at his feet and Reece looked up to see the 222's machine gun in its shielded turret strafing the ground between him and the ditch. The remaining agents dropped out of sight and Reece threw open the vehicle door to see a mass of faces, people chained to the floor. One of them he recognized from the previous day – the girl whom the Gestapo had captured outside his shop. He caught the expression of desperation on her face.

Some of those shackled inside shouted to him, begging him to free them. But one voice stood out. 'Maxime!' it cried. Luc was chained with the others to the floor. 'The photos. I saw the document!'

Three bullets slammed into the van, tearing and buckling the metal. And then a fourth passed Reece's hip. And this one found a mark.

When Reece was a boy he used to go to the pictures. There were films about gangsters that showed men getting shot. The actors would put their hands to their chests, wince and fall to the ground, instantly dead. Very rarely, one would be shot in the forehead and a small black circle without blood would appear. When Reece went to war, he discovered that when a bullet drives into a man's skull it smashes it to pieces, turning the flesh into a pit and sucking the tissue out through the exit wound. On that country road, he watched as a round from the German machine gun tore the face from an old man chained to the vehicle's floor, turning the bones of the jaw and the eye socket into fragments. The man wore the clothes of someone who had once been well-to-do. Now they were stained with oil and dirt.

Luc was still shouting, even more desperate now. 'Maxime! I saw the images. The counter-attack plan. It comes from a German spy high up in England.' He was trying to impart what he had seen. The bullets were going wide – the 222 must have changed direction a little, throwing off the gunner's aim.

'What?' Reece demanded, struck by the information.

'Parade, that's his service name. The plan is called Parade One. It's . . .'

And then, as Reece watched, Luc's body jerked backwards, thudding against the side of the van.

Reece dropped to the ground and scuttled around the side to take shelter behind a wheel. More bullets cut into the ground in front of him as the gunner found Reece back in his sights. Reece could roll out and attempt to take out the gunner with his pistol, but the man was crouched behind steel shielding and the chance would be one in a hundred.

'Maxime!' It was Luc's voice again, weakly piercing through the metal of the van. He was alive, although clearly

67

hurt. Reece turned all his attention to the words he was shouting. 'The photos are in my studio. Charlotte knows my hiding place. They'll . . . sent, but I . . .' The rounds were drowning out his voice.

'Say again!' Reece knew the risk they were both taking, shouting like this.

' . . . says so . . . German radio frequency. I tried to . . .' But his voice was muffled by a new metallic sound, centimetres from Reece, as the wheel in front of him began to erupt. He looked up to see that the Panzerspähwagen's gunner had switched to the autocannon's explosive shells and was targeting him. 'Maxime! Get me out!' and Reece wished that he could but knew it was hopeless; he needed the boltcutters to break the chains and even then he would be dead before he got inside.

The wheel exploded in two. He dived for the ditch, tumbling into it and looking back at the armoured car. It was thirty metres away, no more. And in the distance there was another vehicle closing in – a troop carrier. It was hopeless now.

'Get back. We have to go!' he cried, sprinting for the treeline. They had failed. All they could do now was save themselves. Bullets from the crouching soldier crunched into the van's sides, bulging it, but it was double-layered heavy steel and they didn't pass through. 'Into the trees!'

Hélène leaped up and threw her grenade. At the same moment Reece pulled the pin from his, waited three seconds and lobbed it. Hélène's bounced off the Panzerspähwagen and exploded in a shower of dirt and smoke, but it was too far away to do any damage. Reece saw his lying directly in the armoured car's path and waited for it to blow, but the moment never came. 'Fucking dud,' he growled. They all turned and ran. 'What about Richard?' Thomas shouted, grabbing hold of Reece's bloody, soaking shirt.

'He's dead. We can't go for him!' Reece screamed back, ripping himself away.

They dived into the thick trees, the trunks around them splintering as bullets tore in. A branch fell in their path and they scrambled over it towards their truck. The Panzerspäh-wagen drove over the caltrops but its tyres were too thick to be penetrated by the spikes and it kept on coming, rolling over Richard's body.

Thomas wrenched open the truck door and Reece jumped in the other side. Hélène pulled herself into the back. Behind, they heard a smashing sound as the Panzerspähwagen knocked the abandoned car out of its path and turned up the junction to where they were. Thomas started the engine, but it wouldn't catch, turning over with a pneumonic whine. He tried again as the autocannon from the armoured car started up, shooting into the ground beside them, making it explode in showers of dirt. Then the engine caught and Thomas stamped the accelerator down, jerking them forward. Behind, the gun continued to fire, a couple of shells tearing into the metal of the truck and blowing it away. But the trees they had chained together as a roadblock worked and as they sped away the shells became less and less accurate until they finally ceased and the forest swallowed up the remnants of the German army.

There was silence as Reece and Thomas sat, feverish in their anger.

Thomas glared at Reece. 'All for nothing!' He slammed his fist on to the wheel. The rain was sweeping down the windscreen.

They sped along a dark country lane more used to sheep and geese. After an hour and a number of turns to throw off any pursuit Thomas stopped the van and pulled the creaking handbrake. He stared at Reece. 'That last motorbike. And the armoured car.' Reece knew what Thomas was going to say. 'They weren't part of the transport. They were sent after to warn it. They knew we were coming.' Thomas kept his eyes on Reece for a long time. Then he released the brake and started forward again.

'I know.'

Thomas lowered his voice. 'Do we have a traitor?'

It was a fear Reece had had from the very beginning. All three of the German intelligence services – the Abwehr, SD and Gestapo – had had significant success in infiltrating SOE circuits. He had been on the look-out for a German informant from the beginning, but whoever it was had stayed in a blind spot. And as the truck rumbled through ruts, he berated himself for his blindness, for a failing that had got Richard killed. If Reece's primary responsibility was to collect intelligence on the Germans, he had failed in his secondary: to keep his own agents alive.

'We might.' A traitor. A traitor was lower than the Boche. Two bullets in the back of the head and burial in shallow soil hung over them. But perhaps he was wrong, he told himself: the back-up could have been dispatched for another reason, and then no one's loyalty would be in question. 'We should all lie low for a while,' he said.

'That's for damn certain,' Thomas muttered.

'I'll go to Charlotte to warn her.' He could have sent someone else – it was really Hélène's job as courier – but he wanted to see Charlotte himself. And at least something had come out of the raid: the film and any prints Luc had made from it were hidden in his studio and Charlotte knew where he stashed such things.

He calculated: it was unlikely that the surviving German soldier would have overheard the shouted conversation between him and Luc – and even if he had, unless he spoke good French, he would have understood very little of it – so the Gestapo wouldn't be expecting an attempt to retrieve the photographs. The odds were that they knew nothing of them. Of course, the Germans would have searched Luc's house, but if the photos were well enough hidden, they would still be there.

Reece would go to Charlotte and they would recce Luc's house. If it looked at all like an ambush, they would walk straight past and try again a day or two later. The Gestapo were short of men as it was; they wouldn't have the numbers to keep a squad there for days on end on the off-chance that Reece or another would show up.

As soon as it seemed safe, he would locate the film and prints and make his way immediately to London. A submarine extraction was the quickest and safest way to get home, although reserved for only the most important missions. Yes, it was chance upon chance, but according to Luc there was a highly placed spy in London, and a man like that could kill more men than twenty divisions. Reece resolved to make sure he couldn't operate for long. And then Richard wouldn't have died for nothing. As he thought of Richard, hot anger was supplanted by cold guilt.

He lifted his hands from his knees. They stuck to the fabric and he had to tear them away. He became more conscious of a stabbing pain in his shoulder where the bullet had torn into his muscle. He didn't know if it had lodged in there or if it had passed right through. Either way, he needed it seen to. 'I need a doctor.'

Thomas thought. 'It'll be dark soon,' he said. 'We shouldn't be on the road after that. I know somewhere we can spend the night. I know a vet near there.'

'Good enough.'

'He'll treat you like a horse.'

'It will do.' Treatment by any man who could disinfect and sew a wound would be better than septicaemia rotting him from within. 'I'll go to Charlotte at first light.'

He stared out at the countryside. For the past four years he had thought about death ten times a day – others' deaths, sometimes his own. It rarely had any effect on him now; it was as much a part of daily life as pain. But sometimes, when he saw the life bleeding from his friends, the animal revulsion towards it returned.

He would have to tell London straight away about the failed op. Charlotte would send a priority transmission and Richard's family would receive a visit, no telegram. His role in the war would remain unknown.

They drove through nightfall. Once, in the distance, thin yellow beams from headlights raked the road ahead. They pulled off the road and stayed silent. The lights disappeared and they eased back, driving on for another few minutes before turning up a dirt track that rose in a series of hillocks and pits. All light was gone now, and night birds flurried away, disturbed by the mechanical sound of men. Thomas kept his eyes locked ahead and hadn't mentioned what they had both noticed – that in the time since they had spoken of their destination Reece's blood had soaked his shirt. His head was resting against the window and the bumps in the road were knocking it against the glass, but he hardly felt it. He just felt tired, his mind was heavy and his limbs – he could hardly feel his limbs. What sensation he had was concentrated in his shoulder, burning as if someone had thrust a white-hot poker through his flesh.

After a while he felt a hand on his arm. 'Wake up,' Thomas said. Reece opened his eyes and lifted his fingers to rub them. The jolt of pain in his shoulder made him gasp. He put his hand to it, but Thomas caught it. 'Leave it,' he cautioned.

They had stopped in what looked like a farmyard. Hélène opened Reece's door. She had a web of cuts on her cheek – fragmentation from a grenade, perhaps, or she had fallen against something with thorns.

Reece gingerly squeezed out of the cab, each movement bringing a new stab of pain, and saw that they were in front of a hillside farmhouse. The location gave the advantage that any approach from the main road would be easily spotted. A light came on in the building and the door opened a crack. Thomas helped Reece stumble towards it while Hélène drove the van around the back, out of sight. The farmer, a shotgun in his hand, stepped into the pool of light from the house.

'Are they following you?' he asked urgently. 'You can't be here if they are. Chloé's here.' He pointed upstairs to where the curtains had parted a little.

'She'll be safe,' Thomas told him, helping Reece across the threshold. 'No one's following us.'

The farmer caught his arm. 'Are you sure?'

'Yes.' Thomas's voice was calm and authoritative.

'All right. All right. The kitchen.' He took a look at Reece. 'My God, he's in a state.'

They carried Reece through the rear door into a large stone-flagged kitchen. A grand wooden table took up much of the room and Reece slumped on to it, its contents pushed to one side. 'We need a favour,' Thomas said, lifting Reece's legs up to the wooden surface.

'Go on.' The farmer sounded wary.

'Can you send for Jacques Ferrier?'

The farmer stared at Reece. 'For him?'

'Jacques can be trusted.'

He wiped his hands over his face. 'Yes. All right. I'll send Chloé for him. He should be here within an hour.'

'Tell him your horse is giving birth and it's not going well.'

'All right.'

'Thanks.'

The farmer hurried away. 'You'll be fine,' Thomas whispered to Reece. 'And Chloé's a real looker. Twenty-one. You'll be upright before the night's out, if you know what I mean.'

Reece smiled thinly. Then he lay back on the table to try to blot out the waves of nausea. He felt his mind muddying and slipping.

CHAPTER 6

10 February 1944

In the dark of the farmhouse kitchen Reece woke with a gasp. Pain in his shoulder had jerked him awake and he touched it to find it had been treated, stitched up and bound during the night. But something else had woken him too. A faint sound of shuffling mixed with a metallic clanking: someone moving quietly outside. As the blood rushed back to his head he remembered an op, Richard dead on the road and a traitor.

He rolled over and eased himself from the table where he still lay. He kept low so that his silhouette wouldn't be noticed from outside and felt for his holster and the Colt, but his fingers found nothing. In the moonlight, his gaze fell on a knife block and he crept forward, slipped a long knife from the wood and silently approached the door on the balls of his feet. The terracotta tiles were freezing.

He checked outside the window, but all that was visible was a clear sky pin-pricked with stars. The sound came again: slight, muffled movement, and then a crack as if something had broken underfoot. He pressed the simple brass door handle down and slid outside.

There were creatures out there that he could hear but not see. As his eyes adjusted he managed to make out a barn, a few outbuildings, but little more. The crunching sound of subtle footsteps came from the edge of one of the squat piles of brick and corrugated iron. And it was coming closer.

Reece pressed himself into the doorway, ready to spring forward. A figure in white edged past the corner of the building. By the starlight Reece could make out a gun in one hand and some sort of large metal canister in the other. He crouched. If he waited, he might be able to silently approach them from behind and take them with the blade. He watched as the figure made it to more open ground, covered with the straw and muck detritus of a farm, and then a glint of moon picked out Hélène's profile. Reece tensed his muscles.

'There's no need for that.' The voice made Reece spin around, the knife ready. Thomas was inside the kitchen, his Sten slung over his back by a leather strap. 'She's just collecting milk for us,' he said, putting a match to a paraffin lamp, keeping it low. 'We have to keep our strength up.'

Reece breathed out slowly and placed the blade on the windowsill. He watched Hélène walk quietly back towards the side of the farmhouse. Reece was glad Thomas was there in the night.

'You thought it was her,' Thomas said.

Reece licked his lips. His voice was dry and rasping. 'I did.'

'Well, for all we know, it was. How much do you really know about Hélène?' Thomas replied, gazing back outside into the night.

'No more than I know about you, Thomas.'

'That's true. We have to find out who it was.' The paraffin burned with a faint hiss.

'It could have been no one. Just bad luck. Leave it to me.'

A traitor in the circuit felt a damn sight more painful to Reece than being shot in the shoulder, but it wouldn't help if they all turned on each other. 'We should get going. Better get back to the city before it's light.' Thomas handed Reece a pewter mug of water.

Reece drank, feeling his body soften with the fluid. 'We have to do it soon, before the Germans get to work on Luc and he cracks,' he said. 'Go to your back-up safe houses, break into your reserve identities and be ready to leave at the first sign they're on to us.'

Thomas went over to a heavy wooden sideboard. He lifted a small metal object the size of a coin and tossed it to Reece. 'Have this.'

Without thinking, Reece caught it in both hands and winced at the stabbing pain in his left shoulder. He looked at the object in his fingers, a crushed bullet from a German Radom automatic. He turned it over in his fingers. 'Good luck charm,' he said, putting it in his pocket.

'You'll need more than that.'

The door opened and Hélène entered. She laid the back of her hand on Reece's forehead. 'Well, you're hot, but better,' she said. He nodded. 'If I were your doctor, I would suggest four weeks of rest. I don't suppose you would take that advice?'

'I can't.'

Thomas stared straight at Hélène. 'Someone warned the Germans about the op,' he said.

She stood stock still for a long time, holding his gaze, reading it. 'If you've got something to say, say it,' she said slowly.

'Why are you here? You're not British, you're not French.'

'And yet I'm here, risking my life for it!' It was rare to see her angry.

'All right, that's enough!' Reece cautioned them. They backed off to opposite corners. 'We're doing the Boche's work for them if we go on like this. We have no idea if anyone informed on us. If they did, it will have come from outside

77

the circuit.' He knew that wasn't true, but no good would come of a confrontation. 'Get ready to move out.'

As a boy, Siegfried Klaussmann had lived an outdoor life, combined with conscientious study, especially when it came to the natural sciences, in the hope of one day continuing his studies at a university. His father had been a doctor and was a kind man – respected by everyone, according to Klaussmann's mother. When he had been killed in the closing months of the first war, his mother had cried until she vomited over her son. When she told him that Papa was gone for ever, Siegfried, then fourteen, blinked for a while and started to wail like his mother. The noise alerted their neighbours, who could do nothing but commiserate.

The death of Dr Klaussmann meant that his son had to leave his expensive school and instead join the sons of shoe-makers and clerks in a more modest local academy. By the time he was eighteen, it had become clear that financial restrictions meant there was no prospect of the career he had wanted. Instead, he joined the police and continued his post-school education at the local library and at open lectures.

Early on in his career a colleague had placed a bag containing a bundle of bank notes on a bench in the station kitchen, turned his back and begun pulling crockery from the cupboard. The notes' grimy surfaces and torn edges had served as a metaphor to Klaussmann.

'No, thank you,' he had said, stirring a cup of coffee.

His brother officers didn't know that his objection wasn't moral so much as strategic. Although he didn't want to touch the syphilitic dregs of society, he would have taken their money if he thought it really would be free. However, a man who accepts a bribe one week is the subject of blackmail the next, he told himself. And he wanted to rise.

Now, more than a decade later, he looked grimly on a scene he had never expected. Six soldiers' bodies had been neatly laid out in the back of the army lorry, but their respectful arrangement could hardly make up for the fact that their parents, wives and children would soon be getting letters saying that their sons, husbands and fathers would not be returning. The cold had frozen them stiff and the blood that had soaked their jackets was now dark red ice. At least they wouldn't smell.

'How many were there?' Klaussmann asked the corporal who had manned the armoured car's machine gun and was now staring at his former barracks-mates' corpses.

'We couldn't see fully, Sturmbannführer. I would guess six.'

'When you fill out your report, say two.'

'Two, sir? Won't we look weak?'

'Just do as I say.' He could hardly afford to tell Berlin that the Gestapo had let scores of terrorists run around the countryside, wiping out companies of soldiers at will. Better that there were only two of them and the army's incompetent troops were responsible for their own deaths. He didn't want this man talking out of turn, however.

'Do you have family back home?'

'Yes, sir. In Stuttgart.'

'Friends there?'

'Yes, sir.'

'Close friends?'

'I–I . . .' the soldier stammered.

'A charming town. I know the Gestapo chief there.' He let it hang in the air and the obviously queer twenty-year-old in front of him understood. Klaussmann had a nose for queers. He had no time to deal with this one, though – besides, the soldier would give himself away sooner or later. They had a look about them. 'The dead spy. Have him dissected. Did you see any of the others?'

The soldier did his best to pull himself together. 'We hit one, sir. Here.' He tapped his left shoulder.

'But you had a heavy machine gun and you didn't put him down.' The corporal made no reply. Klaussmann went to the back of the lorry and stared in. This was what he was fighting. But all he needed was one thread to pull.

Winding south through pitch-black mud-flooding lanes towards Paris, Reece realized that it wasn't far from there that, in November 1942, he and Charlotte had parachuted into France.

The moment they touched the ground they had buried their parachutes, scattered snuff on the ground to confuse the Germans' dogs and hidden in the woods until it was light. Then they had walked to the nearby village arm in arm like a pair of young lovers out for a morning stroll in the crisp autumnal air.

Nine months later the Gestapo had kicked in the door of Charlotte's first safe house, allowing the summer pollen to waft in. The house, built in the Marais, east of the Louvre, for a nineteenth-century schoolmaster, was at the end of a little lane lined with trees and bushes. It had two storeys and a spartan attic where Charlotte slept under threadbare cotton sheets. She could receive transmissions there, but it was best not to transmit from where you lived, as the Germans had detector vans. They could find a rough location within fifteen minutes, at which point Gestapo officers with disguised portable direction-finders would move on to the streets to pinpoint the address. But that evening she was already late for her sked and they had taken the risk.

Reece had spotted the men in the street. When they ran into the house they had found him in bed with Charlotte and

Reece had explained that they had been hiding upstairs because 'Sir, we are not married, and she is very traditional, a bit ashamed, you understand.' Luckily, Charlotte's host family were out at the time.

The German soldiers, after making Charlotte get out of bed and stand in front of them so they could 'check for weapons', left, laughing. She had sat neatly on the side of the bed until Reece pulled back the covers and then had lain down, looking at the ceiling. He had covered her mouth with his and she had put her hands to his face.

Later that day Reece had borrowed a camera from Luc and asked a passing man to take a photograph of the two of them sitting on a bench in front of Notre-Dame. When the photograph was printed it showed him looking into the lens. Her eyes were downcast. 'We look like we're on the worst honeymoon,' he had said.

He had woken the following morning to the sight of her at the window, smoking. 'You should go before the others wake up,' she said, waving her hand to where her host family must have been sleeping.

'If you want.'

He dressed and she led him to the door. 'What do you expect from me, Maxime? If we survive, will we go to picture galleries? Or music clubs? Is that us? I don't believe it.'

'It could be true.'

'When you want to, you can leave France. You probably will. One day you will wake up in the sunlight or in the dark, maybe, and you will decide that it's time to leave.'

'What gives you that idea?'

'Experience.'

'Your experience isn't mine.' He had no intention of leaving. He pictured a time, years from then, without the Boche tramping the streets in the summer and the cold drawing their bones out through their skin in the winter. 'What about you? What do you want?'

'I don't think about what I want,' she said, more to herself than to him.

'Why?'

She paused. 'There hardly seems a point.'

'Because you don't care?'

'Because the Germans came through the forest of Ardennes.'

He understood what meaning her words bore: their lives now were not their own, they were in the hands of others. It was a terrible thing, he thought, to see your future dictated by men who considered you less human than them. It was a feeling of bewilderment and impotence. She always left him with the impression that she had given up on the world because it had given up on her.

'Things will change. One thing you can be sure of is things don't stay the same. A little faith, Charlotte.'

And she had retreated into the house, leaving nothing but the smell of her smoke – cheap cigarettes that were more paper than tobacco.

The van stopped and Reece swung his legs out into the dark pre-dawn countryside. They were coming to a halt beside a stream close to the outskirts of the capital. He lifted his bike out, wincing at the pain in his shoulder. 'What will you do with the truck?' he asked Thomas.

'Keep it out of sight for a while, but these plates are false.' He tapped its side fondly. 'We might be able to cover the bullet holes with canvas or something.' The guns were hidden in a metal case welded to the underside of the vehicle.

'What are you going to do now?' Hélène asked.

'Go to Charlotte. Warn her.'

'Take care of yourselves.' Hélène was often the most perceptive of them all and he had no doubt that she had seen what was between him and Charlotte.

'We will. What are you going to do?'

'Take a bath. Hot, if I can. Then I'll go to Mass and say a prayer for Richard. Poor boy. I would go to confession if I could trust the priest. I'll have to make it a silent prayer instead.'

'Do that.'

She embraced him, pressing her cheek to his. Then she did the same to Thomas, forgetting their argument of the previous night, before straddling her bike and riding away.

Thomas embraced him too. 'Goodbye, my friend.'

'Goodbye.'

Reece got on to his own bike and began pedalling, unsteadily at first, unable to put any weight on his left arm, but soon getting into a rhythm.

He passed houses that slowly moved closer together and shrank in size, the greenery around them giving way to pavements and telephone poles. At a half-hearted checkpoint a man on horseback passed by; that was strange, but not remarkable. With petrol so scarce, the only motor vehicles were driven by the Germans or their friends – it was, indeed, shameful to be seen in one these days, marking out young men as *collabos*, young women as the Germans' whores.

A brick wall had bills posted on it. Some were lists of those to be executed, along with their professions, to identify them more closely and frighten those of the same trade; some advertised films: *Les Aventures fantastiques du Baron Münchausen* had been altered, a swastika imposed on the title character's image and the words *Film Boche n'allez pas* across the middle. Corsican tenor Tino Rossi was the musical sensation of the day, exclaimed a third. But each one was covered by a chalked letter V. *Victoire. Victoire. Victoire.* Everyone was certain; everyone trusted that victory was coming. Yet Reece was part of the struggle and, even more after last night, he wished he had the certainty of the young men and women chalking over posters for German films.

He passed a queue outside a greengrocery that must have been a hundred metres long, made up of women wearing hats but no stockings. There was no talk or gossiping among them, he saw; their attention was only on the door that would open an hour or more from now. They had probably been queuing for three hours already and some would have place-holding arrangements with women waiting in lines outside other shops. It was one of the strange necessities of the times.

The morning traffic was on the street now: a postman, a few workers on their way to factories. One threw a glowing cigarette butt to the ground and another immediately snatched it back up and remonstrated with him for the profligacy before placing it in an airtight tin taken from his hip pocket.

Reece passed them and turned up a street where a few stray dogs barked at each other, running up and down the cobbles in search of nothing. There was a strange tang in the air. Hungry, Reece noticed a café just opening, with the owner setting out the chairs and tables in the hope of selling a few croissants to those on their way to work. Reece could wait, though, and stopped for a moment to tie his shoelace and glance up and down the road to make sure no one was standing around for no reason or sauntering casually behind him. It seemed safe. The strange smell in the air was growing stronger and more distinct as he turned the corner into Charlotte's street. A vehicle sped past him, nearly knocking him out of the way. He stared after it. And then he realized what the smell was. As he looked towards

Charlotte's house he saw the windows on the upper storey explode outwards, shattered by the heat from flames behind them.

Black smoke, billowing from the pits that had once been the ground-floor windows, was sending ash through the air, turning it grey and casting a sea of mottled shadows over the ground. Reece stood, shocked, as the remaining glass on the upper floor splintered, the shards falling slowly through the soot. A crowd had assembled below, pointing and shouting. It was as if the febrile raid on the prison transport had somehow followed him here.

A hailstorm of thoughts pounded through his head. It was animal instinct that told him that the Germans had found her, taken her, as they had taken Luc. He felt the pain she would soon feel.

But then something else surged in him: reason crying for attention beyond the reflex. There were no Germans in sight. If it were one of their ops, there would be soldiers or Gestapo officers controlling the scene. And they could hardly be lying in wait for him – the scene was too chaotic, too porous.

So what was it: an accident? A domestic fire? They happened, and the SOE training had warned not to ascribe to human intent what was really the fault of chance, but he didn't trust that prospect at all, not after last night, when the Germans had shown their presence. And above all, he had no time to think clearly; he could only snatch at possibilities.

Then, at the attic window, something caught his eye. Through the clouds of black he saw a figure in a deep red dress looking back at him. She placed her hands on what little glass remained in the window frame. He shouted her name, desperate for her to hear him, but she stood frozen, before stepping back, turning to look at something – or someone – inside the room. Then she dropped to the floor. He ran.

The shouts from the men on the fire engine didn't stop him as he sprinted towards the door, shaking off the hands that grabbed at his clothing and shoving through bodies. Voices were yelling at him to stop. A gang of four militiamen stood around in front of the house.

But he would deal with the aftermath, even if it were at the hands of the Gestapo, when they were both away from the flames' reach. 'Wait! Stop! It's not for you to go in!' one of the militia shouted, grabbing rough hold of Reece.

Reece tried to pull free of the fool who had hold of him, a blond boy barely out of his teens. 'My friend, she's up there, I saw her,' he said.

The boy called to the firemen, who were rapidly unpacking their equipment, ready to investigate the house. 'He says there's someone in there.' He turned back to Reece. 'What's her name?'

'What does it matter?' Reece shoved the militiaman away hard, so that the boy tripped and fell to the ground before scrambling back to his feet and taking tight hold of Reece's lapel. 'What's her name?' he demanded angrily.

Reece regretted the action. The attention would be dangerous right now. He tried to answer the question – but only to discover his mind was a blank sheet. Charlotte was her service name, used only within SOE. She would have a cover identity, but he couldn't remember it. The boy seemed to mark the hesitation. He had likely heard about the raid last night and been told to check everyone's identity.

Her cover name came to him. 'Christine! Christine Tarre. Please hurry.'

'Occupation?' Although Reece was used to the questions, there was an edge to them that was disconcerting, even as he watched three firemen in their protective clothing smash down the front door with a sledgehammer. The young men of the town had been called up for compulsory labour in Germany – those who hadn't run away to join the Maquis rebels in the hills – so these men were older, and Reece felt their slowness. 'I don't know. She's a nurse, I think. I just met her.'

'So she's not your friend?'

Reece tried to bluff it out. 'She's . . .'

'What's your name?'

Reece could see the firemen charging through the house. Their mates had unfurled their engine hose and begun spraying water through the broken windows. He stared again at the attic window. It shimmered through the smoke, appearing then drifting away behind the silky mist. He willed her to come back to it. Once, just for a second, he thought he saw her, and he started to move to the house to get to her, but the militiaman blocked his path and by the time he looked back up the window was empty again.

'I . . .'

Reece was on the verge of knocking this boy to the ground and running into the house to carry her out. But he knew that he could do less than the firemen.

'Papers.'

Reece reached into his jacket breast pocket for his identity cards and felt them in his hand. But they were strange to the touch: all stuck together. He realized they were soaked in his congealed blood. He withdrew his hand, wiping his fingers on the material as he pulled them away. He had to change, to cozen the boy.

'I'm sorry, sir. I've left them at home.'

'At home?'

'Yes.'

'You know that's an offence?'

'Yes. I'm sorry, I do.' Not checking them was a stupid mistake. 'I can go and get them.'

'Go and get them? Of course you can't. Stay here. I'm watching you.' The young man went to a waddling female senior officer and spoke to her, keeping a close watch on Reece. Reece was furious at himself and at the situation, unable to find out if Charlotte was alive, if the Germans were on to them, held back by the watch of this self-important and yet potentially dangerous child.

He stared at the remaining glass in the attic window. It shattered into a thousand pieces and, in its place, fingers of orange flame stretched out and up the blackening brickwork. He caught his breath and looked around, hoping there would be someone who could help. He saw only a growing crowd of the bemused and casually excited, pointing and asking who was in there. A neighbour began wailing for the household until someone informed her that the houseowner had gone on holiday to his mother's in Lyon a few days previously, and she looked relieved.

The militiaman came back, accompanied by the female officer. 'You said –' the boy began, but he was interrupted by a sound like an explosion.

CHAPTER 7

Your cover is the life which you outwardly lead in order to conceal the real purpose of your presence and the explanation which you give of your past and present. The agent must observe self-discipline, e.g. be able to control his reactions in routine controls or if accidents occur. Practise moderation in drink, care in relations with women, avoid celebrations after success, etc.

At the sound of the blast from the house Reece dropped to his knees. Another second and he was peering through a fresh cloud of dusty smoke at the upper floor, trying to fathom what had happened. A battle between Charlotte and some unseen German troops? No, he would have spotted them. Could she have had some plastic explosive hidden there for a sabotage mission? Conceivable, but Reece would have known of it.

As the smoke cleared he saw it was none of these. The roof had collapsed as the timber frame weakened. And it had taken with it half the outer wall of the attic. Where there had been bricks there was now a gaping hole filled with fire and billowing smoke. Slowly, he caught glimpses through the grey mist of a figure charging from one side of the room to the other, as if searching for a way out. He felt as if he were up there with her, trying to find a way down. But as he stared, the heat on his face making him flinch, the figure took form: not her, but one of the firemen, frightened and disoriented by the calamity. The man came to the breach in the wall and called down.

'She's not here!'

Reece couldn't hold back any more. Not caring if it risked undue attention, he shoved his way through the crowd. The young militiaman tried to stop him again but left off when he saw the look in Reece's eyes that said the boy would regret it. Other men were crowding, desperate to get as close to the drama as possible, but he threw them from his path. One took hold of his lapel in anger, until Reece made a fist with his middle knuckle raised into a point and stabbed it hard into the man's midriff, winding him and dropping him to the ground.

'I saw her!' he shouted up to the fireman above. He made it as far as the door, but the sheer heat, blistering his skin, drove him back.

'Leave it to them,' a woman implored, her hands lifted to him. 'You can't do anything.'

Another sound, like a small bomb, made them both stop. The remaining part of the roof had collapsed and more bricks were falling. The top storey of the building was no more than a burning mass. 'Get out!' the chief fireman yelled. The men inside seemed to hear, for they came running out, coughing as they made it to the cordon. Reece spun around, looking for another way into the house. 'She's not there,' the chief fireman barked at him.

The fire crew lifted a ladder to the top floor and their colleague clambered on and began to descend. Then he halted, hesitated and stepped back up one rung. His head was level with the breach and he was looking back into the room. Suddenly, he began climbing again at speed. He scrambled over the ragged layer of bricks and disappeared into the smoke.

'What the hell is he doing?' Reece demanded.

'I don't know,' the chief replied. 'Come out, you fool!'

Voices in the crowd cried out the same and for tense seconds there was nothing but the sound of flames licking at the cracking wood and crumbling mortar. Then the fireman came to the hole in the wall. 'She's in the corner!' he called down. One of his mates raced up the ladder, hand over hand, and into the room, out of sight with the first man.

Timbers cracked and split. More bricks fell. The house wouldn't last long, it was clear, as the flames pushed right up through the roof. A cry arose from the crowd. The firemen reappeared, framed by the tumbling masonry, but they weren't coming unburdened. The first carried something slumped over his shoulder – a charred thing that had once been a woman. The hail in Reece's mind calmed and was replaced by something colder, a settling of frost.

Painfully slowly, the man descended the ladder. Reece looked for movement, signs of life in the body being carried. There was nothing. The fireman came down step by step and Reece fought to get forward again, but the militia had formed a cordon and he couldn't risk being arrested.

The fireman stepped back on to the ground. Three or four others immediately encircled him and took his burden from him, laying it – her – down on the scrubby grass. They formed a kneeling barrier that Reece couldn't see through. Then one stood. Between them Reece caught sight of burnt hair and soot-covered skin. 'Cover her face,' said the chief fireman quietly. 'Give her some dignity.'

'It's the girl who lives here,' said a man standing at the front of the circle. 'I know them. I live over there.' He pointed somewhere to the side.

Reece felt himself pulled into the earth. It was as if something had been cut from him to leave a ragged wound.

'Stay back, friend,' the fire chief said.

'Let me see her.'

'Are you family?'

'Yes, I am.' He felt far closer to her than the people to whom he was related.

'Then you don't want to see her. Trust me.'

Reece gazed at the fireman. The man was doing his best to prevent meaningless distress, but Reece couldn't just walk away. 'I've been in the war,' he said. 'I know what it looks like.'

For a moment the fire officer wavered, then he nodded. 'Let him through,' he told his subordinates. They looked doubtful but stood aside to let Reece view the girl, whose face was now covered by rough hessian cloth, leaving only the dark hair that Reece had let slip through his fingers time and time again. He remembered the sensation now as he stepped forward.

They had always been close to death. He had touched it on the road to Amiens just hours ago when Richard had died in front of them all. Charlotte's old neighbours had been taken by the Gestapo, she had told him back in England. For sure, some of their cohort at the Finishing School had been taken too, now. But her death seemed impossible.

He stopped in front of her, hearing a distant hum from the crowd. The skin on her arms was filthy with soot but here and there he could see scorch marks.

His fingers gingerly reached for the top of the cloth, and he peeled back the rough fabric to reveal the hair, then the charred skin and finally her open eyes. And he felt a hot blade turn in his stomach. Her face. It was burnt and covered in ash, but it seemed . . . His jaw fell in confusion.

One of the firemen put his hand on Reece's wrist, pulling him away. 'My friend . . .'

But Reece's thoughts were rushing. Was her face too wide? The chin too long?

He stared down at the open eyes. They were a watery blue. Charlotte's were green. He knew them better than he knew his own. These eyes were not hers.

A stranger. The woman below him was the same age as Charlotte but shorter, with more powerful limbs. She must be the daughter of Charlotte's host.

'Are you all right?'

'Yes. I'll . . . be all right.' His mind was an upheaval of calculations, of grasped-for hope. He was certain it had been Charlotte he saw on the upper floor, but it was a different woman here on the ground.

Was she still up there and in danger? No, she would have been found too. Either she had run or she had been taken against her will, and he had no way of knowing which. She might still be alive. But the scene before him was no accident. He had to slip away. The police and the militia might climb the ladder and spot something in her room – a transmitter set, code books, her gun – and he had already marked himself out as someone who knew her. He also claimed to have left his papers at home.

He picked up his bicycle and turned quickly, only to find his path blocked by the senior militia woman.

'You were going to show us your papers,' she said. 'Where are they?'

'They're at my house.'

'At your house?' She seemed sceptical. 'Come over here.' She led him up the road, away from the crush of bodies. 'What's your name?'

'Marc LeFevre.' He suppressed his frustration at her petty expression of power.

'Occupation?'

'I run a tabac.' He looked back to where the body lay, once more with a grey cloth over her face. For a moment he doubted himself – had it been Charlotte after all, and he had just wanted so much to think that it was another girl? No, he knew it wasn't her.

'Look at me.' The militia woman was stabbing her finger into his chest. She had small, piggy features. 'Raise your hands.' He did as he was told. He tried to work out what he would do when she put her hand into his jacket's inside pocket and found his blood-crusted papers. He could try to talk his way out, or to run. Running would probably be safer, the chaos around them affording some sort of protection. Her hands went into his jacket's hip pockets. Nothing there. Then she came to his trouser pockets. She stopped, one hand on each. Her right was pressing on a small metal object in his left pocket: the bullet that had been plucked from his shoulder. He cursed the fact that he had kept it. She looked up at him, then slipped her fingertips into his right pocket and lifted out his wallet. 'Maybe your papers are in here,' she said. He watched as her eyes widened at what she found. Two hundred-franc notes. It was probably more than she was paid in a week.

She was corrupt, as corrupt as most of her colleagues, but that hardly meant she wasn't going to take him in. Indeed, maybe she was calculating that a man with this much money in his wallet would be good for more, held ransom to his family. Or perhaps her mind ran in the other direction: a man with this money had friends – maybe he was a black marketeer already paying off the Germans, and she didn't want to step on anyone's toes. Reece tried to tell from her face which way she would jump.

And then the notes were quickly stuffed into her own pocket, the wallet thrust into his hands and she walked back to the crowd, whom she began ordering about.

Thankful for a stroke of luck at last, Reece hurried straight to his bike, picked it up from the ground and cycled away at speed, feeling his bones shake over the cobbles and ruts. Every moment, he was sure that he would be called back, but the demand never came. As he reached the corner he risked a glance over his shoulder. And that was the last he saw of the burning house.

He managed to gain two streets before his feet skidded on to the ground, and he stopped to lean against a tree that had been stripped bare by the weather. He was almost able to order his thoughts now.

It had been no accident. Charlotte had disappeared, and that had been someone's intention. But whose? The Gestapo could be behind it. It could conceivably be part of some plan of theirs to keep her capture secret and to force her to transmit false messages to London. But it was much more likely that they would keep her under observation and try to catch the rest of the circuit when another agent made contact. No, an arrest seemed unlikely.

Equally, it seemed implausible that she was the Germans' source within Beggar and the fire in which she had nearly perished was all part of their plan. And besides: why let Reece remain free?

No, neither explanation fitted the facts. And as the confusion abated it was replaced by a bolt of anger. He picked up his bike, ready to hurl it against a thin wooden fence with all the force he had. But he had an urgent mission now. He had to retrieve the photographs from Luc's studio, and only Charlotte knew where they were concealed.

Formerly a simple garden shed behind his house in Montmartre, Luc's studio was now blacked out and populated with pieces of camera equipment. It was set in a small rear garden, beside which lay an alleyway connecting two quiet streets.

Reece had been there once before, a few months earlier, when Luc had created a number of travel permits for him to visit towns and ports along the Atlantic coast. Luc had enquired why he needed to visit the towns. Reece had brushed him off with an excuse – the truth being that he had been assigned an intelligence mission classified at the highest level. As a former naval intelligence officer, it had fallen to him to recce the harbours and beaches of Normandy and Calais, working out where large numbers of troops could best wade or drive ashore with some protection from attack.

The purpose behind the mission was obvious. Indeed, the German high command had been desperately speculating on the location of the landings for years. Hitler himself had declared that the Pas de Calais would be the Allies' entry point into occupied Europe, but Rommel had pointed to Normandy as the likely jumping-off ground.

If Reece had been in any doubt as to the level at which his information would be considered, it disappeared as soon as he had completed the survey and been picked up in a Lysander that had flown him to an airfield in Hampshire. From there he had been taken in an unmarked government car to a network of bomb-proof tunnels underneath Mayfair. Guards armed with sub-machine guns had saluted as he was led through the austere concrete-block Cabinet War Rooms to a room heavy with acrid cigar smoke.

The Prime Minister, a gaunt American general, a British vice-admiral and Reece's own SOE Officer Commanding had looked at him gravely and asked him to give a full report of his findings. For two full hours he had calmly told them how many men could file off a transport cruiser on to the quays of occupied France in thirty minutes while the RAF fended off the Luftwaffe FW190s.

All the while he had wanted to take the opportunity to grab them by their jaws and demand the invasion come right then because, soon, there would be nothing left of France or its people worth saving.

He recalled that moment as he rode along the alleyway behind Luc's house and peered through a high wooden fence. There was no sign of a Gestapo presence. He returned to the street and approached a small patch of dirt and gravel opposite, where old men were playing boules to while away the day. It was a vision of the France he had once loved: genteel, sporting and jovially bickering, rather than the new diet of contempt and poisonous embraces. The men wore balaclavas against the cold. Meanwhile, at the other end of the green, Reece saw three more of their number holding nets under a tree, waiting for pigeons to come down for crumbs they had scattered. Cold and hunger, Reece thought to himself, were going to kill as many Frenchmen as the German machine. He fantasized a plague that would make the Germans vomit up all the food they had stolen.

He bade the old men a good morning and they replied in kind. 'I'm waiting for a friend who lives there,' he said, pointing to Luc's house. 'You haven't seen him come out, have you?' They wouldn't have, he knew, but they might have seen the Gestapo inside.

'No one's come in or out as long as we've been here,' said one man, taking off his balaclava to reveal a face so gaunt he appeared more a talking skull than a man.

'No, no one,' said another, a little suspiciously. 'Who did . . .' He stopped, and Reece followed his line of vision to catch sight of a German infantry platoon passing by, singing a battle hymn. 'They sing louder when they're nervous. They're always singing louder these days,' he announced. 'They're sending children now – look at them: seventeen, eighteen. And they know the British are coming soon. You listen to me, the battle's about to begin.'

'You said that months ago,' objected his friend.

'And now it's going to happen. You listen to me.'

Reece interrupted. 'Well, I'll come back later. The stench of the Boche, right?'

'Yes, right.'

Reece wheeled his bike away as the men went back to their game. He went to the end of the street and pulled his bike behind a tree and waited. Before long a dirty-faced child, a boy aged eight or nine, walked by, throwing a ball high into the air and catching it. Reece plucked it out of the air and threw it to the child, who chuckled. 'Hello,' he said. The boy smiled in reply. 'How would you like a job? I'm waiting for my friend in the house over there, but I don't want to leave my bike here. If I give you fifty centimes' – he pulled a coin from his pocket and flipped it to the boy – 'can you walk over there and knock on his door?' The child nodded enthusiastically. 'Good. But he doesn't hear very well. So you have to knock for a long time. Try three times. If there's no answer, he's not home and you can go off and play. But if anyone else answers, we're playing a game and you have to pretend you're looking for your friend Pierre and you've got the wrong house. You can't say I sent you. All right?'

'Yes,' the boy said.

'Off you go.'

The boy went to the house. Reece straddled his bike in case he had to leave at speed. The child clacked the knocker loudly enough for Reece to hear and waited. Then twice more. Reece scanned the upper and lower windows for movement or shadows, but there was nothing. Eventually, the boy gave up, shrugged at Reece and sauntered away, his money earned. Reece wheeled his bike back down the alley to the side of Luc's house. The fence was shoulder height, though a crumbling bit of low wall at the far end of it would allow him to scramble over. He clambered on to the bricks, but just as he did so a middle-aged woman strode along the alley, dragging a teenage girl whose face was plastered in make-up. The woman glared suspiciously at Reece.

'Do you know who lives here?' Reece demanded in angry tones. She shook her head. 'Black marketeer. Fucking traitor.' He hopped down. 'Selling meat coupons. I've sent for the Milice. That'll show him.'

At the name of the militia, the woman hurried away, pulling the girl with her. Reece watched them go and then, after checking around, swung over the fence into the garden.

The garden was dead and bare. Luc's wooden studio stood at the end of it, raised off the ground by low concrete blocks, and for a minute Reece waited out of sight behind a water butt to watch for any movement. Satisfied he was safe, he went quickly to the shed. The padlock had been torn off and was lying on the ground, the small room presumably having been searched by the Gestapo, along with the rest of the house. Warily, he looked inside. There was a trestle table with steel trays and bottles of fluid that must have been for developing photographs. Slung from the ceiling was a clothes line with pegs to dry the prints and below it stood a heavy-looking wooden chair with carved legs. Pieces of camera littered the table. In the corner was a radio that seemed to have been cobbled together from two or three other machines – the Germans had restricted the sale of radios to prevent the French listening to Radio Londres.

The floor was swept and scrubbed perfectly clean, Reece noted. But when he looked closer he saw that one plank was off centre compared to the others. With the help of his house key he managed to prise up the wooden slat to reveal a cavity hidden below. He felt hope rising as he groped about inside. But as his fingers found only grime and rough wood it became clear that if there had ever been anything here it was gone.

He stood back up. There was the sound of voices in the alley. He worried that the woman he had spoken to had been only feigning fright at the name of the militia and had in fact gone to find them, or the police, herself. But still, if there was any chance the photographs were still here, he had to find them.

He searched swiftly but thoroughly, turning out the drawers, opening up the radio. Nothing. He went outside, checked the house for signs of life, and then scrambled underneath the shed. It was just high enough for his body to fit under and he groped about, but again found nothing but dirt. He dragged himself back out, covered in soil, and returned to the studio. He couldn't stay long and it looked like he was going to leave empty-handed.

He stared around. And something struck him: the heavy chair was too big for the room. Wouldn't a high stool be more practical for developing? He knelt to examine it. Nothing special. He turned it upside down and it was then that he noticed the very bottom of one of the thick legs was greasy. He looked closer and saw, a centimetre from the end, a narrow score encircling the leg. The line, which looked like a cut from a saw, had been deliberately covered with dirty grease. He pulled hard at the tip of the leg. Slowly, he worked it away until it jerked free. He tossed it aside, peered into the leg and found he was looking at a long, thin metal canister. He pulled it out, the excitement of triumph building, unscrewed the cap and shook out the contents. As he had expected, there were seven or eight false travel passes and identity cards all rolled up.

What there was no sign of was what Reece was risking his life for: a film or prints of the document Beggar had stolen from the SS officer. And with a flash of anger, he guessed what that meant: someone else had found them first. He checked the rest of the chair and all the other furniture for hidden cavities, but he was sure that there were no others. And Luc's shouted words – 'Charlotte knows my hiding place' – had strongly suggested all contraband was hidden together. No, the photographs must have been taken.

Precisely who the thief had been would decide the future of the circuit.

The Gestapo surely wouldn't have left the remaining fake documents; they would have taken them to trace the putative owners. So whoever it was, they knew the circuit's secrets but weren't part of the Gestapo machine.

Charlotte.

And now her disappearance began to make sense. It had been to mask her theft of the pictures.

Reece wiped his sleeve across his face then threw the empty canister across the room. It bounced off the radio in the corner with a ring. Someone had informed on the op designed to free Luc. Someone who wouldn't have risked being in the middle of the firefight. When he had seen her above him through the smoke he had denied it, wanting it to be different, but he could hardly deny it now.

He started to pace forcefully up and down the room to think. But if she were working for the Germans – either voluntarily or under duress – why was there no Gestapo officer lying in wait for him? If she had wanted him caught, there would have been an ambush squad of them waiting at the house.

And one other fact militated against her being a traitor: the Panzerspähwagen that had ended their hopes of freeing Luc from the prison van had arrived late to the battle. That strongly suggested that the Germans had found out about the raid only at the last minute. Charlotte, however, had known before the rest of the circuit and could have warned the Gestapo in good time.

No, no – despite the missing pictures, there was doubt about the situation; her guilt wasn't clear-cut. She was involved somehow, he was sure, but the game itself was still hidden.

And he had no time to think, to remember, to analyse – because no matter what her objective was, he had to warn London what had happened. And without her, he had no way of transmitting.

His best chance would be to contact another circuit and send an emergency message through them. The Fisherman network was based in Amiens so they might also be able to get a message to Luc in the prison there. Besides, the Gestapo had penetrated so many Paris networks he wouldn't know if he could trust anyone in the capital. He had to be wary, more guarded than before.

He glanced at the canister, on its side next to the radio, and a new thought struck him. The radio – he was sure it hadn't been there the last time he was here. And now he noticed that it wasn't a normal household radio; it looked more like the transmitter Charlotte used to send and receive messages. What was it that Luc had shouted from the prison van? Something about Parade One and a German radio frequency. What if Luc had borrowed or built this radio to monitor that signal?

Reece looked over the equipment. The dial looked to be set somewhere around 40MHz – well beyond the normal civilian band. He turned the machine on. Its batteries began to hum and, after checking outside the shed to ensure no one was within earshot, Reece turned the volume up a little. All he heard was static. He moved the dial slowly up and down but found nothing of note. He risked a minute scanning the surrounding frequencies, before he knew he had to leave.

He switched the set off, spun the dial to a random setting, put a match to the remaining forged documents, and prepared to leave.

CHAPTER 8

Wilhelm Canaris stopped to take in the view: snowy Bavarian mountains sprinkled with birds flitting through tall trees. His narrow chest rose and fell as he pictured Alpine milkmaids doing what Alpine milkmaids did in books. And yet the vista was doing little to relax his mood.

That morning an Abwehr agent had acquired a copy of the highly secret notes of Hitler's personal physician, Dr Morell, for the admiral. It had been eye-catching stuff.

It seemed that the Führer wasn't only being regularly injected with extract from the prostates of young bulls – Canaris presumed Eva, twenty-three years Hitler's junior, was the supposed beneficiary of this bizarre treatment – but his days seemed to be a haze of morphine, cocaine, strange bacterial-based tablets to reduce day-long stomach cramps caused by wind, Pervitin, the drug they gave to Stuka pilots to keep them flying for days at a time, atropine, to combat high blood pressure, testosterone, to supplement the bull serum, and a bagful of other drugs to boot. Very discreet enquiries had been made with a psychiatrist, who had confirmed that such a cocktail would most likely place a man on the doorstep of the madhouse, even if he had previously been the most stable of characters. And that was something the Führer had never been.

Canaris hadn't quite decided what to do with the report. For now, it was little more than a personal curiosity, although there was certainly the potential for more active measures further down the line – whether it should be shared with one or two selected individuals or . . . well, that would be decided when the time came. For now, it would remain for his eyes only. And so he placed the report somewhere it wouldn't be stumbled across. It wasn't the sort of document to be caught possessing.

No, not a stable man, Adolf Hitler, but always clever at sowing division. A strangely political beast, Canaris mused. Nature had formed within him an innate talent for placing a knife in a man's hand and pointing him towards a third party. Take today's appointment, for example. It had already set the Oberkommando der Wehrmacht, the closest thing the combined armed forces had to a General Staff, against the army's high command, the Oberkommando des Heeres. With those two bodies at each other's throats like drunks in a beer cellar, Hitler remained unassailable. And that was before you considered the Waffen-SS generals, who would happily liquidate their own families if so ordered by the Führer.

All in all, the fate of the world's German-speaking peoples had never in the whole of history been so enclosed in the hand of a single man. A single man who was being injected with serum extracted from a bull's prostate.

Canaris slipped his hands into his pockets and rose up and down on the balls of his feet, flexing his muscles after the dawdling car journey from the nearby airstrip. After that he strode to the SS guard post to present his identification.

'Heil Hitler!' the guard snapped.

'Heil Hitler.' Yes, yes, Heil Hitler. Perhaps it was a blessing that it wasn't yet *Heil Himmler*. No doubt they had that to look forward to.

The Obersalzberg, the Führer's country retreat for the last decade, was like a state within a state. It even had its own cultural history – a museum's worth of fine paintings and artefacts that had, until just a few years earlier, graced other marble hallways and papered drawing rooms throughout Europe. A self-written history: always the refuge of those labouring under an inferiority complex.

The house itself was really a glorified mountain chalet, and Canaris couldn't help but curl his lip as he reached the white-painted monstrosity. 'May I offer you some tea, Admiral?' asked the subaltern who greeted him. At least there was carpet underfoot.

'No, thank you.'

Without another word, they entered a waiting room with black leather seats. An SS colonel glanced up then looked back down at a report he was reading without acknowledging the Abwehr chief's presence. Canaris was used to that and, although it made things difficult at times, he preferred it that way. He had no more time for Himmler's lackeys than they had for him.

'Would you wait here? He will send for you soon.'

Canaris took a seat. The subaltern clicked his heels and left. The SS officer stalked away too, which was welcome. And so Canaris was left alone to study his own uniform, confirming that it was spotless, until the sound of approaching steps made him look to the doorway in front of him. Momentarily it was filled by a half-hunched, flabby figure walking uncomfortably and unevenly. His right hand was clutching his left wrist, but it could hardly quell the violent twitching that told of a long-term degeneration of his central nervous system. Canaris stood smartly. 'Heil Hitler,' he said, raising his right arm.

The Führer acknowledged the salute, flipping his right palm over his shoulder. The left hand shook and was promptly caught again. Behind him, an Alsatian panted at his heels. Canaris firmly believed the Führer cared more for the dog than for any creature with two legs, including Eva.

'Admiral. I am glad to see you.' He broke a smile.

'My Führer.'

'Blondi, come!' The dog trotted towards his master's heels. 'This way. Have you been offered tea?'

'I have, my Führer.' Hitler led the way, with Canaris and the dog in his wake. Guards clicked their heels as the men passed.

'Someone told me you're keen on cookery.'

Canaris chuckled. 'I confess I am.'

'Yes, I have my spies too, Admiral.'

'If only my own were as efficient.'

'I can let you loose in the kitchen if you like. You might not have tried vegetarian meals.'

'Thank you, but I need to return to Berlin.'

'Of course. In here.' Canaris knew the way, and yet he let himself be led as if it were the first time visiting a friend's new house.

The Führer's study was full of air and light. The decor, personally chosen by him, was pleasant and comfortable – far less imposing than the grey-and-white palate that Hitler and Speer presented to the people of Germany and all the conquered realms. The couches had floral green designs, perhaps in keeping with the theme of nature's bounty that settled on the complex when the SS guards were temporarily out of sight. As he entered, Eva, wearing a yellow chiffon dress and a matching ribbon in her hair, stroked Canaris's shoulder and left the room. He bowed to her graciously, simultaneously noticing two generals in the corner of the room earnestly discussing some pages of a report. He raised a palm to them by way of greeting. He didn't acknowledge Himmler's presence by the window.

Hitler sat and rested his hands, fingers knitted, on a wide desk sporting what appeared to be a rolled-up map bound with white ribbon. He nodded to the Reichsführer-SS.

'We have selected most of the American prisoners we require for Parade One,' Himmler informed the Führer, coming forward. 'We are nearly at full complement.'

'Good. How many more do you need?'

'Oh, a handful. I would say two weeks would see the selection process complete. We have men in the stalags looking for the final suitable candidates right now.'

'May I ask how many of our own men you have?' Canaris enquired.

'More than three thousand commandos, with the core deception units numbering four hundred men.'

'Of course you will require troops who have proved themselves on the field. Not in the eastern camps.'

'You needn't worry about the men of the Waffen-SS, Admiral. They are experienced. Decorated. They are the cream of the Reich. And I am sure you will approve of the field commander.' Canaris waited. 'Otto Skorzeny.'

Hitler raised a cup of lightly coloured tea to his lips and watched.

'Skorzeny is a very capable man,' Canaris agreed. Skorzeny was, indeed, a good choice for a difficult mission. The Waffen-SS lieutenant-colonel's recent daring rescue of Mussolini from captivity in Italy had filled newspaper pages for a week. He had taken a hundred men, flown by glider into the mountaintop ski resort where the deposed Fascist leader was being held, overpowered the Italian guards and spirited Mussolini out to Austria in a light aircraft. Although Canaris had little time for the oafish former dictator, it certainly indicated Skorzeny's courage while clamped in the very jaws of the enemy. Yes, he would be just the man to lead

Parade One on the ground. And once he and his commandos had done their work, Rommel's panzers would sweep in to wipe out what was left of the invasion force. But was Skorzeny clear how his role was likely to end? 'A very capable man,' he repeated. 'And is he aware that the chances of him returning in one piece are comparatively low?'

'He is as aware as you or I. But Admiral, do not write off Otto Skorzeny,' Himmler replied. 'If any man in the Reich can accomplish this mission and exfiltrate unharmed, he is that man.'

'Of course, Reichsführer.'

'And —'

'Although it would be preferable,' Canaris continued, 'if this time we could keep him away from the newsreel cameras upon his successful return. Such exposure may boost morale among the schoolboys and housewives at home, but it leads to resentment in the ranks.'

'You might be correct,' Hitler said, lifting the cup of tea back to his mouth with his right hand before Himmler could reply. His left spasmed on the polished wood and a little of the tea spilled on to his fingers. 'Perhaps you would like to express that to Skorzeny himself?' He smiled genially. 'I am joking, Admiral. But Skorzeny could use your expertise on naval matters for the operation.' Himmler looked as if he was about to loudly object, but Hitler silenced him with a look. Canaris knew that his own presence would be not so much as an expert on naval protocol but as part of the Führer's long-standing strategy of dividing his supporters as much as his enemies. After all, for now, Himmler saw himself as Mark Antony to Hitler's Julius Caesar, but it wouldn't take much to make him Brutus. So Canaris would keep a critical eye on Himmler's commando force, and Himmler would loathe Canaris even more.

Yes, a strangely political beast, Adolf Hitler.

'As you wish,' Canaris replied.

'Has the Abwehr any information on the location of the invasion?' Hitler asked.

'My Führer, you know that I do not make promises I cannot keep. I cannot promise we will gain that intelligence. Perhaps the SD? Parade?'

Parade. It would all turn on Parade. Canaris still wanted that man working for the Abwehr, not Himmler. Perhaps planting the seed in the Führer's mind that the SD were failing to use Parade to his full potential would be the first step on the path.

'We are making every effort,' Himmler responded. 'Parade also does not make promises he cannot be sure to keep. He thinks the chances of gaining that information are low. He will, however, be given access to their army Order of Battle the minute their flotilla leaves port. He will transmit the required details to us within an hour.'

'That will be useful information. Undoubtedly. But unless we have the location of the landings at least a day in advance, Skorzeny could have the greatest units in the world but he won't be in position in time to use them.' It hardly needed repeating, but he quietly enjoyed doing so.

'No doubt that is correct.'

'Who is Parade, anyway?' Canaris asked. 'Is he German?'

Himmler hesitated, as if weighing up whether he could be trusted with such information. 'He's British.'

'One of Mosley's?'

'A sympathizer, but he kept himself off any party lists. We found him in 1936 and told him he could be more use if he joined their government service.'

'Very astute of you.'

Hitler placed his cup down and spoke: 'The quality of his information has been first rate. From now on he is to have his own dedicated channel manned around the clock and you are to put the Abwehr's resources at Himmler's disposal, if necessary, to protect him. We can't let him fall into their hands.'

'He will not, my Führer,' Himmler replied. 'I guarantee it.'

'Forgive an old sailor, Reichsführer, but over-certainty is not helpful,' Canaris interjected, his irritation unusually bubbling to the surface.

'But confidence in the Third Reich is,' Himmler said.

'No doubt.' Canaris settled himself. The Reichsführer-SS had never been on a battlefield. And yet here he was pronouncing as if he were personally in charge of the war effort. This man – a chicken farmer by profession – was as opaque as a clean window: this strategy of his wasn't aimed only at crushing the Allies' Second Front, it was meant to position him as Hitler's successor.

'Show me the map,' Hitler ordered Himmler. The Reichsführer unfurled the large sheet of paper and placed glass paperweights at the corners. It was indeed a map, showing in detail the Atlantic Wall: France's north-west coast with an inland perimeter eight kilometres deep of barbed wire, machine-gun emplacements, land mines and anti-tank defences. The two generals in the corner completed a circle around the map.

Canaris – so many years at sea, so many years on land, spent making Germany stronger, protecting her from threats, building her muscles – watched Himmler's hand tap the map as if he were playing a children's game with soldiers made from tin.

'Rommel's forces have been flooding the fields around strategic locations to defend against paratroopers – the weight of their equipment will probably drown them. The panzers are grouped here, awaiting the invasion. We will keep them in reserve in the . . .'

One of the generals cleared his throat. 'My Führer, before we continue, I must reiterate my firm belief that we cannot rely on the information from this spy. We must . . .'

'Generalfeldmarschall,' Himmler sighed.

Hitler held his palm up. 'No, let him speak his mind.'

'Thank you, my Führer,' the general continued. 'I believe that Rommel is correct – if we hold so many panzer divisions this far from the coast, the Allied bombers would tear them to pieces on the roads before they could arrive to repel an amphibious landing. We must spread them along the Atlantic Wall itself. All the way from here to here.' He prodded the map at the Cotentin peninsula in Normandy and the Pas de Calais.

'Too thin,' Himmler asserted. 'They would be spread too thin.'

'Better than not arriving at all. When we took France it was speed that won the battle, and . . .'

Hitler spoke: 'Generalfeldmarschall, I take your point. We need time to discuss this further, but we have other business now. Shall we speak on Saturday?'

'I would prefer to speak now, my Führer.'

'On Saturday, Generalfeldmarschall.' The officer bowed. 'Gentlemen, I have business now with Canaris and Himmler. You may leave us. Please take some tea if you need refreshment.' The two generals saluted and left the room.

For a while Hitler sat silently with his fingers knitted in front of his chin. Then his fist slammed into the desk. '"I would prefer to speak now, my Führer!" he says. "I would prefer to speak now, my Führer!" I will speak to him when I want to speak to him!' His left hand twitched and jumped on the desk as he shouted. 'He talks of how speed won us France — as if I am not the creator of the Blitzkrieg itself!' His right arm swept through the air. 'Need I remind him that I rebuilt Germany after he and his aristocratic friends left us kneeling to the French? That his loyalty is to me, not Rommel?'

'I'm sure you don't, my Führer,' Himmler replied.

'No. It's better for him that I don't.'

CHAPTER 9

Cover: Identity

A) Your own. Advantages: Your story will be mainly true. Only a limited period will have to be explained away. Records will confirm your statements. Disadvantages: The subversive part of your history may be known to the enemy or to persons who may give you away.

'Hello again, sir,' called the cheery young man behind the till of a well-kept café in Erith, a village south-east of London that had been swallowed into the metropolis, becoming part of it. He drew a stream of steaming tea from an urn. 'Usual cup?'

'Thanks.' The smartly dressed man with neatly lacquered light red hair took a rolled-up copy of the *Daily Mirror* from under his arm and turned it over to study the back page. His lips made little movements as he read the report of a football match.

'Warm the cockles, won't it?' said the young man.

'Hope so.'

The tea was set down. 'Fancy a bit to eat? The Welsh rarebit's good today.'

'Is it? All right, well, I'll have that.'

'Right you are.' The man behind the counter went into the kitchen to put a bit of cheese on toast under the grill. 'Seen anything good at the flicks?' he called out.

'Oh, I don't go to the pictures very much.'

'No?' The young man came back out, wiping his hands on a soggy grey towel. 'Couldn't do without them meself. Only way I get to dream.' They both chuckled. 'Well, I'll let you get back to your newspaper, sir.'

'Thanks.'

The German agent Parade continued reading the newspaper sports pages. Truth be told, he didn't care about football in Germany, Britain or indeed any nation in the world. But it was his cover identity's legend that he had grown up in Bristol, where he had supported the local team, the Rovers. The Wartime League was of even less interest to him than that which had operated before hostilities began – containing, as it now did, a series of cobbled-together sides that sometimes played, sometimes abandoned the match with minutes to spare – but it had to be followed.

He placed the folded newspaper on the café table and looked around at the clientele. Mostly old or feeble. The young man brought him the cheese on toast and Parade gratefully shifted his attention. He had spent many evenings over the past couple of years sitting in this café, killing time.

Another young man – perhaps in his mid-twenties – strode into the café with a huge grin on his face. He was big and broad and wearing the uniform and insignia of a sapper, Parade noted.

'Stone me!' exclaimed the boy behind the counter, rushing out to embrace him. 'It's me brother Phil,' he announced to the three people drinking their tea. 'You on leave or what?'

'Got a couple of days, ain't I?' replied Phil happily. 'Just a couple. Mum's not home, so I come straight 'ere.'

'Don't mind, do you, mister?' asked the younger of the two, taking a seat at Parade's table. 'Not for a hero.'

'Oh, stop that. Just doing my bit.'

'No,' Parade insisted. 'You're all heroes.'

'You off for the big one soon, then?' the younger brother asked.

'Yeah, looks like it. Not supposed to talk, though. Secret 'n that. Just training right now.' He leaned in, smirking. 'But between you an' me: beach training. You know.'

'Yes. I know.'

Parade watched as the two brothers caught up and thought to himself about the young man in a sapper's uniform. *Beach training. Yes, I know. Will your life be one of those on my account this time next week? I have nothing against you, but it's the simple cost of warfare. Millions have died, millions more will die – innocent and guilty all falling together. Why should I care more about you going to your grave than any of those others? Others I have never known and will never know.*

He listened to their chat about where Phil had been and what he had seen. Then, when the time had been killed, he bade cheerio and walked for precisely four minutes to a suburban street nearby. He approached the doorway of house number eighteen, where the render was cracking into spider's webs. He was about to enter when a policeman on a bicycle halted beside him.

'May I stop you for a moment, sir?' the officer enquired.

'Of course.'

'May I see your identity card?'

'All right.' He took it from his pocket and showed it to the constable.

'Thank you.' The officer handed back the card. 'May I ask if this is your house?'

'No, I'm visiting. My brother's widow lives here.'

'I see,' the policeman said, stroking his chin.

'What do you see?' He contrived to sound peeved rather than worried by the policeman's interest.

'Well, sir, it's just, she sounds – her accent isn't English, is it?'

'No, she's Dutch.' Parade changed his voice to sound relieved – he now comprehended the policeman's concern. 'Not German. The Dutch are on our side.'

'Well, yes, sir. But it's as well to keep an eye out, you understand?'

'Yes.'

'Your brother's widow, you say?'

'He died in 1940. He flew Hurricanes.'

The policeman looked at his feet. He was in his fifties or sixties, Parade saw, and skinny from the years of food on coupons. 'I'm sorry for asking, sir. We all owe him a debt.'

Parade felt he had drawn a better card. 'Yes, Constable.'

'Yes, sir. Well, you'll appreciate that I have to keep an eye out.'

'Yes, of course.'

'Have a good evening, sir.' He nodded politely and left.

'Good evening.'

Parade paused for a few seconds and let himself into the house. A youngish woman was waiting for him in the kitchen, sitting at the table, spooning the dregs of a thin vegetable soup into her mouth. She had a slovenly air, as if she never saw other people and had lost all interest in maintaining herself. She glanced at her visitor and cut a slice of bread from a loaf, using it to wipe the inside of the bowl to get the last of her meal. She wiped her lips on the back of her hand and scraped her wooden chair back across the bare floorboards. 'All right, I'm ready,' she said in German.

'Good, let's get on with it,' Parade replied in English. It annoyed him when she spoke German to deliberately flout security protocols, but he knew she did it to rile him so he never reacted.

He hung his hat and coat on the rack and trod softly up the stairs behind her. At the top there was a ladder up into the attic and they hauled themselves up, their feet unsteady on the steel rungs.

The loft had been partly turned into another bedroom, but the job had been left unfinished. There was plywood flooring but no carpet or rug, and the walls had no plaster, only the timbers and bricks that kept out the wind and the rain.

The woman opened a suitcase stowed in the eaves, lifted out a wireless transmitter and placed it on a cleanly brushed table. It came in three grey metal boxes connected by thick wires. She arranged them neatly and placed the Morse key in the correct position for efficient use.

As he took his place on a packing case to encipher a message, Parade shivered. It was one of the coldest nights he had lived through and being inside barely helped. The wind blew through so many cracks in the bricks he might as well have been outdoors — at least there he would have been walking around, instead of slumped over a table for an hour with a sheet of paper, a pencil and a code book. He rubbed his stiff, freezing limbs and shoved his hands into his armpits so his fingers would warm a little. He had to do it every minute or two for the full hour he spent enciphering the words because they kept seizing up with the chill.

Eventually, he had a run of letters broken into groups of five to transmit. The woman took the slip of paper and turned on her set. Nothing happened. He worried, for a moment, that he had wasted those hours trekking through the dark to this godforsaken house and hunched over the table. It would be another hour at least to get home. All for nothing.

'Check the connections,' he said.

'I know what to do,' she muttered in reply. Her accent really was Dutch, as the neighbours believed. Parade had been informed that the SD had recruited her while she was training to teach the violin in Rotterdam. She had, however, never been married, let alone to Parade's non-existent brother.

She checked the connections. If the batteries were flat, they would have to spend another two hours sitting in the semi-dark while she charged them downstairs then brought the set back up to send the message. He thought hard about leaving it for the night and returning in the morning.

She removed the batteries and cleaned all the connections with a handkerchief. Finally, she put the headphones back over her ears and switched on again.

For a moment, there was nothing. Then the sound of static through the earpieces told them that the equipment had sparked into life.

'Thank God for that,' Parade muttered.

She tapped out the code to establish that someone in Germany was listening. They were. She pressed the Morse key back into service, transmitting her safe code to say that it was her and that she wasn't transmitting under duress. The code was accepted and returned with a reply code. Satisfied, she began to transmit. *Plans for large rehearsal for beach landing Hemsall Sands Dorset 16–20 Feb. 40000 British 12000 Canadian troops. Will approach from Portsmouth in 9 tank landing ships. Escort 2 corvettes 2 motor torpedo boats. Will include live fire exercise. Suggest E-boat interception 0700 16 Feb. Confirm. Now know that Maxime organizer of SOE network Paris recently briefed Churchill. Subject of briefing unknown. Ends.*

She removed the headphones. 'This man Maxime . . .' she said.

'You've done your part. That's enough.'

Yes, the message would be enough to put the Gestapo, Abwehr and SD on full alert. A man who had recently briefed Churchill would be the most hunted agent in Europe, Parade mused. He would be lucky to last a week in the open.

*

How to carry out surveillance
Position of watchers. The distance between the watchers and the quarry should vary according to the circumstances. It is often better to use the other side of the road. With a team of watchers it is useful to change position occasionally (e.g. when turning corner).

Sturmbannführer Klaussmann clambered into his sleek motor car to find that even the leather was freezing. Schmidt took the front passenger seat. 'It should only take ten minutes,' he informed his superior.

'Take your time,' Klaussmann replied, settling in. Schmidt had recently been transferred to Paris. It was his first posting outside Germany and only his second overall. And Klaussmann felt that Schmidt showed promise – he was bright – but he had the perennial problem of young men: they were always trying to run ahead, certain they knew better than the generations who had come before them. Still, it was in the nature of young men to be reckless, and incumbent on those of the older generation to instruct them in the necessity of everything-in-its-place, he reminded himself. He also felt a degree of paternalistic pride in moulding Schmidt to be a good officer. There was only so much that the Gestapo training academy could teach; the rest had to be learned on the job. 'Make it a smooth journey.'

He had much to consider on the way. He had now been sent two messages informing him of the actions of the spy network. The first had identified Luc Carte, allowing Klaussmann to arrest him at the bar in Montmartre. The second had warned of the raid on the prison transport to free him. Carte would therefore be the key to taking the network.

He looked through the polished window at the posters that his men had put up around the town: decrees about curfew times, about gatherings of more than three men. He pondered what he would have done if French tanks had rolled into Berlin and parked in front of the Brandenburg Gate. If that absurd self-appointed 'general' de Gaulle had started writing German laws. Would he, Klaussmann, have joined a hit-and-run brotherhood set on driving out the French? He didn't think so. Cutting telephone wires and breaking locomotive engines seemed tawdry, really. He had no great desire to die on the field of battle like a Wagnerian hero, but at least it wouldn't feel trivial. Sneaking around in the night, firing from tree cover, too frightened to show one's face. Yes, that was about the size of the French. Terrorism was their level. And they couldn't even do that without the British pulling their strings.

The car moved through the centre of the city before turning north into the narrow streets of Montmartre. They stopped in a pleasant winding street and, if you just stood and looked along it in the crisp wintry light, you could believe it was twenty years earlier. 'You know, we're the ones preserving this,' Klaussmann said as he stepped out of the car and swept his hand across the scene. 'This history. The twentieth century is a battle between National Socialism and Communism. We want to preserve what is good – it's the Reds who want to knock it all down. It's all they know.'

'Yes, sir.'

He hoped Schmidt really did understand. The Reich wasn't perfect, but it was necessary. Warfare was a noble construct prosecuted in dirty circumstances, and it was down to the Gestapo to clean away the dregs. That was something that had to be done once in every generation, he believed. He recalled chaotic times in the previous decade: hungry dogs tearing rubbish apart, grown men and women walking in their wake to search for food. Humans no better than animals. A breakdown not just of society but of natural and racial order. That couldn't happen again. No, it couldn't happen. And so he and his brethren would hunt down all those who might bring it about.

They walked to the house where Luc Carte had lived. Some old men were playing boules on a patch of grass beside it, but they studiously ignored the Germans' presence. The house had been searched two days earlier, the night they had arrested Carte, but nothing of note had been found. Klaussmann, however, wanted to look for himself.

'Good. Let's go in.'

Once inside, he and Schmidt spent two hours checking for anything that would lead to the spy network. And yet, by the end of it, they had nothing to show for their time but pained backs and dusty knees. Frustrated, Klaussmann went into the rear garden – a small kitchen garden now devoid of fruit and berries – and stared at the house. A dead garden, a dead end. A waste of time.

'What are you doing?'

He looked around for the wheedling voice. A small child – a girl with curling fair hair underneath a bright orange woollen hat – was peeping over the fence to the side of a tatty shed with covered-up windows. The older children were wary of the German uniforms, but the youngest had grown up with them and seemed to regard the big men in grey as part of the landscape.

'I'm looking for a friend of mine,' Klaussmann replied.

'Mr Carte?'

'That's him.'

'He isn't here,' she said brightly, happy to help an adult with her knowledge.

'So I see.'

'He's my friend.'

A woman's voice called out, worried. 'Françoise!' Klaussmann saw a thin woman in her thirties emerge from the girl's house. 'Come in.'

The girl ignored her. 'Who are you?'

'Come into the house, darling,' the woman called, walking cautiously towards the girl. 'It's too cold to be out.'

'Go to your mother,' Klaussmann said.

'He said I'm his best friend.' The girl started walking towards her mother. 'He has other friends, but they're not the same.' She reached her mother's outstretched arms.

'Wait,' Klaussmann said sharply. The girl looked back. The woman tried to gather her up and lift her away. 'I said, wait.'

'Sir, she's only six,' the woman pleaded.

'Tell me about his other friends,' Klaussmann instructed the girl, ignoring her mother. 'Mr Carte. His other friends?'

'Ummm.' She looked skywards, as if the answer were written in the clouds.

'When do they come?' he gently nudged her along. 'What time of day?'

'Sir!' the woman said.

'Be quiet,' he replied, lightly, so that the girl wouldn't take fright. 'Do they come when it's dark?'

The girl thought it over and nodded. 'Sometimes. Usually when it's the day.'

'The day? That's nice. I like it when it's the day. Do you? You can play in the garden.'

She grinned and nodded more vigorously. Her mother looked distressed, but Klaussmann's eye told her to hold her tongue. 'Do you know any of the friends who used to come to Mr Carte's house?' She shook her head. 'Did any of them ever say their name?'

She thought hard. 'No.'

'Oh, well. He was lucky to have you as his friend.' He looked back to the house. They might as well leave and try something else.

'But I saw one once.'

He stopped. 'Who?'

'One of the men.'

'When?' Although he felt the thrill of urgency, he kept it out of his voice.

'Grandpapa took me for a walk once in the Tuileries Gardens and we went to see Napoleon's tomb and went into a tabac, and I saw one of Mr Carte's friends in there. He worked there.' The girl's mother winced involuntarily. The girl noticed and looked confused. 'Mama?'

'Give me your hands,' Klaussmann said. He stretched his arms up as if he were reaching for the sky. The girl copied him and he took hold of her wrists. She giggled as he lifted her up and over the fence so that she could no longer see her mother. He knelt down to her. 'Did you like that?'

'Yes,' she chuckled.

'Good. Now, can you remember the name of the tabac you saw the man in?'

'Ummmm. No.'

'Can you remember the street it was on?' She shook her head. 'Oh, that's a pity. Because I like that man and want to meet him.'

'Oh.'

'Can you remember where it was?'

She shrugged. Then her expression brightened. 'There was a man like you in there.'

'A man like me? Wearing clothes like these?' He pulled at his uniform.

'Yes. He was carrying lots of them.'

'Lots of them, you say. I see. Aren't you a clever girl?'

A few minutes later Klaussmann climbed back into the car. Schmidt was waiting for him. 'There's a tabac, somewhere between the Tuileries and the tomb of Napoleon, where some of our officers get their uniforms cleaned. Find out where it is.'

'Yes, sir.'

He pondered for a moment. 'Schmidt, you're a father.'

'Sir?'

'Tell me.' He turned to his subordinate. 'The girl back there. Say the mother knew something but refused to speak, would you have done whatever it took to the girl to get the woman to speak?' Schmidt thought for a moment and nodded slowly. 'Good.'

PART TWO

CHAPTER 10

Reece checked the peeling café sign. LA CYGNE. The bistro was his emergency contact point for the Fisherman circuit in Amiens and he needed to get word to London as soon as he could of the disaster that was engulfing Beggar.

The establishment was in one of the town's lively squares, and all around there was a constant tapping from the articulated wooden soles that had replaced leather due to the shortages. Reece glanced at the sign as he stepped into the café, ambled to the bar and took out a copy of *Le Matin*. He pulled it apart and left the front page on the seat beside him as the initial recognition signal.

He ordered an egg sandwich, having realized that he hadn't eaten since the previous day, handing the waiter his ration book to have the coupons neatly clipped out. He wondered what his fourteen-year-old self would have made of such an age, when France, the world's great nation of gastronomy, was reduced to hunger en masse. It was hardly the worst of the privations the country was enduring day by day – indeed, one part of him felt guilty that he could afford to eat at all, with his forged rations coupons and bank notes dropped by London – but there was something talismanic about food. Many of his warmest memories of his adolescence were formed around meals with his family, watching their penniless artistic friends stuffing down canapés and gulping champagne before staggering home to unheated attic rooms. France in all her ludicrous glory.

'Not much custom today?' Reece asked.

'Not much,' the waiter replied, wiping the bar.

'Times are tough.'

'They are that. They are that.'

'I have to look after my brother's family too, while he's working in Germany,' Reece told him. 'The Obligatory Work Service.'

'We all face it, though I've been lucky so far.' The waiter sighed as he served another customer.

'Well, good for you. It's tiring, I hear.' He looked up at the waiter. 'I'm so tired today I can't stand up.'

The man noted the second code and glanced at the front page of *Le Matin* on the seat. 'You're not alone. A friend of mine was telling me that his business is doing so badly he's exhausted himself with any work he can find, just to keep going. And he's a mechanic. A skilled job.' Reece recognized the counter-signal.

'Poor man. I could put some work his way.'

'Well, be my guest. I could give him a call.'

'I would appreciate that.'

The waiter went out to the kitchen and Reece returned to his newspaper. This was always a tense time. He had made contact with a stranger whom he hoped was a friend in the struggle. But that man could be an imposter, he could have switched sides, he could be incompetent or under surveillance. Reece watched all around for anything out of the ordinary – a pair of customers with lots of coupons or too well fed for their poor clothes – or something so deliberately banal that it cloaked something more dangerous. All he saw was a young family outside, pressed together as they waited for a gas-powered bus. The youngest child was screaming and his mother was trying to cuddle some warmth into him.

The newspaper front cover carried a leading article denouncing the prostitution of French society that had been ended by the arrival of the German troops in Paris: 'That clear day in June, 1940.' France had become effete and lowly, the article said. The people had been secretly and invisibly enslaved by a corrupt ruling class. But all that had changed now and true patriots were signing up to help their German protectors by joining the militia. *That clear day in June, 1940.* Even the weather was up for revision, it seemed – the day had been anything but clear, Reece knew. It had been a day when the air was heavy with soot, the Germans having bombed a petrol depot outside the city. It had been months before the trees and buildings were clean again.

He hadn't seen it, of course, but he had heard. The first reaction had been shock – for months, the French authorities had spun stories about the under-nourished German soldiers who existed on eggless omelettes; how they would crack under pressure due to the psychological effects of their brutal training methods.

And then the Wehrmacht had driven up the boulevards, fully equipped, well disciplined and revelling in their victory over the people who had defeated their parents twenty years earlier. It had taken them mere hours to fan out and take over the city. Reece sat wishing that time could somehow turn back. That the French army deserters would this time stay at their posts. He was glad he hadn't seen it. There would have been something even more galling for him about watching the jackboots march towards the Louvre than seeing them now mill around it. Nowadays he knew the soldiers and Gestapo thugs to be worthy of his contempt more than his fear.

But had Charlotte secretly wished the French army's defeat? Was she one of those who had lined the Champs-Élysées for the Germans' daily victory parades? He couldn't tell. He searched for clues in the days and nights they had spent together. There had been no spark of triumph in her eyes when he talked of the fall of France. There had been tiredness only, he was certain. When she had returned his touch it had been unflinching.

It was two hours before the waiter spoke to him again. 'We were talking earlier about a friend of mine,' he said. 'He's over there.' He pointed to a man in his twenties wearing a cap and overalls, pushing counters around a backgammon board. Reece had seen him enter some time ago and had wondered if the man were Fisherman's organizer but had been careful not to pay undue attention.

'Thanks.' Reece paid the bill and sauntered over.

'Mind if I play?' he asked.

'Please do,' the man replied. Reece drew up a chair and they played silently until the last customer had left, half an hour later.

'It's been years since I was here.'

'It's a nice town when you get to know it.'

'I'm Maxime.'

'Of course you are,' replied the man. Reece looked at him properly now. There was something very English in his bright blue eyes and blond hair. The Nazis, of course, would have claimed him as one of their own. But now that Reece listened for it, there was a slight Anglo-Saxon deadness to his French accent. 'I'm Sebastien.'

'I need to get a message to London. My wireless operator's gone.'

'Gone? They got him?' Sebastien's eyes flicked up in concern. It was a shared worry; every agent felt for every other one. Reece was grateful for the unintended gesture of solidarity.

'Her. I don't know. She's gone.'

'You'll forgive me if I ask you a few questions,' Sebastien said.

'I'd expect nothing less.'

'Who trained you in hand-to-hand combat?'

'Silent killing?' he said it quietly, in English. 'Eric Sykes.'

'What was your final test at Beaulieu?'

'We had to plant dummy explosive under the 9.24 to London just outside Brockenhurst station.'

'Seen any British films lately?'

Reece thought for a second. 'I saw *Shadow of a Doubt* when I was back on leave for a week.'

'Tell me about the plot.'

'It's a Hitchcock. A girl thinks her uncle's a killer. Kills women for their money.' Sebastien nodded. 'Can you put the safety catch back on?'

'It doesn't work anyway,' Sebastien said, withdrawing his hand from his pocket. 'Spanish crap we were handed by some comrades from the Civil War. As likely to blow up as fire an actual round.'

'Perhaps that's why they lost.' Reece was bitter about the defeat. The Republicans had their faults, but the loss to Franco had paved the way for Mussolini and then Hitler; if only Britain and France had seen where it would lead. Time was a litany of missed opportunities to hold back a tide of mud.

'Perhaps,' Sebastien said. 'My pianist's next sked will be tomorrow 11.15 a.m.'

'I need it sent now. Priority channel.'

'OK.'

Reece was beginning to feel more confident. This man, Sebastien, seemed efficient. Testing Reece, even after he had come out with the recognition pattern, was a sensible added layer of security. He appeared to be a man whose lightness of manner masked a sharp judge of character. 'And there's something else. I need to get a message to one of my men who's in the prison here. It's top priority.'

'I sympathize, old man,' Sebastien said. Reece believed him, but sympathy was free; what he needed was action. 'But the chances of getting a message to someone in the prison are pretty much nil. We've tried before.' It was an answer Reece had been hoping not to hear. 'He'll be in the Gestapo section. After they've interrogated him, they'll probably execute him.'

'We have to try,' Reece said. He was resolved. He had lost Richard; he wasn't going to lose Luc too.

'We'll give it a go, but it's like I told you. And, well, God knows what state he'll be in.' He paused, giving Reece time to take in what he had said.

'How soon can your pianist transmit?'

Sebastien pushed away from the table. 'I would say about three minutes from now. This way.' He led the way outside and around the back of the building to a rear entrance. Stairs led to the upper floor. 'The weather's good today,' he called up the stairs. A rotund man in his thirties with wisps of brown hair over his ears peeped through the bannister before retiring out of sight. Reece and Sebastien reached the landing and entered the only room. It appeared to be a box room full of junk and broken furniture. The rotund man had a small revolver in his hand, which he placed on a footstool when he saw all was well.

'We need to transmit, priority channel,' Sebastien told him.

Fisherman's pianist made no reply but pulled a red leather briefcase from under a heap of broken wood. He cleared space on a rickety desk and opened it to reveal a transmitter of the same model as Charlotte's. He took a pencil and paper, ready to note down and encipher a message, and waited.

Reece had prepared a short message. It deliberately left out some of the details because the more details there were, the more likely it would be that the SOE leadership would want to start directing him; and he wanted to run this op in his own fashion.

'"From Maxime, Beggar circuit. Photographs of document show German D-Day counter-op designated Parade One. Believe Germany has spy in British intelligence service name Parade. Op Beggar Sixteen to regain captured agent failed due to sabotage. Circuit may have a traitor."' That detail was too dangerous to conceal, painful as it was. Sebastien raised his eyebrows but said nothing. '"Charlotte missing. Request Charlotte real name and address. Understand security, but utmost importance."'

There might be something in the document that could lead them to the German agent. The chances of getting to Luc were slim and, even then, he would be able to provide them only with what he could remember from the document detailing the Germans' counter-attack against D-Day. But Charlotte had the photographs themselves. Reece would find her and, if she were still loyal to SOE, she could give them to him and he would take them to London. But if – *if* – she were with the Germans, he could still force some information out of her. After all, she would have seen the pictures too.

And he had his own reasons for wanting to find her.

The wireless operator set about enciphering the message.

'An op against the invasion?' Sebastien looked grave. 'What are they planning?'

'I don't know.' Reece shook his head in the grievance of failure. 'Were you in uniform before this?'

'RAF. I was here when the Krauts invaded.'

'Then you saw what happened. They destroyed us by coming through the Forest of Ardennes when we weren't expecting it. If they have another trick up their sleeve, it could mean another rout. How many from the Expeditionary Force did we lose in '40? Sixty thousand dead, almost the same POW. That's one in three men dead or captured. And they weren't making amphibious landings – whatever Parade One is, the invasion force is going to be far more vulnerable.'

There was a pause as they considered the consequences. 'Do you have any sources who might have heard something?'

'One or two who occasionally pass us bits of information, but –'

'Ask them. Keep it as hush-hush as you can, but ask if they have ever heard Parade One mentioned. Anything at all. The clock's ticking and right now we have nothing.'

'I'll see if I can turn anything up.'

They were silent for a while, watching the rotund man enciphering the message and listening to the sound of the clicking wooden soles in the square outside, as if they could provide a comment on what had been said. Eventually, the wireless operator nodded, opened the window to string his aerial outside, and sat down to tap out the transmission. He said nothing when he had completed it but sat back and nodded again.

'Do you want to wait for the answer?' Sebastien asked, checking through the window. 'We probably won't get it before curfew.'

Reece checked his watch. It was only 3 p.m. Curfew would be six hours away. 'I'll wait.'

'All right. What now?'

'There's something else. This set, can it tune to 40MHz?' It was the frequency that Luc's radio had been set to. It was worth a try.

The pianist spoke for the first time. 'Just about. But that's nowhere near our frequency band.'

'Do it anyway.'

Sebastien placed his hand on the man's shoulder to tell him to follow Reece's instructions. 'Fine, but there won't be anyone there,' he muttered. He placed the headphones back over his ears.

'Leave them off. We want to hear too,' Reece told him. The man shrugged and held the headset between the three of them. Reece could detect light static rustling from the padded earphones. The operator spun the dial to the right and the static became louder. The three of them crowded around, listening intently as the man searched for a signal. They watched for the needle on the meter to twitch. It stayed resolutely stable. 'Nothing there. I told you,' the man muttered again.

'Keep trying.'

'Nothing better to do today? All right.' He gently moved the dial again, up and down, without any change in the sound of sea waves from the earphones. 'How long do we keep doing this?'

'Keep going.'

The pianist shrugged at Sebastien and returned to cycling up and down the frequencies around 40MHz. Three hours later, Reece went down to the café to bring them some sandwiches and coffee. When he returned, he found the pianist in a state of excitement.

'I thought I heard something. Just for a second,' he blurted out.

Reece put down the food and stared avidly at the set. He needed a breakthrough. He deserved one. For another twenty minutes the operator twisted the knob here and there.

'There!' Reece cried with elation, pointing to the needle. Sebastien woke from a doze. 'It's moving.'

'Bloody hell,' the wireless operator said to himself as the black needle seemed to tremble just a millimetre and back.

His brow furrowed, deep, fat lines appearing in the flesh as he tried to find the point that had latched on to the ghost of a signal. He turned back and forth, feather by feather. 'There.' And as he lifted his fingers away, the needle stayed put just above its resting point. It had found an electrical impulse in the ether. 'Can't hear a sodding thing, though.' The lines in the flesh of his brow doubled in thickness. Reece could no longer hear the sound of static and could only watch as the pianist fiddled with the dial once more. Then the man's mouth seemed to open a little in surprise. 'What's . . . here, listen to this.' He offered the headset to Sebastien, but Reece took it from his fingers and pulled it on. Underneath a loud buzzing he heard what was unmistakably a human voice. The pianist turned up the volume to its maximum level and Reece pressed the earphones tight to his head, blotting out all other sound. Yes, a human voice, metallic and distorted by distance and electronics. It was coming in waves, becoming louder then fainter again, but the needle was twitching up and the signal getting stronger. 'USS *Colorado*, USS . . .' The signal was lost again. Static. Reece waited, holding his breath to minimize any sound. The rain was pattering through broken windows.

'Do you . . .' Sebastien began.

Reece held up a hand to hush him.

And then the voice returned, louder now: 'USS *Texas*. USS *Texas*. HMS *Rodney*. HMS *Rodney*. HMS *Warspite* . . .' until it was overtaken by static.

'What is it?' Sebastien mouthed silently.

'Lists of ships in English. Battleships. HMS *Rodney* – she's a Nelson class, I've been on her. *Warspite*'s almost as big.' He paused. 'They're just the ships that would spearhead the invasion flotilla.'

'Just lists of them? Nothing else? No orders or questions.'

'Nothing like that.' Reece listened again. He caught only the briefest sounds.

'What does it mean?'

'Christ knows.' There was no more. 'Could the signal be coming from Britain?' There was a chance that it was Parade himself sending his information to Berlin.

'Possible,' replied the operator. 'But it would have to be a hell of a strong transmitter. More likely somewhere in France. And they're speaking in Clear – they can't be agents.'

'So whatever their op is, it involves our battleships,' Reece said to himself. 'Listen, say you were Rommel looking to defend against the invasion. What sort of strike op could you mount if you knew the major battleships coming?'

Sebastien pondered. 'No idea. I mean, maybe you could attack them in port before they embark? But that's a pretty tough mission for the Germans. Some other sabotage, maybe.'

Without more information, they wouldn't come up with a better idea than that. 'It's possible. Well, keep monitoring it. As much as you can.'

Klaussmann and Schmidt, now wearing plain clothes, stood at the back door to the tabac in the rue du Haut Pavé. Klaussmann glanced up and saw a curtain in the flat opposite ripple; he would go around to speak to the owner later.

Schmidt managed to slip the catch on a small window and reach through with a looped wire to unbolt the door.

'Good work,' Klaussmann told him.

Once inside, they immediately saw the well-used steps up to Reece's attic bedroom. As soon as they were up, they closed the blackout curtains and Klaussmann divided the room into metre-square sectors in order to go through them methodically. 'Not so quickly that you miss anything vital,' he instructed Schmidt. 'The last time, you went at it like a bull.' He started examining his first sector.

'Sir?' Schmidt said, holding up a pair of boots. They were caked in thick mud.

'Could be something – receiving a supplies drop – or maybe he just went for a walk in the countryside with his girlfriend.'

They went back to their search. Klaussmann shook out the meagre bedclothes and checked the mattress for signs of the stitching having been opened. When he came to Reece's bedside table, he lifted the Proust novel *À la Recherche du temps perdu* and leafed through it. He recalled a night in May 1933 when he had stood in Berlin's Bebelplatz before a huge, burning pyre. Students from Humboldt University, under the watchful and approving gaze of Joseph Goebbels, had removed all the library books by restive Jewish authors and thrown them into the flames. No doubt copies of this one had been among those consigned to the pyre.

'Anything in it?' Schmidt asked.

'Not that I can see,' Klaussmann replied, placing it back on the table. He shifted his attention to the flooring but stopped and turned back. Something seemed out of place. 'Have you ever read this book?' he asked.

'No, sir.'

'It's hard going,' he said thoughtfully. 'Too hard for a simple shopkeeper.' He lifted it again and began examining the pages more carefully, holding them to the light from the window. 'Look here.' He pointed to the final blank page. 'You see these little marks?' There were a few small light brown strokes on the page. 'It could be invisible ink. It often leaves a few stains, as you can see.' He stroked the paper, feeling for any indentation, but couldn't find any.

'Shall we send it for testing?'

'Yes. And keep the place under observation, around the clock. If he comes back, we have him.' He tapped the book. 'Making invisible notes. I wonder if he's the organizer,' he said. 'Well, we'll find out sooner or later. Never be in a hurry – let him make mistakes. Such as using the wrong kind of book.' Despite the fact that they would have to wait, he felt pleased with himself, and with the lesson it had provided for Schmidt.

'I see, sir.'

'But we know we are on the right track. So return to what you were doing. If he's made one such error, he's likely to have made another.' Klaussmann himself went back to methodically searching his area. 'After this, we'll . . .'

'Sir.' Klaussmann looked over to see Schmidt run his fingers along the top of the skirting board. 'Something here, I think.' He took his pocket knife and inserted it behind the wood.

'Be careful how you do it.' Schmidt managed to gently ease the wood away, revealing a small cavity. He slid his fingers in and drew something out, a small box made of card. He opened it to find a handful of .32 hollow-point rounds. 'No doubt now,' Klaussmann said with satisfaction – satisfaction at what they had found and satisfaction with Schmidt's work. 'Well done.' He clapped Schmidt on the shoulder. 'We'll finish up here then we'll call on the neighbours. We need a physical description of this man.'

CHAPTER 11

Security of organization
Security standing orders
i) No member will be told more about the organization than is necessary for him to do his job.
ii) No member will attempt to find out more about the organization than he is told.
iii) Members must only use the service names of all other members.
iv) No member will carry arms unless a cover story is impossible, e.g. during wireless transmission or reception. Where an agent carries a weapon, he must be ready to use it.

11 February 1944

At 3 a.m. Sebastien, organizer of SOE's Fisherman circuit, sat on a felled tree outside Amiens with a knife in his gloved hand, cutting chunks of cheese by the light of a blue-bulbed pen torch. He was struggling, the cold air freezing the cheese as hard as wood. 'Funny, when I was at the family place up in Yorkshire, I always used to miss the French cheese most,' he said, popping a piece in his mouth. He drowned it in a swig of genuine red wine. 'Now I would kill for a bit of good English Cheddar.'

'Hello Tractor Three, this is Beggar. Hello Tractor Three, this is Beggar. Acknowledge. Over.' Reece spoke into a microphone for the twentieth time. He was enveloped by the machine: an aerial strapped to his chest, batteries and electronic boxes on a belt around his waist and the headset over his ears. The S-Phone, heralded as a miracle of clandestine field communication, was in fact little more than a glorified radio. It allowed highly directional narrowcast communication, so it was difficult to intercept – even if an eavesdropper knew the right frequency – unless that listening post were in the direct line of transmission. Yet an agent on the ground was able to speak to an officer in a plane forty or even fifty kilometres away, so long as they were precisely facing each other. 'Hello Tractor Three, this is Beggar. Hello Tractor Three, this is Beggar. Acknowledge. Over.' The only reply was static, and he didn't want to be here all night. Unlike a drop reception – which took at least ten agents and resistants to set out the flare path, hurriedly unpack the weapons, money and gifts from their big steel containers and hide the containers in the woods or down farm wells – there were only two of them tonight, skulking at the edge of the wood, but still the plane would be a big Hudson flying low and Reece was wearing radio equipment that could be detected.

'You must have something very important to talk about,' Sebastien said laconically. 'No, don't worry, I won't ask,' he replied to Reece's stern look. 'I've been here a while myself and would like to see the dawn of 1945.'

Reece steeled himself. When the reply to his radio message had said that the deputy director of SOE F section was going to make a night flight through flak to speak to him, it wasn't going to be good. He thought over the report he would write: filling in the details about the German spy and knowledge now of a plan that appeared to involve the battleships spearheading the invasion.

'Hello Tractor Three, this is Beggar. Hello Tractor Three, this is Beggar. Acknowledge. Over.'

Reece wondered if Parade had been recruited as he had been: to work for an ideal; or if it had been on purely financial terms, paid in Swiss francs. Perhaps, even, this man had seen which way the wind was blowing in 1940 and had decided to get behind the force that seemed to have destiny in its palms. Agents had volunteered for every conceivable reason; some for none.

Reece wanted something – anything – that would put Parade in his sights. Parade could, he knew as well as anybody, sit in a London drawing room and dig a grave for twenty thousand men. A soldier will obsess about a man across the field pointing a rifle at him, a sailor about the opposing man at a wheel, a pilot about the man under the Plexiglass canopy with machine guns at his fingertips. But Reece saw his opposite number quietly walking between Whitehall offices, gathering knowledge as he went, building it into a far more dangerous weapon.

'Hello Tractor Three, this is Beggar. Hello Tractor Three, this is Beggar. Acknowledge. Over.' And then, finally, a rough, distant reply: a voice buzzing through the wires. 'Hello Beggar, this is Tractor Three. You're faint, but we can hear you. Over.'

Reece felt relief. He knew the voice as that of his Officer Commanding, Major Daniel Delaney.

'Good to have you with us, sir. Over.'

'Report. Over,' Delaney said.

'Yes, sir. I believe our attempt to rescue Luc was betrayed. They were expecting us. The prints and negatives of the SS document have been taken from us. I believe by Charlotte. Break.'

'Acknowledged. Over.'

'Charlotte's gone, sir. I don't know if she's the informant, or she's in hiding or if they've taken her. But she could have had the Gestapo waiting for me when I searched Luc's house and she didn't, so I'm not convinced she's working for them. Over.' He didn't like revealing to the OC how much in the dark he was, it wasn't strategic, but he had no choice if he wanted to get the job done.

'Hardly conclusive. Over.'

'Roger. But no matter what, she has the document or she's seen it. She's from Paris, so chances are, if she's gone to ground, it's there. I can extract the information from her. Do I have permission to locate her? Over.'

'No, you do not! Going after Charlotte's a fool's errand – and going on what you've said, she's almost certainly working for the Germans or in their custody. They'll take you in an instant. Luc has seen the document. He must be able to remember more. Contact him. Over.'

'Even if the Nazis don't execute Luc as soon as they've interrogated him, making contact will be nigh on impossible, sir. We need to find Charlotte. Over.'

'And you're the last bloody agent I would send. If she's working for them, then they're on the look-out for you. And if she isn't, then God knows what game she's playing, but you're not likely to find her. Over.'

Reece watched the moonlit skyline for the Hudson's approach. It would be making a drop somewhere nearby. Possibly it would be landing and taking a few agents home, although that was tricky, requiring a big field for take-off. 'Sir, I'm the only one who can find her. Over,' he said.

'What the hell's got into you? I've given you your orders. Over.'

'Nothing has got into me. I am focused on my mission, sir. And there are facts on the ground of which you are not apprised. Over.' He was angry that Delaney couldn't see the right course of action, that Charlotte was the key. It all turned on her, not Luc. Delaney's approach would undermine the whole mission.

'I'm apprised of more than you would possibly believe,' Delaney replied slowly. 'Your orders are to contact Luc and recover as many details from the document as possible.' His voice relented. 'You've been bloody successful for a good long time. You know what's coming. We need you A1 fighting strength for that. When your mission is complete, do you need to come back for a couple of weeks' leave, to see your family, recharge the batteries? Over.'

'Sir, all I need is Charlotte's real name and address. Over.' He held out little hope that his plea would be answered, but he had no more facts or argument. Chains of command existed of necessity, but this time one could well destroy all that he, the circuit and the whole of SOE had bled for time and time again.

There was more static as Reece waited. 'Look,' Delaney eventually said. 'I'm not happy about telling you this way, but you're not giving me much choice. There's another reason we can't put you in danger right now.' Reece waited. 'We might be sending you on another reconnaissance op to the locations of your previous recces. We need more details of the ports there. Then you'll come straight home to brief us. With what you know already, we just can't risk you getting taken. Do you acknowledge? Over.'

Reece understood. Another reconnaissance op to the prospective landing beaches and then to the War Rooms under Whitehall, with Churchill and two staff officers in a smoke-settled room. It would clearly be a vital mission and one that they couldn't risk the Germans becoming aware of.

Much as he disliked it, Reece knew what he had to do. 'Roger,' he said. 'Over.'

'Your request to pursue Charlotte is denied. Follow your orders, or come back and I will appoint someone to take over your current role. Those are your two choices. Will you comply? Over.'

There was no way he could return now. It would be a poisonous end to his long mission in France. But that didn't mean he wasn't angry.

'Wilco. Over.'

'Then you have your mission. See it through. Out.'

Reece tore off the headset and would have cast it to the ground if he hadn't heard Sebastien clear his throat behind him. 'Everything shipshape?' he asked.

Reece wondered how much Sebastien had heard and how much he could have reconstructed from one side of the conversation. But he couldn't let Delaney throw everything away on a misjudged plan. He would have to follow both tracks at once. 'You said you might be able to find someone with access to the prison.'

'I can try,' Sebastien replied cautiously, 'but the chances are slim.'

'Do your best.'

'I will. I couldn't help but overhear some of that,' Sebastien told him.

'I'm sure you couldn't.'

'We all have disagreements with the OC from time to time.'

'We do.'

'But I have to know. If I help you, am I committing mutiny?'

Reece considered for a while. 'Sometimes we know better than him, right?' he said. But it wasn't just that he was convinced going after Luc was likely to fail. If he was honest, he wanted to go after Charlotte because he wanted her in front of him. If she were loyal to him and to the service, then he had a duty to her. And behind it all, he wanted to believe that throughout their time together in England and France he hadn't been a dupe.

In the field, loneliness was a danger for the agent – they had all been told that again and again during their training, that it allowed enemy agencies a way in. And he had to admit to himself that the solitary existence he had lived had got to him. So when the relationship with Charlotte had formed it had been a crutch. In the bitter winter, there had been, simply, someone in the same room as him.

And so he had qualms when it came to finding Charlotte. He didn't want to discover it had all been a trick. He had tricked and used others – sometimes good people who were just reluctant to help – in his own mission, but each time he had done it for what he unflinchingly knew to be the restoration of decency to a world on the brink.

If she were with them, she didn't even have the thin excuse of having been brought up smothered in the ideology of National Socialism, like the young soldiers tramping the streets in *feldgrau*. If mindlessly following Nazism made one guilty – and he believed that it did, even those soldiers still had minds to think and reject it, to desert, malinger or rebel – then choosing it, seeking it out, was a capital crime.

So if, as Delaney presumed, it was Charlotte who had informed the Gestapo of the raid, leaving Richard dead on the road, then Reece knew he would ensure there was justice. He had to be just enough to extract it.

Sebastien leaned against the mottled bark of a tree and looked up to the slice of the sky where the unseen aircraft must have flown. 'Do you need me to hide you for a while?' he asked.

'No, I need to find someone,' Reece replied. 'I have to go back to Paris.'

Just after 7 a.m., Klaussmann read a brief message from the French tax records bureau. The owner of the tabac was, as the neighbours had claimed, one Marc LeFevre. He had bought it two years earlier and the only address for him was the shop itself. No more information. Klaussmann went to the window in thought. 'This man and his comrades were taking a severe risk, hitting the prison transport.'

'Yes, sir,' Schmidt replied.

'So they must have been desperate to liberate their friend.'

'What is happening to Carte, sir?'

'The SS garrison in Amiens is under Obersturmbannführer Baumann. He's working on the man.' He cleared his throat. 'Baumann's committed, I'll give him that, but not made for these affairs.'

'Has he got anything from the prisoner?'

'He said he'll update me "in due course", which makes me believe he's got nothing. Now.' He tapped on the window to underline his point. 'The English cell failed to free Carte but got away mostly intact. I imagine they will try again to either free or contact him.'

'You think LeFevre has gone to Amiens?'

'I think there's a good chance. I don't want to hand it all to Baumann, so we'll go ourselves. A bit of pressure and one of the local terrorists might let something slip.' Klaussmann smirked. 'It's old-fashioned legwork.'

A junior officer from the Amiens SS garrison drove Klaussmann and Schmidt around a series of locations and businesses suspected of being actively sympathetic to the Resistance: a couple of cafés, a bookshop, a car-repair garage. Questions about Marc LeFevre were met with blank stares. Overall, the two Gestapo officers came up with nothing and returned, frustrated, to the train station just before 1 p.m.

A dusting of snow lay on the ground like lace when they set foot on the platform for Paris. Porters stood idly around below red swastika-emblazoned banners.

'If you see him, arrest him immediately. You understand?' Schmidt instructed two SS guards. 'And make sure whoever replaces you understands too.'

'Yes, sir. We were all briefed.'

'I'm sure you were. But I wanted to remind you.'

Klaussmann spoke. 'Schmidt is my hand of efficiency,' he said with a smile. 'I know you two men will do well.' The SS troopers saluted and went to their posts.

Klaussmann brooded as he waited for the train. Six mothers back home would already be screaming their throats raw for what the British spy had achieved. He thought of his own mother, when she had received the letter telling her that her husband would not be returning from the previous war: the look of desperation in her eyes. The others, and many more, would be like her. The needle-pricks of terrorism were not without cumulative effect.

'Excuse me, gentlemen.' A girl with skin stretched over her bones like cheap fabric trudged towards them, carrying a bundle of firewood. They parted to let her pass between them. She dropped a couple of sticks and Schmidt immediately picked them up from the ground.

'Allow me, miss,' he said, offering to take the full burden from her.

'No, thank you, sir,' she sighed, passing on.

'You did well to offer,' Klaussmann informed his assistant. 'We must maintain relations as well as we can with the population. Do you want to stay in France?'

'I like it here, sir.'

'Yes, it's a pleasant posting. Better than Kiev, at any rate. I can help you remain.'

'Thank you, Herr Sturmbannführer.'

Klaussmann appreciated the formality. And he was looking forward to continuing to mould Schmidt into a good officer. It would be a point of pride.

On the other side of the entrance hall, Reece walked through the station's double doors, clutching his backup set of identity papers. They identified him as a boat mechanic named Maurice Vert from Caen in Normandy and were the ones he had used to gain access to the Atlantic ports for his previous reconnaissance mission.

The snow was beginning to come down in earnest, whipping around him and settling on the ground. He had a cheap purple scarf wrapped around his face as protection and he bound it tighter as he felt his jaw becoming numb. It must have been ten degrees below zero on the centigrade scale – so cold that his lungs struggled. It seemed to him that ice crystals were forming within them in sympathy with the air outside. He was tired, too, after the previous night and could have gone to sleep, blanketed by the falling white dust.

He pondered the day ahead of him: back to Paris to find Charlotte. To help her evade the Germans or to track her down like quarry? He couldn't tell. He wanted to find her hiding from the Gestapo, but if it turned out that she was a German parasite, he would have to swallow down the vestiges of his feelings for her and treat her as he would any other *collabo*.

He approached the doorway to the platforms. Two SS troopers were checking identity papers as people filtered through. Reece was confident his sallow skin and the bags under his eyes would appear to be no more than the effects of overwork and poor nutrition, rather than anything that should arouse suspicion.

'Papers.' Reece handed them over. The German, who looked no more than seventeen, examined them closely, rubbed the paper between his finger and thumb and looked at Reece.

'Sir, that's my train,' Reece said, huffing warm breath into his cupped hands and pointing to the locomotive arriving on the platform just a few metres away. He did his best to look politely put out.

The man glanced over his shoulder at the train. 'All right.' He handed back the identity card and pushed Reece towards the platform. The arrogance was the only thing left of teenage childhood, Reece understood.

As he stepped out on to the platform a welcome thought crept into Reece's mind: that his luck might hold at least until he got to Paris.

He also knew such thoughts were the quickest route to getting killed.

He hurried towards where the locomotive was waiting, like a giant black dog. People were spilling in and out of the carriages: old men, thin girls; a few throwing their arms around people waiting for them. Many looked like walking mounds of clothing, wearing layer after layer against the cold. They were all moving, shuffling around to generate a bit of warmth in their limbs, producing a strange tide-like motion along the platform. And then two figures caught Reece's eye: a tall SS major and a younger man in a Gestapo leather greatcoat speaking to a French policeman on the platform. The policeman looked surly but nodded at whatever he had been told.

Reece stared at the face of the officer in SS uniform and a flash of recognition appeared in his mind. He stopped dead.

Reece had done his best to disguise himself, wrapping the scarf around his face, but it had been only three days since Sturmbannführer-SS Klaussmann had entered the Lapin Agile bar in Montmartre and looked him straight in the eye before dragging Luc away. Three days for a memory to fade, for the photograph to turn blank in the sun. It wouldn't be enough to blot out the memory of a Gestapo officer who had spent years tracking faces. Reece's mind tumbled with thoughts of escape, but he kept his nerve. The only weapon he had was the knife on the underside of his lapel, and panic would send him to the gallows.

Klaussmann glanced at Reece. His eyes ranged up and down Reece's dirty clothes as if they were an identity card offering a second story on the owner. Reece felt the scrutiny and steeled himself to run; if he saw any recognition in the man's expression, he could bolt across the tracks and scale the fence before the Germans could move on him. But although he would have the start, he would also have to weave, to avoid any bullets.

And yet Klaussmann immediately returned his attention to the policeman and didn't look back. Reece waited, watching. More passengers scurried through. Still nothing. He risked sauntering away a few paces to buy a newspaper from a stand and casually walking past the two Gestapo officers, all the time ready to make a dash for it.

' . . . to that tabac,' he heard Klaussmann tell his assistant in German. Reece tensed. They were talking about him. They had to be. They may not have recognized him, but they were surely looking for him. If they knew where he worked, they must know his name. And if so, had they somehow also found his photograph? That would make the danger ten times worse, and no doubt they would insist on all men removing scarves from their faces.

He looked to the brick wall, plastered with a list in Gothic script of the Resistance members who had been executed that week, along with the photographs of others who were being sought. Money was on offer to anyone who could locate these men and women who had slipped away. He couldn't help but think of what the Germans would do to him if they caught him.

'Yes, sir,' replied the junior officer.

The station guard blew his whistle as a warning that the train would soon be moving. It would be the best way to get away from Klaussmann – turning around and leaving the platform would bring more attention. Reece therefore walked briskly towards the closest carriage. He climbed through the door into the narrow corridor and into an empty compartment. From where he sat, he could just make out Klaussmann and his assistant, apparently giving the policeman some final instructions, before striding away out of Reece's sight. He relaxed into his seat and checked out the other window. Just the fence and a white sky.

And then there was movement on the platform. Klaussmann had returned. He and his junior were making their way straight for Reece's car. The train was beginning to move now. Reece jumped up. He had to decide: he could leap out, but that would only attract the Gestapo officer's attention. He would have to run for it if he did that. No, it was suicide. Klaussmann's hand was pulling open the door. He would have to brazen it out.

Klaussmann hauled himself into the corridor, followed by the other Gestapo officer. They nodded politely at Reece. 'Excuse me, gentlemen,' he muttered, and got up to leave, as if offering them the compartment to themselves.

'No, no, stay,' Klaussmann replied, motioning for him to retake his seat.

Reluctantly, Reece did as he was bid, smiling in thanks.

He berated himself for not somehow avoiding this needless, pointless danger. Even the simple proximity to Gestapo officers made his skin bristle with loathing.

The two Germans removed their coats before sitting, showing no sign of recognizing him. And then Klaussmann's gaze fell to the scarf wrapped around Reece's face and his brow furrowed. A pang of worry grabbed the British agent, but he had no choice. Gingerly, he removed the scarf.

'I would prefer our own men on the gate,' Klaussmann told Schmidt, ignoring the Frenchman and turning to peer through the window at the SS troopers.

'I'm sure they will do their best, Herr Sturmbannführer.'

'One's best is no help if it doesn't get the job done.'

It was a testing time. Things were tense in the service – not just in France but in Germany too. Thousands of Gestapo and SS officers had returned beaten and frostbitten from the Eastern Front, driven back by the brutish Slavs, and many of them held a grudge against their brother officers who had been stationed nowhere more dangerous than Brussels. They would have dearly loved to supplant any man seen as failing in his job. Everyone could feel invasion in the air and only fools believed that the Allies would have no hope of success – already there were rumours of senior Party members spiriting away plunder to Swiss bank accounts and setting up escape lines to Argentina or Brazil. Like dogs when all the food has gone, they were beginning to watch each other, marking out the weak to be sacrificed when the time came.

All of that made the soil rich for suspicion between the services too. The Gestapo and SD may have been spiritual allies, but still they competed for the patronage of Himmler and that bred the rivalry of brothers born a year apart. Indeed, possibly the single line on which their interests coincided was an intense distrust of the Abwehr. There had long been suspicions that Admiral Canaris harboured anti-National Socialist beliefs – and he had a lisp that made him sound just like a queer, they said. Yes, Canaris was too slippery, too inscrutable. Thankfully, the Führer's hand was on Himmler's shoulder. There would be a reckoning soon, and the Reichsführer-SS would undoubtedly triumph.

The train took them out into the countryside, through a dense, skeletal forest rapidly turning white. On the opposite track a massive machine passed them, travelling in the other direction. Like a skyscraper turned on its side and with a giant pipe piercing the sky, the railway gun – artillery powerful enough to shoot huge mortar shells right across the Channel – seemed like a sleeping metal beast.

A few minutes later they drew into a small town. The snow outside the window formed a blurring, rushing sheet. The wind had picked up too, whistling and forcing its way through every nook and hole in the sides of the carriage.

Klaussmann crossed his arms for warmth and his eye fell on the dirty Frenchman in front of him, laboriously reading the words of a newspaper. A typical workman, probably. Klaussmann wondered, in fact, if the man could be of use – a different perspective. There would be little things that he understood about France and French life that would pass a Prussian Gestapo officer by. It could be instructive to Schmidt as well as himself.

'Sir,' he began. Reece looked up. 'I am Sturmbannführer-SS Klaussmann. Schmidt here and I were just remarking on the beauty of your country.' Reece didn't move. 'And not to mention the beauty and elegance of your maids. They are so – what is the word that you use? *Elegante.*'

'That is the word, sir,' Reece replied.

'Even in Germany we read poetry about it.'

'I don't read books, sir.'

'No, no. Of course. You are a working man.'

'I fix boats.' Reece looked attentive.

Klaussmann decided the man was a simpleton. The train halted and a few people pulled themselves into the carriages. 'Working with your hands,' Klaussmann said, directing the words at Schmidt, almost as a rebuke to the junior officer. 'Do you know Amiens well?'

Reece looked uncomfortable. 'I am sorry, I am not from the city.'

'No? It seems to me a pleasant town.' A young woman entered the carriage from the corridor. She was looking down at the ticket in her hand as she slid the door open on squealing hinges. The noise made her look up sharply and she caught her breath as she spotted the two Gestapo officers. She began to withdraw, but Klaussmann stopped her. 'No, no, miss, do come in. Please. There's a place free for you just there.' He pointed to the seat beside Reece. She hesitated. She was dressed up for a day out, with a pink hat and gloves, trying to keep up the travel standards of the previous generation. She carried a matching pink case with copper-encased corners that was damp with melting snow.

'There are other . . .' she stuttered, looking out into the corridor, carpeted with the slushy footprints of those who had tramped along it.

'I wouldn't hear of it. Please.' He motioned his hand to the seat. Reluctantly, she entered the carriage.

Reece and Schmidt both rose to take her case from her and place it in the overhead rack. Schmidt was about to say something, but Klaussmann gently tugged him back down into his seat. 'It's only natural that she would like one of her gallant countrymen to aid her,' he said, chuckling genially. 'We must remember our place in this country.'

'You are our guests, sir,' Reece said, lifting the case.

The train jerked violently. It could have been a set of points, but Klaussmann suspected they had, in fact, shaken over a spot where one of the *réseaux* had blown the tracks, necessitating a rushed repair-job. The motion knocked Reece against the young woman. And that was when Klaussmann noticed something about the Frenchman, something that fell into place.

Reece saw Klaussmann's eyes narrow. 'I'm sorry, miss, my fault,' he said, sliding the case into the rack above them. The girl, too, looked concerned for some reason that Reece couldn't see. Was it the presence of the two Gestapo officers?

'Do you know,' Klaussmann began, stretching back into his seat, 'I have heard your countrymen speak so highly of your national cuisine that I am in a permanent state of hunger.' Reece watched him pull a small leather-bound note-book and pen from his breast pocket, scribble something upon a page, tear it out and give it to his junior officer. 'Take this to the dining carriage. Make sure it's prepared like I ask. I can't stand undercooked chicken.'

'Yes, sir.' He got up and left.

'Now, sir, miss,' Klaussmann said, addressing Reece and the girl. 'I have a confession to make. You may have heard terrible stories about the men of my nation and our stern ways, but I must say that we have the hearts of romantics when it comes to the countryside. Just look at this,' he said, wafting his left hand towards the stark fields and twisted, naked trees that were speeding past. 'Look at that fine old church. Its tower has stood for five hundred years. That village.'

Reece followed the pointed index finger. He could barely see through the snow now; it was like looking through a moving and wailing gauze of brilliant white. But there was something strange about Klaussmann's insistence. He didn't trust it for an instant. And then he noticed a different movement: a twitching in Klaussmann's other hand. The tips of the fingers seemed to be itching for the gun holster strapped to his waist.

Reece's nerves sharpened, watching for more. And in the spectral window reflection he caught sight of the SS officer's eyes. He wasn't looking at the church or the village, he was watching Reece.

In an instant Reece saw what had set this fat Boche oaf's heart beating: a spreading dark, painful patch on Reece's shoulder. The stitches on the bullet wound had opened when he fell against the girl and he hadn't noticed.

He jumped up. Immediately, Klaussmann went for his Luger. The girl screamed. Reece knew there would be a second before the barrel was pointing at him. At this distance, he couldn't miss. Reece's only choice was surrender or a bullet. But he couldn't let himself be taken to undergo the interrogation in which he could spill so many secrets, even landing his fellow agents in the Gestapo's hands. He was ready to throw himself into the course of the round rather than that. He just wanted it to be quick.

And yet, another second, and the gun wasn't in Klaussmann's hand. The Gestapo officer was overweight, clearly unused to combat, and he was fumbling with the holster clasp. Reece saw a chance and grabbed hold of Klaussmann's thick wrist, trapping his hand on the fastening. They fought, muscle against muscle. Reece strained, overstretched, to keep his opponent from drawing. Klaussmann tried to throw him off, twisting away, but Reece was younger and stronger and used his weight to pin the German to the seat. He held the other man's hand in place, refusing to let the gun emerge. If he could wrench Klaussmann's arm away and draw the Luger himself, he could put a bullet in him and get free.

But then the Gestapo officer seemed to have a burst of strength and his elbow cracked into Reece's cheekbone, knocking him back. The motion of the train overbalanced him and he fell back on to the seat. In a moment the gun was in Klaussmann's hand and pointing at Reece's chest. Reece froze.

'*Halt!*' There was no triumph in Klaussmann's eyes, only grim determination. His voice steadied. 'Don't move.' It was the moment Reece had expected since he saw the Germans on the platform. Klaussmann had him cold. Now he wouldn't have even a quick death. If Klaussmann wanted him alive – barely, with a bullet in his gut – he had him. Reece could almost feel the shackles snaking around his wrists, the cosh breaking his bones. He clutched for the L-pill disguised as a jacket button, ready to rip it from its threads and crush it between his teeth, robbing the Reich of its prize. Death would be painful, but swift, they had told him. Better than the agonies of torture in the Gestapo cells. His fingers found the small rubber-encased glass phial and subtly snapped it from the fabric. Klaussmann noticed the action and readied to fire. 'Stop.'

And then, out of the corner of his eye, Reece saw sharp, speedy movement. The girl had pulled her case down from the overhead rack and was swinging it hard at Klaussmann. She missed, and its copper-tipped corner smashed through the window, letting a flurry of snow blow into the compartment and scattering a rain of glass fragments to the floor. But the movement pulled her into Klaussmann's line of sight, forcing him to try to push her aside.

At the same moment, Schmidt pulled open the door, flanked by two soldiers with MG 42 Spandau sub-machine guns. It was clear that the note Klaussmann had written had been nothing to do with food and everything to do with going for reserves. Reece was caught between the two, but suddenly there was an exit. It was barred, but it was a route to freedom.

'Gentlemen,' he said emolliently, releasing the suicide capsule and jumping up with his arms open, hoping to buy a second to find a way out. Amazement at the scene flashed across Schmidt's face.

The confusion offering Reece a glimpse of escape, his hand snatched his lapel knife from its thin sheath and levelled it. For a single heartbeat, he looked into Schmidt's eyes, seeing nothing but bewilderment. Behind Schmidt, the two soldiers lifted their weapons. Reece did the same, pointing the arrow-like tip of his blade at Schmidt's neck. And as everything seemed to slow in time, he threw himself forward.

Klaussmann's pupils enlarged as he watched. He saw the girl in pink fall away, more shards of glass tumble to the floor and the spy's blade cut through dust suspended in sunbeams. To his eyes, it seemed to hold, somehow, in the air, before sweeping forward and forward, and then through the skin of Karl Schmidt's throat. It sent, as Klaussmann watched, a thin line of blood spurting up the wall and on to the face of one of the soldiers. Then Schmidt's body folded into itself and crashed backwards, knocking the guards away. His stomach turned.

He had seen blood spilled before – it had run like a stream along the floor of interrogation rooms – but then it had been men and women in civilian clothes or naked, strapped to tables and chairs. Now it was a man in a leather greatcoat clutching his fingers to a red bubble bursting from his neck.

Klaussmann kicked the girl aside and jumped up to better reach his gun. The spy's back was to him and he would have a clear aim. He pulled his Luger from its holster, raised his arm and aimed for the back of the man's head. His arm was trembling a little with the adrenalin as he touched the trigger, but the shot, he knew, was true.

'Stop!' he cried. 'He's mine!' The two soldiers, raising their Spandaus to shoot, halted as ordered. Reece spun around and saw the arrow-shaped Luger now pointing at his chest. Klaussmann steadied his hand and breathed out, as he had been trained years ago.

At first, he didn't know why a bolt of pain as sharp and sickening as any he had ever felt was racing through his body, up from his pelvis. Then he looked down to see the girl's black-shod foot retreating from his groin, where it had slammed into him. The shock flowed through, buckling his knees, but no electrical pulse of thought had told the muscle in his finger to cease squeezing the trigger. It pulled back until the metal met the metal behind it.

CHAPTER 12

The sound of the explosion passed Reece well after the bullet did. And by the time he heard it the round had grazed his hair, passing within a few millimetres of his skull, and smashed through the mouth of one of the soldiers, leaving a ragged and dirty hole in his cheek. The other soldier dived to his side.

'Get out!' It was the girl, shouting at Reece. Klaussmann was crumbling, but he still had his gun. 'Get out!' Even in the chaos, Reece was grateful to her for his life.

As he scrambled to escape he felt the train slowing in its motion. More points or hasty repairs were forcing it to lose steam. He leaped over the body of the dying Schmidt, who was trying desperately, raspingly, to breathe, despite the air flowing out of his throat. One of the soldiers was holding his hands to his face and whimpering while the other crouched in the corner like a beaten animal. He made a feeble attempt to grab for Reece as he ran past along the corridor, then through a sliding door into a carriage chosen at random. He found five Frenchmen inside, carrying crates of wan vegetables.

'The Boche!' Reece shouted.

After four years, everyone in France knew the story. One of the men tore off his pale blue overcoat and threw it around Reece's shoulders, but it would hardly help; there was no hiding him. Only the land outside presented a possibility. The train was German territory but, in the countryside, he could hope to evade them. He stared through the window into the white gale. He could just make out that the train was crossing a bridge. Beneath it, a dirty brown river was flowing, barely visible between breaks in snow-covered ice.

He heard two shots behind him, dulled by wood and glass. He guessed the girl's life was gone. Silently, he thanked her again before grabbing the handle on the external door. He hesitated for a moment. It was a fraught escape.

One of the Frenchmen closed the sliding door to the corridor, holding the handle as tightly as he could to slow any entrance, but almost immediately someone on the other side attempted to draw it open. A few centimetres of space opened up between the door and the frame and a black gun muzzle thrust through.

No, there was no other way, Reece knew. He forced the door outward, the wind resisting his strength before wrenching it from his hand to slam against the outside of the train. Instantly, a surge of snow swept into the carriage, coating the floor and seats; it flew into Reece's eyes and hair, scratching and freezing the skin of his cheeks.

He stood on the threshold to the open air, looking down through the swirling sea-like white mass. The bridge was lined with a low brick wall running no more than a metre from the train. Beyond it was the sleet-filled air and the surging river.

'Go!' growled the man holding the door as one of his friends rushed to help him keep it closed. The gun barrel flashed and the window to Reece's side immediately shattered outwards.

'Good luck!' one of the Frenchmen shouted in heavily accented English. Reece caught his breath, charged forward and leaped as far and fast as he could, lifting his feet like a long jumper to clear the wall, with nothing but hope to lift him over it. He trusted his life to the wind and the snow. For a moment he was in a white world without form, his shoes scraping the edge of the bricks as he passed over them.

And as he twisted in the air he saw someone at the open doorway: a figure in SS uniform framed by the wood. Klaussmann was levelling his gun once more. Reece saw another flash from the muzzle.

Clouds seemed to slip past him, and time stretched like gossamer as he dropped through the gale-whipped white ocean, down towards the river.

Daniel Delaney's staff car rolled through oily puddles on a narrow road deep in the Essex countryside. The window was partly open and heavy winter mist was condensing on the wool of his jacket.

He was tired of uniforms. He had been nineteen when he was first commissioned into the army. It was the last year of the Great War and he had seen action, although not the worst of it. In 1920 he had emerged from the armed forces and matriculated at King's College London, to read French. One of his classmates was an Austrian named Elena and he had fallen in love with her for the best part of a year, during which time she tried, and failed, to make him a Communist. After that they had remained close friends and when she had returned home they had continued to write long letters to each other. After the Anschluss the Gestapo had beaten her to death.

Delaney read the news in a letter that Elena's brother had written. It had watery blotches through the ink. Delaney had despised the Nazis before that, but an hour after slipping the letter back into its envelope and placing it gently into the bottom drawer of his writing desk he had re-enlisted with the aim of ending the lives of as many of them as he possibly could. He hoped they would feel more pain than she had over the hours and days it had taken to kill her. After time in Army Intelligence, he had been approached to join the nascent Special Operations Executive as deputy director of the France section.

Thoughts of Elena came into his head from time to time, unannounced, and – truth be told – unwanted. He had a job to do and the anger that still smarted impeded him. They came now as he climbed out of the back of his car and he had to remind himself of the day's purpose. In front of him, American military police sentries guarded a gate through a wire fence topped with barbed wire. Also at the gate, waiting for him, was an American lieutenant from the combat engineers.

'Major Delaney, please show your identification to these men and then follow me,' he said. Delaney did as he was asked, returned the guards' salute and followed the eager young man through a second fence, one bedecked with camouflage drapes that made it difficult to see clearly into the camp. 'Welcome to the First United States Army Group.'

In the distance he saw rows of tanks, all neatly assembled. Scores of barracks huts could have held many thousands of men. A company-sized number were drilling on the central parade ground at the heart of the camp. Like the tanks, the men were just about visible from the road, but only at some distance.

A small party was watching the company march and wheel. An American general with short, neat white hair, a British brigadier in a beret and a third, who wore his preferred army uniform – that of a colonel of the Queen's Own Hussars – puffing on a fat Cuban cigar. 'Glad I'm not taking them into battle,' the latter said to the other two, receiving chuckles in return.

'I'm glad no one is,' added the general.

The colonel with the cigar turned to see Delaney's approach. 'Gentlemen, I have business to attend to,' he said, before shambling away. Delaney followed him towards a line of tanks. They walked slowly. Churchill was a rock for the people of Britain, and he moved like one, as if each step he took were a defensive line to be dug. They were discreetly followed by two men in plain clothes who kept their distance but maintained a watchful eye on their charge. 'Damn nuisance after a while,' Churchill muttered, jerking his thumb at them. 'Think I can't take a bath without the Nazis attempting to kill me. Have you been here before?'

'No, sir.'

'Ah,' chuckled the Prime Minister. 'Then you must see the party trick.' He beckoned to a pair of American sergeants who were comparing lists on clipboards. They dutifully walked over. 'Gentlemen. Would you show the major here just how manoeuvrable your tanks are?' The men grinned and went to the nearest vehicle. They lifted metal weights from its tracks, took hold of opposite ends of the tank and lifted it into the air. They threw it up and let it fall to the ground and bounce a few times before gently wafting in the breeze. They replaced the weights. Delaney went over and stroked the rubber-plastic. 'Don't think about poking it with a pin. It will create the most almighty bang,' Churchill said. 'A thousand of them here now. Inflate in five minutes, you know, and each one packs down into a single crate. We can move an entire mechanized division on a lorry. A most excellent game.' His voice fell and a more serious look appeared on his face. 'Nothing is without cost, of course.'

Delaney understood. Somewhere along the line, someone was paying for the ruse. 'Who are the men?' Delaney asked, indicating the troops who were still drilling, although their movements were ragged.

'Medically unfit. And have you seen those?' The Prime Minister pointed to a line of jeeps. Delaney approached the closest. It was a shell of plywood and painted cardboard. 'The RAF has obligingly allowed one or two Luftwaffe reconnaissance flights to briefly penetrate. Just long enough to catch a glimpse.'

Delaney thought it over before returning. There was always a danger of overplaying the hand, which would result not only in the Germans discovering the trick but realizing the reason for it. 'Have they taken the bait?'

Churchill dropped his voice to a near-whisper. 'Indications from Bletchley suggest so. Herr Hitler is focusing all their attention on where our ghosts are heading.' He prodded his toe into the ground and dug up a little soil. '"All warfare is based on deception." Do you know who once said that?'

'No.'

'A Chinese general. Long ago. Five hundred years before the Romans even set foot on this land. Nothing changes in time.' The men finished their drill and the American general and the British brigadier walked towards one of the huts. Churchill settled himself on to an empty packing case. He sat uncomfortably, as if he wanted a backrest. 'Right, what do you have for me?'

'Maxime reports that the stolen document refers to a German spy in London with high-level access,' Delaney said. He said it directly and simply, as he knew Churchill demanded.

'Does Maxime, by God,' the Prime Minister growled. 'The game's afoot, then. What about 5?'

'MI5 will take any opportunity to turn London upside down. They're ready.'

'Hmmm. No doubt. And I suppose Himmler will hear the commotion if they do,' Churchill mused. 'Though if there really are any bad apples in our barrel, the clamour might make them so frightened they call home and we can pick up their transmissions. Dirty business.'

'It is, sir.'

Churchill stared at the ersatz tanks and jeeps. 'Well, then, I suppose it's time to unleash the dogs.'

'Yes, sir.'

Churchill glanced over Delaney's shoulder. 'Well, that was quick.'

Delaney looked around to see a tall, slim man wearing a pinstripe suit. 'Hello, Evans,' he said. Huw Evans was MI5's main liaison officer with SOE and MI6, which ran its own intelligence-gathering operations throughout Europe. It couldn't have been an easy role to play and Delaney respected him for it.

'Delaney. Prime Minister,' Evans said as he came close.

'All warfare is based on deception, did you know that, Mr Evans?' Churchill asked, puffing out another acrid cloud from his cigar.

'I didn't, sir. But I think that's a wise thing to say.'

'Hmmm. Yes, perhaps it is. But wisdom tends to be forgotten the second the balloon goes up.'

'I saw Maxime's report. Time for us to swing into action, I would say.'

'I would say so too.'

No flowing water met Reece's feet as he crashed into the river, but something solid. As the shock of the impact buckled his knees he believed he had somehow missed the river and fallen on to hard land. Then he plunged through the snow-covered ice into the depths below. And the world disappeared from his vision. The freezing water choked from him what breath he had, the air blasting out as bubbles that he couldn't see – it would have been a yell had it not been smothered by the dark water. As his panicked senses adjusted to this new world, he realized what had happened and, with only the barest of thought, a primeval desire to live took over. He told himself to stay alive.

Reece had learned to swim as a child in a country river just like this, but then it had been a summer holiday at his grandparents' home on Long Island and the flow had been nothing compared to the torrent that now dragged him along. Even as he struggled to work out which way led to the air, he kicked with his feet, emulating the strokes he had practised when younger, and he windmilled his arms, desperate for movement.

At first his movements were too chaotic to propel him in any direction. But then his actions seemed to unconsciously unite in purpose and he felt himself moving, slowly rising up. As he drifted through the dirt he felt sure that there was air within reach, if he could just stretch his arms to it. They lifted above his head, higher and higher. But then, just as he felt certain he was about to make it out, his searching fingers were stopped by a layer of ice, filtering the grey light and keeping him from the air he needed.

As his lungs burned he thrust both his palms up and pushed, trying to force his way to the sky. But the solid ice wouldn't crack or yield. He felt all around, further along towards the bank, where it was mottled with vegetation frozen into it, but it was just as hard. Desperate now, feeling his life slipping from him, knowing he had only seconds left before consciousness would leave him, he formed his right hand into a fist and punched upwards as hard as he could. But it failed to break through.

He punched again. And again, with all the strength he had left. And that time, hard enough to fracture the bones in his hand, he felt cracks threading through the ice. One more strike and shards of the ice came away from his knuckles, and then, with both hands, he reached up and grabbed hold of the broken edges of the glassy sheet, wrenching himself upwards and throwing his head through the surface.

He gulped down air and falling snowflakes. It seemed as if he had burst from one world into another. He spluttered as he sucked in as much air as he could, giving himself seven or eight lungfuls before resting then tearing away more ice, clearing and scrabbling a path through it towards the weed-tangled riverbank.

He dragged himself through a crowd of reeds, shivering, up the mud and filth of the bank, his body numb and his heart thudding like a marching army, until he collapsed on the hard earth, thankful for whatever bestial part of his mind had saved him from drowning in a freezing river.

Slowly, as he lay there, his vision turned into colours and lines. The sky became a cream-hued sheet peppered with dark treetops. The mud between his fingers sopped to the ground and his body shook all over as snow drifted over him and settled on his chest.

Barely conscious as he was, he knew he had to check for pursuit. He scanned all around: no, the train had disappeared and no one was in sight.

He pulled off his jacket and shirt, wrung them out then pulled them back on as some protection against the chill before slumping back down, trying to recover. Little by little, his lungs returned to normal and he checked himself all over. Klaussmann's bullet had missed him. It was a reprieve he hadn't expected but for which he was thankful.

The leather shortage meant that most wallets were nowadays made from cardboard. It was luck that Reece had kept one made from leather because as the river had closed over him the water had soaked the material to seal in its contents, keeping his identity card intact.

He drew it out as he approached the checkpoint into north-western Paris some hours later. It had been a hard, bitingly cold tramp for a while, and he had had to keep moving or risk hypothermia from his wet clothes. But the snow had ceased and then a delivery van caked in dirt had given him a lift for most of the distance from the small town in which he had found himself. The driver had let him out a couple of hours' walk from Paris and now he was approaching on foot. He wasn't the only one – there was a constant stream of men and women in and out as the townsfolk made journeys by any means they could to country cousins in order to scavenge some fresh food. They returned with pork, butter and eggs and Reece let the swell of sated bodies swallow him up and bear him along.

It felt good to be lost in that melee for a while. The occupation had set so many against each other as they fought over scraps, but even in the cold, these people coming back to town with full bellies were happy and there was an air of camaraderie that he had missed. Life in the circuit was a strange, divided one – bound hard to the other agents and yet rarely seeing them in order to maintain security. Charlotte had been an exception – and, he feared, a lapse.

And so as he walked among these people he chatted about trivial things – the state of the road they were on, whether a new film was any good – giving him respite from the thoughts of what he was immersed in. They were good folk and knew nothing of what he had been through.

He wanted to stay among them, to go to their homes. One was highly knowledgeable about Fauvist art and he and

Reece discussed Chagall, neither mentioning the artist's enforced flight to America. Another invited him to eat at his house that night – so long as Reece could bring coupons to cover his meal, of course – but Reece could neither spare the time nor risk the danger to the man's family that would come from harbouring him for the evening.

They were the France he had known, these men and women: romantic about painters, cheerful in food and wine. He watched them walking, satisfied with what they had begged from their rural relations, joshing each other. And all the time they talked Reece became more determined to recover what he could of that for the nation.

Once they were inside the city he bade goodbye to his new friends and set off on his own path.

As he walked his mind turned to the man whose throat he had cut – the only good Gestapo officer was a dead Gestapo officer, of course, so Reece hoped his death had been a slow agony – and to Sturmbannführer Klaussmann. The Gestapo were after him and had his description, but how much else they knew about him or the circuit he couldn't tell. That meant that all the while he was trying to find Charlotte the Gestapo would be right behind him and his task would therefore be intensely more difficult.

At least he had gained one piece of vital knowledge: Klaussmann had mentioned the tabac to his junior officer so Reece couldn't risk going back there. He would have to shelter elsewhere.

He had ordered Thomas and Hélène to break into their reserve cover identities and safe houses – and, precisely to defend against hostile infiltration, only Reece had known those details, so they should be secure, even if Charlotte were working for the Germans. He could stay with one of them for a day or two.

What else could she have told them? She could have said that SOE had acquired the file but the only one who had seen it was Luc. And she could tell them about Reece. She could tell them much about him – how he looked, how he slept.

But she wouldn't know that Luc had managed to tell Reece there was a spy in London. So that man wouldn't have known to go to ground. Special Branch or 5 would therefore still have a chance of hunting him down – if Reece could just get hold of the photographs.

It was a strange triangle: Reece, Charlotte, Parade. Three agents with different masters, all watching each other. All with different reasons.

Charlotte. Reece wanted to know what could have turned her against her country. There were *collabos* everywhere, from the Fascist-copy Parti Franciste to the Carlingue, who were motivated by little but the plunder they could steal from those they turned over to the Gestapo. Charlotte had never seemed to him in the least bit covetous – she was almost ascetic at times, her eyes passing over material things as if they were objects without substance – but equally, the sheer conformism of Fascism seemed as alien to her character as snow to the desert.

And yet, that was if she were indeed working for the Third Reich. But if she were being held in one of its cells, she would likely be thinking of little else but that Reece and the circuit would come for her. He wasn't even sure if he wanted that to be the case because, if he failed her, or if he were forced to leave her to rot, the worm in his soul would be worse than if she were a traitor.

The sun had set by the time he padded on swollen feet through the checkpoints, down through the city itself and across the Île de la Cité, the island in the Seine where the great cathedral of Paris stood, offering sanctuary to those who needed it. He stopped, barely able to walk another step, in front of the holy edifice. It was here that he and Charlotte had once had their photograph taken.

In need of warmth and rest, he staggered through the entrance archway, surrounded by moulded saints, past the candle-lit bronze crucifix of Napoleon III, into the nave of the church. A service was underway and he dropped into the last pew to watch a choir of boys singing below the majestic stained-glass rose window: an open flower with a thousand coloured petals. He had been brought up without religion or belief in anything beyond the physical world – his sense of what was good and what was not had arisen from an innate sensibility rather than a priest's words. And yet, as the Latin Mass blanketed him the sound was full of comfort. He stayed for another half-hour, hearing the music and the words from the pulpit, until he felt able to walk on.

Through paved streets and cobbled lanes he trudged, footsore, until he stood outside a dusty closed bakery south of the Champs-Élysées. The faded turquoise door to its right was bereft of a number but there was a panel of frosted glass. He clacked the knocker, more in hope than confidence that it would be answered. And yet, a few moments later, through the glass, he saw someone approach. It opened warily, to reveal Thomas's eyes, narrowing at the sight before him.

'What's happened?' Thomas asked in a low voice, casually drawing Reece into the flat.

'Charlotte's disappeared.' Reece explained all that had happened since the attempt to free Luc. 'I was nearly caught. I think they know who I am.'

'Shit,' Thomas muttered. 'Do we need to clear out?'

'Not yet. We have to track Charlotte down. She has the photographs.'

'How? We don't even know her real name.'

'There's something she told me once. It might help.' He hoped it would. He had doubts, strong doubts. 'But listen, I need to sit down before I fall down.'

Thomas led him into a single-room flat with one corner dedicated to a miniature kitchen. 'Are you hungry?' he asked.

'Yes.'

Thomas went to a cupboard and retrieved a loaf of black bread and a little dried sausage. Reece could see it was the last that he had – all that was left in the cupboard was a bunch of carrots. Everyone ate carrots endlessly these days because they weren't rationed, some eating so many that their skin gained an orange tint.

'My wallet's full of coupons, but there's nothing in the bloody shops to spend them on,' Thomas said. He went to a small stove, poured sawdust into it and placed a pot on top, stirring oats into watered-down milk to make a thin porridge. He unwrapped a little stick of cinnamon taken from the back of the cupboard and grated it into the pot so there would be some flavour. Reece tore into the bread and meat. There was a pile of books in the corner. He noted a few of the authors: Kafka, Freud, Zweig. 'Before they're burned,' Thomas explained quietly. 'I know, it could bring attention. But we all have to try to save something.'

Reece stared at his food. The lives in those books, the lives that wrote them. All destined, perhaps, for death.

'You're filthy too. Want some fresh clothes?'

Reece felt itching grime all over his body. 'I would, thanks. Is there any chance you have access to a radio – not civilian, something like Charlotte's set? Something on high frequencies?'

'No, sorry.' Thomas sounded bemused. 'I've just got that thing.' He pointed to a radiogram in the corner of the room. 'What do you need it for?'

'I can't tell you.' He was desperate to try again to listen to the transmissions he and Sebastien had come across. If they never found Charlotte, this might just be another way to unravel Parade's plan. Yet internal security demanded that information be shared only if strictly necessary – failing to observe this rule had brought the circuit to where they were now: Richard dead, Charlotte absconded. He had told Thomas about Charlotte, but that had been necessary because he needed Thomas's help to look for her.

Thomas gazed at him then went to a cupboard and lifted out some clean clothes. He put a small pot of water on the stove and took a thin, hard bar of soap from a drawer under the sink. 'When it's warm you can wash with it,' he said. They sat for a while until Reece had eaten. Then he peeled away his clothes, washed in the lukewarm water and pulled on the underwear and shirt Thomas had given him. He was surprised how much better he felt for being something close to clean, with some food in his stomach. He felt able to plan now.

'So, we find her,' Thomas said.

'We find her,' Reece echoed resolutely. Find her, know her – although even if he discovered her in the Gestapo's cells and every splinter of evidence showed that she had been loyal to SOE from the beginning he would have to admit to himself that he still knew her only on the surface, like a figure passing by a mirror.

'Good. Then how do we go about it?'

Reece tugged the curtain from the streaked window and checked outside. He let it fall back into place. 'She used to play piano in bars.' He had tried to think of anything else that would give them a clue to finding her. Her clothes had been supplied by SOE; she had never discussed her schooling or her job, other than playing piano. Each time she had told him which part of Paris she was from it had changed. Direct questions about her earlier life had been shrugged away. Reece had cudgelled his thoughts, grabbing for just one unrecalled piece of information that could help, but little else emerged. She had kept it all back. He had to admit she had been more careful than he had.

'So? We can't ask about her if we don't know her real name.' Reece reached into his wallet and drew out a folded photograph. He opened it out to show the picture that had been taken of Charlotte and himself in front of Notre-Dame.

'It was for cover. When we had to present as a couple,' Reece said in reply to Thomas's surprised expression. He could see the scepticism in the way his friend's mouth turned in response. He tore the photograph in half, ripping himself out of the picture to leave Charlotte. Her eyes were on the paved ground, as if sadness had enveloped her.

'All right, it's a start, but are we going to show this around every bar in Paris where they had live music? It would take a month to go around them all – and the Gestapo would get wind pretty quickly.'

'We can narrow it down. She said she played for Sorbonne students.'

'So we try the Latin Quarter first, but that's still forty bars.'

'It's a chance.' He drank some warm water. 'Have you got a map?'

Thomas tossed a stack of junk off the lid of a trunk. He hunted through and stood up a minute later with a creased map in one hand and a thick book in the other. 'This might help,' he said, holding up the book. It was the *Pages Jaunes*, the city business telephone directory.

'You're right about that.' Reece took the map and unfolded it on to the bed. A wave of tiredness hit him and he wavered.

'Look, give that to me.' Thomas took the *Pages Jaunes*, leaving Reece to slump back against the wall in tiredness, and flicked through the sections – legal services, butchers, coal merchants – until he found the section for bars. He went through the listings, noting some down on a pad. Reece watched him for a minute but struggled to keep his eyelids from falling. He lay down on the bed.

He woke with Thomas's gentle grip on his shoulder.

'I didn't know whether to let you sleep properly.'

'No, I can't. Not yet,' Reece mumbled.

Thomas held up the notepad. 'We have this. The most likely bars.' He sat on the bed, giving Reece time to come back to life. 'The Latin Quarter's where I first lived in Paris,' he mused. Reece knew that Thomas had studied architecture in the city for a couple of years. 'It was a hell of a lot more exciting than Aberdeen, I can tell you that. So many people. Parties all the time. Music. Poetry. So much dreadful poetry.' Reece chuckled. 'A bit different these days.'

'That's for certain.'

'When do you think it's coming?' Thomas asked.

Reece wanted to tell him that in a few months' time an armada of ships would power through the waves and British, American and Canadian troops would stream on to land to hammer the Boche into the ground. He couldn't. 'I don't know,' he said. 'But I do know that what we're doing, you and me, right now, is important for it.' There was silence as they both lost themselves in their thoughts.

'God, I could do with a decent meal. A shopkeeper up the road has bought a pig for his cellar,' Thomas said. 'He's promised me a couple of bits. The heart, if I'm lucky.'

'Tasty.'

'I was thinking of raising a couple of rabbits in here,' Thomas added, looking around the room.

'Sounds easier.'

'Yeah. I could break a rabbit's neck, but slaughtering a pig takes some nerve.' He went to the sideboard and took a small wooden box from a drawer, opening it to reveal two sugar cubes wrapped in pristine white paper and offering them to Reece. 'Here. You could probably do with the energy.'

'Thank you,' Reece said. He knew this was as much as Thomas would have for a week. He placed one in his mouth and savoured the sweetness. For a moment, it was almost like the time before the war. The other cube he carefully put inside his jacket pocket.

'Here's one. A German says to a Frenchman, "I hear you're eating rats now." The Frenchman replies, "If only! All the real rats are gone. Now we only have ersatz rats."' Thomas raised a smile. 'Why don't we hit Maxim's while Göring's there?'

'Don't think you're the first to come up with that idea. He has all the tables around him cleared and his guards wouldn't take kindly to any attempt.'

'A bomb – the RAF?'

'Very difficult to be so precise. And we would kill a lot more Frenchmen.'

'Perhaps, perhaps,' Thomas said. 'You know something? I'm glad they're looting the country.'

'How so?'

'Because for the first few weeks after they arrived the French were all frightened of these huge, efficient warriors.

Then they began stuffing their suitcases with jewellery and the French realized they're little better than petty criminals. Do you know what I heard them called the other day?'

'Tell me.'

'Colorado beetles. Because they eat all the potatoes.' He laughed. Then he sighed.

'How many bars do we have?' Reece asked, pointing to the notepad.

'Twenty-eight. Shall we go now?'

'Later tonight,' Reece replied. 'I've got something else to do first.'

'Do you need anything?'

'Yes. A sledgehammer.'

CHAPTER 13

Move by day and stick to roads, unless circumstances require you to move by stealth (e.g. in prohibited zones). Do not move in a group of more than two. At night, if you meet a motor car or bicycle, hide. Beware of curfew and dusk hour. Move at rush hours.

Jeder einmal in Paris — 'Everyone one time in Paris' — had been German military policy since 1940. All the troops would visit once. It was to be a playground for the tired servicemen, led through the city by the *Guide Aryen*, which told them the best places to enjoy themselves before they returned to their bombing missions, undersea hunts or bitter fights caked in the sand of North Africa. The *soldatenbordell* — soldiers' brothels — in which women were forcibly penetrated scores of times each day for fifteen minutes per soldier were not listed in those publications. Reece guessed that the seven or eight guffawing young soldiers entering what looked to be a requisitioned hotel near the Trocadero were there for that purpose.

When Hitler visited Paris after its capture in 1940 he had been famously photographed in the hilltop Trocadero park of gardens and small palaces with the Eiffel Tower below, brooding in the background as if it were awaiting his departure. Since then, German soldiers had slung a banner from the iron edifice: *Deutschland siegt auf allen Fronten*, it read. 'Germany is victorious on all fronts.' They had had to climb up to hang it because the French had cut the power cables to the lifts.

Reece glanced at it now as he rode in the evening darkness and trusted the day would soon come when the banner fell and the Nazis' stench no longer hung over the gardens.

The street was virtually empty as he cycled – even in the city centre, petrol was so scarce that you could watch a major road for an hour during the day and see just ten cars go by. Buses had fallen in number by three quarters, replaced by cycle-taxis sporting slogans such as 'Speed, comfort, security' and by horse-drawn carriages. It was strange to Reece that the new-found quiet of the streets seemed not charming but oppressive and ominous. Perhaps it was the fact that you now heard conversations conducted on the other side of the road – no one's life was private any more. All words had to be considered before they were uttered.

He pedalled past the Trocadero and stopped in front of two large iron gates opposite the Museum of Mankind, the seat of learning and culture that had been the headquarters of one of the very first *réseaux*, back in 1940. That year seemed a lifetime ago. Paris was another city now – one that, as the cars and crowds had left, had become cleaner, less abrasive and quiet as the grave. He despised how deathly it seemed under the palm of the German officers who swarmed about as if they belonged there.

After chaining Thomas's bike to a tree he clicked together a padlock that his fellow agent had found in a wooden lean-to at the bottom of the garden behind his flat.

That was also where they had found a sledgehammer, which Reece had wrapped in newspaper pages. Thomas had offered him some old sheets from *Le Temps*, the journal of record that had closed two years previously after refusing to print collaborationist propaganda, but Reece had eschewed even that subtle act of defiance and found a few abandoned pages from an officially sanctioned rag in the gutter outside.

He had strapped the tool to his back with rough garden twine. As he rode, it had chafed long red lines in his flesh, but that was hardly the worst of his privations now.

In front of him, a series of square columns constructed from white stone blocks rose five or six metres tall. They were set into a high wall that extended to the left and right, curving around to enclose a roughly triangular area of ground, each of its sides about two hundred metres long. Between the stone columns two intricately cast iron gates stood closed.

There was no one on the street, but just to make sure Reece stopped for a minute to fiddle with the front wheel on his bike, watching up and down. After that he stood, stretched and sidled over to the nearer gate. Peering through, he saw that everything was in perfect darkness. Whoever had designed the gates had made it difficult to get through them, but there was a full metre's gap between their tops and the stone slab above them – the streetlights, painted blue for the blackout, cast no light at all that high off the ground.

Picking locks, scaling walls and slipping through windows had been among the skills he had unashamedly enjoyed learning in the Finishing School, and this wrought-iron barrier was far easier to climb than the sheer walls of the large houses he had shimmied up and down. His toes found willing holds and he almost walked his way to the top, before winding his body through the gap to scramble down to the ground.

He checked back through. A policeman was sauntering in his direction, but he didn't appear to have seen Reece enter. All was well and Reece slipped along the path, lit by the faintest blue glow from outside the gates, among the aristocratic dead of Paris.

To his left he spotted a wooden board with *Cimetière de Passy* carved in cracked and weathered letters at the top. The few notices pinned to it fluttered in a light breeze. He flattened one against the wood. With a pencil torch he could just make out the writing. It explained a little of the history of the cemetery and mentioned a few of the famous residents: Debussy was under its soil, it seemed, as was his rival Fauré. Reece was tempted to visit the tomb of Manet, whose paintings had been his favourite as a child. But the grave he needed to find was not listed on the notice; he hadn't expected it to be, of course, and he set off again in search of it.

Luckily, Passy was one of the city's smaller graveyards, with only a few hundred occupants. If it had been Père Lachaise, it would have taken him days to go through it all. Family tombs sprouted everywhere, many with small altars sporting ornate crucifixes and flowers. Stars of David appeared here and there on gravestones too. In the low light, carved angels appeared threatening, ready to leap down from their plinths.

On Reece's left a famous actor lay rotting in his casket; to his right, a minor noble in a baroque mausoleum. He read all the stones as he passed, attempting to correct his course in the hope that they were grouped by era but soon realizing that the dead had been thrown in at random, wherever a space had appealed to the family. It would be a long night. A few stones with the year that he was looking for – 1940 – caught his eye, but the precise date was wrong.

For two hours he tramped the freezing lanes and mounds of the cemetery, shining his pencil torch here and there, and by the end of it his hands were stiff with pulling aside encroaching weeds. More than once he considered calling it off and running back to Thomas's flat, where there was a semblance of warmth and some – meagre – food to fall into his stomach. But always, the next few minutes could be the ones that brought him to his quarry.

And finally, just after 9 p.m. he stood in front of a modest grave and knew he had found it. The plot had a headstone that had once been white and was now yellow with lichen. Reece's gloved fingers traced the man's name – Dubois – and, crucially, the date he had died: *11 Juin 1940*. That was three days before the Germans had entered Paris, making it the day Charlotte said her father had died. She had also told Reece that he was buried overlooking the Eiffel Tower, and only Passy cemetery, built on the low hill, could offer that, so Reece was sure this was the old man. He gazed at the headstone then took the sledgehammer in his hands and smashed the stone to pieces.

Shards flew left and right; large chunks fell into the sod. The weight of the steel tool pulled Reece around as he brought it down five times, cracking the headstone into smaller pieces. Then, when it was wholly broken up, he dropped the hammer and surveyed what he had done. There were fresh flowers on the grave. He kicked them aside.

It felt good to exert himself like that, to break and to destroy. He had nothing against the dead man and he felt a pang of guilt for destroying the monument, but Reece's purpose had to be served, for all their sakes. And he had done far worse.

He then went to the two closest graves and repeated his actions, throwing flowerpots and smashing the wings of an angel. Having finished, he wiped the sweat from his brow and hands and pulled his shirt from his chest to let cool air down his front. He cleaned the handle of the hammer with a cloth to remove any fingerprints and threw it into some bushes at the foot of the furthest surrounding wall before walking back the way he had come. The sound of the breaking stone might have alerted a passer-by, and he had to get out as soon as possible.

Parade peered out into the night, watching for the German bombers he was, in some ways, inviting to drop their loads on London.

He might even have met some of the pilots, rubbing shoulders with them in beer halls. He had spent a year in Germany as a student and those twelve months had opened his eyes to something new. It had begun when he had joined a student club made up of aristocratic youths who liked to fence with live blades. The *mensur* society, he had been instructed, was the highest form of honourable living in such an effete age. They would be the officers of tomorrow. If their nation and the British ever came to blows again, it would be these young men who would lead the charges.

And some, he soon found, went further than idle expectation. Some desired such a day, such a year, such a time.

The new Chancellor was a jumped-up little corporal and the nation's noble natural rulers would rein him in when they desired to do so, they had said, but for now he was useful. In fact, it might be amusing to go to his forthcoming victory rally in Nuremberg. Parade had readily agreed, intrigued by the possibility of seeing such a man in the ascendant.

That night had been like nothing he had ever seen or experienced before.

He would never forget the power of it all. Searchlights had swept the clouds and picked out a Zeppelin, floating above them like a call to greatness. Bodies of men had wheeled and marched, the will of each individual becoming subservient to the commonality. All of them chanting the name of the man who would bring their nation to its true destiny.

He heard that chanting still as he looked into the London night. It was echoed in the wailing sirens that warned of approaching bombers. For a minute, there was nothing at all, then dull puffs of flak and, finally, the whine of engines and thud of falling bombs. None were close, but the sound rippled through the air.

He pulled back from the window. It was uncovered, but the light from the attic's weak, red-painted bulb was unlikely to be seen from below. Still, he would remember to put up a curtain next time. In fact, he looked around for something to cover it now, as he listened to the tap of the Morse key sounding the rest of the message: *USS North Carolina BB-55 added to invasion naval flotilla. Now steaming from Pacific expected arrival Portsmouth eight days. Arm 9 x 16 inch mark 6 guns . . .*

But then there was a different sound, one that made him alert: a creaking of wood. That noise was common in the house, but it seemed unusually close and vivid. He turned around and looked towards the trapdoor leading down into the house. Staring back at him, amazement set into them, were the eyes of the thin policeman he had spoken to the previous day. The man's head and chest were in the attic space. They both looked at the woman sitting at the wireless set operating a Morse key.

'The light . . .' stammered the policeman, unable to say anything else. 'You . . .' Then he stopped and rapidly descended the ladder to the landing.

Parade didn't waste a second. He leaped for the trapdoor and dropped straight to the landing floor, bypassing the ladder. 'No, wait!' he cried at the officer, who was backing away from him.

'Who are you?' But the policeman didn't wait for a reply and attempted to pull his truncheon from its leather strap before changing his mind and charging down the stairs.

Parade followed, grabbing for him, but the constable was beyond his reach.

'You've made a mistake!' Parade shouted.

'Spy!'

Parade tried to speak, but his breath was taken up by the chase. They both jumped the last few stairs, but the older man stumbled as he did so and Parade managed to get hold of his jacket. It wasn't enough, though, as the policeman shook him off and charged into the kitchen. A loaf of bread sat on the sideboard, a long, serrated knife beside it. The policeman grabbed it, but he hadn't been trained in such fighting and he jabbed it into the air in front of him without skill.

'Wait,' Parade breathlessly told him, holding up his hands. But the officer seemed now to be over the worst of his panic and was edging towards Parade, more confident now he was armed and seemingly determined to do his duty. He thrust the blade forward in short little stabs towards Parade's midriff.

Parade, however, knew what he was doing when faced with an armed man. He parried away a strike of the knife, took hold of the policeman's wrist with his right hand and broke his nose with his left. Blood and tears immediately sprayed, but the officer refused to let go of the weapon. Instead he used his body weight to throw them both against the sideboard. Out of the corner of his eye Parade saw his wireless operator framed by the kitchen doorway, her hands over her mouth. 'Don't . . .' His words halted as he felt something thud into his thigh. He looked down and saw a trail of liquid leaking from his limb. A moment later he felt the pain as the blade was drawn out. He parried it again as it came towards his stomach then hooked his arm inside the policeman's elbow, twisting the knife away. For the last time it thrust upwards, but this time it found a new direction, up into the man's midriff.

Parade held the officer to him and looked into his eyes. Something was leaving them, and the man's torso began to sag. They were locked together for twenty seconds as the officer's lips trembled in an attempt to speak, but no sound came. Parade set the man down on the floor. Blood soaked them both and the white linoleum.

The woman's mouth hung open.

Parade put his fingers to the man's neck, then to his wrist. He stood slowly, his knees creaking. 'I'll deal with it,' he said. 'Continue the transmission.'

'You want –'

'I said, continue the transmission! This is not your concern.' He wiped sweat from his brow and followed her up to make sure she did as she was told. He watched her tap out the words:

Transmission resumes. Arm 9 × 16 inch mark 6 guns 20 × 5 inch. Call sign NIBK. Command Vice Admiral Hustvedt. Officer complement 120–150. Experienced. Capacity suggests central use in Parade One. Ends.

An answer was received immediately, asking what had interrupted the message. *British officer discovered us. Now dead.*

The transmission now complete, Parade returned to the kitchen. He took a sheet from a pile of washing in a tin bath, folded it in two and rolled the body on to it. It would absorb some of the leaking blood.

'When I was a student, we used to come here to pick up girls,' Thomas said as he and Reece paced a dingy street that seemed to have been squeezed between two other much more respectable thoroughfares. The pavement was hazardous, the streetlamps having been turned off to save electricity, forcing them to rely on a weak electric torch. They had spent an hour walking from bar to bar, having quiet words with landlords and waiters, discreetly showing them the photograph of Charlotte and placing a few francs on the table to jog memories. No luck had followed, no one recognized her face or the name Dubois. 'This is a bit of a twist on that.'

'I came here with my dad sometimes. He liked the music clubs too.'

'Think it will ever be back to how it was?'

'Yes, I think so.' He hoped so, years in the future, when the Boche were back in their holes. There would always be the spectres of *feldgrau* and black boots in the background, though.

He and Thomas descended the steps into a club to find it sparsely populated. What customers there were looked glumly into their drinks while a violinist with a long white beard sweated over a tune that he had obviously been grinding out for decades. An old waitress strode between tables, presenting drinks.

'What would you like?' she mumbled, a line of spittle falling from her lip to her chin.

'Two grenadines, please,' Reece said, a friendly expression on his face.

'Is that all?' She looked sceptical.

'Also, we're looking for someone.' He pulled out the picture and placed it on the table, telling her the sparse personal details he thought it safe to reveal.

The woman picked it up and inclined her head to one side. 'She's a pretty girl, but no, I don't know her. Now, do you want those drinks or not?' A small puddle of spilled red piquette had seeped into a corner of the photograph and Reece wiped it off with his sleeve.

'I'm sorry, no, thank you,' Thomas replied. The waitress rolled her eyes as they stood to leave. They sauntered out once more into the clear night.

'Where's next?' Reece asked out on the pavement.

Thomas consulted his list. 'That one, then one more in the next street.'

They tried the remaining bars but, just as with all the others, their hopes rose when they showed the photograph of Charlotte and fell when no one showed any sign of knowing her.

As they dejectedly left the final club on the list, they stopped outside the German bookshop on the place de la Sorbonne. 'See the bomb damage?' Thomas said. 'Communist *réseau* did that in 1941. This Jewish boy, Tommy, took his father's copy of *Das Kapital*, cut out the pages and put a bomb inside it. He simply walked in, left it on a table, and a minute later, *boom!* Germans scraped off the walls like . . .' His voice drifted away and Reece followed his line of sight. Young men leaving a cinema were being herded to one side by police and Gestapo men to have their papers checked. 'For the Obligatory Work Service,' Thomas muttered. Two were thrown in the back of a grey army truck and driven away. A third was about to be but was shoved back when he suffered a severe coughing fit that spoke of tuberculosis.

They trudged back to the safe house. Thomas settled into an armchair and draped his jacket over his knees. 'What now?' he asked.

'I have an appointment in the morning,' Reece said wearily. 'It might work.'

'Well, you can have the bed. I'll be all right here. You need some rest.'

CHAPTER 14

12 February 1944

Just after 8 a.m. the following day a woman dressed in a brown fur coat arrived at the entrance to Passy cemetery, passing colourful posters stuck on the cemetery walls. Some of the bills advertised continuing performances at the cabarets and were illustrated with pictures of topless girls riding horses across bright stages. Some were smaller and full of close type under the headline *Vengeance*. These informed readers how best to resist the Occupation without endangering themselves or their families.

A wiry little man was waiting for the woman in front of the iron gates, the gates Reece had scaled the previous night.

'My name is Dubois,' the woman said. 'You sent a message to my house,' she said.

The man stammered nervously and took his cap from his head. 'I'm very sorry, miss. I saw the damage as soon as I got in. I start at six, sharp, so it's all tidy by nine. Sorry, miss, I'll take you there right now.'

'I know the way.'

'Sorry, miss.' He led her quickly between the graves and watched as she stopped in front of the first headstone Reece had smashed to pieces. She looked down on the stone slab at her feet. 'Terrible people, miss. They're not right in the head, whoever did this. Three graves they did. No reason for it, no reason at all. But the police know, and they're on the look-out.'

'You told the police?'

'Yes. First thing my manager did after he looked up your address.'

The woman looked dissatisfied. 'Did they break any others?'

'Just these three. I found this in the hedge, you see,' the caretaker said, fetching the sledgehammer Reece had used from behind one of the grander monuments.

'Do the police know about this too?'

'I told them. As soon as I found it.'

'So it's not yours?'

'No, I don't have anything like this,' he replied.

She looked between the graves. Her father's lay in the middle and had suffered the most damage. The tool had been brought specially for the act and then thrown away, having served its purpose. That purpose had been to break up her father's headstone; the attack on the neighbouring gravestones had been a half-hearted afterthought.

She had thought she was hidden, but someone was coming for her.

A bus swerved to avoid Reece as he turned out across a junction into the avenue de la Bourdonnais, alongside the Champ de Mars, where so many revolutions had started and ended.

He raised a hand to the bus driver in apology, but the woman behind the wheel shouted something at him and he returned to his train of thought. He forced the pedals around faster, clunking the chain that was wiping gritty oil on to his ankles. He was tempted by the roadside kiosks – the brief breakfast Thomas had managed to scrape together had barely lined his stomach – but he couldn't stop. His body had been exhausted and he had slept later that morning than he had intended.

He was therefore relieved when, a few minutes later, he arrived at the cemetery gates. However, when he looked, he saw something wrong, something unexpected. The gates were unlocked and ajar, whereas they shouldn't be open for another half-hour. He glanced around. There were a number of people about: on their way to work, or returning from hours of queuing outside grocery shops with measly wares. But no sign of her. He stepped cautiously through the gates, seeing the graveyard in the daylight for the first time – mounds of graves and splendid family tombs cracking under the weight of time, but apparently empty of the living.

He stole up the first, steep stretch of path, where most graves were old and simple. There was no one in sight and he tried to work out if a caretaker had opened up and gone home or retired to some hut.

He walked on, watchful, a few more metres to where he knew the path bent to the left and opened up the vista of the graveyard: hundreds of plots and headstones, miniature temples with altars dedicated to family saints. His feet crunched over stones and hardened soil. To remain unobserved, he slipped into the portico of a white stone sepulchre with ivy creeping up its walls and a long-extinguished candle on a narrow altar. The ceiling had part collapsed, leaving chunks of masonry on the floor. It would do for an observation point. A large brown rat ran from behind the altar, out on to the path.

Reece scanned the cemetery, looking first towards the top-left-hand corner where Charlotte's father's grave lay, the headstone lying in pieces. When Charlotte had told Reece that her father had died just before the Germans entered Paris and was buried overlooking the Eiffel Tower, it was just about the first and last time she had ever let him into her real life. Now, he was using it as bait to draw her in.

No one around. It would be safe to explore further in. He began to step out but halted sharply. Two people were emerging from behind another serpentine coil in the path: a small, slim man and a woman in a brown fur coat.

He knew the way she moved. The way she turned her body.

It was the first time he had seen her since the flames had risen around her in her safe house. It felt like he had opened his eyes into bright, piercing sun: the truth was there, presenting itself to him, but it was hard to make it out amidst all the noise and glare. He was wary that his will would twist the facts, making her loyal still to her country, when such loyalty was a chimera. He told himself to keep something back.

Carefully, he edged out, ready to call over, to have her explain what had happened. But the sound of rapid footsteps clipping behind him made him stop once more. A German corporal was running up the path.

Reece drew back inside and crouched. He couldn't yet tell the true nature of the situation – whether the German had come to arrest him or her. Stealthily, he took one of the chunks of stone from the floor to use as a weapon. It was heavy and pointed and he could wait until the soldier passed and then stave in the back of his skull. But he would have to wait.

Charlotte continued walking, deep in discussion with the small man to her side. She hadn't seen the German. The soldier drew level with Reece. Hidden in the tomb's shadows, he lifted the stone.

'Miss Dubois!' cried the soldier.

Charlotte looked up. 'Where have you been?' she replied. The same tones as ever, slow and deep. 'You were meant to be here half an hour ago.' The tension left Reece's muscles as the undeniable realization crashed on to his shoulders.

It should have been obvious from the start. France had turned blind eyes and deaf ears to all the horrific sights and sounds around. Its people had pretended their friends and neighbours weren't informants and collaborators. He had pretended that Charlotte wasn't among them. Now the part of him that had known all along was asserting the truth.

He let his hand fall to his side, the stone cracking against the top of the altar. The sound was followed by a shallow echo.

At the noise, the German stopped and looked around. Reece pressed himself to the wall, just metres away from the man, holding his breath and trusting himself to the shades, ready to spring out if he had to. Now he could no longer see them; he could only listen, blind.

He heard a footstep. Then more, slowly coming closer. They were heavy, crunching the winter frost and stiff twigs underfoot. The soldier.

'Is someone there?' the corporal demanded. Two more footsteps. But the German must have heard only a sound behind him, unsure where it came from. Another footstep and another, but they were moving away from Reece – to the opposite tomb, it seemed, which had an iron gate across its entrance. Reece stowed himself behind the altar. He heard the gate on the other sepulchre open on whining hinges. Then another sound, like a stone kicked against a wall. He chanced a glance out. Rats were scurrying under the gate, away from whatever the soldier had booted at them. Would the soldier check the white stone tomb in which Reece was crouching? Maybe he could slip out while the German was still looking into the one across from him, and run, like the rats, around the back of the shrunken Grecian temple. He readied himself to do it, but then the *feldgrau* jacket turned towards him and he dropped down behind the altar again.

He picked up the stone and tensed, ready to attack. He would take the soldier first and seize his gun. Then he would face the other two.

The footsteps crunched closer on the path. The sound changed, clicking on the stone steps up into the portico. Something moved in the shadows, scuttling over Reece's foot. Another rat in the gloom. From where he waited Reece could hear the corporal's breathing, hoarse in the cold air. Another stride inside the sepulchre and he would be within striking distance. Reece's hand was so tight on the stone it ached. Another step in. It was time.

'What are you doing?' It was her voice. Irritated and demanding. Reece held himself.

The German snapped back to her. 'I apologize. Just rodents.'

'Leave them to the rat-catcher. We're leaving. Now.'

'Of course. The car is waiting.'

Reece listened. The jackboots tapped once more on the stone step and then out on to the softer path.

Those few words of hers told him everything. Now he knew her for what she was something hardened inside him.

'All right,' he heard her say. He chanced a look from the shadows. The soldier had his back to Reece. And finally, she came into his line of sight, her dark hair falling across her cheek. She pulled it behind her ear. He remembered that action too from before. 'I'm coming now.' They moved along the path.

It passed through his mind that he could attack. He could rush out, knock the German's legs away and strike him down with the stone. But if the German were alert, he could well minimize Reece's attack, and then it would be three against one.

Besides, he needed to question her about the photographs of the SS document – where they were, what she had seen in them – and that could hardly be done here. No, he had to wait. He slipped out from behind the altar and pressed himself to the wall, watching them filter via the path towards the exit. As they reached it, he crept out.

The small, grimy man was nervously squeezing his cap in his hands as the other two disappeared from sight. As a car started up, Reece emerged and strode to the entrance. The little man looked surprised by his presence.

'Good morning,' Reece said, affecting a calm air, as if the man had simply failed to notice him enter earlier.

'Good morning.'

Reece looked along the road. There was only one car in sight. A black Citroën Traction Avant. Only the Germans and collaborators had cars at all, and the black Traction Avant was known as the car of the German intelligence services. He had seen men and women bundled into these cars, their eyes closed up with bruises. But Charlotte wasn't a prisoner: the car was hers. He saw it at the end of the road.

'You're open earlier than I thought.'

'We had to. For someone important.'

'Who was that?' Reece asked.

'I shouldn't say,' the man replied, a little warily now.

'No, you're very professional, aren't you?' Reece said, smiling. 'I hope you're paid properly.' He wished there was time for a more subtle approach, but he had only seconds. He drew his wallet from his pocket. 'Can I buy you a drink as a token of appreciation for your work?' The man hesitated and glanced around. Then he peered at the twenty-franc note in Reece's hand and the tip of his tongue touched his lower lip. He was clearly struggling with the idea of revealing the woman's name – after all, telling people names was something that got you into trouble these days.

'I . . . really, sir, I shouldn't.' He seemed tempted, but the risk of German fury outweighed the money. Money wouldn't be enough.

And then Reece noticed a ring of keys swinging from the man's hip. Among them was a small metal object: a weight that perfectly equalled the daily meat allowance – a popular keepsake among hungry townsfolk who wanted to ensure they got every gram to which they were entitled.

'Do you eat well? How would you like extra coupons? A full three months' worth.' Reece pulled from his pocket the book full of coupons – freshly delivered in the last drop – that Thomas had given him that morning to replace those destroyed by the river water. 'You could have beef on Sunday. Would you like that?' And that was the man's price. He nodded greedily and snatched for the money and coupons. Reece held them away. 'What's her name?'

'Dubois. Clémence Dubois,' the caretaker said reluctantly.

And then Reece had her first name to add to the family name he had seen on her father's grave. He knew her from beginning to end.

Clémence Dubois. It was hard to attach it to the woman he had known as Charlotte. It seemed far less real, less natural, to him than the name he had repeated by night and day.

Reece handed over the money and the coupons. There would be no going back now for the man. 'Her address?'

'I don't know. I was only told Miss Dubois would be coming.'

'Do you know anything more about her?'

'Nothing.' He twisted his cap in his hands as if it could offer him some protection against whatever he was getting into now. 'I was just told she was coming, that's all. She was upset about the headstone. Her – her father's headstone,' he stammered. 'It was broken up. Thieves, or . . . or . . .' He stared at Reece as something dawned on him.

'Did she say where she was going?'

The man hesitated. Reece gave him a five-franc note. 'She didn't say anything to me. But she told the driver to go to Saint-Cloud.'

'Where in Saint-Cloud?'

'She didn't say. She just said Saint-Cloud. That's all.'

That meant it was to an address they went to frequently. Reece dropped his attempt to appear calm and ran to his bike. He couldn't let Charlotte slip away into the streets of Paris.

He set off at speed in the direction her car had taken, towards the city centre. The conversation with the caretaker had lasted barely a minute and cars drove slowly these days, running on low-grade fuel. If they were heading for Saint-Cloud, a working-class commune on the western edge of the city, they would cross the Seine at the pont de Saint-Cloud.

He sped along the avenue Paul Doumer in their wake, towards the huge bois de Boulogne park, hurling around corners and between other riders, some of them shouting at him in anger. There were no more than five vehicles sputtering along the route de la Reine and he wove between them. Then there were two more cars on the steel bridge to Saint-Cloud: a battered old dark-red Peugeot and a black Citroën. Her car.

The thought that she was inside somehow gripped him in a tight clasp and he squeezed on his brakes. His heart beat hard, more than the sprint behind it. The Peugeot steered in front of him and he was grateful that it would hide him. He

199

needed time to decide on his course of action. A direct assault on her right now would be impossible. No, he had to see where she was going and only then form a plan.

The Citroën pushed on over the Seine. A police van crossed Reece's path, and he heard singing from inside: *Allons enfants de la patrie, le jour de gloire est arrivé.* Singing the Marseillaise was illegal. The only people who would do it in the open were those already on their way to the execution grounds. His knuckles turned white on the handlebars as he remembered Luc, now facing the same fate, at the hand of the woman in the car.

They passed into the poorer suburb of Saint-Cloud and the car turned into a dead-end street lined with houses built in the nineteenth century for the artisans and skilled workers romanticized by Zola. The bricks had been baked locally and laid unevenly and the timbers were bowed. And yet there was a sense of unity there, as if the street and its residents had all made peace with their fate.

Dismounting at the mouth of the road, he saw the car stop in front of one of the houses, one with an elm tree outside. A child's swing hung from the thick branches.

Charlotte emerged from the car and went in through the front door. Reece propped his bike against a hedge and fiddled with the chain for a few minutes, pretending that it was causing problems. He could have skulked behind trees or in shadows and attempted to remain unseen, but the location was too open – someone passing by would have seen him and become suspicious. No, right now, the best option would be to hide in plain sight.

The corporal also got out of the car, and idly stared around, his gaze eventually falling on Reece. Reece shrank down, hoping the man would ignore him. But his luck didn't hold.

'What's wrong with it?' the man shouted over in German-accented French.

'Twisted,' Reece replied. He cursed inwardly. It would be impossible now to follow them without being challenged.

'Need a hand?'

Reece considered. If he got chatting to this man, he might be able to draw out some information about Charlotte – where she went, whom she met. But just as he was about to accept the offer she came out once more, having changed into a cream skirt and jacket and a yellow overcoat against the frost. 'No, I'm fine, thanks,' Reece called, turning his back to them.

'Please yourself.' The man helped Charlotte into the car, settled himself into the driver's seat and drove away, leaving Reece by the side, watching their departure. He couldn't follow them, but now he knew where she lived.

He remounted his bike and rode into the commercial part of Saint-Cloud to buy the necessary tools. In a side street he found a hardware shop and picked out a kitchen knife with a wooden handle. There were more lethal-looking blades there, but the one he came away with would do well enough and would raise less suspicion if he were stopped. A radio in the corner was whining out a man's voice. 'Henriot is on,' the shop-owner informed him, pointing at the machine. It took Reece a few seconds to grasp that he was expecting Reece to show an interest in the furious words of Vichy's main propagandist.

Reece stopped to listen for a minute, as the man seemed to want him to: some sort of test, perhaps. It was the normal torrent of hatred. Last night's RAF raid on Lyon had left hundreds dead, it seemed. It was doubtful if that was true.

No, France wasn't short of collaborators, radiating through the airwaves or hurrying on the pavements of the towns and cities. They all had their reasons: a belief that Catholic France had been brought to its knees by atheists, Jews and Communists; greed; a desire for power over others in a life spent in servitude; sheer hunger. But it did make Reece consider that Charlotte must have a reason. Whatever it was, it had brought her to the Germans, or the Germans to her, and he tried to work out if that motive might be something he could follow and use.

When Henriot had finished, Reece continued browsing in the shop, picking out a few more items; a multi-tool knife that he selected after opening out ten of them, a length of strong twine and a few small screwdrivers. He placed them all in a small cloth satchel that cost six francs.

When he came to pay for the knife, the shop-owner charged him double because he didn't have one to bring in to exchange. 'The metal shortages, right?' the man said, a faint suspicion in his voice.

'It broke and my wife threw it away,' Reece replied. The man shrugged and reiterated the increased price.

On the way out, walking along the street to where his bike was chained, Reece tried to picture her with the face of the young German he had killed with his stiletto knife during the ambush of the prisoner transport to Amiens. It would be easier, he thought, if he saw her as a German soldier. Reece had felt nothing but adrenalin when he slipped the blade into the man's lung and windpipe. Nazis were inhuman beasts. There was no point crying for them, no more than you would cry for a pig on its way to slaughter.

He saw her death as the final frames in a movie reel: a depiction of life, but unreal. The previous scene had shown them together in her bed, their bodies hot in each other. It dragged him away from his purpose, sapping his will to end it all with her hollow death in a narrow street. And yet the arithmetical calculation of her death against thousands of Allied troops was irreproachable.

He slowed his step, considering. Was there another way? He could contact Fisherman, give Sebastien her name and let them hunt her down and dispose of her. But there wasn't time for such an op. And it would raise many questions about how much he knew and when.

He found himself back at the entrance to her road. He steeled himself and rode in, continuing to the end, passing gardens that had been turned into tiny, impotent farms. Many of the houses looked closed up, although any tell-tale wooden boards across their windows would have long since gone into stoves for warmth. One house had a number of women coming and going, all carrying cooking pots: a communal kitchen set up to save on precious gas.

He returned to her house. There was no light on and no other sign of life when he rapped loudly on the door, ready to rush anyone who answered. He circled around to the rear of the row. There was a tumbling fence behind the house and he easily scrambled over, hoping that no one had noticed him enter, then he approached a back door that looked as if it hadn't been opened that century. On one side, a small wooden outhouse blocked it from the neighbours' vision. The other side was open, though, so he would have to work quickly and hope no one was watching.

He crouched and examined the lock. It was an old-fashioned design. He took the multi-tool clasp knife and a flat-headed screwdriver from the satchel then inserted the screwdriver into the lock, turned it as if it were a key until he felt it connect with the metal inside, putting pressure on the mechanism. Holding it in place with his left hand, he took the clasp knife and selected a tool designed for removing stones from horses' hooves. It was long and thin, with a hook on the end, and would do as a pick.

Like a dentist probing a gum, Reece delicately felt around with the hook for the furthest pin in the lock. He found it and pushed it up until he heard it click. He withdrew the tool very slightly until he found the next pin and kept going until all were aligned in their slots.

He turned the handle and pulled. Nothing happened. It was still locked. He cursed and reinserted the pick, feeling about for a pin he had missed. There it was, right at the back. He pressed it into place and tried the handle again.

This time, it turned, and he pushed the door open, stepping through into a chilly room with a hint of damp in the air – clearly once a workshop. Her father had been an engraver, she had said. Deep-welted wooden benches sprouted iron clamps and there were examples of the man's intricate work covering the walls – bronze medallions, steel discs, copper plates. He had had talent, Reece could tell. One thing was absent, however: there were no tools to be seen, for this was a workshop without a workman. It had been preserved only as a spotless and dustless memorial. He couldn't help but wonder if anyone would do the same for him. His recent life, the actions he had been forced to accomplish, would hardly be looked upon with such unadulterated admiration.

The workshop led to the kitchen, equally spotless, with copper pans hung by size on the walls, gleaming even in the jaundiced light. A *tat-tat-tat* came from somewhere, a tap dripping into a deep square enamel sink.

He went on, into a living room with old-fashioned furniture. It could have been the home of a proud artisan family before the first war, with children running around and a mother instructing them on their catechism. The front door to the house opened directly into this room. He examined it: a single heavy lock that he would most likely hear turning. There was also a circular staircase that led to an upper floor. Reece guessed there would be two rooms above, no more, and perhaps not even that many.

Climbing up, he indeed found two doorways. Picking one, he stepped through to find a room both empty and full. The master bedroom, it had neat furniture: a small but well-made bed and a dressing table with a triptych of mirrors. But there was nothing of the detritus of everyday life. There was no discarded comb, no book left open, no jacket sleeve trapped in the door of the wardrobe. There was, as in the workshop below, an overriding atmosphere of preservation – as if it were being maintained as a memory, not a living place.

And beyond that, Reece could tell that there was something else missing. Something that would ordinarily be there but wasn't – yet he couldn't identify what it was. His eyes raked the bedroom: the well-formed casements, the smooth floorboards, the bed jutting against a painted plaster wall. Somewhere, there was a blank space.

He had no time for the absence, however: he had a painful task ahead. He stalked out, into the other bedroom. And then, without warning, her eyes were boring into him, making him stop and stare back.

On a mantelpiece above an iron fireplace the photographic image of an eighteen-year-old girl looked out at the world with curiosity, and perhaps a sense that she barely belonged in it. The sepia print shaded her skin a caramel brown, but the hair was dark and the eyes as hooded as they always would be. She was shading them from the sun, leaving most of her face in deep shadow. It was a summer holiday, perhaps, freezing in time a moment without guard.

So this was her room, her life, her image looking back at him. It made it harder to fulfil the duty he had been set. Now he, too, had stolen in to subvert and betray.

He lifted the picture so that his face and hers almost touched. Who had taken the photograph? Her father? Her mother, maybe, or a boyfriend. Perhaps just a friend. Even then there had been something in her expression, deep-set into the lines and curves of her face, that said there was a gulf between her and everyone and everything around her. He put the photograph back.

Outside, a slate-grey cloud slid across the sky. He recognized some of the clothes in an open wardrobe – those she had worn in England and some she had worn in Paris. So she lived in this house, her family home. Why? The Germans could have given her a huge apartment seized from an unfortunate local. Sentiment, it must be, though that seemed out of place in a woman who gave her services to the Nazis.

He went through her washbag, the books on the shelves, the few souvenirs on her desk. After that, a more thorough hunt: turning out the contents of the desk in her bedroom and the chest of drawers in the larger bedroom; feeling behind the wardrobes for envelopes taped to them; shaking out books and examining the furniture. Then down to the ground floor and through the kitchen and workshop. Nothing.

There were no negatives, no prints, and nothing that told him anything more about her. He went back upstairs and sat on her bed, his fingers searching for the here-and-now question: The photographs could come or go, but when she stood before him would he be able to go through with it?

He would do, he told himself, what he had to do. No more, no less.

She was no more than an informer, and the standing sentence had to be applied. He needed her alive for just long enough to tell him if she still had the photos; if she didn't, he had to extract from her anything she had seen in the prints. After that, she was as much Boche as the Germans in uniform. He loathed the last two years of his life as much as he loathed what she had done.

Pats of rain began tripping down the glass of the window, looking for gaps between the frame and the brickwork, thin passages into the building.

He gazed at the ceiling, listening to the rain become heavier, feeling it on the air, little daylight now coming through. The ceiling had spores of black mould at the edges. On the walls were a couple of framed prints. Monets. A Degas showed ballerinas at a bar. There were books of piano music on a shelf, a dark wooden metronome beside them. And yet, again, as he looked around the walls he was sure there was something missing, something that he had grown used to seeing in rooms like this. He sat there for a while, thoughts tumbling through his mind.

The sound of a key turning in the lock downstairs was a knell for him, dull metal falling upon dull metal.

Siegfried Klaussmann sat at an ornate Louis XIV desk at 11, rue de Saussaies. Despite the urgency of what he had just been told, he couldn't stop himself mentally replaying the moment when he had failed to pull his gun in time and the British spy's blade had pierced the throat of Kriminalassistent Karl Schmidt.

He pushed his chair back and stood to smooth down his uniform. He thought through the *Eidsformel der Schutzstaffel*, the SS oath of loyalty he had once taken: *I swear to you, Adolf Hitler, as Führer and Chancellor of the German nation, loyalty and bravery. I vow to you, and to my superiors designated by you, obedience until death.*

He couldn't help feeling that when Marc LeFevre had cut a ragged hole in Schmidt's neck it had been an attack, however small, on the German nation that Klaussmann had sworn he was loyal to. He could now think of little but finding the spy and watching while he was beaten to the ground, his broken wrists bound behind his back.

And now, standing in front of Klaussmann, was a man who might be able to aid him. He was an oily little man, a caretaker who maintained Passy cemetery. On the desk was a picture drawn by a police sketch artist to Klaussmann's own description of Marc LeFevre. The caretaker had confirmed that this was the man who had been asking suspicious questions and had then covertly followed a French woman and her Wehrmacht driver. Klaussmann could only speculate as to who this woman, Clémence Dubois, could be. Could she be the mistress of a senior German official? Possibly. It was also conceivable that she was attached to one of the SS units made up of French volunteers, or one of the other security forces. But he would consider her later. For now, capturing LeFevre was his only concern.

'When?' Klaussmann demanded.

'About an hour ago, sir. I came straight here. As fast as I could. I knew I should tell you because the lady he was following and asking about was telling one of your soldiers what to do, so she must be with you gentlemen . . . but I had to stop at the checkpoints and –'

'Give me the address.'

The man handed over a grubby slip of paper with a street address in Saint-Cloud written in a surprisingly neat hand. 'I had to take it from the register book, sir.'

'What register?' Klaussmann asked, going to a large map on the wall and searching for the short lane documented on the paper. 'The register of burials?'

'That's right, sir. It's how my manager got her address, and then he sent a messenger there first thing this morning.'

Klaussmann tapped a thin line on the map, lettered with the name of the street. The place where he would cage the animal Marc LeFevre. 'You did the right thing. Just the right thing.'

'Will there be —'

'You will be paid for the information. So long as it is accurate.' The man smiled broadly. Klaussmann addressed his adjutant. 'I want to know who this woman Clémence Dubois is. Find out if she's in our files. She must be linked to him somehow — and she had a Wehrmacht driver. But we can't wait — get a squad together to bring him in.' He handed over the address the caretaker had supplied. 'He'll resist, so make sure the men are ready.'

CHAPTER 15

How to defend yourself against surveillance
Do not go straight to your destination. Make use of a vehicle, either public or private. If you use the former, board it on the run. If you use the latter, do not take one which offers to pick you up, and start by telling the driver the wrong destination. You should never take a vehicle right up to your destination but complete the journey on foot. Make some innocent visits on the way. Visit at least one crowded place. If you suspect you are being watched, check up to make sure that you are really being watched. You may easily imagine that you are being watched, especially if your nerves are strained.

At the sound of a key turning in the lock Reece could feel the moment of necessary action creeping in. When the door eased from its tight wooden frame his fingers twitched to the twine and his eyelids lifted once more to the wall above him. And it was then that he realized what was missing in this and the other bedroom.

In every French house he had entered as an adult, there had been a crucifix above the bed. When he was a boy the houses he had visited with his father had been occupied by atheists who sneered at the religious peasants, but now, even in intellectual homes, let alone this one, owned by a simple artisan engraver, they had become more fashionable – no longer to protect against the influence of the Tempter but to show deference to the ultra-Catholic sensibilities of the militia and the Vichyites.

The absence had to mean something, but he put it to the back of his mind.

The moment came nearer, sealed in as the door below slammed shut. He heard a car leaving and sat up, waiting to hear if her footsteps would climb the spiralling stairs. If it were her, it would have to be the knife, face to face, with the blood and chaos that would come with it. For all that it made no difference in the end, he didn't want it to happen that way. There should be some dignity for them both. He wanted to preserve something of the old world, where such madness was still madness, rather than the everyday. At least with twine around her throat, he wouldn't soak his hands in blood.

But the steps shuffled into the kitchen, and Reece heard her opening cupboards, arranging plates. He went to the doorway, listening for further movement.

She returned to the living room and began humming something to herself. He crept through to her parents' room and lay on the floor, his ear to the boards, trying to hear the tune and the words. Really, he was hoping for a clue, anything that would let him into her thoughts, anything that would show him the path she had walked for them both to end up here.

He had to decide exactly how. There was a chance she was armed, or she might have a gun stashed somewhere, so charging down the stairs at her was a big risk. Even if she had no weapon, she had been through the same hand-to-hand training as him. Sheer strength was important in such fights, but it wasn't everything. And he had no idea what the Germans had taught her.

It would be best to take her by surprise, unseen. But if he waited up here until she happened to come upstairs, she might never come – who was to say she hadn't just returned to complete some task before going straight back out again? Any theatricals designed to bring her up the stairs – deliberately making a noise, perhaps – would be more likely to send her out calling for the Feldgendarmerie.

He moved noiselessly to the top of the stairs, but a knock on the front door made him freeze. The sound was a quick, urgent *rat-a-tat* and he could just make out Charlotte striding quickly to the door.

'You're early,' she said. Reece retreated silently to the bedroom. He heard the front door close and someone enter.

'We had to be.' It was another woman's voice. It was older and creaking, almost drowned out by the rain outside.

This changed everything. The presence of someone else – even an old woman, as she seemed to be – cracked his intention apart. Better to abort an op and plan a new one than try to adapt to unpredictable circumstances.

'Come in,' Charlotte told her.

'Are the others coming?'

'Yes.'

More coming. Reece cursed his luck.

'Have any more . . . gone?' the old woman asked.

'Not that I've heard.'

'Well, that's something.'

Could he distract them somehow and make a run for it? Perhaps.

There was another knock at the door. Charlotte answered without a word and more people came into the house. 'François now,' a man's voice said.

'Are you sure?'

'Yes.'

'Oh.'

Reece had little chance against them all. He could only hide. His best option would be to remain in the master bedroom. Charlotte was less likely to go in there. If she – or any of the others – did, he would slash with the kitchen knife and charge for the door, hoping to get away before they realized what was happening.

He pulled the door closed. There was a lock on it and he considered turning the key, but that would only seal him in and alert anyone there to the fact that someone was inside.

Then, from the room underneath, he heard a strange sound. It was Charlotte, quietly singing in a language he didn't know. The song had a supplicatory, devotional quality.

How long could he wait? What if they were going to spend the night here? He had to think of a way. He rubbed his brow. What if . . .

'Hello?'

The voice made him catch his breath. The single word had come from the other side of the bedroom door. It was female. Curious.

He stepped back and crouched, pointing the tip of the blade at the doorway, ready to spring and run.

'Hello?' it repeated, uncertainly now, with a note of concern, or worry. An idea came upon Reece: he could use her as a hostage, grab her and hold the knife to her throat until he could get out of the house. Below him, the singing stopped abruptly. He tensed. He heard steps clicking up the spiral staircase. It was going to happen now. He had no choice. He wrenched the door open and grabbed the figure in front of him. And then he stopped, amazed.

It hadn't been a woman's voice he had heard; it had been that of a boy aged around ten years old with golden hair matted with rain and a shallow circular cap on the crown of his head. Two interlocking triangles forming a six-pointed star were picked out on the cloth in silver thread. The shock, the impossible situation, stayed Reece's hand and the boy shook free and began to scream. Someone with an adult's heavier step was on the stairs and Reece jumped back into the room and threw the door closed.

No crucifixes above the beds. That prayer-like singing. They had been telling him who Charlotte was. But how could that fit with what he knew she had done, with who he knew she worked for? It made no sense to him.

'There's a man!' the boy screamed.

Even before he heard it he saw a small hole punch through the wood of the door. He dropped to his side, tumbling down, a bullet just missing him. In the living room chairs were being turned over and people were rushing around.

Two more rounds slammed into the wall beside him. He raised his knife as the door itself burst open. His eyes met Charlotte's. Dark and hooded as they had always been.

Her mouth opened. She had a clear shot. He could see right into the barrel of the gun, a small white semi-automatic, and waited for the impact. Her finger seemed to twitch. The gun remained frozen, pointed at him. But no bullet burst from its pipe.

Below, he heard the last person leave the house, out through the back door. Then there was silence.

'Maxime.' Her chest rose and fell with the breath of the word. He waited. It was up to her now. He wasn't going to beg for his life, and there would be no point anyway; she was going to do what she was going to do. He saw her lips form words, but the sounds made no sense to him. And then they seemed to weave into words. 'On your front.' He didn't move. 'I said, on your front.' Slowly, he lay back, his feet towards her, and turned on to his stomach. He couldn't see her, he could only see the window and the dimly lit day. The sky seemed to be nothing but pouring rain.

'You don't need to do this, Charlotte,' he said calmly.

There was a pause. 'Put the knife down.' He felt its warm metal in his fingers, but it was useless now. He placed it by his side. The dull steel, grimy with the dirt and oil of his fingers, contrasted with the swept-clean floorboard.

'You don't have to.' He felt the floor against the palms of his hands. At least it would be clean. There wouldn't be the pain, the weeks and months of pain, of captivity at the hands of the Gestapo. He waited for it, more calmly than he had ever thought he would. Maybe because there seemed nothing left for him to do. Still, he waited.

Still, no shot came. Only the sound of his heart beating against the floor.

He turned his head to see the muzzle of her gun still trained on him. It was as if they were staring at each other through a tunnel. 'Who else is here?' she demanded.

There was no point in lying. 'No one,' he said. He tried to understand what she wanted. Was she going to try to wring information from him, as he had planned to do to her? He would make her sweat for anything he gave up.

He watched as her eyes flicked to the stairwell and back to him. 'You're a fool for coming here.' She backed out of the room, taking the key from the lock.

A glimmer of strange, unexpected hope rose in his breast. Could she really be leaving him? It could be some sort of trick. She took another step towards the stairs.

Then something made them both stop. It was a sound from the street: the noise of cars arriving at speed through water-filled ruts and their doors being flung open. Charlotte rushed to the window and stared out. 'Klaussmann,' she said under her breath.

Klaussmann. He had tracked Reece like an animal.

Reece could hurl himself at Charlotte and take a bullet but hope he could still wrestle the pistol from her grip. He would never be able to fight his way out – the Gestapo would have the house surrounded within seconds – but he could try to take one or two of them with him and then end his own life with the gun. A thousand men were dying each day in Italy, Africa and the Far East, and few of them had volunteered, as he had. He crouched, readying himself.

'Out there!' she shouted. He didn't understand. Then he followed the line of her pistol. She was pointing to the landing, where a window in the rear wall of the house let grey light filter down the stairs. 'The window. Move!' She levelled the semi-automatic at him once more. 'Or I'll shoot you myself.'

He rushed for the window, seemingly reaching it in a single heartbeat. The sound of splintering wood told him the solid front door was being kicked in. He grabbed the bottom of the window and heaved it up, allowing a blast of cold air and needle-like rain to prick the skin of his cheeks.

What was in her mind, the weave of her strategy as she wrenched him away from Klaussmann's grip, was a mystery. And that made her almost as dangerous as if she were handing him over.

Without looking back, he pulled himself through the opening, instantly feeling the rain soaking him through and adding to his weight. A few metres below, he saw, three men had guns trained on the kitchen door. Black hats protected them from the cascading weather but, for now, also hid him from their gaze.

'Up!' she hissed, pushing him. 'The roof!' He stared up and felt a gush of cold, harsh water pouring into his eyes. Another sound told him that the front door had caved in. He grabbed the iron drainpipe on the side of the house and swung around it, scrabbling for footholds, his feet kicking at the bricks.

'Search it!' he heard a voice shout in German from inside the building. He pulled himself upwards towards the edge of a flat roof, one hand bracing him to the drainpipe and the other stretching up as far as it would reach. He heard scrabbling behind him. It had to be her, but he couldn't take the time to check as his feet found a shallow ridge of bricks and he grasped for the lip of the roof.

The clouds above were so black and thick it was like night. He glanced down. A white flash right across the sky lit her face as pale as the dead.

He tried once more to gain the roof. The sky churned with sound as his fingers rose higher and higher through the torrent, water running down his sleeve on to his chest, but he couldn't quite reach.

'Up there!' a man shouted. A clean-shaven face stared up from the ground. The muzzle of a gun followed.

Reece had no choice. He kicked with his feet and launched himself upwards as best he could. It was a choice between the hopeless action and certain capture by the men below. He lifted into the air, springing from the shallow ridge. And his hands caught on crumbling, soaking brick.

He swung up, trying to find some foothold on the sheer surface. '*Halt!*' he heard. A volley of shots erupted through the rain.

For the last time, he kicked up, and this time his foot found a notch in the brickwork, just enough to propel himself over the lip of the roof. As another sheet of lightning lit the scene, pain shot through his muscles.

'Maxime!' he heard Charlotte shout. Another bullet tore past him, shattering one of the cheap bricks into fragments.

He dropped down on to his front and looked over to where she was, on the ridge of bricks beside the window, holding on to the iron pipe.

217

He had no idea who she was. He could leave her now and run – somehow, somewhere. And he would more likely survive without her. He could leave her to face whatever punishment her German handlers would place before her – it would be a sort of bestial justice, he told himself. Another bolt of lightning lit the world like a flashbulb, flattening it, robbing everything of depth and nuance.

He thrust his hand down. She grabbed it and he pulled as she scrabbled upwards. Another bullet sped past, but a crash of clouds overhead drowned the sound. She hung from him until her feet found the bricks and she dragged herself, like he had, over the edge of the roof.

They lay there for a second before jumping up to face each other. He needed to know if he had saved her only for her to turn him in, or if they were going to run together. Her white-handled gun levelled at him once more.

'I will shoot you if I have to!' she shouted through the rain. He knew that was true. Whatever her game or strategy, she was playing it to the end. He would have to bide his time before he could join it or turn it on her. He opened his hands to show he had no weapon. 'Break the drainpipe. Quick.'

He went to the pipe and kicked it again and again, but it was solid iron and the bracket held. He looked over the edge. A man was climbing out of the window, reaching for the drainpipe. Reece threw down a loose chunk of cement. 'We have to go!'

'You first.' She kept the pistol pointed at him. The garden below now held two Gestapo men, and in front of the house he made out three black cars and an officer in SS uniform loudly barking orders at an underling. Reece didn't need to see his face to know that it was Klaussmann. There was no way down. The only way was across the rooftops. 'Do it,' she said.

He charged towards the next house. It was one of a line of five or six, with two-metre gaps between their roofs. As he ran he listened for her footsteps to say she was coming after him, but the cascading water made it impossible to hear. As he reached the edge of the building he lifted his feet and burst over the gap. He was in the air, willing himself forward.

And then a thud as his feet found the solid surface. He skidded, unused to the action, falling to his knees. The sound of another impact behind him made him whirl around to see she was with him still, crumpling to her knees but immediately righting herself and training the pistol on him. Whatever the game, she was risking herself and she had bound him into it. For a moment he thought of dropping from the building to the ground or leaping for the branches of a tree – something so risky she would never dare follow. But until he knew she meant to kill him he was safer running with her than from her.

'Keep going!' she yelled.

He was about to sprint away towards the next roof, but a dark movement some distance behind her made him stop. A figure was rising up and over the edge of the roof of her house. 'They're coming!' he shouted. She glanced over her shoulder.

He ran and jumped again, this time landing without stumbling. She did the same. He chanced a look back and saw the Gestapo officer standing on the edge of the first roof, seemingly deterred by the jump. Instead the German pulled a gun from his pocket but if there was a shot it was swallowed by the thunder.

They ran and jumped again. And again and again, until they reached the end of the street, where it met the main road.

At the final house some sort of solid workshop or garage abutted the building and they dropped on to it, landing softly and rolling on to their sides as they had been trained for parachute drops. They clambered down to the sodden earth and pressed into the wall, gasping for air, sucking in rain, feeling it trickle down their throats. Reece chanced a look around the side of the building, back into the street they had just left. It was worse than he had expected. Ten or twelve men, guns in their hands, were coming towards them. Then he spotted something. A possible route away that the Germans wouldn't see they had taken.

'There!' he said, pointing to a manhole cover at the edge of the road that didn't quite fit the hole in which it had been placed. She spun around and covered him with her gun. His fingers, frozen with the cold, barely worked as he prised then wrenched the metal upwards. It lifted aside to reveal a ladder built into the brick walls of the sewer. He dropped into it, landing waist deep in water and filth. The pipe was just high enough to stand up in.

The sudden expulsion of the glimmer of light above him told him she had followed him. She dragged the steel cover back into place and they were in utter darkness. He heard her scrabbling down the ladder to the bottom. He didn't know if the gun was still in her hand. Then the only sound was the lapping of the filthy water around them and their own breath.

'Where do we go?' she asked.

He reached into his jacket pocket and found a box of matches. He managed to pull one out and tried to light it. It flicked across what he thought was the striking surface, but there was no spark. It must be too damp. He tried again, but he could tell the thin match had snapped in the middle. He cast it aside and tried with another. Then another.

'We can't wait. Come this way.' He put his hands out and felt for the wall, his legs swishing through the waste. As he lifted one, the current nearly toppled him and he fell against the side. 'Be careful,' he said. His voice echoed until it drifted off into the tunnel and he glanced upwards: the manhole cover wasn't moving so they seemed to be safe. He felt his way along the wall, with no idea where they were heading. They walked on for a few slow paces. 'Who are you working for?' he asked, hardly expecting an answer. There was silence but for the sound of their own movement through the water. 'Do you have the photos? Where –'

'You're in no position to ask. I still have the gun.'

'Go to hell,' he muttered. He calculated that if she were going to kill him she would have done it by now.

'You think I'm a traitor.' And then her voice again. 'It wasn't me who betrayed the circuit.'

'What?' he exclaimed, incredulous. He stared back to the void where her words had come from.

'It wasn't me.'

'Then who?'

'Germany has a spy in London.'

'I know.'

'Do you?' She paused. 'Do you know that he is watching you? You, Maxime. He wants you caught. He told the Gestapo about the op so that you would be taken.'

'You're lying!'

'Why would I lie now? Like this. The pistol is in my hand, not yours.'

Reece had informed London of the raid on the prison transport. Parade could well have found out from a source in London, not in Beggar, and then passed the information to the Germans. Maybe there was no traitor in the circuit after all. But he was far from convinced by her words.

'What does he know about me?'

'I don't know. I only know that he has been watching you.'

Did he know about the recces to the beaches of Normandy and Calais? That was the secret Reece could reveal to no one. 'Tell me who he is. Tell me what he's planning.'

He heard her breathing hard. 'He's SD. Whatever he knows about you, it wasn't from me.'

He wracked his mind. Why would she lead him away from the Gestapo rather than put three rounds in his chest and hand him over if this weren't true? And if Parade were SD, her readiness to expose him pointed to her being of one of the rival intelligence services. The escape from the Gestapo ruled them out. 'So you're Abwehr.' She made no reaction. He experienced a flicker of satisfaction. Knowing who she worked for was a first step towards knowing her. 'What do you know about his op?'

'I know they need two things to execute it: your army Order of Battle, and where you're going to invade. Parade can give them the Order of Battle, but not the location.'

That meant there was still hope to destroy Parade's op.

'Who is he? What's his cover identity?' Reece heard his voice echoing. 'Charlotte. Tell me how to find him. Do what's right.'

'I don't know.'

'You know something!' His words bounced all around them. He heard his own frustration, the anger barely contained within it. 'You must know something.'

There was a long silence, then the answer came through the dark like a whisper from an unseen spirit. 'I know he's killed someone.'

'Who?'

He could no longer hear her body plunging through the water. 'A British official, a man who found him transmitting.'

'A policeman? MI5?' It was something, a scent to follow. A way to recover Reece's mission, and the last two years of his life, from catastrophe.

Her voice was quiet, as if it were coming from a long way away. 'I don't know. It was his last sked, but I can't say when that was.'

'Who told you about him?'

'The people I work for. Don't ask me about them. I won't tell you.' He believed her. 'Be careful, Maxime. Parade has a source tracking you. You can't trust anyone.'

'Where are the photographs?' She didn't answer. 'They could lead us to him. Do you still have them?' Still no answer. 'If you have them, tell me.' He went back towards her and put his hands out, feeling through the dark, but he couldn't find her. And then he realized it was because she wasn't there. 'Charlotte!' he cried.

In the distance there was a flicker of light. A spark. The spark became a flame in her hand from a gold-glinting lighter. She was at a crossroads in the pipes. He saw her eyes lit by the flame.

'You're not the first I've lied to, Maxime. I don't have a choice now.'

He didn't doubt that she had lied to him and to others many times. 'You do. We can get you out.'

'Your faith. You always had faith, Maxime. I have none. No. It goes round and round like the hand of a clock. Until someone smashes it to pieces.' He began to walk towards her. She snapped down the lid of the lighter in her hand and the blackness enveloped them once more like a shroud. 'Stay away.' And the sound of her movement became distant.

He waded on to where he had last seen her and rounded the corner, but it was all darkness. He berated himself for

223

rushing in without watching her for long enough to know her strategy. His idiocy had let those vital photographs disappear with her.

How could he salvage something from the situation? He thought quickly. First, he had to let SOE know about her. And from then on, there was only one option left, hard as it might be. The pictures of the Parade One document were gone, but Luc had seen them. He might have seen something in them that could lead them to Parade and the op he had set up. Somehow, he had to get a message into and out of Amiens prison. He waded away in the impenetrable dark, searching for a way out.

Wilhelm Canaris looked out of a second-floor window on to a wide street of old houses. Charming little Bayreuth, where the proto-National Socialist Wagner had staged his epic performances. Canaris had never been one for the bombastic tradition and had, if truth be told, preferred the work of Slavic composers. That was not something he would be mentioning in front of the Führer. He lowered his gaze and returned his attention to the room. It was ornate beyond compare: gilt-edged mirrors lined the long far wall, an emerald-green harpsichord reputedly played by Bach stood in the corner, but what dominated the room was the long table covered in silver dishes of food. Those brief patches not sporting poultry or game were decked with crystal vases of flowers. Canaris wrinkled his nose at the lack of subtlety. They might as well have had a couple of whores set up in the corner.

There was an unpleasant noise too. It was the noise of dirty, starving men with poor table manners stuffing any and all the food they could down their necks. Canaris masked his disapproval as he watched them: two men, each with one hand free and one cuffed to the chairs upon which they perched as they reached for the meat and wine. They wore unclean uniforms of American airmen, a lieutenant and a buck sergeant. Behind them were two Waffen-SS guards, and sitting opposite was Otto Skorzeny, the hero-paratrooper chosen to see Operation Parade One through to its ground-shaking and bitter conclusion. He had red wine in his glass and a thick cut of pork on his plate, but both remained untouched. The American sergeant kept staring at the long, deep scar that ran from the left side of Skorzeny's mouth almost to his ear, a badge of honour from his Vienna university duelling club.

'It is how long since you had good food?' Skorzeny asked in heavily accented English. The two men just looked bemused at the question. 'Years?'

'Years,' confirmed the American officer. The NCO to his side just glanced at him and went back to tearing meat from a chicken leg with his teeth.

'I am sorry that is the fact.'

'Not as sorry as I am,' muttered the lieutenant.

'What is the food like where you are? I have never been in one of those camps.'

The American looked sceptical. 'Like shit,' he replied. 'Like eating shit.' Skorzeny smiled genially. Canaris went back to the window. Of course, Parade One was a form of warfare, but he wasn't delighted at the prospect of mixing it with conventional soldiers. 'You want to swap places?' said the American officer.

Skorzeny almost laughed. Canaris was well aware that he enjoyed the limelight and public adulation that his daring rescue of Mussolini from house arrest had brought him. He also clearly enjoyed lording it over captured foreign troops. 'I do not think that.'

The lieutenant spluttered on some food and washed it down with thick red wine. The sergeant said nothing but seemed to be following the conversation keenly.

'Lieutenant, I am more old than you. I have been in this war from the beginning. I know what it is to be hungry and to want a bath and clothes.' The lieutenant looked down at his soiled jacket. 'I can give you this. Your men this. From one officer to another officer.'

The American drained his glass and set it down on the table. 'Sir, we are both officers. You're right about that. But before I was a pilot I was on Wall Street, and I knew when someone was about to offer me a deal.'

Skorzeny nodded curtly. 'Yes. I will get to the point. I will make you and your men comfortable. It will not be like this every day, but you will have good food and more space. In return, you must be a teacher.'

'Teaching what?' The pilot picked a slice of white cheese from a tray and bit into it.

'English. Common English. Our translators have to hear your radio news programmes for reports of the war and they find it difficult to understand common American language. People who sound like you. Not people who sound like teachers.' The sergeant tore into a fistful of beef without a word.

'Sound like I do?' The lieutenant smiled, placed the cheese on the plate and stood up. The guard behind him made to take hold of him, but Skorzeny waved him away. 'You think I'm a fucking idiot? That I don't know what you want to understand "common American language" for? What you're listening in to?' The American leaned over the table, scooped a handful of fruit salad from a bowl and smeared it into his mouth. 'Obersturmbannführer,' he said as he chewed, the mashed fruit cascading down his front, 'go fuck yourself.'

The guard leaped forward and smashed the butt of his pistol down on to the back of the lieutenant's head and dragged him back, dropping him to the floor. The guard kicked him but was rewarded only with a sharp peal of laughter from the man.

'Stop that,' Skorzeny ordered the guard. The SS man stepped away.

'There is nothing I can do for you,' Skorzeny said irritably. 'I made a good offer. It would be good for you and your men. Perhaps it would keep you all alive, and this is the answer you say to me. There is nothing I can do for you.' He turned to the guard and spoke in German. 'Just take . . .'

The American sergeant spoke through a leg of chicken. 'I'll do it,' he said without looking up. 'I don't care, I'll do it.' He continued gnawing at the bone.

'Sergeant!' the lieutenant shouted, pushing himself to his knees.

'Take him out of here,' Skorzeny ordered the guards with a thin smile. They lifted the pilot up, undid the metal handcuff that bound him to the chair and dragged him out of the room.

'I'm ordering you –' the lieutenant began. A blow to the stomach silenced him and then he was gone.

'It don't mean nothing,' said the sergeant. 'And I don't believe you'll give this to the other men, but I don't care. You want to know how we speak? How we say goodbye? Sure, I'll tell you. Sure. Listen to our newscasts? No, sir. I know what you really want. You're listening in to our communications. Who's going where. That's pretty clear. But you see, I don't care. I'll do it. It's not my war.' He reached for the wine glass and refilled it from a decanter.

Skorzeny smiled. 'I am glad. We will take you to somewhere more comfortable. One of our own barracks. You will have your own room and will eat with our men. I cannot give you this' – he swept his arm across the table – 'but it will be the food I eat. My men eat. We can arrange for a woman if you want. We have places for that.'

The sergeant reached for the bowl of fruit and bit into something soft. 'Yes, I want that.'

The two guards returned. 'Take our friend here to Sommerfeld. He will know what to do.' They saluted and led the American soldier away.

Canaris took a seat at the table, viewing the debris from the American pilot's brief defiance.

'We expect the Allies to be at their most vulnerable four hours after they make land,' Skorzeny told him. 'Their communications will be stretched and they will be exhausted from fighting their way off the beaches but not yet relieved by a secondary infantry wave. When I consider them to be at their weakest I will signal for the commando units to engage. I will then personally command the Parade One deception units. We estimate two hours for the deception to reach peak effect, wiping out much of their armour and scattering the infantry.'

'The strength of the assault units?'

'Six thousand paratroopers; two thousand infantry; one panzer division; four fighter-bomber wings.'

'The expected casualty rate?' Canaris asked. 'Theirs, not ours.'

'From the deception wave, thirty per cent. From the assault wave, an additional forty per cent. The rest we can leave to run around the countryside and we'll mop them up later with regular units. They won't pose any danger to us.'

'And casualties among our men?'

'Ten per cent. They are itching to begin. Their names will be in the history books.'

'No doubt.'

'Is there any word on where the invasion is coming? Anything at all?' Skorzeny asked.

'Rumours. Nothing we can act upon.'

'Damn it. Sitting around waiting.'

There was silence as Canaris thought of the young, dirty buck sergeant who had been bribed with food to betray his country. How cheap the price. Canaris wondered if the man would ever come to regret it. He would have to return home one day – unless he wanted to live out his years in the Reich, of course, but that seemed unlikely.

And Canaris wondered about Skorzeny too. A man of action, yes, but was his mind as sharp as his aim? If it was, he could be of use. For one thing, he would be party to information about Parade One that even the admiral would be kept from. The question was whether Skorzeny's true loyalty was to Himmler, Hitler or the Fatherland – for the three were rarely one and the same.

Hard men, such as Skorzeny, always believed they were impervious to persuasion, and that itself made them susceptible to it. He would have to be handled with caution, though, like a piece of machinery with sharp edges.

'What about the pilot?' Canaris asked. Skorzeny held his gaze, unblinking. 'Yes, I presumed so.'

'Why waste food on him?' the paratrooper explained. Canaris went back to brooding. 'My grandparents had a farm in Westphalia.'

'Oh yes?'

'When I was nine my grandfather took me to watch him kill a pig. He stuck it in the throat with his knife. It took more than a minute to die, running around its sty, trying to find a way out. I've never forgotten it.'

'No, I don't suppose you would. Are you suggesting that Parade One will have all the Allied troops responding in a similar fashion?' Canaris asked.

'I tell you so. I've seen crack troops fall apart when they don't have strong leadership. This plan will turn them all into that pig.'

'I see.'

'It's true,' Skorzeny confirmed. 'Yes, we need good fortune too. But God has been behind us so far.'

Canaris glanced at the table. 'Even God can swap sides.'

CHAPTER 16

13 February 1944

Delaney's shoes trod softly as he approached the map room, the heart of the Cabinet War Rooms. The huge depictions of the globe that gave it its name filled every wall, portraying the movement of troops and materiel through the various theatres of war. Naval officers brooded over the speed and trajectory of their forces in Europe, Africa and the Far East. In the corner of the room, the Prime Minister sat spitting smoke from a cigar. He was in civilian dress this time: a three-piece suit with pinstripe trousers. It might have been dark blue, but the unnatural light rendered anything dark into black. Beside him was a nearly empty bottle of brandy.

'Good morning, Major,' he said gruffly.

'Good morning, sir.'

'I would offer you a cigar, but I don't have many left. They're from the president of Cuba, and Special Branch smoke one from each box just to make sure they're not laced with strychnine. Damned impudence, if you ask me. No doubt they draw lots to be the lucky guinea pig. What do you have for me?'

'We have located one of our agents whom we thought we had lost.'

'Your demeanour suggests this tiding carries a mixed blessing.'

'You might say, sir. Her service name is Charlotte. She was part of Beggar circuit.'

The Prime Minister looked up. 'Beggar, eh? Go on.'

'We lost track of her for a few days.'

'And this disappearing act was not sanctioned?'

'It was not.'

'And?'

'And now she's gone to ground again.'

'She's what? She's gone to ground? They're not cricket matches, Delaney. You can't keep losing them and no real harm done. Well, what about her?'

'She's suspect. Maxime believes she's Abwehr. He initially thought she had been inserted into Beggar to collapse the circuit, but now he's not so sure. She's given him some information.'

Churchill chewed on his cigar for a few seconds. 'Plot and counter-plot. Hmmm. Give me open battle any day,' he said. 'All right, go on.'

'She said their spy over here has killed someone, an official.'

'Does she know any more?'

'No. No details. It sounds like she had it third-hand.'

'But she wants us to know.'

'Yes, sir.'

'Well, that's interesting, isn't it?' Churchill stared at his knuckles, deep in thought. 'So if she's Abwehr . . .'

'Why is she trying to expose Parade? Yes. A very good question.'

'And the answer, Delaney?'

'I suspect she has a personal relationship with Maxime.'

'Mixed loyalties?'

'It could explain her behaviour.'

Churchill rapped on the table. 'Indeed it could. Indeed it could. And if that's so, we must wonder, mustn't we, what she has got out of him in return. What Canaris now has at his fingertips.' Churchill's voice darkened. 'What the Austrian corporal knows.'

'I think it would be limited.' Churchill glanced at him over his glowing cigar and muttered something inaudible. 'She might be useful to us,' Delaney continued, 'if she can somehow monitor what they're saying in Berlin about Parade. If we can get it out of her.'

'I see your point. Yes, that little insight would be rather useful. But I think that's down to Maxime, isn't it?'

'Yes, sir.' There was a pause. 'You want to know how much I trust her.'

'I do,' Churchill replied.

'Not a great deal.'

'No. No, you're not a very trusting lot, are you? Still, I suppose that keeps you breathing.' Churchill rose from the table and leaned against a low wooden cabinet, stretching his legs. 'What about Maxime?'

'I told him we were sending him back to recce the landing points. Sir, I . . .'

'I know, I know. Your objections have been well noted.' He went to the central map, which showed France. He was unsteady on his feet and Delaney suspected he had been up all night, powered by drink. 'I've just had a war council with the Admiralty. They're more worried about the weather than anything else. Strange, isn't it? We're playing a blindfold game of chess with our agents' lives, and uppermost in their mind is whether it's going to be a sunny day.' With his forefinger, Churchill traced a rocky and wavering line from Normandy to Calais. His finger quivered as he reached the northern port. 'Not even thirty miles from Dover,' he said under his breath. 'We could do it in two hours.'

'They know that too, sir.'

The Prime Minister peered closely at the narrow stretch of water that had secured Britain's safety but which now acted as a barrier to France's liberation. 'Yes, they do. Hitler knows it well.' He traced his finger along the coastline again. 'I've had experience with marine landings,' he mumbled. He stared at the port marked in red on the map then returned to his seat.

'Sir, Maxime believes –'

'Maxime, Maxime.' Churchill undid his tie and threw it on the table beside him. He opened his collar and rubbed his neck. 'This is a dirty business. I don't like descending into the mud of it.' Delaney had seen him drunk before, but never with this pang of self-loathing on display.

'Neither do I, sir.' He meant it. Because the operation engulfing them had been Delaney's idea, but he often felt as Churchill did now.

'No, I don't suppose you do. But when the final clarion call sounds it will be my name at the bottom of the page. History will judge us both; yes, indeed. But it will judge me far harsher, Major. Far harsher.' He lifted his glass but found it empty and dropped it back on the table, where it tipped over and rolled along the wood before falling to the floor and breaking, to leave needle-like shards in the worn carpet. Churchill muttered something to himself, a sentence growled under his breath.

'Sir?'

The Prime Minister thumped the table. 'I said that, when we come to the end of this, there's going to be a reckoning!' he snarled. 'Such a reckoning that the Devil himself takes fright.'

When he was dismissed half an hour later Delaney headed out through a corridor of cream-painted bricks. As he was about to pass the final sentry post, Huw Evans of MI5 entered carrying a pair of hefty briefcases.

'Going to see the old man?' Delaney asked.

Evans nodded. 'What sort of a mood is he in?'

'Dark.'

'That's all I need today. I've already had a damn curt enquiry from 6 asking what the hell's happening with the Special Duties flights.'

'Bloody RAF's talking of diverting some of the pilots to other squadrons. Just when we need them the most,' Delaney told him. 'What the RAF fail to understand is that if they don't let us do our job they'll be coming up against every German fighter from here to Berlin on D-Day.'

Evans nodded an agreement. 'Is there anything you need from 6 in the Bordeaux area? They have a good source there now inside the Gestapo *Hauptquartier*.'

'Bordeaux?' SOE's Bordeaux circuit, Scientist, had been one of the largest and most successful, until it had been infiltrated by a French collaborator. Most of its agents had been dragged to German concentration camps. 'Nothing specific,' Delaney said. 'But an update on their working practices and personnel is always useful. We're trying to re-establish a good network there.'

'I'll keep you in the loop on what they find out.'

'I would appreciate that.'

Reece and Sebastien shivered in the corner of a mechanic's shop in a shabby part of Amiens. It was dark but before curfew and they were doing their best to avoid the tearing gusts that seemed to come directly from the Arctic.

'Has your pianist kept monitoring that frequency?' Reece asked.

'He's been glued to the set. He said he twice heard voices again and it sounded like those same ship names repeated over and over. After a minute of that each time he lost the signal. Hasn't found it again. Any idea what it signifies?'

'Not much.' He kicked his feet to make the blood flow. 'I've –' He broke off at a sound outside, something scraping on the floor. Then a melody whistled by someone unseen. Reece recognized the tune: *Le Chant des Partisans*, the anthem of the Maquis.

Sebastien responded with the same song and a man came slowly through the doorway.

'Relax,' the man said in French-accented English. 'Relax, *mon cher*.' He grinned.

'This is Alain,' said Sebastien. Alain took out a thin home-rolled cigarette and made to strike a match. 'Better if you don't – we don't want the light,' Sebastien admonished him.

'Ah, don't worry,' Alain reiterated. 'The sausage-eaters are all in their beds now.'

Reece politely placed his hand on Alain's. 'We don't all want to end up behind bars,' he said.

'You are too nervous, Englishman.' But still he replaced the match in its box. He swapped to French. 'Well, to our business this evening. I understand you want a little information from the prison.'

'We do. Can you supply it?'

'Can I supply it?' he mused. 'Can I supply it?' He gazed at the two agents. 'Yes, I can. But will I supply it? Well, that is another question.'

Reece realized he was in a negotiation. 'How can I convince you?'

'I would say five hundred francs would convince anyone,' Alain replied. Reece grimaced at the words. He was used to dealing with resistants committed to liberating their country from the Germans or frightened civilians who just wanted to keep their heads down. Those who wanted to make money from the occupation were unwelcome acquaintances. 'My brother is a Communist, but not me,' he went on. 'No, sir, I believe capitalism is the way to freedom.'

Sebastien spoke up. 'You know that we're going to win the war soon. The invasion is coming. You'll help us liberate France.'

'And I wish you all the luck in the world. Really I do. But for now I want to be paid in cash, not in liberation.' He shrugged genially.

Reece took Sebastien to one side. It was clear that they would get nowhere with this man. 'Do you have the money?' he asked.

'I can get it.'

Alain called over to their backs. 'And gentlemen, this is not a situation where you haggle over the price. It is five hundred francs.'

'You'll have it,' Reece told him, returning.

'Well, then I can tell you that your friend is still alive, in the prison.' A wave of relief washed over Reece. Then there was still a chance to recover the information in the SS document and find the spy in London. 'But not for long. They will be taking him somewhere else soon. They have big prison camps in Poland and Germany.'

'How soon?' Reece demanded urgently.

'I wouldn't be informed until the last minute. I just organize the staff rotas.'

'You have to ask him what was in the photographs. He'll understand what that means. And you have to write down exactly what he says.'

'Ask him?' Alain said, surprised. 'I'm not asking him anything. I thought you just wanted to know his situation.'

Reece took a hold of the man's arm. 'We need you to take him a message and bring us the reply.'

'Are you mad?' He tore his arm away. 'You think I can just wander in and out of the fucking cells asking them questions? I can tell you if he's still alive or where they've transferred him. I'm not going anywhere near him.'

'Shit,' Reece spat. He broke off and walked away. 'Is there any way at all you can get to him?'

'How?' Alain was becoming irate too now. 'I work in the office, not on the wings. If I look slightly out of place, they'll do to me what they do to your people. I'm not doing it for any money.'

Reece paced up and down. 'Give me a bloody cigarette,' he muttered.

Alain offered him one and a match. Reece lit it and threw the match to the side still alight.

'Maxime,' Sebastien said. He pointed to the ground. 'Oil patches, you know. We don't want the whole place to go up.'

Reece ignored him and drew in a lungful of tarry smoke. He had failed to rescue Luc from the prison transport and then, through his ignorance of her – of her game – he had let Charlotte escape with all she knew. He had failed twice. He wasn't going to let it happen a third time. Often it was hatred of the Nazis that motivated him, seeing their brutal arrogance infect the streets of his youth; sometimes it was a desire, like Hélène, to see the world made better; but now, here and now, he felt a simple sense of duty: he would get to Luc to save him and gain the vital knowledge that he held because it had to be done and he was the one standing square in front of the task. 'I'll go in,' he said.

'How?' Sebastien sounded amazed at the idea.

Reece blew the smoke out of his nose. It burned on the way out. 'We create a diversion – a night attack while most of them are asleep. Grenades on the front gate. There'll just be a few guarding the exterior, won't there?'

'Maybe seven, eight,' Alain replied uncertainly.

'So we let them spot us outside. Some run out after the rest of you. Once they're out of sight of the guard post, I impersonate one of them, wearing their uniform, and slip back in behind them. In the confusion, they won't be looking for one man trying to get in. I speak good German.'

'There will still be guards everywhere,' Sebastien objected. 'As soon as the siren goes they'll all jump up, ready to shoot.'

Reece turned his head away, ignoring the objection. 'What's it like inside our friend's wing?' he asked.

'It's a corporal in charge at night,' said Alain. 'Skinny little runt. Looks like he still sucks his mother's tit.'

'We don't have another option. This op has to happen,' Reece told Sebastien. He turned to Alain. 'Can you get me a uniform? Steal one. An NCO would be best.'

'The laundry room isn't exactly high security,' Alain replied. 'I can get in there.'

'No doubt you will name a price now.'

'Oh, I am not a greedy man. Another five hundred francs will be enough.'

'Agreed,' Reece told him, caring little about the price. 'I would guess the boots would be harder to come by?'

'Yes, they don't send them to the laundry to be cleaned.'

'No matter. With the raid on, no one will be looking at my feet.'

'It's suicide. Too risky,' Sebastien blurted out.

'We have no choice. I'm telling you, we have to make contact with Luc. If you've got another idea, let me know right now.'

Sebastien took a cigarette and thought it over. 'No, as it is, it's too risky – too many variables – what if they don't come out of the gates when we attack but shoot at us from the walls? But listen. I've got a way to increase our chances. We put it to London months ago, when we wanted to free a group of resistants, but they refused. This might twist their arms.'

'What is it?'

'Operation Jericho.'

CHAPTER 17

14 February 1944

SOE's London offices were in a nondescript block in Baker Street, lending the service the nickname the Baker Street Irregulars, after the benign street gang that occasionally aided Sherlock Holmes. At 7.30 a.m. Major Delaney arrived to find a deciphered message on his desk from Fisherman. He read it, lifting a cup of tea to his lips.

Message from Maxime Beggar circuit. Item secured in Op Beggar 4 lost. Only chance to secure information is urgent approval of Op Jericho. I will infiltrate. How soon can op be executed?

The cup slipped from his fingers and tea spilled on the desk. His assistant stopped typing a letter and looked over. 'Something I can do?' she asked.

He stared at her. 'Bring me the Jericho file.'

'Yes, sir.'

'Then . . .' He broke off. She looked at him expectantly, waiting for him to continue. He wanted to tell her that the fate of the second front, still months away, could be decided that day. That the invasion was on a knife-edge and the German counter-plans could destroy it in the blink of an eye. He couldn't. Like Churchill and so many others, he had to pretend that the chances of success were far higher than they really were, that the men in the gliders and landing craft were far less vulnerable than he knew them to be.

'Sir?'

'Then call the War Rooms. Tell them I need to see the Prime Minister immediately.'

At the same time, on the outskirts of the city of Amiens, Alain tramped through a muddy lane to his job at the prison. He stopped to pick up a cigarette butt. There were still a few puffs left on it and his freezing fingers shook as they struck a match. The tiny glow of heat brought his veins to life and he realized that up until then his hands had been entirely numb.

It was hard lighting the fag – it was damp and smouldered rather than burned. Eventually, he managed to draw a little smoke from it, soothing his lungs and mind as he gazed up at the seven-metre walls surrounding the jail.

For a moment he seemed to wake from a dream – was he really doing this? He normally left the heroics to others. If the Germans got even a sniff of what he was up to, they would . . . well, they would do to him what they did to the poor bastards inside.

He could hear the rattling of keys on the other side of the steel door. What should he do? Turn around and run? Feign illness and go to ground?

One thousand francs. And all he had to do was steal a uniform. It was good money. Very good. But who needs good money when you're in the grave? The key was shoved into the lock. A hidden man's boots stamped on the ground in an attempt to keep warm.

Should he go through with it or find an excuse and back out? After all, the Germans weren't even that cruel – he had known harsh times all his life and this wasn't as bad as some he had been through; the politicians in Paris didn't care any more for working men like him than the Nazis did.

Perhaps if he told the Germans what he had been paid to do, they would pay him for the tip-off. Twice the cash and no risk at all. It made sense. Yes, that made sense.

The key turned slowly, thudding away the tumblers. The door opened and he stepped through it.

He was going to back out.

Reece and Sebastien watched Alain disappear into the prison. They turned back to their path, sauntering along the road, gazing at the fields around them, chewing some black bread they had bought on the way. 'We're about two kilometres due east of the city right now,' Sebastien said.

'Right.'

'You see how the prison's shaped like a cross? Those are the soldiers' barracks.' Sebastien pointed to opposing ends of the horizontal beam of the building. 'There should be about seven hundred inmates; a hundred or so are women. It goes up and down depending on how many have come in overnight and . . .'

'And what?'

'How many have been executed.'

They stopped walking and Reece glanced up at the high walls, seeing friends, comrades, falling before the machine guns. There was a stench in the air that wouldn't leave the prison, the smell of what the Germans used it for. After a while, he spoke. 'How many of them are resistants?'

'About a third. The rest are mostly in for petty stuff – theft, that sort of thing. You really think you can just walk in there?'

'If there's enough going on to distract the Germans, yes.'

'For a suicidal plan, it's probably the best method of suicide,' Sebastien muttered.

'All right. Where do we head after the op?'

'That way leads to a little town named Albert,' Sebastien said, pointing. 'No garrison there, so it's quiet.'

'Fine.' Reece gazed around, away from the prison. Despite the pain from his tired body, the sight that met him seemed to chime with something in a part of his memory that had rarely seen the light of day recently. In front of him, sharply contrasting with the wet and dirt and corruption now in every brick of Paris, were fields and rising hills, small birds flitting between finger-like branches, a white sun in the pale sky and no sound but their own breath. He took another moment to breathe and allow himself to remember what France had been.

Alain glanced at them through a barred window, watching as they walked away. His cigarette was definitely out now, damp and lifeless, but it still clung to his lower lip. He tramped through clunking gates and doors until he reached the administration wing, where he spent his time arranging staff rotas and detailing what the prisoners had brought with them and what they were to be given back when – if – they left. The two columns rarely tallied. Anyone foolish enough to declare a valuable item to the receiving officer would never see it again.

He felt relief now that he had decided to back out of the plan and satisfaction that he had thought of a way to get paid nevertheless. The stairs were wet with mud brought in on leather boots. As he stepped up to the next stair, he slipped and fell to his knees, to the amusement of a pair of Germans passing him on their way down. He smiled, in on the joke, allowing them to enjoy it. One said something to the other in German and the second one laughed. Alain smiled again and resumed his journey.

'He says the floor is as wet as your mother was for him last night.'

Alain turned and forced a smile. 'He is very droll.' He turned back and went on climbing.

'He says ten francs was too much, though.'

'Does he?' The humiliation began to light in his cheeks.

'Hey, why don't you do for me what she did last night?'

Alain gritted his teeth and continued climbing up to the next floor. Then he felt a hand jerk his collar backwards, pulling him off balance. He grabbed the bannister and waited for the two men to leave him alone.

And as they descended the stairs, something fell into place. He would wipe the smiles from their faces.

He spent the morning performing his normal routine. At lunchtime he ate his black bread spread thinly with margarine, a poor substitute for the sweet butter he used to eat, then at 1.30 p.m. he paid a visit to the staff toilet on the ground floor, taking a large bag with him. It was a stinking place, always awash with a centimetre of stale water on the floor. No one ever bothered to clean it. Even the inmates' stalls were cleaned regularly, if perfunctorily. But the staff toilet also happened to be next to the laundry room. He came away with a sergeant's trousers and jacket.

That evening Alain delivered the bag to Sebastien's safe house. Reece handed him an envelope with one thousand francs and Alain counted the cash.

'Your friend is in the east wing. I couldn't tell which cell, but there aren't many there.' That would make it harder, Reece thought, but there was no helping the situation, and no reason for thinking Alain was lying about not knowing Luc's exact location. 'Count your friend lucky they haven't sent him to one of the camps yet.'

'Number of guards?'

'Normal rota for tomorrow. Fifty-two French working in eight-hour shifts. I don't know about the Germans, but about thirty normally.'

'All regular men?' Reece asked, checking the uniform. It should fit him, more or less.

'Yes.'

'And everything else is as you told us? Mealtimes, that sort of thing?'

'Everything's normal, as far as I know.'

'Good. All right. Is there anything else you can tell us that could help? Think. Anything at all: a broken pipe, a fight between inmates. Anything.'

Alain pondered for a second. 'It's freezing inside, though I doubt that makes a difference,' he said.

'Probably not.'

'Then I wish you luck. That's all I can think of.'

Reece nodded his thanks. For a moment he wondered if he should be suspicious about Alain's sudden enthusiasm for the plan, but he decided that he was just being overcautious.

They waited for five minutes without saying a word, in case anyone had seen Alain enter, and then he left and Reece returned to the parlour, where Sebastien sat shuffling a pack of cards in the dark. Across the room from him, Thomas and Hélène were eating omelettes made with powdered eggs and carrots. Reece gazed at them in the gloom. He still couldn't discount the possibility that Parade had an informant within Beggar, but he had little choice about having his fellow agents there for the op. He needed all the hands he could muster; even with Sebastien's circuit joining them later, they would be short on bodies.

In order to maintain security he had had one of Sebastien's men bring Thomas and Hélène to Amiens without telling them where they were going or what the operation was to be and since then he had watched them at all times.

Thomas finished his food and ambled over to the table, where Sebastien dealt a hand of whist. Reece took the opportunity to hand over his cards and join Hélène. 'How are you feeling?' she asked.

'We'll get the job done.' He couldn't help being cagey. 'How are you bearing up? It's a long time since you saw your family.'

'God, it feels so long. London's promised me a week's leave next month. They're trying to co-ordinate with the Canadian army so my husband can get leave too and we can spend it together.'

'I'm sure he would appreciate that as much as you.'

'I haven't seen him for nearly two years. It's tough. Really tough. Do you have someone back home?'

He thought of someone holding a lighter as they stood waist-deep in water. Then the flame flicking off and nothing but the tunnel. 'No. No one.'

'I'm sorry,' she said, in her strange Québécois accent. 'You need to find someone, someone who actually likes you, not just some young girl impressed by all your war stories. Don't sit around in some country house chasing girls from the village, or whatever it is you do.'

'I'll do my best.'

'We need more coal for the fire,' Sebastien said, throwing down his hand. 'You're clearly dealing from the bottom of the deck anyway.'

'Bloody right I am,' Thomas replied.

Sebastien went out through the French windows at the rear of the room that gave access to the garden. Reece heard him knock into something outside.

Then the French windows opened again. 'Did you forget something?' Reece asked. Receiving no reply, he looked around. Sebastien stood in the doorway, but his figure wasn't the only one framed by the night sky. Behind him were two leather-coated Gestapo men with guns pointing into the room.

Reece threw himself to the side, desperately searching for some sort of weapon. One of the Germans knocked Sebastien out of the way and shouted at Reece to stop. Behind them, a powerful electric torch shone into Reece's face, blinding him.

At the same moment, the front door seemed to break in two. A shot was fired, but he couldn't tell from where and all there was was confusion. The last thing he remembered was the butt of a pistol thudding into the base of his skull.

CHAPTER 18

During interrogation

i) Speak slowly, clearly and firmly. Do not answer simple questions imme-diately, and hesitate with the more difficult ones. Similarly, keep an even level of preciseness, i.e. do not overdo the detail in replies to easy questions and then 'forget' everything with difficult ones.

ii) Remember that shouting, bullying, coaxing, joking, sentimentality, etc., is all an act to make you afraid, angry, hilarious or sentimental and thereby lessen your vigilance.

iii) Avoid replies that lead to further questions. All your answers should end in a cul-de-sac. Do not help the interrogators by adding unsolicited information . . .

iv) Do not express personal affection or interest in anybody.

15 February 1944

He was drowning. His mind and flesh told him so. He was in a ship leaving Dunkirk and it was going down. A thousand bodies around him were falling to the bottom of the Channel. He saw them all, soldiers with empty faces, grasping hands, brine flooding their mouths.

But then it was no longer heading for England, it was heading for a cold French beach, and the ship, packed with eager young men, was powering towards the harbour even though it had been torpedoed from below, tearing its metal body apart and letting the sea rise over them all.

When he opened his mouth to yell out, to make it stop, freezing water poured in and he choked. The water streamed down his throat, wracking his body with sharp pain.

'Stop it now.'

He barely remembered himself. His name was out of reach, like the coast. But something, somewhere, was telling him he had to forget. He had to keep something locked away.

He should have died, it said, he should have crushed the L-pill between his teeth rather than be taken.

And as he came to himself so did that memory. His recce mission. If they found out where he had been, they would understand the significance and those blank faces would be filled. Ten thousand boys would fall through the sea because of him. He had to keep it locked away from them.

'Pull him up.'

It was a man's voice. A moment's pause, then Reece's head was wrenched back by his hair and a rag torn away from his face. He spewed cold water over himself. He tried to open his eyes, but the moment he did so a glare of intense light burned his irises and he shut them tightly again. He felt himself thrown into a chair and straps wrapping around his wrists and ankles.

He shook his head, willing his eyes to open. Splinter by splinter, his eyelids lifted. The light was ferocious, but after a few seconds his vision adjusted and he could make out two arc bulbs shining straight into him. Silhouetted against them were dark faces. Then the silhouettes pulled away and all that was left was the white glare. He tried to put his hand up to block it out, but it wouldn't move.

A man came into his line of vision and peered down.

Klaussmann. Klaussmann had found him.

Reece tried to focus on the here and now, to prove to himself that he was conscious and awake and in charge of his own body. He could resist.

Above was a concrete ceiling. He had to remind himself of what was going on. Yes, the Gestapo's favourite interrogation method: they would forcibly submerge him in a bath of ice water until he passed out or told his captors everything they wanted to know. To know it was to have some semblance of control over it.

'Your name is Maxime. Well, that's what your circuit call you.'

Reece's mind raced forward. How did Klaussmann know that? Had it been Charlotte? Had she tricked him again?

Klaussmann waited a while before speaking again. 'What's your full name?' Reece did his best to look dazed, to play for time before he came up with a strategy for evasion. 'I've been here before, Maxime. More times than I care to remember,' Klaussmann sighed wearily. 'Would you like me to turn the lights off? I can do that.' Reece stared at the wall, playing dumb, half dead, secretly bringing his mind up to speed. Klaussmann waited. 'You've only been through the play-acting at Beaulieu, haven't you?' A pause. 'When were you there? Forty-two? Forty-three? Ah, the rose garden must have been charming in the summer.'

Klaussmann was right – at the Finishing School they had gone through mock interrogations, dragged from their sleep and subjected to hours of questions and mild physical pressure, informed that it was nothing compared to the violence of a real Gestapo interrogation. Reece realized that Sebastien and the others would be in another of these rooms or waiting in a cell.

He focused. He had to predict how this would play out. Klaussmann would begin with innocuous questions such as when Reece had trained at Beaulieu and the questions would slowly become more dangerous and the methods more brutal. Agents were trained to hold out against the pain for at least forty-eight hours, to give SOE a chance to limit any damage – change codes, send any surviving contacts underground. He planned to defy it for longer. But the beaches, the meeting with Churchill. That information could change the course of the war. It had to be hidden as deep within himself as it was possible to plunge such a truth.

He looked at Klaussmann from top to toe, fully awake now. The last time their eyes had met the German had been scrabbling for his gun and Reece for the blade underneath his lapel.

'Would you like me to turn the lights off?' Klaussmann repeated.

The lights hurt and Reece wanted respite from their glare. But what he needed more was to understand what Klaussmann wanted.

'Where am I?' he managed to splutter.

'Oh, somewhere.' Klaussmann waited. 'Would you like to know? Well, I will make a deal with you. I will tell you where we are if you tell me something utterly without importance about yourself. You can choose what it is.' Yes, that was how the interrogations would begin, Reece told himself: seemingly unimportant information at first. Nothing operational. Then more and more demanding, closer to the bone. Coming more to himself, he tested the leather cuffs around his wrists. Klaussmann watched him. 'You can tell me about Clémence Dubois.' Despite himself, Reece looked up. Her name sounded strange coming from the German's mouth. Perhaps it shouldn't have done. Abwehr officers would have been pronouncing her name for a time. 'I have her photograph.' He beckoned to a subordinate, who handed him a white folder. Klaussmann pulled out the sepia-toned picture Reece had seen in her bedroom – the one perhaps taken on holiday. Her dark eyes, shaded from the sun, were the same, looking sadly through you to a point in the distance. On paper, as in life, they never saw you.

But Reece realized something: Klaussmann didn't know who Charlotte was. He didn't know she was with the Abwehr. If he had known, he wouldn't be asking Reece about her. Not so directly, anyway. The animosity between the intelligence services had kept her unknown to him.

And Klaussmann's question also suggested that none of the other people who had been in Charlotte's house had been picked up. Luckily for them, they had run when Reece's presence had been detected and had all gone before the Gestapo arrived.

Klaussmann gazed at the image. 'She's very beautiful.' He placed the photograph in the folder and handed it back. The other man brought him a wooden chair. 'I will explain something.' Reece sighed deeply, his lungs beginning to work again in their natural rhythm, his head clearing. 'It doesn't matter where we are. What matters is that we have as much time as we need.'

'Tell me who informed on us.'

Klaussmann seemed unperturbed. 'If I gave you a name, would you even believe me?'

'Try me.' He knew that he wouldn't be able to trust it, but he clutched at the straw.

'Not yet, my friend. It is an exchange. First you tell me something, then I will tell you something.'

'I'll tell you nothing.'

'Well, then,' Klaussmann said, getting up from his chair. 'I have been polite.' He walked out of Reece's sight. A fat man, stripped to the waist, strode in front of Reece and pulled a cosh from a loop on his belt. In reflex, Reece tried to lift his hands to ward off the blow, but they only strained against the leather straps. The cosh came down in his eye socket. Reece heard Klaussmann's voice again. 'I won't warn you again, Maxime.'

Three hours later, Reece's body was a map of what the guards had done to him. Dark patches spread here and there, cut through by red lines and yellow pools of liquid under the surface.

Two men, covered in sweat like Reece himself, were taking it in turns to beat his bones with their coshes.

'Stop it now. Leave us,' Klaussmann ordered. Reece lifted his bleeding face. Klaussmann settled himself into the chair. He was holding the Proust novel in which Reece had recorded the movements of German officers who visited his shop. 'Our regiments. You have been busy,' he said, lifting the book. 'Now, let us start again.'

Reece gazed at him. 'Will you . . . tell me something?' he rasped. His throat was dry through thirst. He wheezed air.

'Perhaps.'

Klaussmann looked into Reece's face, now a seething and torn mass of craters and bulges. Slowly, the British agent's eyes lifted to meet Klaussmann's. The lids closed in pain and suffering and the head lolled to the side. Reece's lips came together and he attempted to speak, to drop a word or two, but the sound was caught in his mouth and his tongue refused to function properly. 'What?' Klaussmann asked, bringing his face closer.

Reece lifted his forehead then crashed it down on to the bridge of the Gestapo officer's nose, smashing the cartilage outwards. Klaussmann roared in pain and threw himself backwards, almost tipping over. Reece's lips spread and he panted in shallow laughter. Then something metal cracked into the back of his head and it all turned dark.

CHAPTER 19

16 February 1944

When news of Reece's capture crossed the desk of Major Daniel Delaney the following morning, he sat back in his chair, passed his hands across his eyes and saw again the face of his one-time-girlfriend Elena, who had been beaten to death by the Gestapo. But he had been through such news too often to be disabled by it.

He went directly to the Cabinet War Rooms, to find Churchill in conference with Huw Evans from 5, and showed them both the message he had been sent. The stamp at the top, 'Most Secret Sources', indicated that it had come from the codebreakers at Bletchley Park, who had been intercepting German intelligence and military traffic.

It contained a message sent by a minor Gestapo officer, one Major Klaussmann, to Headquarters in Berlin.

'Just tell me what he says,' Churchill said gruffly. There was a half-eaten plate of spam and bread on the desk beside him. Churchill had his own bedroom in the bunker and sometimes barely saw daylight for forty-eight hours. 'No time to trawl through German cables.'

'It looks like Maxime has been caught. We can presume he's being interrogated.'

'How long do you think he'll hold out?' Churchill growled. 'We don't want all of this to be for nothing.' Evans took the signal to read it through.

'It's hard to say. Bletchley is deciphering the cables as top priority.'

'You think Maxime will survive the interrogation?'

'Perhaps. At least Jericho will give him a chance.'

'Evans?' Churchill said.

'I say Jericho's the best chance we have, Prime Minister,' he replied. 'I'll speak to 6 as well to see if they can find out anything in the meantime.'

'Do it.'

Reece lay on the concrete floor of his cell, his swollen and bruised eyelids drooping. During the night, every time he looked to have fallen asleep, the guards had either sprayed him with water from a hose or administered a beating, and each time he had felt his mind and his resolve weakening.

In the course of their training, Reece and the other agents had been taught that, if captured, it was best to go along with instructions – but to do so slowly. Always make the Germans wait for a second before acceding to their demands, they were told. That way, for a moment, you are in control. Outright defiance simply gives them an excuse to kick you into submission. So when the guard told Reece to stand he sat for a couple of seconds, as if deciding whether this was what he wanted to do. Then he stood, only to find he was so exhausted he had to use the wall to brace himself. The guard pulled him around and cuffed his hands together.

'Out,' he was ordered.

'Where are we going?'

The guard's only answer was to jab him in the back with his cosh. Reece hoped he could hold out again today. The longer it went without him breaking, the colder the trail for the Gestapo to the rest of the circuit would be.

The resistants' cells were in the horizontal bar of the cross-shaped prison, guarded by Germans. The ordinary criminal prisoners were guarded by French warders in the vertical bar. A central tower where the two beams intersected allowed the Germans and the French warders to keep an avid watch on all the prisoners.

When Reece was shoved into the interrogation room he saw Klaussmann, as before, with the ghost of a smile on his thin lips. Reece was strapped into the chair, although this time his head was restrained too. He didn't resist; there would be no point. He did notice some bruising around the bridge of Klaussmann's nose.

'We spoke yesterday of your trip to Saint-Cloud,' Klaussmann said, wandering over to the corner of the room. 'Do you know it well?' Reece looked the Gestapo officer up and down. 'Had you been before?' So, Klaussmann's plan was to get to him through Charlotte. Did they have her? Had she been with them all the time after all? The silence was filled by the click of the guard's heels on the concrete floor and the swish of a cosh raised. Klaussmann lifted his palm to stop the man. Air wheezed through Reece's throat, in and out. 'If you will only tell me if you have been before, you can have some food and water. Would you like that?' Klaussmann took a pack of Turkish cigarettes from his pocket. He lit one. 'Would you like to smoke?' Reece shook his head. 'Very bad for the lungs. But your lungs sound bad already.' He took a long draw. 'So let's start again. Do you know Saint-Cloud?'

'Go to hell.'

An unseen fist cracked into Reece's jaw. He felt it dislocate then snap back into place with searing-hot pain. He wanted to put his hand to it, but they were held by the leather.

'I said, do you know Saint-Cloud?' This time the fist thudded into his temple.

Hemsall Sands was a short and isolated stretch of the Dorset coastline in southern England. Part of a wide bay, it had a beach that began as sand at the shoreline but soon became pebbles further back. It was topped with large grass-covered dunes, and behind them a road led to a small village consisting of a handful of houses, a shop, a church and a tiny village school. The village had recently been evacuated, however, and the beach covered with lines of spiralling barbed wire and huge iron tank traps.

Some way along the coastline, low cliffs hovered over the sea. On one of the cliffs, the German agent Parade stood with a telescope wrapped in sacking and propped up on a low brick wall. The targets he was watching were too far for binoculars to be effective. He looked one more time along the forlorn beach that had been turned from a place where families would take giddy children to one where men would have their clothes and flesh grabbed at by spiked wire while mortars fired over their heads. Then he scanned the horizon again. Nothing.

He looked over to the village. There was the little Norman church, forlorn in its churchyard peppered with leaning gravestones. There the shop and there the single-room school. How many of its past pupils were now readying to embark for France? Hard to say. He spun back to the simmering sea, peering east. Empty as ever. He spat on the ground. They were . . .

Wait. There. Yes, there was something: a grey mass suspended on the horizon, appearing around the headland. Finally.

It was steaming from Portsmouth, Parade knew, as he refocused the telescope. Good, not much longer to wait. He drew his jacket tighter – it was a cold morning, but he was in light civilian wear so that if a patrol happened to come across him he could claim he was merely a lost holidaymaker.

The flotilla, stretching three or four kilometres in full, drifted across the open sea, its lines solidifying into a corvette leading nine LST tank landing ships, each carrying four hundred British and Canadian soldiers and sailors. Nipping along their sides was the motor torpedo boat escort. Parade checked his watch. It was 6.50 a.m. He had suggested the E-boats intercept the flotilla at 7 a.m. The E-boats must be close now, their powerful diesel motors thudding them through the waves – so long as they hadn't run into a Royal Navy patrol in the Channel. That was entirely possible, of course. If so, it would spoil what the German high command no doubt considered an excellent round of practice for the Kriegsmarine, gearing up to repel D-Day just as the Allies were preparing to prosecute it. A show of strength and shark-like stealth by the Germans today would also put the fear of God into the Allied troops – and strength of morale would be as much a factor as the strength of arms that day.

At 6.58 a.m. the convoy was about half a mile offshore. The LSTs – 'Large Slow Targets', to their sardonic occupants – took up their positions in a ragged line, waiting for the signal to approach the beach and rehearse rapid disembarkation. In order to acclimatize them to the chaotic noise of an amphibious landing, the corvette began to shell the beach. Parade watched the shells land and blast the pebbles into the air, sucking dark sand into high vortexes that spread over the beach.

The corvette should have been monitoring the open sea, but Parade guessed its crew was focused on the beach, watching the explosions send up plumes of dust. Through his telescope he saw the E-boats speeding in at forty knots.

As they approached through the freezing water he thought of the young man he had met in a café in Erith, the one who said he was about to receive beach training. But he thought of him only briefly. There were, simply put, a billion young men in the world. Not all of them would be grieved for.

The first the LSTs knew of the E-boats was when the side of the middle craft erupted like the sand on the beach. Parade watched as the steel blew apart. Another second and the boat was listing in the water, then rolling over like a shot animal. Another explosion erupted in its rear, flames spreading across the deck. Shells continued to rain on the beach as the gunners on the corvette failed to spot the danger that was now upon the flotilla.

Then another LST, and another, shook with explosions – torpedoes and surface guns buffeting them from side to side. Those few boats left undamaged were scattering, but they were heavy, slow-moving vehicles built for stability on the Channel crossing, not for speed. The first one hit was beginning to slip down into the water. Hundreds of men in battle dress, weighed down with equipment, were jumping from its side. Parade couldn't hear, but he knew they were crying out for help. Then the E-boat cannons opened up on those in the water.

Suddenly the shelling from the corvette ceased as its commander became aware, and its guns swivelled towards the German boats. But it was too late – the German raiders had already turned and begun dashing for the open sea, leaving a churn of men and torn metal. Carnage was all around, as if the sea itself had torn the boats to pieces: two of the LSTs were engulfed in fire, three more were nearly submerged and, as they sank, they sucked scores of men down with them.

Parade scanned the scene. He guessed that there were two hundred men in the freezing February water, most with large packs strapped to their backs. Some were struggling feebly towards already overladen lifeboats, although there would be little point. Most were simply sinking, their arms above their heads, reaching out for a rescue that would never come. Some of the lifeboats were limping towards the shore. A few sodden packs were floating on the surface, their pale owners now drifting downward, no longer able to cry out for help.

It appeared to Parade that of those men here who had seen the sun rise, one in two would see it set again. It had all taken four minutes.

Around a hundred and fifty thousand troops would land or wade ashore on D-Day. If the Kriegsmarine could repeat the sort of success he had just witnessed, that would mean an entire city of men at the bottom of the sea. They were men with names and wives and sons and homes, just like the men before him, screaming to the sky as their limbs became colder.

And this is war, he thought to himself. *I did not choose it and it is a necessity of man. This will not be the last time.*

He mentally noted the destruction, the number of deaths and how the boats had panicked, and retracted his telescope before placing it inside a green knapsack and walking away along the cliffs.

'The police have been going door to door,' the woman told Parade the moment she let him in that evening. 'They were here two days ago.'

'CID?'

'No. In uniform.'

'That's better.' He set down a bag of groceries by the front door. 'What did they say? Tell me exactly.'

'They said a constable on this beat hadn't returned to the station on Friday. Had I seen or heard anything? A fight or anything like that.'

He nodded. 'And what did you tell them?'

'I said I hadn't seen anything at all. But they'll be back, I know they will,' she said, her voice straining. They began to climb up to the attic.

'Don't worry. They have no idea he was here.'

She lifted her hands in supplication. 'I want to move. I can't stand it here any more.'

'You can't move. This is where you're staying.'

'Then I want to go out sometimes. And I want money to do it.'

'All right, all right.'

'Thank you.' She sounded relieved.

'Now stop talking about it.'

'This business, it feels like we're –'

'Don't think about it. Just do your job. This one's priority channel, you understand.'

'Of course I understand.'

They reached the attic and she assembled the transmitter. And then it was time for the message Parade wanted in SD headquarters immediately: *Op at Hemsall Sands good success. 6 of 9 LSTs sunk. Estimate 1800 dead of 3600. Discovered captured SOE agent Maxime briefed Churchill on invasion landing beaches. Real name Mark or Marc Reece. Captain ex naval intelligence. Ends.*

Parade spent three hours smoking cheap gaspers and struggling to read a book about English mediaeval history by the light of the cheap bulb above them. He couldn't concentrate; his mind was too active, thinking about Maxime.

The man in France who, after five years, seemed to be the key to final victory.

His thoughts were interrupted by the arrival of the reply, which the woman took down: *Personal congratulations Reichsführer-SS Heinrich Himmler.*

He read through the words a few times and wondered what those congratulations would be worth when the war was over; what he could buy with them. He called to mind seeing Himmler that night in Nuremberg at the 1933 rally. A little man, he had seemed. No smaller than Hitler himself in sheer size, but without the power and fury of his master. Men would listen to Himmler, respect his orders, but they would never follow him as they would follow the Führer.

'You said you would do something about me being cooped up.' The woman was talking to him. He snapped back to London in 1944 and his mission now. 'I want some money. And to go out sometimes. I'm going mad, staying here all day and all night.'

'It's not safe.'

'I tell you, I'm going mad. Let me go out. I'll be discreet.' She sounded as if she really were on the edge.

'All right. All right. I'll see what I can do.' He went downstairs and out to the telephone box at the end of the street. He asked the operator for a number in London that rang only once before it was picked up.

'Hello?' he heard a tinny voice rattle through the line.

'It's Huw Evans,' he said. 'We've had some trouble. My wireless operator wants to go out on the town. I need a bit of cash.'

There was a distorted sigh. 'Or what?'

He pushed another gasper between his lips and lit the end. The glow flickered in the misted-up telephone box like a lantern. 'Or it's all over, really.'

CHAPTER 20

Clothes
These should either fit the locality (e.g. seaman's jersey near docks) or be
inconspicuous by their neutrality. In any case, they should be dark rather
than light in colour. It is advisable to anticipate any change in the weather.
It is sometimes very useful to change all or some clothes en route.

17 February 1944

Klaussmann rubbed his eyes. He hadn't slept well. It was
8 a.m. and he had spent the night at a hotel in Amiens, rather
than go to and from Paris while the spy was being interrogated. The bed had been softer than he was used to, and his
back had been in pain half the night. He cursed the prison
commandant, who had refused to allow the spy to be taken
to Paris – he had got a sniff that the man might be important
and wanted to keep the prize close.

Again, without meaning to, Klaussmann thought of those
few seconds on the train when the British agent had evaded
him to put a knife through Schmidt's neck. He suppressed a
tide of anger and frustration that threatened to rise and inter-
fere with his rational thoughts.

As soon as Klaussmann had fulfilled his promise to the
Reich by extracting as much information from the spy as he
possessed, he would allow the anger to surge up and cause
the man as much suffering as he could take. Yes, he told himself, sentence was a necessary part of judgement.

His thoughts were interrupted by a knock on the door to his suite. A young Gestapo officer was waiting with another message – one from Berlin's secret source, it became apparent. This one had been circulated to all Gestapo offices. Klaussmann opened it and lay it on the table to read as he lifted a cup of tea to his mouth. As the china was about to touch his lips he stopped. The cup hovered in mid-air before he placed it back down on the table. 'My God,' he muttered, taking the message in his hands and running faster and faster through the lines.

'Good news, sir?'

Klaussmann allowed the man the indiscretion of asking questions of him. 'We might have a very important man in our custody.'

Reece opened his eyes. All he could see was blurring water. The sting of the ice would have made him wince, but his muscles had failed. He tried to remember if he had been awake minutes or hours.

He knew that, deep down, he was someone; he had a name and a place and a home and a country and he was somewhere other than in this freezing water where his muscles were unable to work. He was spinning, sick, afraid of what was happening to him, what would come next.

And then something was grabbing him, pulling him out into cold air, dragging him upwards from the point of death. He felt himself strapped into a chair.

'You have been awake for three days, Captain Reece,' said a voice through the darkness of his failed vision. 'You want to sleep, don't you?'

He did. He wanted to be unconscious and to sleep and then remember who he was. And he realized that this man in front of him knew his real name. It was bewildering.

'I can do that. I have power over what happens to you. You can sleep in a bed. All you have to do is talk to me.'

At the edge of his mind, in the twilight of thought, he could feel memories slipping in. Days without sleep, hours in cold water, submerged until his heart stopped beating and cold fingers wrapped around his hands and feet to drag him away into death. Then lifted up into the shivering world and his own muscles shaking him back to life. A painful and dreadful life.

Each time it happened he felt that another part of him had been taken away, a tiny grain of himself that he had clung to drifting out of his grasp. Whether it was hours ago or days ago he didn't know, but the grains of resistance had slipped from his fingers and he feared that the man doing this to him knew that.

'Winston Churchill. You spoke to Winston Churchill. What about?'

Reece's mouth opened and strings of water cascaded from it, some entering his throat to make him cough. His mind had divided into confusion. *Delaney said you're going back. Recce the harbours. The invasion.*

'I . . . no,' he mumbled, his tongue too cold to work, his lips blue and frozen in place.

'Again.'

And he was plunged back in. His eyes closed and darkness turned black. He was there for hours, it seemed, before he was up again, his brain suspended in ice. Delirium seemed to wrap its palms around his mind.

'Winston Churchill. You spoke to Winston Churchill. What about?'

And then a new vision entered his head. Charlotte in the sewer below Paris talking about Parade One. '*I know they need two things . . . your army Order of Battle and where you're going to invade.*'

266

'Please. Please.' *Distract him. Deter him. Keep it to yourself. Feed him something. The circuit. Their lives, your life. Worth it. Worth the secret.* 'I'll . . . tell you about the network.'

'I'm not interested in your petty crimes. I want to know what you spoke to Churchill about.'

'Beggar. Luc . . .'

'Again!'

'No!'

And he clutched for that grain of himself again. *Lie. Make it up. Trick him as long as you can.*

'Liberation. We talked . . . liberation of Paris.'

There was a pause. 'When you tell me the truth this will end. Again.'

And Reece was back in the water, feeling his veins wrenching out of his flesh. He became nothing but water. And then he was being spoken to again in the air.

'Now, the truth.'

The scene before him faded into blank. He felt himself vomit, his chest heaving as if it had been jerked by an electric current, but all that cascaded down his chest was more filthy water.

'Fine, if you won't help yourself, we have to do something different.' Klaussmann beckoned to one of the guards at the door. There was shuffling and the sound of whimpering. Through the icy fog, Reece could make out more bodies shuffling in front of him. The mist began to lift and he saw a young face that he recognized. Hélène stood before him, her blouse and skirt torn away and her hands shackled. Her mouth was gagged with a dirty rag.

'What you are going through is nothing to what my men will do to her,' Klaussmann said simply. 'You will be in the same room, as it happens.' Hélène's eyes opened wide and she began to implore Reece as best she could, unable to speak. Hélène, who had volunteered to come to France so that her son would never grow up in a world where the Nazis smothered other people's lives. 'You will watch her face as it happens. You will choose then to tell me the one thing I am asking. But by then it will be too late; she will have suffered such harm she will never recover. And then we will cut her so that she bleeds to death in front of you.' Hélène sank to her knees and lifted her bound hands to Reece, and then to Klaussmann. 'Save her from that. She's a good person. You can save her from that. The information is information we have anyway. We only want it confirmed. You can save her.'

Reece shook his head.

At that, Klaussmann nodded to one of the guards. The man untied the gag in Hélène's mouth. As it was removed she began pleading.

'Please, Maxime, don't let them –' she cried.

'I can't . . .'

'My son! He's two. Don't let him lose his mother. Please. Please, Maxime!'

He looked into her eyes and clutched for that grain one last time. It was telling him that he must not speak. That the words would cause something terrible, far more terrible than his or her death. That truth would kill them both a thousand times over, it would lay waste to nations and turn the soil to whirlpools. He tried again to control his own thoughts, but something had happened that last time his mind had been frozen in the water and at the sight of Hélène on her knees the truth of who he was, was out of his reach.

The word dripped from his mouth, so quietly that only Klaussmann could hear it. Little more than a breath.

'Invasion.'

And Reece knew that deep within himself a fracture had opened.

'What about the invasion?'

Reece could feel ice rush through his stomach. Then something else. A blow from something metal, doubling him up, making him cough out more words.

'A recce.' He could see nothing but figures in a blue mist.

'Speak to me.'

There was something comforting about the voice.

'I had to survey the harbours.'

'Where?' Klaussmann demanded.

Reece shook his head.

'Where? Tell me now.' He paused. 'Do whatever you want to her.' Hélène cried out as the material was stuffed back into her mouth. 'Then hold his head up so he can watch as you cut her throat.'

'No, please,' Reece begged.

'Where will the invasion arrive, Captain Reece?'

'I don't know.'

'*Where?*'

'I swear I don't know. I don't know!'

A knife was pressed to her throat, the point breaking through the skin to leave a prick of ruby blood, and she screamed his name. 'Maxime! Maxime!'

And at the sound, echoing through his mind so that nothing else existed, he split in two. In a single breath, in a moment when he seemed to fall from the cliff, he spoke. He told them everything he knew or had guessed: where. How strong a force. The ships they would use. Each word burned in his mouth and spilled from his lips. Each sentence was treason to himself.

All that he had suffered – the months of hunger and isolation and suppressed fear; the hours when he told himself the end justified the means – all had been turned back on him, weapons now for his enemies, not for his friends. It was an immolation.

With all that he was, he wished for it to be over – for everything to end, for God to lift his hand and sweep it across the world, turning it all to darkness.

He knew that it was night outside.

CHAPTER 21

18 February 1944

At 6 a.m. a tannoy sounded in the pilots' sleeping quarters at RAF Hunsdon in Hertfordshire, forty kilometres north of London. The two-man crews of 140 Wing of the 2nd Tactical Air Force were heard to swear when the order was given for them to assemble in the briefing room at 8 a.m.; only the appearance of the messing assistant with cups of tea quietened down their complaints.

The wing, made up of pilots from the New Zealand, Australian and Royal Air Forces, flew Mosquitos, the fast light bomber that carried out the nearest thing 2 TAF had to commando raids. The twin-engined Mossie could fly at 600km/h, precisely drop four 200-kilogram bombs and turn for home before the Luftwaffe knew it had arrived. The Mossie was an ugly machine – no one pretended otherwise; it wasn't woman-sleek like the Spitfire. It looked like a bull, and it hit harder. The 2nd TAF had already carried out a precision hit on the Berlin radio broadcasting system, cutting off Hermann Göring's speech halfway through his address to mark the tenth anniversary of the National Socialist German Workers Party seizing power. It had earned them the highest respect in Bomber Command.

Even before they peered through the windows – steaming up again as they were wiped clear – the men knew the conditions outside. In fact, looking out hardly helped, since a cascade of thick snow was blocking out the sun and pitching the whole land into a winter half-light. They could hear the gale-force winds, though, howling the snow into something close to a blizzard. For the previous forty-eight hours all but the most urgent flights had been grounded; and those days had been clearer than it was now. It seemed the briefing they were being summoned to could hardly be for a mission – just going up in this weather would be far more dangerous than any German fighter patrol.

The snow frosted their skin as they hurried to the mess then on to the bus that took them to the aerodrome a little more than a kilometre away. Desperate for the warmth of the hut, there was another barrier before they entered: for some reason, there were RAF police guards on the door and identification had to be presented before they could be admitted. They had already flown secret missions against V1 launch sites in France and now joked, uncertainly, about the additional security.

Waiting inside the hut were their Air Officer Commanding, the Group Intelligence Officer and Group Captain Percy Pickard. At twenty-eight, the tall, blond, pipe-smoking Pickard was already a national hero, due to his starring role in *Target for To-Night*, a heart-soaring propaganda film that showed the bravery and level-headedness of the bomber crews. When the eighteen pilots and eighteen navigators of 140 Wing had assembled, still attempting to return the blood to their chilled limbs, Pickard stepped to the front.

'Your mission for today is a very special one from every point of view,' he informed them. 'There has been no little debate as to whether this attack should be carried out, and your AOC more or less had to ask for a vote of confidence in his men and his aircraft before we were given the chance of having a crack at it. It can only be successfully carried out by low-level Mosquitos and we've got to make a big success of it to justify his faith in us and to prove further, if proof is necessary, just how accurately we can put our bombs down.' He opened a large wooden box and took out its contents. 'This is a model of your target for today.' The thirty-six airmen examined it. 'It's still snowing and the visibility is not so very good, but we can get off the deck all right. I've just had a final word with Group on the phone and they've given us the OK to go.' He paused. 'It's a job of death or glory, boys. If it succeeds, it will be one of the most worthwhile ops of the war. If you never do anything else, you can still count this as the best job you could ever have done.'

His words resounded through the room, but they all knew the difficulty involved and as the briefing ended they drifted to the tea urn or the windows and stared out. For two hours they did little but watch the snow pour down and tell each other that it had to clear.

And yet, by 10.45 a.m., when the men hurried out towards their machines, their lips cracking, it had worsened. The gusts were threatening to rip the windsock from its moorings and dash the crates to the ground before they had even left the English coastline. The cloud was no more than thirty metres from the ground and there was something of a shroud about it. The airmen could barely believe the op was on, but they checked each other's life jackets, climbed into the aircraft and set their minds to the task. Within seconds, thirty-six Rolls-Royce Merlin engines turned over and the planes trundled forward.

With the sound of their engines for once engulfed by the roaring air around them, the aircraft of 140 Wing 2 TAF took off in three waves, their pilots praying that they wouldn't crash into each other in the poor visibility. First the New Zealanders, then the Australians, then the RAF pilots, who were to be the reserve, in case the first two waves failed to achieve their precision-strike targets.

In that case, the British planes would sweep in and bomb it all to pieces.

Reece was pushed naked through the door, to find that there was no one in the interrogation room. He guessed the beating he was about to receive was to soften him up for more detailed questioning about the invasion – when, how many men, what armour would support them. He felt empty of hope as his wrists were bound in leather cuffs and hoisted to a hook in the ceiling. He hated himself for being weak and revealing the secret that he had known was the one truth he had to guard with his life, no matter what they did. As the rope was pulled tighter and his wrists lifted higher, the ligaments in his shoulders began to strain and tear, but he tried not to cry out, knowing that it would do nothing but encourage them. He bit his tongue and wished not that he had a gun or a knife but only that he had the L-pill, the little glass capsule of potassium cyanide, within his reach. The rope tightened and he felt the bones in his shoulders dislocate.

'Are you enjoying yourself?' one of the guards asked. 'We are.'

Reece groaned in pain.

'We have you for your whole life,' the other man called over. 'We end it when we want. Your life belongs to us.'

The door opened. Reece attempted to turn his head to see who had entered, but it doubled the burning in his shoulders. And he had no need.

'You two out,' Klaussmann's voice ordered. 'Captain Reece. My superiors in Germany are very interested in what you have been saying. You have told us the most important thing so there is no reason not to give us some more trivial details. We let you sleep last night and we will let you sleep again tonight, so long as we speak just a little today.'

'I can't tell you more. I can't.'

'You will, Captain Reece. You must believe me on that.'

As 140 Wing reached the English Channel, the murky water below swirled as if countless creatures were fighting below its surface. In Mosquito HX922/EG-F, Pickard's navigator, Bill Broadley, pointed through the Perspex window to their port side, where their fighter escort of Typhoons shimmered and moved into their bodyguard positions on the bombers' wingtips. The escort would fly at their side when crossing the sea and approaching the target, on the lookout for German fighter patrols. They would then hover above the Mossies as the bombers hit the target. 'We're bloody lucky they found us,' Pickard said through the intercom. The wing dropped down, speeding at fifteen metres above the surface of the water to avoid detection by the German radar. The target was an hour away. They accelerated to 400km/h. 'Damn blizzard,' Pickard said through the intercom as they reached the halfway point across the Channel. He counted his aircraft. Four of the Mosquitoes were already missing, and he guessed – hoped – they had turned back after being separated from the others by the thick snow. 'Right. Radio silence from now on.'

He pushed on until, at 11.57 a.m., 140 Wing reached the town of Doullens, and turned south-east, above a brilliantly white landscape that reflected what light the sun could force through the clouds. Two more minutes and they were over the town of Albert, following the straight old Roman road south-west. Pickard's heartbeat rose with the sound of his plane's engines. And then he saw their target: Amiens prison in the snow.

'Captain Reece?' Klaussmann said. He drank some water and held the glass in front of Reece's dry lips. 'How many men will the American government be committing to the invasion?'

He had betrayed them all. He had betrayed himself, his circuit and all those men who would be wading ashore under a hailstorm of German bullets. He had lain awake all night clawing at his scalp, as if he could tear away his weakness and guilt. He knew what he had done: he had condemned hundreds of thousands of men to death. He had condemned France to endless night under the German sky. He wished he had died in the drop into France, or on the road to Amiens, instead of Richard. He wished himself dead now.

'No, I can't.' His voice was thin.

'We already know, but my superiors want to confirm it. Superiors – we all have to deal with their whims. How many men?' And as Klaussmann said it, he heard a distant buzzing in the air and looked towards the sky.

At 12.02 p.m., two minutes behind schedule, the first three of the six New Zealand aircraft dropped to just four metres above the ground, bursting past sparse hedgerows at 300km/h. The lead pilot gripped his control column so hard that the frozen skin on his knuckles cracked. Then he pressed the button to release two 200-kilogram bombs.

The first was an armour-piercing munition designed to break through the wall; the second was packed with high explosives, designed to blow everything to pieces.

The bombs struck the base of the eastern wall of Amiens prison and thudded to the ground without exploding. The pilot jerked his column back, climbing as quickly as he could, straight up, to clear the wall that rose above him and threatened to smash his crate to firewood. The bricks were so close he could have reached out and touched them. Another second's delay would have seen him the first casualty of the op, dead before it had even begun. But, praying for speed and time, he just made it, tipping over the height of the wall and passing so close to a German guard in a watchtower he could see the tip of the man's cigarette burning red. The soldier was too shocked to fire the machine gun he was manning and the aircraft's slipstream made his cigarette glow brighter before it fell to the floor of the watch post.

The second plane followed and dropped its bombs. Then the third, each one fighting to ascend vertically before reaching the double-layer brick wall that had stood for the best part of a century. The German guard now grabbed his gun and pointed it at the fin-like tailplane of the fourth Mossie. The aircraft was in his sights but he never got the chance to pull the trigger because, below him, the eleven-second fuse on the first bombs activated, blowing a hole in the base of the wall about ten metres from the front gate. Then the second bombs. Then the third. And then the fourth. And at last there was a gap in the wall five metres wide.

The shockwaves from the blasts carried through the main building, making the floor shiver.

Klaussmann blinked and looked to the ceiling, as if he would be able to penetrate it with his stare. The roar of planes overhead was so fast and close that he instinctively ducked. 'What . . .'

'An air strike,' Reece rasped in English. 'Jericho. It's Jericho.' He began to laugh and silently prayed that it would kill them both. 'And the walls came tumbling down.' The explosions felt like a balancing of the scales. He had betrayed himself and all those men in the landing craft. Jericho felt like the wrath of God coming down on him and Klaussmann to scour away the stain. Vengeance in fire and shaking earth.

They heard more engines coming in – three New Zealand planes breaching the northern wall as their mates had punched a hole in the eastern – and the floors trembled again, harder and louder.

'I . . .' Klaussmann began, trailing off without completing his thought. He pulled himself together and strode to the door. 'Go and find out what's going on,' he ordered the two guards who had been waiting outside, stunned into inaction.

What was going on, Reece could hear, was a torrent of noise from the cells, as if the Tower of Babel were coming down. The prisoners were shouting to each other, saying that the outer wall had been knocked to the ground. 'Do you hear me, Klaussmann?' Reece cried with what strength he had left. 'The walls came tumbling down!'

Above them, the lead Australian aircraft swept in above the main building. Its target was the mess hall, where the German guards were assembled for their midday meal. It dropped two more bombs straight through the roof, crushing the wooden tables underneath and sending the German guards scrambling away, and soared off as the munitions blew the windows and walls outwards in a cloud of splinters, leaving the guards torn and dead in the dust.

Four more bombs fell from the other Australian aircraft, slamming into the tip of the opposite spur of the building, each one placed and chosen to free the prisoners from their cells. And so shockwave after shockwave from the high-explosive munitions wracked through the prison structure, each time blasting more cell doors from their hinges.

Reece twisted around to see Klaussmann screaming at the two Gestapo men. 'They're hitting the –' And then Reece felt himself flying through the air.

For a time, there was nothing but darkness. Darkness and a sound like a distant whistle. Gradually, the whistle became howls, screams and cries.

When his eyes opened, he was enveloped in a brown mist. It settled on him, stinging, gritty and dirty. He rubbed it away and it turned into a foul paste squeezing out of the corners of his eyes. Many voices were shouting, desperate pleas for help, French and German mixed into each other. Reece's whole body felt numb until, in a rush like a tidal wave, the pain hit.

The jolt of it lifted his shoulders, creasing him in the middle. And it was then that he realized he was no longer hanging from the ceiling. More than that: as his eyes focused, they saw that the whole ceiling was gone; the solid masonry and rough plaster that had stood for a century now lay on the floor. The hook from which his wrists had hung was embedded in the cracked wall.

He struggled up, his hands still bound by the leather straps.

'*Halt.*' He felt it as much as heard it. '*Halt.*' It was feebly whined out in German, robbed of its power. Prostrate in the doorway, Siegfried Klaussmann was staring at him, face-up, from the floor. The Gestapo officer stretched a hand towards him, but it was no longer a hand; all the fingers had been shorn off. His other palm pushed weakly at a heavy wooden beam across his chest. Through the blurring dust, Reece's eyes met his. And Klaussmann seemed to understand how things had changed. He tried impotently to scrabble away through the dirt, the debris of the war that had come closer to him than he could ever have imagined. 'Please help me,' he said faintly. Reece hauled himself to his feet unsteadily, one of his knees feeling swollen or even fractured. He felt as hollowed out as the building that had buried them both. 'Please help me.'

Raw with the pain, Reece stumbled over, resting for a moment against what was left of the door frame, now nothing more than a testament to Reece's captivity. Outside was havoc without end. The brown cloud hung everywhere like thick smog, so that he could see no further than he could reach. The railing along the edge of the landing had been blown away, leaving a sheer drop into the ocean of spiralling dust. Bodies brushed past him – prisoners or guards, it was hard to tell and impossible to care, when they had all been plunged into the same chaos. Reece gazed at the man at his feet. Then he dropped to his knees and placed his palms under the wooden beam. It was heavy but gave way a little. Klaussmann, too, put his good hand under it, pushing as hard as he could, and between them they managed to shift it little by little off his chest. Reece slumped against the wall, his ankle burning. As more bodies seethed past him, shouting that the walls were down, he stooped to drag Klaussmann further out on to the landing.

'Thank you,' the German wheezed.

'Who gave me up?'

'I . . .'

'Who informed?'

'I . . . The messages came from Berlin,' Klaussmann replied, grimacing in pain. 'They wouldn't tell me. A secret source.'

From Berlin. A source secret even from the Gestapo's own officers. It had to be their man in London.

'Have you heard the name Parade?' Reece muttered.

'What?'

'The man who put me here.' The one who had torn the flesh from Reece's wrists and back, sent blood coursing down his beaten skin. The one Reece would do all these things to, whose eyes Reece would look into at the payment of account. 'What do you know about a spy in London?'

'Nothing. I swear to you that I don't know. Please help me.'

With his hands still bound, Reece pulled Klaussmann further on to the walkway. And further. And then Klaussmann understood. Reece stamped on his face and rolled his body to the edge of the landing, then over once more, through the gap in the guard rail and down through the smog. Their eyes met once, a flicker, and then Klaussmann's turned downwards, looking to the ground. Reece watched him fall through the smothering dust and crumple into the floor below.

In the war, every payment was short, and this was all Marc Reece could extract. But he enjoyed seeing Klaussmann fall.

He stood breathing, his sleeve held over his mouth and nose to filter out the harsh brick dust. His body ached, but his muscles were becoming stronger. A German guard charged past him, ignoring him entirely, and Reece tried to understand where he was. Somehow, providence from above had turned his fate on its head. That meant the prison walls had been bust down and the prisoners must be streaming out. He had to seize the moment; for the moment, now, was with him.

If he found Luc, he might salvage the mission to expose Parade. Something Luc had seen in the photographs of the document could lead them to the spy.

He grabbed a prisoner who was making for the stairway. 'Do you know Luc Carte?' The man stared at him without comprehension. Reece shook him. 'Do you know Luc Carte?' he repeated.

'No. Here,' the other man said, taking Reece to the side, where a door's broken and twisted hinge was protruding from the brickwork. 'You need to be free.' Reece used the torn metal as a saw to cut the leather cuffs on his wrists.

'I need to find Luc Carte.'

'Try in there.' The escaping prisoner pointed to the warders' room. 'They have the list. And the keys.'

Reece didn't need to be told twice. He limped towards the room, gaining a little strength with each step.

The door, like most others, had been blown out. Inside, it was as dark as hell.

'Who's there?' a voice called out in German.

Reece spun around to its source. 'It's fine,' he replied in the same language, crouching slightly. 'Where's the Sturmbannführer?'

'I don't know,' the voice said, before turning into a deep, retching cough. Through the gloom Reece saw a slim man crawling, spluttering uncontrollably. 'Why –'

Reece lifted a brick from the floor and brought it down on him.

When he was finished and the guard's body had stopped trembling he stripped the body and donned the uniform. It was too dark to find any list and the papers and files had been blown haphazardly across the floor. He would have to find Luc another way.

Out on the landing the dust was settling, coating everything, like the sleet outside. The streams of prisoners running for the spurs of the cross, where the opposing exterior walls had been destroyed, had become a tide. And yet, as Reece stared around, he saw some inmates standing inside their empty doorways just watching hundreds of men and women run for their lives and their freedom. He thought of looking for Hélène and Thomas, but he knew securing the information from Luc and getting it back to London was the priority. He just hoped they had escaped with the others.

Every second brought the arrival of German troops to the prison closer but, without knowledge of Luc's location, he had no idea if he had escaped – and without keys, there would be little Reece could do about it if he were still locked in his cell. He had to think what he could do. As he tried to form a plan, he spotted a uniformed figure on the ground floor below, a German guard waving a sub-machine gun in the air and loosing off a few shots to keep back a group of prisoners. Reece shouted to him in German. 'Hey, we need help!'

'What?' the guard shouted back.

'Here. Come up.'

'I can't.' The soldier turned his gun back towards the Frenchmen in front of him.

'The Sturmbannführer's orders.' The soldier below hesitated, but decided he had his orders and dashed up the stairs to the first floor, where Reece was waiting. 'We need to find a prisoner. Luc Carte. He knows who did this,' Reece said, sweeping his arm around. 'The Sturmbannführer wants him taken away before his friends do come.'

'Before what?' The German soldier looked confused by the strange wording.

Reece realized his mistake. He had to cover it. 'I'm sorry. I grew up in the Sudetenland. We speak differently. I can forget sometimes. Quickly – we need Carte now.'

The guard seemed unsure but pulled a ring of keys from his belt and hurried along the walkway, with Reece following. They approached a cell where the door had been thrown off its hinges and now lay uselessly on the concrete walkway. 'That one,' the German said. Reece's spirits rose at the sight of the empty doorway. He must be out.

But as Reece approached the German shouted into the room in French, 'Are you Carte?' And Reece looked inside to see a man covered in dust. His eyes met Reece's and widened in shock. 'I said, are you Carte?' The guard raised his gun.

'Yes, sir,' Luc whimpered.

'He's all yours,' the guard muttered to Reece. 'Here.' He handed Reece a cosh from his belt. 'Use it if you need to.' Then he rushed back down the stairs.

Reece checked behind him and hurried into the room.

'Maxime?'

'Yes. Come on, we have to go.' He pulled Luc towards the open doorway.

'No.' Luc tore away from him.

'What? It's open – the walls are down.'

'I can't.'

'What do you mean?'

'If I run for it, the Boche will arrest my whole family. My sister has two daughters.' Reece realized he was right. The repercussions of this raid, of the freeing of hundreds of prisoners, would be felt by many more people than just the inmates themselves. And he understood why those other men had been standing at the opening to their cells, just watching while others burst through the walls, away from Germany and into France.

He dropped his voice to a whisper. 'When we hit the transport I only heard you say there's a German spy, Parade, and the op is Parade One. What else did you see in the document?'

'It's a counter-attack against your bridgehead on D-Day. There were maps of the north-west coast: one of Normandy;

one of the Pas de Calais. Each one had beaches and harbours marked on it, with German battalions moving
towards them. They must be the different possible invasion
points. The plans show the counter-attack for each one.' So
the Germans had been unsure where the invasion was
coming – and then Reece had talked and told them. But
there would be a time for self-recrimination. 'There was a
typed sheet; it said Parade was a Fascist recruited before
the war.' It was something, Reece noted, something about
this man. 'And there was an address that it said will be used
to train special units for Parade One. Number 2, rue de
l'Église.'

'There must be a thousand rues de l'Église in France.
Which one?' Reece demanded.

'I don't know.'

'Anything else at all?'

'That's all I can remember. Maxime, I –'

Suddenly, they were both knocked to the floor. Another
explosion was shaking the building, bringing down grit from
the walls. Reece couldn't understand what it could be – the
planes had roared away minutes ago. Then he realized:
the ammunition store. 'I have to go.'

'You can leave me here. I haven't told them anything of
use,' Luc said plaintively. 'After two days I gave them your
cover identity – I was sure you would have broken into your
reserve identity. I don't even know what it is. I didn't tell
them about the photographs, and I'm being sent to a prison
camp now. You can leave me here.'

Reece was torn. He understood Luc's fears, but the day
before, Reece had told Klaussmann all. Somehow, he had
been given another chance, to undo some of that damage. If
Luc stayed, sooner or later the Germans would interrogate
him again.

'Luc, you're brave. I can't tell you how much braver you've been than me. But we can't take the chance. I . . . I told them things.' He felt Luc's gaze burn into him. 'Now they'll question you again. They could bring your sister before you, and you know what the guards will do to her.' Visions of Hélène entered his mind. He shook them and the moments of self-treachery away. 'The best chance you have is to escape. Find your sister and tell her to hide with relatives.' He saw the conflict on Luc's face: the danger of running against the danger of staying.

'An escape line?'

'We'll find one. Come with me.'

Reece reached under Luc's arm and hauled him to his feet. 'I can't walk so well. They worked on me.'

Reece could see that his ankles were swollen and puffy. The joints had surely been beaten again and again. 'We'll make it.' He supported Luc's weight as they made their way out on to the landing.

CHAPTER 22

Detective measures
Penetration. Double agents. Discretion needed in recruiting men and in contacting other organizations. Double agent may work well for an organization for a long time before any arrests are made.

Hundreds of prisoners, men and women, had fled through the broken walls, but many others remained, and an awful wailing now filled the air, the sound of human pleading. It rose all around and, as he reached the ground floor, Reece realized that it was coming from mouths buried under rubble. Here and there, men and women were desperately digging through broken bricks to save their friends.

'I'm a doctor!' a Frenchman cried to Reece in German, seeing his stolen guard's uniform. 'Help us – he needs to get somewhere I can treat him.' Reece knew that he had no time, he had to get away. There was more at stake than the lives of one or ten or five hundred men. He ran towards the opening in the wall. 'Boche shit!' he heard the doctor scream at his back.

'I'm slowing you down. You have to run,' Luc said urgently. He reached into the back of his own mouth and pulled out something white, a false tooth. A tiny glass capsule came out of it. 'I've got it ready in case they catch me. Look, so many are getting out.'

Reece knew he was right. Luc had a good chance, but Reece's was better. 'Goodbye,' he said. 'Good luck.'

He wished he could find and free Hélène, and the other agents too, but if he got Luc's crumbs of information about Parade back to MI5, perhaps they could use them as a first step to identifying the man; or perhaps the address, 2, rue de l'Église, already appeared in Army Intelligence files and an op could be mounted to uncover exactly what the counterattack entailed. In such exigencies, friendship and loyalty were burdens to decision.

So he clamped Luc on the shoulder and charged away, scrambling over piles of broken wood and brick. And then he was out into the air and the dim snow-filtered sunlight. The brightness shimmering off the white blanket made his eyes hurt as much as the dust that had coated them and he had to turn away for a moment.

'You, come on, this way!' a voice shouted. It was the guard with the sub-machine gun he had left a minute earlier. But immediately, a noise was drowning him out. A plane – a bomber – swept overhead, its twin engines sounding like a swarm of wasps. Reece could make out the RAF roundel on its side. And right behind, mirroring the Mossie's movements, was a Luftwaffe FW 190.

'Go on, boys!' screamed the German guard. 'Kill the bastards!' The 190's guns opened up, shooting a line of black flies against the white sky. The first burst missed, soaring away into the distance, but the second found its mark. As one, the bullets cracked into the British aircraft's tailplane, sheering it away and crippling the bomber. Unable to fly, the Mosquito shivered in the air and began to tumble. The German cheered at the sight of it falling to the frozen ground. Reece knew in his bones that the two men in that plane had died to save his life. He felt guilt mixed with hatred towards the man beside him. He walked sharply away before he did something stupid that would scupper his mission and his freedom – the mission and the freedom that those men had died for. 'Hey, come back!'

'The Sturmbannführer has orders for me,' Reece called over his shoulder.

'Coward.'

Once around the corner, he ran to the opposite wall, the east, where the first gap had been blasted. Through it he could see the main road, with houses on the other side. Streaming through were local people, rushing to help pull the injured and the dead from the rubble. He fought his way through, enduring the hate-filled stares of the townsfolk, and then he was out on to the road.

He scanned the open fields opposite and, spotting no German patrols, sprinted across the soil, all the while glancing back towards the prison, wondering if he had abandoned more of his agents to prison camps. Scores of prisoners were running in every direction. Guards were now pouring out from the prison too, some with dogs straining against chains.

Reece tore away his soldier's tunic and dropped it to the hard soil. He had to get back to London. He had to tell them what Luc had seen. As he ran, he passed a small copse where the wooden frame and metal controls of Mosquito HX922/EG-F lay struck into the hard earth. He saw eight local people dragging the broken bodies of Group Captain Percy Pickard and Flight Lieutenant Bill Broadley from the mud-flecked wreckage.

Charlotte gazed through the sleet-soaked window of a dark car. They had been driving for fifteen hours already. Through Strasbourg, across the border to Stuttgart, and on to Berlin, in the east. Along the way columns of troops and armour were rolling from the Fatherland towards the French coast to defend against the coming invasion.

'Do you think we'll win?' the driver asked her as a convoy of armoured cars sped past, destined for the Atlantic Wall.

'Who's "we"?' she replied, under her breath.

She had visited Berlin once before – as an eighteen-year-old girl. Paris had been gay in the late twenties, but Berlin was like a circus run by madmen. She had stayed out all night, dancing; flirted with men and had them ply her with drinks until she left without telling them. She met artists, musicians and an actress who always wore men's clothes.

Now, houses and restaurants were without roofs, their windows blackened by incendiary bombs. People stood about staring, as if they, like her, could think only of the same structures lit up at night, full of life – unable now to recognize the corpse of a building in front of them. The hundred-thousand-strong military marches along these boulevards had been the dividing line between the world of hedonistic joy and this one of deprivation. Berlin had been born, developed tumours throughout its flesh and was now dying with fluid in its lungs.

'How far is it?' she asked.

'A few minutes.'

The car turned on to Tirpitzufer, bouncing through weals in the road caused by the ice and Allied bombs, and drew up outside the building at number 76–8. Its neo-classical facade had all the austerity and conformity of the Nazi era but without the grand ambition. It was a second-wife of a structure – there to continue the tradition, without any of the expectations that had gone before it. Camouflage netting was strung across the street to obscure it from the air.

The security officers minutely examined the papers that identified her as an Abwehr agent and checked her name against a list of those expected to arrive today. When this, too, approved her entry she was escorted up to the third floor, led along a corridor and shown into a soundproofed meeting room with a window looking down over the street. It contained only a polished table, five wooden chairs, a larger leather-bound chair at the head of the table, a board on which papers could be clipped and a black Bakelite telephone.

After placing a folder containing the fruits of her theft from Beggar on the table, she went to the window and lit a cigarette, letting it burn as she looked down on the people outside. She could hear their thoughts: a mish-mash of continued and unswerving belief in the Führer, Folk and Fatherland from some; an understanding that the war was lost from others. From the rest, there was only helplessness in the face of a brutal destiny. Her cigarette seared down.

When it had nearly burned away a man entered the room. He came in alone, although a younger man appeared to have accompanied him thus far and was now waiting dutifully outside. Admiral Canaris, wearing his naval uniform, sat in one of the discreet wooden chairs, not the leather one, and opened the folder, examining the photographic prints and negatives within. On the wall above him a clock swung its brass pendulum in a regular motion: left, right, left . . . Opposite it was a large framed portrait of Adolf Hitler.

'I expected these days ago, Miss Dubois,' he said.

'The Gestapo were looking for me. I had to remain out of sight for a while.'

'Troublesome people. But you made it in the end. These may prove useful to us,' he said, placing his hand on the envelope.

'Have you seen Parade's latest sked?' She spoke through blue smoke.

'A little more about their invasion planning, but nothing spectacular. However, something has happened that touches on our project. It begins with Sturmbannführer Klaussmann.'

'That man's a pig.'

'Well, he's a roasted pig now. The RAF hit Amiens prison four hours ago and he was inside at the time.'

'Good.'

'Yes, I imagined you would say that. I would like you to attempt to clarify something. Parade alerted the Gestapo to your cell's attempt to free your comrade on the road to Amiens, but I am still unclear as to how he gained that information in the first place. Is it possible that he has a source within Beggar itself?'

'It's possible. But I transmitted the plan to hit the transport to London in advance. So it's more likely his source is in London.'

'Yes, that seems more likely.' He was thoughtful for a moment. 'Now, something else you should . . .'

The admiral's young adjutant entered and handed Canaris a slip of paper. He read it and handed it back. 'Tell him to stay where he is. This is not the time.' The young man left again. 'Miss Dubois, I apologize. As I was saying, something else you should know is that, when the airstrike hit, Klaussmann was interrogating your circuit organizer.'

'Maxime,' she said quietly.

'Maxime. He was arrested in Amiens on information directly from Parade himself. Curious, isn't it, how this man seems focused on having Maxime caught? It seems almost . . . personal.' He studied Charlotte. 'Would you care to know Maxime's condition?' She shrugged. 'Well, in any case, it's actually a little hard to assess, since the object of the airstrike was clearly to free as many prisoners as possible. He is now hiding in a French ditch somewhere – the same for the rest of his circuit, as it happens.' He watched for a flicker of emotion at the news. 'It seems he held out against Klauss-mann for two days, but I'm afraid his resolve was not unlimited.' She placed her cigarette in the ashtray. 'Had it not been for the airstrike, Himmler would have kept it secret that he was in Gestapo custody. Luckily for us, the RAF drew some attention to the prison.'

'Lucky,' she said.

'Well, then. Our best course of action would seem to be to continue our attempt to identify Parade.'

'All right.' She blew a line of smoke out of the side of her mouth. She was certain that Canaris was party to the plan-ning of Parade One – even though he refused to divulge to her exactly what it entailed, beyond that it was a counter-attack to the Allied invasion. What he wanted was the identity of the spy. But Himmler was keeping that information to himself, apparently revealing only that Parade had been watching Reece. 'What will you use Parade for?' Whatever it was, Himmler would not be happy.

'If I need you for any duties, you will be informed, Miss Dubois. It's best not to pry beyond your current responsibil-ities.' He placed the folder in his briefcase and knitted his fingers together on the polished table. 'Bear in mind that I took something of a chance with you. The position of your race is more precarious than ever.' He checked his wrist-watch. 'I have an appointment with the Führer. There is something I am to observe, and he's not the sort of man you keep waiting.' He bade her goodbye and she watched him leave, his young adjutant in his wake.

She waited a minute before leaving too. As she stepped out on to the street Charlotte thought back to her eighteen-year-old self. Goebbels had since closed all the theatres, but the cinemas were still open. Perhaps there was one she could sit in and work out her next move.

She walked a few roads lined with ornate lamp posts, many of them bent in the middle or lying on the ground. Men in once-fine clothes pulled handcarts bearing their few remaining possessions. A pair of women wore black crêpe dresses, clinging to custom as a crutch.

Something rose in the air, a whining sound that warned bombers would be above them in seconds. And something else: palls of thick grey smoke pumped from the ground to hide the city from the aircraft overhead. It seemed the whole city was on fire even before a single plane had been sighted.

A dirty white tram came to a rattling halt and its passengers spilled out, running for cover. Charlotte hurried in the wake of a score of aged people, down some steps into a dank cellar that smelled of urine. The wooden door closed and they were in perfect darkness, listening to the distant thuds and closer shouting. One of the bombs must have hit the building above them, because the ceiling shook and dropped flakes of wood.

'God watch over us!' an old woman began to whimper. 'Forgive us for the sake of your Son.'

'For his sake, be quiet. It's bad enough without you,' a girl's voice ordered her. 'I have to go to the welfare office. We haven't got a single slice of bread. It'll be closed by the time this is over.'

Someone lit candles and, as the soft light glowed, Charlotte saw they were in a chamber with close to twenty others huddled on benches. The room connected to another that looked to have a similar number of occupants. It was impossible to say how many more chambers there were beyond. They were designed like that, she knew, so that if one room panicked, the contagion wouldn't spread to the others.

'Is there another way out of here?' a young man asked.

The girl ignored him and began to sing a song with a childish music-hall rhythm. 'Everything will pass over; everything will have an end. Every December has a May . . .'

Canaris's car came to a halt in some godforsaken field around a kilometre from the cliffs of the northern coast. It had been an eight-hour drive into the night and his muscles were aching. As soon as he hauled himself out he felt the sea salt settling on his skin, carried by a wet haar. He pulled his collar up a little. He was getting too old for such foul weather.

He stepped out to see a few planes idling nearby, including a Fliegerstaffel FW 200 Condor. So the Führer had arrived. Canaris steeled himself a little. Two members of Hitler's personal guard armed with Werke sub-machine guns saluted him, and he returned their salute.

'Heil Hitler.'

'Heil Hitler.'

'The Führer requests the admiral's presence on the viewing platform.'

'Lead the way.' They took him by red-tinted torchlight to a wide platform held up by scaffolding. A clutch of eight or nine figures was already aboard it, lit amber from an unseen source. Canaris walked over and, politely declining the offer of aid, climbed the metal ladder. Each step clanged out as he rose up, cursing the weather again. A couple of flaming torches were burning at the top – an unnecessary bit of Munich-rally-era theatrics, he felt – allowing him to make out all the faces he had expected to see and had seen up close more times than he cared to remember: Hitler himself, Himmler, Jodl, Rommel and a few other assorted Wehrmacht luminaries. And one more: Otto Skorzeny was the only one wearing camouflage fatigues rather than a heavy overcoat. Black in the firelight, the long, deep scar that ran from the left side of Skorzeny's mouth almost to his ear made his face more unattractive than it had been before.

Skorzeny was watching a scene played out in the shallow valley between them and the coastline. A model Allied camp, complete with command post, vehicles and anti-aircraft defences was being picked out piece by piece by a roving red searchlight.

'Heil Hitler,' Canaris said, raising his arm. The Führer flipped his palm over his shoulder. 'I apologize for my lateness. A matter I had to attend to overran.'

'No matter,' Hitler said, as he returned to scanning the camp in front of them with a pair of field glasses, following the moving scarlet beam as it alighted on a Sherman tank – a model, Canaris presumed – and then a large wooden hut that looked like a communications post. There were soldiers in the camp too – some were mannequins, but there were at least fifty corporeal men milling around, some patrolling the exterior, wearing American uniforms. Canaris guessed they weren't really POWs but civilian prisoners dressed in the clothing as practice targets. Skorzeny stepped forward and bowed. Canaris reciprocated, his bow a touch shallower than the younger man's. 'Skorzeny, will you instruct the admiral?'

'Yes, my Führer,' he replied. 'But I think the admiral is about to see for himself.' He pointed further along the valley to where black shapes were speeding through the dark. The searchlight swung around to make them glow red like the torches. Twenty jeeps were racing through the dark, men's faces crowded into them, ten in each vehicle, it seemed. Their engines had been muffled but still whined, and the smell of their petrol fumes seemed to sweep up and over the watchers on the platform. Without apparent cause, every one of the patrolling guards fell to the ground. 'Silenced weapons,' Skorzeny told the men on the platform. They mumbled approval.

'Who are the defenders?' Canaris asked.

'Undesirables.'

In the distance a few of the men in the camp stopped still, seemed to understand what was approaching and then began to sprint away from the incoming vehicles, dropping weapons and helmets as they ran. Scores of troops jumped from the moving jeeps, which crashed through the camp, knocking down posts and tents. A few of the incoming soldiers leaped straight on to the escaping men. Canaris noted one shadow flit between tents, apparently unseen by the attackers, and scramble under the fabric side of a tent to hide inside, before one of the incoming soldiers with a large pack on his back ran over and stopped to listen. He shouted something into the tent – a recognition sign, it seemed – then slit through the fabric with a knife and slipped inside. Canaris heard the man within scream, then the attacker dragged him out. The roving red beam fell on them as the attacker seemed to calmly draw his knife through the man's neck until it lolled to one side and the soldier tossed him to the ground.

'They've been assigned specific targets,' Skorzeny informed the men on the platform. 'They have located them all.'

Canaris heard sharp whistles, and the men, as one, ran out of the side of the camp. The whistles were immediately replaced by the diesel sound of panzer engines. He hadn't seen the five gross metal beasts which emerged from dark camouflage netting to speed into the camp. But instead of the rattling carnage sound of their machine guns, the turrets were shooting horizontal spits of flame a hundred metres long. When the jets hit the tents and wooden huts they exploded into fireballs, consuming all around them. Canaris gazed up at the yellow-tinged sky.

After half a minute there was little left but burning debris. A couple of voices in the camp were crying out, their strangled sound carried on the wind.

'Ninety-eight seconds,' Skorzeny announced to the assembled watchers. 'And we can get that down.'

'The Flammpanzers?' enquired Canaris.

'First the commando assault, then the deception phase, then the Flammpanzers will come in to ensure there will be no prisoners we have to feed.'

'Your men have taken Pervitin?'

'They could go for days.'

Hitler was listening to their discussion without comment. 'No doubt. No doubt,' Canaris replied. 'What is the latest regarding Parade?'

Himmler chuckled. 'Our man seems to have an aspect of genius about him.'

'I'm glad. What form does this genius take?'

'He has identified a secretary at the British Army Intelligence corps with Communist sympathies. This woman now believes she is passing vital information to Moscow in order to ensure that the future of Europe is red.' Himmler laughed out loud. Canaris had to give Parade his due – it was a delicate move.

'And what has she told us?'

'The Allies are still planning for an amphibious landing in the summer. As soon as the precise locations and the army Order of Battle are decided she'll pass us the names and mission objectives of every officer from Eisenhower down.' Canaris could smell Himmler's breath. It smelled of garlic. 'Skorzeny's commandos will clear the path for the Parade One deception to deploy. With the information from Parade's new source, our units will take control of the artillery without too much trouble. We now expect a kill ratio of around fifty per cent of their infantry, forty per cent of armoured brigades.' He stepped back, allowing Canaris to see Hitler's eyes locked on his own, searching for something. 'You agree, of course, Admiral?'

'Yes, Reichsführer.'

Much as he would have liked to disagree, Canaris saw that Himmler's plan had been well conceived. There were thousands of Skorzeny's men in French barracks, pressing rounds into magazines, waiting only for the enemy to come into view. Canaris watched two hundred of them hunting through the camp for anyone or anything left to kill.

When it is all over, we will have to keep these wolves in cages, Canaris thought to himself. *Before they devour their mothers and their fathers.*

The soldiers in the camp regrouped. A squad of three broke away and started jogging over to the observation platform.

'Would you like to meet some of the men?' Himmler asked Canaris, shooting the Führer a quick glance lit by the flames.

'I would indeed.'

The squad arrived and scaled up to the wooden platform as if they were walking on the street. They stood, stinking of sweat, their guns in their hands. One's chest was soaked in dark, sticky fluid.

'Heil Hitler!' they declared, snapping to attention. The Führer watched them.

'Men,' Skorzeny called to them. 'You did well. Fast. Now I introduce to you Herr Admiral Canaris.'

Canaris lifted his hand, ready to return a salute. But it never came. Instead the three men raised their silenced pistols and pointed them directly at his chest. He froze. Skorzeny strode in front of him and their eyes met.

'Wilhelm Canaris, I arrest you for treason against Adolf Hitler and the German Reich.' He punched hard into Canaris's stomach, crumpling the older man to his knees like paper.

'My Führer . . .' Canaris groaned, unable to think how to continue: Plead? Deny? Out of the corner of his eye he saw Himmler break a smile and Hitler raise his binoculars once more to view the defeated camp in front of them all. Skorzeny grabbed Canaris by his hair and wrenched his head up. Canaris's spectacles fell to the wooden floor and he could see only blurring figures. 'I have –'

Himmler strode over. 'You think I don't know what you are planning? You think I haven't been watching?' He nodded to Skorzeny, who pulled a pair of steel handcuffs from his pocket and shackled Canaris's wrists together. Canaris felt his heart beating irregularly. It occurred to him that he might be having a heart attack. He guessed what was coming soon, and it might well be preferable if his heart stopped beating now. He began crawling towards the edge of the platform. The fall wouldn't kill him instantly, but it might halt his heart. Then a hand, too strong to be Himmler's, took hold of his collar and jerked him back. A car drove up and a man jumped out, leaving the door open. A black hood was pulled over Canaris's head. He heard Himmler's voice. 'Just wait, Admiral. It will come.'

PART THREE

CHAPTER 23

Marc Reece lay on his bed, looking out at a London sky. The blue expanse was pricked with white barrage balloons. When he had first left the city for France they had been numerous. Now they were a contagion. As the morning spread, the promise of a true summer to come was noticeable in the heavier air.

He had spent many mornings staring listlessly through the metal-framed window since he came back from France. It had been deep winter then and the fingers of the oak tree outside had dripped day in, day out from the rains. But over the months he had seen them bud red-brown with the spring breeze then burst into waxy green as summer sun forced through the recalcitrant clouds so they now provided thick hiding spots for crows and magpies.

He had watched the first changes as he recovered from his injuries – those inflicted by the German whips and those by the bricks that fell on him when the bombs dropped. When he felt able to, he had started seeing people socially, trying to return to some sort of normality, even if it were just for an afternoon. Some of his old friends from the private boarding school in New Hampshire were over, stationed along the south coast and desperate to see London and the old, quaint English villages. 'How're the proper English girls treating you?' one had asked. 'Being friendly enough?'

'They are,' he replied.

He thought of Charlotte from time to time, but less than when he first arrived back. He had made an effort to divert himself from those thoughts.

And, undoubtedly, in 1944, Britain was a happier nation than France. Yes, the rationing was the same, but the police patrols were far fewer and less threatening. The plays and books were largely uncensored and free to poke fun at anyone – even, within reason, the armed forces. And there wasn't the anger and humiliation that rang on the paving stones of every street in every town across the Channel. Instead, there was a belief that destiny was finally on Britain's side.

Loose lips, they had been told, sink ships, and most newspapers had been circumspect about reporting the fact that hundreds of thousands of men – British, Commonwealth, American, and free forces from the occupied nations of Europe – had thronged the towns of southern England one week and seemingly disappeared the next. But many lips were discreetly talking of ships and of landing craft and gliders to convey troops behind the German lines. They were talking of a final confrontation with the Nazis.

The very minute Reece had arrived back, he had informed Delaney of what Luc had seen in the photographs: that Parade One was a land-based counter-attack against the bridgehead; that Parade was a Fascist recruited before the war; and that an address, 2, rue de l'Église, was to be used as a training point for the op. Then there was what Charlotte had told him earlier and he had already transmitted: that Parade had killed a British official.

Luc himself had turned up two weeks later, having come via Spain, but had been unable to add anything to the intelligence.

It was then that Reece told Delaney he wanted to go back and see it through. 'You're exhausted,' Delaney had replied.

'You're not ready for the field. You need to rest. Get your head straight. You're a timer down to the last second.'

He argued, of course, but Delaney was adamant. He wanted to work? Fine. The Finishing School needed good conducting officers who had been in the field. There was a new initiative, joint with the American Office of Strategic Services and the Free French, to drop three-man teams behind enemy lines just as D-Day hit, and Reece's experience would be invaluable.

Without joy, he took the job. It would be a contribution – something, even, to set against the way he had already betrayed them all.

He spent two months filling the new agents' heads with the reality of life under occupation: the sensation of being buried that comes when you can't trust those around you. The grip around your chest as you wake up with a false name ready. He didn't tell them the worst of what he had lived day by day. They probably had vague suspicions. Some were eager; some grim. Few naïve. It was different to how it had been at the beginning, when none of them knew what they were getting into. He wished them luck.

And all the while he waited for word from Delaney that the information he had so nearly died for had led to the German spy. The telegraphed vindication of what he and the others had been through.

But his hope counted for little as, bit by bit, it all came to nothing. It was, said MI5, no surprise that a spy for Germany had a history of Fascism, and they could identify no one in their own ranks or elsewhere who fitted the bill. MI6 managed to find a hundred rue de l'Églises – a clutch of them in Paris alone – but none stood out as significantly more likely than the others as the location of the training station.

And there was no link to a British official's death that Special Branch could dig up. 'It's just not enough,' a superintendent told Reece in Delaney's office. 'A place. A time. That's what we need. We can't put five men on every death of a tax inspector or town-hall clerk. We have other work. I'm sorry.'

Each time the news was relayed to Reece he felt a burst of anger that he experienced as a barely controllable urge to go out into the street and throttle the first person he saw. He told himself that it was the result of his failure to find Parade and to complete his mission. It wasn't, he told himself, the three days he had spent in the pain of death and of death postponed. Nor the self-hatred that gripped his mind because, when the time had come, he had broken and told them what he knew. Each night, he slept for a few hours, waking at slight noises outside or a blade of light through the curtain.

He thought about Parade as he walked down the street, mulling the fact that he could be passing the unknown agent at that very moment. They could have exchanged glances on the Tube. It could have been the man who asked him for a match in the cinema or held the door open at the Lyons Corner House. From time to time he had heard warnings on the radio about vigilance against foreign spies and he had wondered if the man reading that warning had even the faintest idea of what lay behind it.

As Reece's frustration grew he found himself staring at maps of the French coast. Somewhere on this stretch of land falling into the Atlantic Ocean the Parade One units would be waiting with their secret plan to drown the Allied troops in the breaking waves. He stared at the pages until his vision blurred.

But today he had decided on a new course. He would no longer sit around frustrated at Special Branch's lack of progress. They couldn't devote the time to the search, he had been told. But he had so much time to sit and do nothing but think, it was driving him out of his mind.

Dressed in a grey suit, Reece walked quickly to the local library near his flat in Dulwich, south-east London. 'I need to read some newspapers,' he told the steely white-haired woman with outsized spectacles at the enquiries desk.

'Which ones?'

'All of them. For the last two years.'

She sighed and pointed him towards the newspaper room. 'They're bound. You can't take them away.'

'I understand.'

For the next five hours he leafed through page after page, looking for reports of unusual deaths or disappearances of government officials in the London area at least a few months earlier. Whenever he found one, he noted down the location and any details.

So Reece sat in the cold library, watching the lacklustre bulbs drop a little illumination on to people huddling together for warmth around the desks.

Delaney had pointed out that they didn't even know for certain where in Britain the man had been killed. That was true, but if Parade was embedded in the highest levels of British intelligence, he was likely living in the London area. Reece's research therefore came up with three plausible incidents within the previous twelve months: an Air Raid Precautions warden found drowned in a canal in Hackney; a council official who disappeared while assessing damage at a bomb site in Richmond; and a policeman found stabbed in an alleyway in Erith.

'Damn it, Maxime. Leave it to the professionals; 5 knows what it's doing,' Delaney said angrily. They were in the anteroom to his office in Baker Street. His secretary rose and discreetly left.

'How many of them have been a field agent in enemy territory?' Reece returned in the same tone. 'None, I bet. I have. I know far better than they do what to look for.'

'Such as what?'

'Choice of weapon. Location. Something small that you only recognize from experience.'

Delaney glared at him then led the way into his office. A slim man was in the corner, drinking a glass of water. 'This is Huw Evans,' Delaney told him. 'He's our liaison from 5.'

'Hello, Maxime,' Evans said, placing his glass on the windowsill. 'I wanted to tell you in person that we're on top of the investigation, and it's progressing. Of course, any information you can add will be gratefully received and considered. You might find the nugget we've missed.'

'Go through the newspapers, like I did. There must be something there.'

'Leave it now,' Delaney interjected. Reece threw up his hands in exasperation. It was no better than the last war, when aristocratic imbeciles had been chosen to direct battles fought by a hundred thousand men. He went to the window. Outside, a group of nurses were talking to American airmen, sharing cigarettes. Reece glanced suspiciously at Evans. 'Anything you can say in front of me, you can say in front of him,' Delaney informed him.

Something seemed to close over Reece like a cloak. It was the sense of fury at himself that he had come to know as his constant shadow, creeping behind him from the second he woke to the one before he drifted into light, interrupted sleep. 'I told them everything I knew. The invasion points.'

'I know.'

'They'll have sent it straight to Berlin.'

'Yes,' Delaney sighed. 'They will.'

'We could change the plans, make land somewhere else instead. We . . .' He was grasping at straws, trying to quell the anger.

'We've been through this. We can't just change the plans. It's not like we picked the invasion zone out of a hat. We need deep enough harbours for the troopships, wide beaches for the landing craft; it needs to be the right distance from Paris but close enough to England for the RAF to cover us . . . Twenty different factors. You know this as well as anyone. All we can do is attempt to discover what Parade One is – how the hell it involves our warships or that bloody radio frequency – and pray it doesn't cut our boys down on the beaches.' Reece turned away and stared into the corner of the room. In another office someone was talking into a telephone. Delaney paused, considering something. 'Look, there's something you should know. A someone, really. Someone we have in custody.'

CHAPTER 24

2 June 1944

In the towns and cities of France, everyone knew where the Gestapo beat, drowned or shot the foreign agents they caught. The German authorities made a point of advertising – sometimes even exaggerating – their presence as a method of cowing the local population into passivity. But the people of London rarely wondered where captured German spies were held and interrogated.

Reece stood in front of a grand stucco mansion. Numbers 6–8 Kensington Gardens had been built to house dukes – prime ministers, even. And now in its five interrogation rooms and thirteen cells it held the failed agents that Germany had sent to Britain by parachute or via ship from neutral nations. Its wartime name – the London Cage – was probably a deliberate ploy to tell its new inmates that their stay would be brutal.

Reece was wearing his uniform, that of the Naval Intelligence Division, for the third time in three months. The first had been for his full debriefing on arrival in Britain; the second when he had been decorated. He could barely remember what medal had been pinned to his chest. He thought one day he would care a little more than he did now.

Evans stood beside him, smoking the last of a gasper. He finished it and tossed it to his side. 'Right, let's go in,' he said. A Blue Cap military policeman on sentry duty opened the door and Evans led the way in through a linoleum-floored lobby that had once been expensively decorated. Slivers here and there of thick wallpaper told of what the house had been and who had lived in it before it had been handed to the War Office.

The sentry, whose knuckles were bruised, opened a metal cabinet, selected a bunch of keys and placed it in his pocket before descending a set of steps into the basement. The top of the stairs was guarded by a private with a baton who saluted as they passed. It felt strange to Reece to smartly return the gesture. Had he spent the previous four years in uniform, no doubt it would have been second nature, but he had instead lived as a strange half-breed of civilian and serviceman.

'Mind your head. Ceiling's quite low,' Evans said. Their feet made the wooden steps creak.

At the bottom, the Blue Cap led them through a tunnel-like corridor hewn out of what had probably once housed the washroom and the cold store. It had the musty smell of age-ing wood. 'Worst bloody ones, these,' he said, reaching into his pocket for the ring of keys.

Evans nodded and pointed to the last of three metal-reinforced doors in a row. 'That one. I'll do it.' The sentry handed him the keys. There was a peephole on the door, covered by a metal disc, and Evans lifted the disc to look through. 'All right,' he said.

He selected a key, inserted it into the lock and twisted. But it wouldn't turn properly. He took it out, examined it and tried a second time. It clicked into place. He drew it out, pushed the door open and spoke in a low voice. 'See if you can get anything more,' he said, standing aside.

'Hello, Maxime,' Charlotte said. She was sitting on a low wooden bed attached to the wall. It had a sheet, a blanket and no pillow. 'I thought they would send you.' She spoke in French.

Evans went to the corner of the room, crossed his arms and remained quiet.

'Why are you in Britain?' Reece asked her, simply, in the same language. For a second he felt a flash of that white anger: an unthinking, reflexive fury that seemed to light without a spark. He forced himself to regain control.

'Can I have a cigarette?' He reached into his pocket and drew out a silver case. It had been a present from SOE. Agents were given them as tokens of appreciation, and as valuable items should they ever have to barter for their lives. 'You're still using it.' He lit one and gave it to her.

'Why did you come?' he repeated.

'You know that I worked for the Abwehr. It no longer exists. Canaris has been arrested. He will probably be executed.'

'Are you here to swap sides? Again? The Abwehr recruits you to infiltrate SOE and now it's on its knees you think it's time to change once more?'

She paused. 'No, Maxime. No. I have always worked for Britain. In a sense,' she said. The smoke rose in front of her lips. 'Canaris recruited me. He's as horrified by the prospect of a Nazi Europe as you are. He's been removed because he's been plotting against Hitler. Identifying Parade was part of that – Canaris would have told you about him when we knew who he was. I'm here to help you now if I can.'

'Do you expect me to believe this?'

'I don't know, Maxime, I really don't.' She looked at Evans. 'Do you believe me?'

'The jury's still out,' Evans replied in English.

Reece had presumed Evans spoke French, but it was useful to have it confirmed. The smoke filtered through the air.

'I've lied to you many times,' Charlotte continued. 'I wouldn't blame you if you think I'm lying now. I'm not. We're in England now. It can all come out.'

Reece watched her, wondering if there was any way to tell if her words were honest. After what they had shared, he wanted them to be the truth. But that was the danger: he *wanted* it to be the truth. And so he doubted himself as much as he doubted her.

'Go on,' he said.

'Canaris made me report on the circuit. He wanted to know what your plans were and how close you and the Americans were to invading. I think he was going to give you Parade's identity and the details of Parade One if, in return, you gave him a role in the new government when you defeated Hitler. He wanted the Nazis gone, but he was going to keep it from you until you agreed.' Reece knew from Delaney that this was the story she had told before. Of course, that didn't mean it was true. 'He has files somewhere about the SS too. The crimes they are committing. It's all a crime.'

'How did Parade know about me?'

'I don't know, but it wasn't from me,' she said.

'Can you prove that?'

'You know it couldn't be me. Someone gave you to the Gestapo in Amiens. How could I have known where you were? I had no contact with the circuit then. Canaris said Parade had got the information from a source in London.'

It fitted together. The only ones who had known the plan were Reece, Sebastien and London. She had known nothing of it. But his anger at her for duping him remained, and he wanted to make her feel it. Even if she had never betrayed the circuit to the Gestapo, she had betrayed him in another way. He wanted to turn the screw.

'How do you know about Amiens at all?' he asked.

'From Canaris. He has sources in the Gestapo. He was the one who warned me that the raid to rescue Luc on the road had failed and they would be coming for us. He says Parade has very high-level access. That's why he ordered me to take the photographs when the op failed. I was to save them from the Gestapo. Canaris wanted to identify Parade and inform you, but now he doesn't have the chance. So I'm here.'

'Where are the pictures now?'

'Canaris had them when he was arrested.'

Reece looked to Evans, to see if 5 knew of any conflicting evidence.

'It's possible,' Evans said. 'We've known for some time about Canaris's anti-Nazi sensibilities.' So her story was plausible – but then she had had time to come up with a plausible cover.

'What about the fire at your safe house?' Reece asked.

'I set it to keep the Gestapo away from me while I disappeared. And before you bring up the girl who died there, she was my host's daughter, and don't shed a tear for her. She was spying on me – she had a German boyfriend. Her death was two birds with one stone. I did what had to be done.'

'I was there,' he said. He relived those moments, not knowing if she were alive or dead; if she was in the hands of the Gestapo or giving them orders.

'I saw you.' She lifted her eyes to him. They were dark in the low light. 'You don't know how much I have lost. So many things.'

He wanted time to filter out what could be real from what had to be false. But he didn't have that time. 'Later, when I found you at your family home. Are you Jewish?'

She tucked her hair behind her ear. 'Half. My mother's side.'

Evans piped up from the corner. 'We're believing her on that. We've looked into it — she knows a little Hebrew, the prayers. Canaris has recruited a number of Jews and given them Abwehr papers so they can escape.'

'Hardly conclusive.'

'I could have killed you there,' she said. 'Instead I saved your life and told you all that I knew about the spy.'

'Have you heard any more about him?'

'I've told Delaney everything.'

'So you say,' Evans said in a low voice. 'How do we know you're not keeping anything back?'

'I suppose you don't,' she replied.

'What happened to your mother?' Reece asked.

'Oh, not the Nazis. No, she died before they came. Some of my family, though.'

'I'm sorry.' He was. He thought of his parents' artist friends, fled or taken away, wherever they were now.

Her eyes stayed on his, her pupils shrinking as they took on a faraway look. 'We will live,' she said.

Some of the fight went out of him. He took a place beside her on the bed. 'What do I call you?'

She shrugged. 'What do you want to call me?'

'Charlotte.'

She dropped her cigarette on the floor. 'I prefer it. My real name reminds me too much of the past. It feels like someone else now. I want to help. If I'm out of here, I can do that.'

'Evans?' Reece said.

'I'll speak to someone,' he replied. 'But it's not my decision. There are regulations.'

'I know. I'll wait,' Reece told him. 'What were your orders, when you were recruited to the Abwehr?'

'I was to report back to Canaris whatever intelligence you gained of the Gestapo or SD.'

'Why didn't you inform us when you came over in '42? Tell us who you were and what you had been sent for. Work for us directly, not for Canaris's personal game.'

Her eyes met his. 'I still have family over there. Canaris is protecting them. Was protecting them. You would do the same for your family, I think.'

He nodded, understanding. 'So why didn't you come over as soon as he was deposed? You've had months.'

'I was in Germany when the Abwehr was destroyed. First, I waited to see if he could regain control. They had him under house arrest for a while, then they released him and I thought perhaps he was safe, but when they arrested him again I knew it was all over. I crossed the border to Switzerland and came from there.'

Reece rested his back against the wall and stared at the ceiling. He was tired. He wound his shoulders back, to ease the stiffness. When he shut his anger away, he believed what she was saying.

There was a long silence.

'What's happened in the last few weeks. In the war?' she asked after a while. 'Being here is like being buried.'

'We're driving the Japs out of India. The Russians are still advancing in the East.'

'Good.'

There was a silence while he watched her stand and lean against the wall, her arms folded. 'Do you want anything?'

'A warm blanket. Something to read. I haven't read a book in months.'

Evans cleared his throat. 'I'll send you one. I'll tell the guards that you're with us but we need to clear the formalities. They'll make sure you're fed well, not treated harshly. I think it will take a couple of days.'

'I can wait. I've been waiting a long time.'

A noise rose from outside the cell, the sound of someone kicking a door. Then a maniacally strained voice shouting the first words of a song: *Die Fahne hoch! Die Reihen fest geschlossen! SA marschiert . . .*

It was the Horst Wessel song, the Nazi Party anthem, Reece noted. A German proud to defy his captors. Then there was the jangling of keys, the sound of the metal door swinging open and feet scuffling on the concrete floor.

Charlotte went to the door and gazed at the peephole, covered from the other side. 'It's a strange feeling,' she said. 'To betray both sides at once. To aid my friends by working for their enemies.'

'Do you ever forget who you are really working for?' Reece asked.

'Sometimes.'

'Is that true?'

'Sometimes.' She touched the peephole with her index finger.

CHAPTER 25

Alibi

In addition to your cover background, you must have an explanation ready for every subversive act, however small.

The 'alibi' should be as near the truth as possible, provided that it is not suspicious. Time can be expanded. Dates of events can be transposed. If you do this, make sure you allow for different circumstances on different days, e.g. do not say you had been to the market if there is no market on the day for which you give your alibi, although there was one on the day of the events of which you have transposed.

A few minutes later Evans and Reece stepped out into the street. 'What are your impressions?' Evans asked.

Reece brooded on what had been said. 'I believe her.'

'Yes, so do we. Not without reservations, you'll appreciate, but that's our overall conclusion.'

'All right.'

'Which way are you headed?'

'Charing Cross. You?'

'The same.'

They set off, barely exchanging a word until they reached the huge Victorian station with its sweeping iron ribcage. Evans looked over to the wooden departures board. 'I'm on the 5.47.'

Reece checked the clock above them. It was 5.43. 'Mine's in fifteen minutes,' he said.

'I expect we'll run into each other again, Captain. Look after yourself.'

Reece bid him farewell and watched as Evans hurried towards the platform. He checked the wooden destination board for his own train. He glanced at the 5.47 on platform three, Evans's train. It was calling at Clapham Junction, Balham, Croydon and a few other stations.

Reece stood for a minute, waiting for his platform to be announced, contemplating all that Charlotte had said that day. All that she had revealed of herself. He couldn't help but feel fury at her deceit but pity for what she had lived through.

The board changed and Reece's platform was displayed. He walked towards it, still thinking. As he passed the entrance to platforms three and four he glanced in. He saw the guard raise his green flag and the 5.47 begin to move. Slowly, at first, a walking pace, and then a gentle canter as it departed the station. And yet there was one man left on the platform. Evans. He was sitting on one of the benches some way up the platform, casually reading a newspaper. He had clearly been there a while and was making no attempt to board the train, even though it was still quite possible to do so. Reece was about to call over to him, but then he saw Evans stand, move to the adjoining platform and fold up his newspaper. The train there was just closing its doors. Reece looked up at the platform destination board. And as he looked down the roster of stations, his stomach clenched: Dartford, Slade Green and Erith.

Erith, where a police officer had been stabbed and his body left in an alleyway, the life having poured out of it.

Reece stared at Evans's retreating back. It was probably nothing: a slight coincidence. But . . .

He pulled back, behind a hoarding advertising chocolate that no one had the coupons for any more. And he resolved that as soon as Evans boarded the train he would slip into a rear carriage and follow him, just to observe.

Everyone on the platform boarded the train. Doors slammed closed. Reece was itching for Evans's back to turn so he could just gain the last car. But then the engine whistled and only then did Evans climb aboard, and the train begin to move. There was no way Reece could board without sprinting for it and attracting attention, especially from Evans himself. As it left the station he swore under his breath, angry at his failure.

What now? Delaney had told him to drop it and leave it to 5. There was no chance he would comply with that order. The next Erith train was in twenty minutes from the same platform. He paced up and down the concourse as he waited.

It was an uncomfortable thirty-minute journey, when he caught it, stuffed between servicemen on leave and commuters. Upon arrival, he found his way, with some difficulty, to a dull suburban street that had been the police officer's last known location. There was no sign of Evans, that was sure.

Could it have been in this street that a police officer had interrupted Parade while he was communicating with Berlin? It was certainly a good place for a transmission. Reece knew from France exactly what was required: a quiet road with roof space or somewhere to hang an aerial. All the houses here had attics that would do fine. And a long straight street would allow the agent to keep watch for detection vans.

He looked along the road. The attic windows were all empty. And then a figure passed behind one of them. And something black seemed to be trailing out of it.

Reece began walking to the house.

'Good evening, sir.'

He spun around to see two policemen approaching him, one with a short, neat beard, one clean-shaven. 'Are you looking for someone?' asked the bearded officer.

He didn't want the attention. Not yet, while he had only the vaguest of suspicions. 'It's a bit embarrassing. My friends live in this street. I'm afraid I've forgotten which number.' He checked up at the dark house again.

'Well, tell me their name and we can see if we can find them for you.'

'It's Watson. But really, I'll be all right on my own.'

'It's no trouble for us to check. We'll accompany you as you look.'

'Why?'

'You see, sir, it's the evening and you're calling at people's houses. And something happened in this street or nearby a few months back. So I'm just making sure you really do know people here.'

Reece turned away. 'I've had enough of this,' he said, striding off.

'Please wait, sir,' the officer said, catching him and taking hold of his arm. 'I would like to ask you a couple of questions.'

'Get your hands off!' Reece growled, pulling free. Then he felt the other officer grab him more strongly from behind. Without thinking, he broke the man's hold and raised his forearm, ready to snap it into the first man's windpipe, but caught himself just as his arm began to move. For a moment he had felt his arms bound and his face plunged into freezing water. He gasped for air as the officers pinned him to a wall and pulled his wrists behind his back.

Huw Evans, standing back from an attic window, watched as the handcuffs were locked on Reece's wrists.

'Christ,' he said. 'Cut the transmission.'

'What?' the woman replied, looking up from the Morse key.

'I said, cut the transmission. Now!' She immediately tore away her headphones and turned off her set.

'What's going on?'

'We need to move. Pack up.'

CHAPTER 26

3 June 1944

'I should have you damn well court-martialled,' Delaney growled as Reece sat slumped and unshaven in the chair opposite, having been pulled from the police cells an hour earlier by a pair of Red Cap military policemen.

'So why don't you?'

Delaney stabbed his forefinger on to a single sheet of paper and pushed it across the desk. It was a report from a radio listening station. 'One of our posts monitors an SD station outside Berlin. At 8.15 p.m. last night it transmitted a code that means something like: "Why have you ceased transmission?" Eight fifteen happens to be just when the plods say you were starting a commotion in the street.'

Reece felt a surge of elation. It was a weak connection, but a connection all the same. 'It's Erith, isn't it?'

'It's possible. Don't get your hopes up. We've searched all the houses in the surrounding streets. Nothing yet.'

'Evans was on a train to Erith, after we saw Charlotte. From Charing Cross.'

'And do you know if he got off there?' Delaney asked.

'No.'

'Then it's probably coincidence. And not even much of that.'

'He said he was getting another train . . .'

'Maxime, I know Evans. I've known him for years. He's got a full service record without any question marks over it.

And 5's dogs went through all their people as soon as you brought it to us that Parade existed. He's clean.'

Reece had to admit the evidence was thin. And yet . . .

He shook the thought from his mind for now. They had a real lead to work with. 'What about this SD station?'

'It communicates with one in Paris. In Billancourt, to be precise. That's an industrial area, right?'

'Yes. In the west. Working class – a lot of factories.'

'Well, the maps show a rue de l'Église there. The street's mostly warehouses. We have one of them under surveillance and we're sending a reconnaissance plane over right now. But we have to get in there. This op seems to be Parade's poisonous offspring, so there might be something that leads us to him.'

Reece stood and paced to the window. He understood the reason that lay behind this conversation. 'You're sending me back,' he said.

'I need you to infiltrate the location, find out anything that tells us what they're planning or anything that could identify Parade.' The river surge of emotions was chaotic: trepidation, yes, but heat at a chance to return to the Germans, in some form or another, what they had inflicted on him over the course of three days in Amiens. 'Hélène and Thomas are back in Paris. She's attached to Schoolmaster circuit. Thomas is unassigned. We'll let him know you're coming. Make contact and execute the op. Find out what you can, then Hélène can have it transmitted.'

He thought of the previous day in the Cage. 'How plausible is what Charlotte said about Canaris?'

Delaney shuffled a few papers on his desk. 'We've been in contact with the admiral for years.' Reece was astonished, but betrayed little of it. And she was telling the truth. Blameless? No, she was far from blameless. But she had had a reason for what she had done. What he felt had no name, but relief flowed below its surface. 'He wanted Hitler dead and buried as much as we did. He's done us a few favours. I can't go into too much detail, but he's provided some first-rate intelligence about troop movements and German influence in neutral nations: Spain, Switzerland. Helped us know whom we can trust there, and whom we can't.'

'You believe her when she says Canaris inserted her into the circuit to keep tabs on our invasion plans, and she stole the photographs so he could trade them for immunity and a role in the post-war government?'

'Just the sort of thing he would do. He has principles, but looking after himself seems to be high up the list. We have one of his anti-Nazi circle over here now, trying to make a deal.'

'What sort of deal?'

Delaney studied Reece. 'They remove Hitler and his cadre and we leave Germany in possession of its conquered lands to the east. To act as a bulwark against Soviet expansion.'

'Then her story fits.' He wanted it to fit. 'What reports do you have of Canaris now?'

'It's not looking good for him. The Reich Main Security Office has taken over. A pity for us.'

'The deal Canaris's man is offering – will you take it?' Reece asked.

'Not my decision. Thank God. Some people high up are considering it. They're looking at what Europe might look like after the war is over – we can't go from fighting Nazism to fighting Communism in a matter of weeks. That really would mean total collapse.' He knitted his fingers together and rested his chin on them. 'Total collapse,' he muttered. 'No wonder Winston's a lush, with that sort of decision on his shoulders – sending armed men to death or glory is easy;

trading innocent lives for security is far harder.' He pursed his lips. 'Enough of that. You'll go to Paris.'

'Send Charlotte with me.'

Delaney pondered wordlessly for a minute. 'Yes, all right. But watch her.'

Carrying a canvas holdall, Huw Evans took the Underground to Bethnal Green in the East End, lifting his hat to two young women on their way back from a long factory shift. He had taken his wireless operator to a guest house in Bloomsbury, where a single, shabby room would be her world for a few days. Tonight he would be using an alternative means of communication.

The Tube was stuffy with pipe smoke and warm bodies. It had been drizzling almost constantly, so the air was damp too. He was glad to get out of it and back to street level.

In front of him was the York Hall public baths, a solid building of two storeys built twenty-odd years earlier. It was half an hour before closing time, so when he entered the entrance lobby he found only a bored-looking old woman crocheting baby clothes behind a desk. 'One for the first-class baths, please,' Evans told her, passing over a few coins. She counted them meticulously then handed over a small paper ticket and pointed him through.

He passed into a deserted communal changing room, stripped down and took a brown bathrobe, wallet and shaving bag from his holdall, stowing the rest in a shabby wooden locker. The sign for the first-class baths was in a finer script than that for the second-class. There was a distinction even here, it seemed.

Barefoot, he trod through into a large room filled with a deep, light blue pool reeking of ammonia. He padded around it, towards a pair of rooms set in the opposite wall. Steam was filtering out from the one on the left. The other would be the Russian sauna – dry heat. He checked inside this one first. It was empty of occupants. He moved on to the steam room to his side. When he opened the door a wave of steam made his face burn a little. It was a room of substantial size, with pine benches and little puddles of warm water on the floor. Through the thin cloud he could see, at the end, two figures moving quickly apart. He walked towards them.

As he got closer he could make out a thin man in his forties with sparse, damp hair sprawled across a bald pate. The other figure was a blond boy aged perhaps seventeen, drawing himself into a corner. 'Get out,' he said. The boy scrambled off his bench and ran out of the door. Water was dripping from the ceiling and running down white-tiled walls.

The other man stood up. 'That boy approached . . .' His accent was a southern Irish lilt, but that of an educated man.

'Shut up, Ryan, for Christ's sake.' The man stopped moving, and a look of shock swept across his face. 'I couldn't care less who you fuck.' Regardless of what Evans said, the man, Ryan, gathered up what courage he had and began walking carefully towards the exit. Evans reached into his shaving bag and pulled out an old-fashioned cut-throat razor, which he opened out to show the long, curved blade. He blocked the other man's path. 'Don't. Sit down there.' He pointed with the razor to a bench in the middle of the room.

This was already a disturbingly unpredictable moment for Evans, not knowing for certain how Ryan would react. He wasn't happy about using the Fenians as a conduit for his communications with Berlin, but the supposedly neutral Irish favoured a Nazi victory over Britain and would secretly pass Berlin anything they could that would hasten such an outcome. Evans's handlers in Berlin had pointed him to

Ryan as the best contact if he needed to communicate outside his normal method. And the emergency method would make Berlin recognize the efforts he had gone to in order to send the information.

Ryan's lips trembled as if he were attempting to form words, but then he meekly acceded to the demand and sat on the bench, his arms wrapped around himself. Evans opened his wash bag once more and pulled out a small paper packet. He placed it gently on the bench. Ryan stared at it. 'That's right, you can pick it up,' Evans told him. Ryan's fingers went nervously to the package. 'Open it.' He still had the razor in his hand. Ryan opened the packet and pulled out three photographs. His eyebrows lifted as he stared at them in bare comprehension. 'I want you to send these to Berlin.'

Ryan stared up at Evans. 'I . . . I don't . . .' he stammered. 'I work at the Irish embassy. I . . .'

'I don't have time for this, Ryan. Send them to the SD.'

Ryan stopped speaking and a smile broke out across his face. 'Who are you? No, I understand. No names. What is this?'

'Look at it.'

Ryan looked more closely at the photographs. Two showed maps, and one was a document divided into two columns, marked 'codeword' and 'clear' – a list of codewords to be used during the coming beach landings: landing points, ships and regiments. If the Germans were monitoring the Allies' radio signals, they could precisely follow the progress of the invasion and work out the weak points.

'Sir,' Ryan said happily, 'this will do us a great service. Defeating the Brits –'

'Be quiet. You think I'm doing this for your shitty little rebellion?' He paused. 'How many potatoes does it take to kill an Irishman?' He waited. 'None.' He smirked, watching for a reaction. 'Quite good, isn't it?' Colour rose in the seated man's cheeks. 'How long to get it to Berlin? Can you transmit?'

'Transmit, no. But I can have it on an aeroplane to Dublin in the morning, I would say. I will have to find an excuse, but that's . . .' He saw the impatience in Evans's face. 'And they will take it straight to the German embassy. I expect it will take them no more than six hours to get it to their government. All in all, less than eighteen hours, I would say. Will you . . .'

'Tell them that by the end of tomorrow Parade will have access to the full Order of Battle.' The man's eyes widened again. 'Be here. Have a plane waiting and the German embassy ready to receive it.'

'Yes, I will.'

'And something else. Pass on a message: the SOE agent named Marc Reece will be paying a visit to Paris soon. Tell them to spare nothing to find him. Do you understand?' The man nodded rapidly, his eyes fixed on the weapon still in Evans's hand. 'I said, do you understand?'

'Yes, yes. I understand.'

'Good. Don't fuck this up.' Parade lifted the razor very slightly. 'Clear?'

'Yes. Clear. It's clear.'

Evans eased the razor back down. Without another word, he left the bath house. He stopped outside to light a gasper. Truth be told, he couldn't stand these absurd, sophomoric theatrics – he was hardly going to spread a minor diplomat's arterial blood all over the walls and bring the police running, but it was probably necessary in order to tell this cowering little man and his Pope-fellating friends that Germany's agent was committed right to the end. So they had better be committed too.

He slowly looked back at the white building. The Irishman would be hurriedly dressing, repeating the messages over and over in his mind, making sure he didn't forget a word, hoping this would bring triumph for the cause and fame for himself.

And what will you do when we succeed, my Irish friend? You have sown the wind. Will your whole nation reap the whirlwind?

CHAPTER 27

4 June 1944

'You two must be important,' said a fat, leering lieutenant-commander as Reece and Charlotte climbed into the fast Motor Gun Boat in Plymouth harbour late the next morning. The rain was pouring down. 'We had to be rerouted for this.' He held out an oily hand for Charlotte as she stepped down on to the deck, barely visible in the dark. She politely ignored it. 'Lots of funny business about right now. Seen them boats made outta cardboard in Dover harbour?'

'No.'

'To keep Jerry confused about when and where we're coming, I heard.' He looked to Reece for comment but gained none. Reece had had too much practice at keeping his mouth shut to reveal all to a minor naval officer. 'All right, I know, I know.' He looked out to sea. 'Leading Hand!' A young man came quickly from the rear of the boat. 'Get our two guests a couple of oilskins. We don't want them freezing on the way over. Some hot drinks too.'

'Thank you,' Reece said.

'It won't be a pleasure cruise – bloody tight storm out there,' said the boat captain as he peered out to sea. 'Ever been on an MGB?'

'No.'

Charlotte shook her head.

'Well, we're bloody quick. Like a rat up a drainpipe. We'll be going twenty-five knots, so get below and hold on.'

'Do you understand the mission objective?' Reece asked. 'If we see an enemy vessel, you are not to engage it. We have to lie low.' This op was more important to Reece than any he had been on. Ten times a day he still felt the sting of how he had betrayed his fellow agents, the millions of men and women fighting the Reich, and his own years of sacrifice, when he had talked. This could reverse some of the shame and damage. It was a shot at redemption.

'I've been in this game for a few years,' the hefty captain replied. 'I'll get you there. By hook or by bloody crook.' Reece understood that the man looked buffoonish but was determined to fulfil his duty.

He and Charlotte went below and kept as warm as they could while the engines started up and drove them out into the open sea to bash through high grey waves. Bristling with weapons – cannons, machine guns and depth charges – the gun boat was heavy for its size, but the engines were powerful and busted the vessel through the water at a speed that would make it hard for any boats in the Kriegsmarine to catch.

The straining motors made the metal floor thrum underfoot and their throats tasted the diesel fumes mixed with salt from the air. They were given hot tea and glasses of rum to keep out the cold.

At a wooden table bolted to the floor, Reece took two RAF aerial reconnaissance photographs from a pocket in his backpack. Also within were a set of lock picks, a camera, a pair of dark glasses, a small battery-powered microphone connected to an earpiece, two large glass phials containing powders – one red-brown, the other white – and a thin strip of metal about thirty centimetres long.

'Delaney wanted us to make contact with Thomas, and then the three of us hit the warehouse. After that we RV with Hélène and she has the intelligence transmitted. But that's a wrong move – it's safer if I infiltrate alone. So we'll go straight there and contact Thomas and Hélène afterwards,' he said as the boat heaved and rolled. 'The warehouse is on the riverfront in Billancourt. The Free French have scouted it for us. The building's square – maybe fifty, sixty metres each side. Flat roof. Two storeys.'

'Entry points into the compound?'

'Single. The front gate, guarded by four uniformed soldiers. This post of theirs is raised a couple of metres off the ground.' He pointed to a guard post. 'Another guard makes rounds from time to time. The *réseau* had a peek in when the gates opened but saw nothing useful. The road itself is a bit of a backstreet.'

He pointed it all out on the photographs, taken by a reconnaissance flight and passed on by Delaney. They showed the square warehouse surrounded by a high fence. On one side was a large courtyard. There was a normal-sized door into the warehouse, and next to it a very wide sliding door for vehicles.

'Are you going over the fence?'

'It's too risky. Barbed wire, and the guards can see it from the front. But the French have found one way in that the guards can't see from where they are.' He tapped a point in the middle of the courtyard. 'There's a drain here for the run-off in the courtyard. It empties out into the Seine. The *réseau* checked the outlet and it's wide enough to get through. But it's barred.'

'You'll cut the bars?'

'It would take an hour to saw through. I'll have to use these.' He held up the glass phials of powder. 'Thermite. I just need you to distract the guards at the front. They'll be bored and looking for any distraction.' From a side pocket in his bag he took a pair of time pencils – SOE's specialist detonators, which looked like innocuous small metal pipes – and two tennis balls. He opened a hidden split in the rubber to reveal what was inside. 'They're flares. Good for one minute. There's an empty house opposite. Cover the flares in wet newspaper to get some smoke going. The timers are set to three minutes. Make sure you're clear.'

She nodded. 'Are you sure you don't want a weapon?'

'We can't. We'll be breaking curfew and there's a fair chance we'll be stopped.' He wished he could have taken his Colt, but a gun would have increased the danger. And infiltration in daylight would be too risky.

'If you don't come out?' she asked.

He lifted the glass of rum to his lips. It had left a slick of moisture on the nicotine-stained and metal-scratched wood. 'Get back to London as soon as you can.'

'All right.' She met his gaze. 'Do you trust me now, Maxime?'

The question was as insidious as a chemical in the blood. She didn't expect the truth, of course. She was just testing what he would say, how he would act. 'Do you think I should?'

'I can't make you. But I want to know what you'll say to me in return. I want to know if you'll lie to me. I think I want you to lie to me. Lying can be a kindness.'

'Perhaps.'

'No more than that? You won't answer the question? Well, another that you won't answer: do you think you will ever forgive me for what I did?'

'Working against me?'

'It wasn't against you,' she corrected him. 'It was with you but without you seeing it.'

He knew she was right. But he still wanted to punish her. To turn the screw. 'You can dress it however you like. It was still a trick.'

'It was a necessity.'

'You could have told me.'

'I couldn't have –'

He grabbed her wrist. 'No! You could have done. I would have seen to it that you and your family were safe,' he whispered angrily.

Her eyes flared. 'Don't be an arrogant fool. It's dangerous.'

He let go of her wrist and took a pace back. They stared at each other while they both cooled down. 'Let's try to get some rest,' Reece said, taking control of his voice.

He struck a match and lit the corners of the two photographs, dropping them into a metal pail as the boat continued to rise and fall. Every time it took a big wave head-on they would lift into the air and thud back down to the rock-like water below when they had cleared it.

After a while they saw the round moon appear through the Plexiglass. And then, sailing across it, the masts of the French ketch that would take them to the coast.

After transferring to the fishing boat they slipped through the heavy afternoon rain.

Later, close to Brest on the coast of Brittany, they clambered into a dinghy, and were taken to a deserted cove. From there they walked to the railway station hand in hand like the first time that they had arrived in France together, and caught a train to Paris.

Close to its destination, the train rolled past a column of German military vehicles full of soldiers. Reece noted the battle-hardened look they wore.

CHAPTER 28

Detective measures
Agents provocateurs. Sometimes after small fry (black marketeers, etc.).
More dangerous ones provoke subversive talk (by violent Nazism as well
as by pretended patriotism), offer services, pose as members of subversive
organization, ask for help as RAF pilots, escapers, etc., trap friendly
police who let them pass control with arms, bogus clandestine newspapers.

5 June 1944

In the darkness before dawn, their footsteps rang off cracked
pavements in Billancourt, western Paris. A seller of black
bread rolls walked disconsolately past them, wordlessly offering his wares on a wooden tray. 'We don't have any money,'
Charlotte told him.

They turned into a short road with five or six warehouses,
the rears of which must have looked out on to the wharf. A
dog was pawing through a heap of rubbish and it whimpered
and trotted away when it saw them approach. Reece immediately saw which building was the target. Four German
soldiers in Waffen-SS uniforms stood in front of a gate that
was wide enough for a lorry to pass through.

They walked straight past to the next corner. Reece
reached into a buttoned pocket inside his pack. He drew out
and swallowed a pill, watched by Charlotte. Within a minute
the tiredness left him and he felt like running, but the Benzedrine washing over him wasn't clean, it was full of grit.

From there Reece carried on around the block, leaving Charlotte in place to divert the guards' attention.

He strolled down to the wharf front and carefully picked his way along the shoreline, past industrial relics: mooring points and rusting metal cranes that had once lifted heavy goods from barges. He gazed across the water to the heart of Paris. Without wanting to, his mind travelled back to when he was a boy and had walked along the water's edge, with friends, with a girl, when things were better. They had to be better again soon.

After checking around he knelt and grabbed some dirt from the ground, smearing it across his face and hands as camouflage against the dark, before creeping forward until he was behind the warehouse's riverside fence. It wasn't hard to spot the drain on the riverbank that took away the rain-water from the warehouse courtyard. It was concrete and less than a metre wide but with a thick steel bar across the middle, preventing all but a child from shimmying up it. Reece took the two glass phials and unscrewed their tops. The red-brown powder was iron oxide – rust – while the whitish powder was aluminium. He poured them both on to a sheet of paper, carefully mixed them, then poured the mixture back into the phials. He tied each phial on top of one end of the bar. He took the strip of metal – magnesium – divided it in two and inserted the two lengths into the mixtures. Then he put the dark glasses over his eyes, drew his cigarette lighter from his pocket and lit the end of the magnesium ribbons, and stepped back three paces.

The magnesium flared with a blue-tinted flame. A few seconds later the flame hit the mixture of rust and aluminium and, as it did, a flash erupted, the glass phial exploding. The brightness of the thermite reaction hurt Reece's eyes behind the specially treated glasses and he felt the intense heat – thousands of degrees high – on his face. The flame was so bright he couldn't see the mixture within it, but almost immediately he saw the steel bar begin to melt underneath the core of the flame. In less than ten seconds the thermite had melted right through each end. With a thud, the middle part fell to the ground. As the remaining thermite dripped on to the wet bottom of the pipe, it flared once more, cracking the concrete. Reece put the glasses away, waited for the reaction to die down then smothered it with mud.

He crawled into the wet pipe, lighting the way with his pencil torch, hoping there would be no bend or kink to squirm around. Luckily, it proved to be straight, slanting up to the ground. It was a foul crawl, but he had been through worse. About fifteen metres along, he could make out what had to be the drain inlet. He dragged himself underneath the iron grille, through which water was dripping. He waited, listening for the sound of footsteps. There was a sound, indistinct, that came to him distorted by the concrete passage – distant shouting, perhaps – but it died away. He stretched up and gently pushed the heavy iron grille away. Then, carefully, he lifted his head through.

He found himself looking at the heels of two black leather army boots. The guard had his back to the drain entrance. Reece immediately drew back down, watching the grey-clad legs. He had to decide what to do. The grille was still out of place and he was exposed. He gingerly reached up, but then stopped. The guard was beginning to turn around. Reece got ready to retreat down the pipe. But then something made the guard turn back. Shouting. Faintly, Reece heard the word 'Fire!' It had to be the flares set by Charlotte. The guard muttered, '*Scheisse,*' and dropped a cigarette end before striding away.

Quickly, Reece hauled himself up, quietly replaced the grille and ran to the rear of the building. So far, it was working.

All the windows on the building had been boarded up, no doubt to stop anyone looking in as much as to prevent light escaping during blackout. The warehouse had a door that would have led on to the riverfront, had the fence not been there, and Reece set about picking the ageing lock. When the tumblers fell into place he opened the door a fraction, saw all was dark, and stepped in.

It proved to be a short, empty corridor with metal stairs leading to an upper floor – where the offices were, Reece suspected. That would be the primary goal. He climbed noiselessly to find a landing with two doors, both bruised and scraped. There was no sound from either and he pushed the first open to be met with an unpleasant smell. By the light of his pencil torch he saw he was looking at a foul latrine. He pulled back and went to the other door, where a dim light was leaking around the edges. As he opened it, he made out a neat office and a candle burning on a wide, untidy desk. Beside it was a bottle of schnapps and, right behind it, a man was slumped in a plump chair, his eyes closed. He was using his jacket, which bore the insignia of an SS rifleman, as a blanket.

Reece had no weapon except his lapel knife. He drew it and held it ready, carefully listening to the man's breath. It was deep and long, faintly snoring. Reece would have liked to search the room, but the sleeping man was too much of a risk, so he eased himself back and drew the door towards its frame. As it moved into place, the hinges emitted a short, sharp whine. Reece stopped and watched the German, waiting to see if the breathing would change. By the orange candlelight Reece could see he was a big, barrel-chested man who had squeezed into his uniform. To his relief, the deep breaths continued just as they had. He began to back out. And then the man's eyes flicked open. In the warm light they were a watery grey and they fixed on Reece in a moment.

'Sorry, I was looking for the latrine,' Reece said in German. For a moment, the man in the chair looked confused and pointed out, towards the other door. But then his line of sight fell to the knife in Reece's hand. Reece knew it was time.

The soldier jumped up and threw himself at Reece. But as he did so Reece pulled the door further towards himself, bracing it with his foot, and the rifleman crashed into the wood, rebounding off it and staggering back. Reece stepped forward, his knife tip pointing at the German. The big man responded by grabbing a solid-looking wooden stool and hurling it effortlessly at Reece's arm. It smacked his hand open, knocking the knife somewhere under a cloth-covered table. The soldier glanced to his side and Reece saw where his gaze was heading: a pistol in a holster a couple of paces away. The German went for it and Reece charged forward. The soldier had his hands on the gun when Reece landed within arm's reach of him, spun on his left foot and stamped with his right on to the German's knee. Even without the cracking sound Reece knew he had fractured the bone. The trooper froze for a moment, both hands on the leather holster, his face blank in amazement, before crumpling to his side, falling with a cry of anguish on to the broken joint and knocking over the candle. Its light extinguished with a wisp of smoke.

In the dark, Reece grabbed the man's thick hair and brought his knee up hard into the temple, stunning him more. Then he clamped his right elbow under the German's chin. He seized his own wrist with his left hand and tightened the grip on the man's neck, cutting the carotid artery, restricting the flow of blood to the brain, tighter and tighter, until there was no flow at all. He felt the trooper desperately struggling, his hands clutching faintly at Reece's arm. He fought hard, but Reece felt him growing weaker by the second. After half a minute the struggle became little more than a shuffling, and then it stopped altogether. Reece listened for breath, but it had ended. He let the German slump to the floor in the blackness. He checked the man's wrist and then his neck. There was no pulse.

By the light of his torch Reece dragged the body behind a large trunk and stowed the gun and jacket there too. The guard gone, he began to search the room. He looked over the desk, but the only papers were unimportant chits for rations and fuel. Two of them were authorized with a small, tight signature. Reece looked at it and his eyes narrowed. It was a name he knew. Otto Skorzeny's rescue of Benito Mussolini had been trumpeted in the controlled French newspapers as much as in the German press and now his name had turned up in the Paris warehouse. Whatever Parade One was, it seemed that Skorzeny was commanding it.

There was nothing in the drawers except for a few pens and pencils. Given the importance of the facility, that suggested more sensitive documents were hidden somewhere.

He quickly looked around and began pulling the furniture away from the walls. In the corner, veiled by a cloth-covered table, he found a small grey steel wall safe. For once he blessed his luck that the big trooper had woken up. But he still had to get it open. It had a single dial to spin and presumably three numbers to find from the sixty on the dial. Reece examined it closely but there was no clue as to what the combination could be.

He took the small microphone from his pocket, held it against the metal two centimetres to the right of the dial and placed the earpiece to his ear. He turned the dial gently, notch by notch, listening to the tumblers clicking, as he had been instructed at the Finishing School. Each sound was light and thin, until the number thirty-one fell harder. He had one. Then *click click click* the other way and the six slotted into place. A rustling sound above made him catch his breath, but it must have been a bird settling on the roof. And then more turns and the number two locked in. He took the steel handle and lifted. The door opened and he was presented with two buff brown folders. He checked behind him. There was no sign of anyone close, and he pulled out the papers. One contained records for personnel. Reece turned on an electric lamp on the desk and rapidly photographed the records. The men detailed, mostly Waffen-SS but a few from the Heer and Kriegsmarine, and one from the Luftwaffe, had impressive war records. Many had been decorated. Reece replaced the papers and opened the second folder.

Five pages detailed nearly twenty Allied battleships and cruisers that would form the backbone of the invasion flotilla, naming their officers and specifying in detail the range and destructive power of the armaments carried. With that level of detail it could only have come from someone inside the Admiralty. Behind the documents were maps in small and large scale of the French coastline – the maps Luc had seen in the photographs, the maps of the possible invasion points and the German counter-attack plans in each case. The marked beaches were labelled with German regimental numbers, all grouped on the edge of the page as 'Parade One'.

At the bottom a number of lines had been typed – the names of Wehrmacht and Waffen-SS commanders to whom the map had been circulated, it appeared, and expression of the classification level. Below that there was one more point of information: 'Parade to provide army Order of Battle, officers' names and precise regimental objectives upon departure from port, to enable operational activation' stood out in black letters. That meant that Parade – or one of his sources – was in a role whereby he would gain clearance for the Order of Battle as soon as the flotilla started steaming for France.

Reece knew that there would be a precise list of who would be given details of the flotilla and that it would be divided into two classes: those who needed to know before departure and those who didn't need to know until afterwards. The fact that Parade or his source was on the list and in the second category would narrow the search down for 5. But they would still have to find him before he transmitted the information.

Reece photographed the pages under the lamplight. He didn't have much time now. He replaced the folders precisely as they had been and turned the safe dial back to where he had found it.

From there, he stole down the stairway and found a large door on the ground level. He passed through, and a change in the air – colder, harsher – told him he was in a vast room: the main warehouse space.

In the dark, Reece decided to chance his blue-bulbed pencil torch. Its ghostly beam searched through the room. Just below the ceiling a metal gantry ran around the walls, accessed by a series of ladders. The glimmer fell on a few pieces of machinery pushed to the side of the room and on the wide sliding door along the side leading to the courtyard. But the strangest sight was a structure beside Reece. He stared before walking over and right into it, struck by how out of place it seemed, the strangeness accentuated by the blue glow.

It was a perfectly constructed army post set up at one end of the huge warehouse floor, complete with power supply, telephone lines, maps pinned to boards and desks. But what was strange was that all the maps and signs were in English. The officer's jacket slung across the back of the chair was American. He checked the insignia on the uniform: US infantry. It was an American command post in a Waffen-SS training facility. It had to be for training for some sort of sabotage mission, but precisely what that mission would be was not yet clear.

Beside the hut a series of tables were laid out with British and American weapons in neat rows, arranged by size. On the wall there were maps with Allied units marked on them, vectors showing intended movements. Points marked with red pins seemed to intercept the Allied forces close to the coast. Above the maps were large photographs cut from newspapers of the Allied commanders – not just Eisenhower, Patton, Montgomery, but a score of other brigadiers and generals. This seemed much more than the Germans simply knowing their enemy.

Reece looked around and, as he peered to the other end of the warehouse, he saw three metal beasts lurking in the gloom. A Sherman tank with standard American markings sat beside a jeep and a British half-track; they must have been seized in battle – perhaps in Italy or North Africa.

He took a pencil and paper from his breast pocket and noted down the names of the senior officers that the Germans had been learning to identify on sight. He took the camera from his pocket and recorded the scene as best he could with the weak torchlight. He was halfway through his task when he stopped.

There had been a noise – not a single sound but a mixture of small thuds and murmurs. Somewhere in the building there was movement, and it seemed to be coming closer to him. It was approaching from the short corridor he had come down, thus shutting off his primary exit route. He hurried to the sliding door leading to the exterior. There might be guards outside, but he didn't have much choice. He tried to force it, but it was locked. He could hear voices now, and the door behind him began to open.

His only chance was a ladder that led into the metal gallery above.

He had just enough time. He scrambled up the rungs, emerging through the walkway the same second the door pushed open. He pressed himself against the wall. The gantry was a little below the ceiling, perhaps ten metres from the floor. It had wide safety bars at knee and waist height and was strewn with debris from whatever use the building had been put to before the Boche had arrived: boxes, lumps of wood, spools of used and dusty cable. He gently placed one of the spools across his midriff and a tin canister in front of his legs as he turned to watch the entry of whoever was coming in.

A single man, dimly lit by electric lights in the corridor, walked into the room. He stopped, reached into his trouser pocket and pulled something out. A moment later he was lighting a cigarette, and the glow provided just enough warm yellow light for Reece to see that the man's uniform wasn't *feldgrau*. But then he flicked the lighter off, and all that he could make out was the cigarette's smouldering tip as the man went to the side of the room. Reece watched him move into the shadows. And then there was a metallic thump and a line of bright bulbs suspended from the ceiling blazed on. For a moment, Reece was dazzled by the sudden brightness, but his vision adjusted and he looked down to where the man had thrown the master switch. His clothing, indeed, was far from the German grey: it was the olive-green jacket and tan trousers of an American infantry major. The major removed the cigarette from his mouth. 'Get a damn move on, soldiers!' he shouted out into the corridor, in English and with a wealthy New England accent.

Reece's mind raced between possible explanations for the American's presence. It could hardly be some sort of behind-enemy-lines op if the man was in uniform, so was he a POW? There were no camps in Paris. Whatever it was, the prospect of an ally raised Reece's spirits.

Slowly, more men, dressed in the uniforms of American enlisted soldiers, filtered in, babbling in a variety of American accents. They were dragging their feet, bored with their surroundings.

Cautiously, Reece began to stand. But the entry of another man into the room made him freeze. This one was in German uniform and he had a sub-machine gun slung over his shoulder. A guard, it seemed. Yet he was mixing freely with the Americans, who didn't seem bothered by his presence. His suspicions piqued, Reece slunk back to the floor of the walkway and kept watch.

He counted around twenty Americans by the time they were all assembled. Five, in tank crew uniforms, ignored the others and wandered over to the Sherman. They sprawled on it without interest while the others assembled, chatting among themselves. After a minute or two the major called them all together. He seemed to be issuing orders that Reece couldn't hear. Most went over to the command post and discussed the maps. Others went to the arms station and busied themselves dismantling, cleaning and reassembling the weapons. All the time, Reece watched, calculating the risk of waiting or of asking for their help in overpowering the guard and running.

Before he could come to a conclusion the door opened again and another man entered, this time wearing the uniform of a Waffen-SS officer. In an instant Reece recognized Otto Skorzeny. And a new explanation for the Americans' presence began to form in his mind.

Skorzeny nodded to the American major, who commanded his men to halt and stand at ease before beckoning over the tank crew's sergeant.

'Where are you from?' Skorzeny asked, in precise but heavily accented English.

'A state called Utah, sir.'

'Ah, is that where your Mormons are from?'

'Yes, sir, the Church of Jesus Christ of the Latter-Day Saints is very important in our state. But I'm a Catholic myself.'

'Do you have anyone who misses you?'

'You mean a girl, sir?'

'Yes, a girl.'

'Well, I've been going steady with Anne for about a year and –'

The American major interrupted. 'Does Schwartz pass the test, Colonel? Every man has his backstory well practised. Each one is individual and unique to that man.'

Skorzeny thought for a moment then nodded again. '*Beeindruckend*,' he said. '*Viel Glück*, Scharführer Schwartz,' he told the tank sergeant.

'*Danke*, Herr Obersturmbannführer,' the sergeant replied in native German.

'*Sieg Heil!*'

'*Sieg Heil!*' the sergeant repeated, clipping to attention and saluting. Skorzeny clapped the major on the shoulder and left.

'Back to drill,' the major announced in English.

They went back to their tasks. Reece watched one of the men at the command post pick up the receiver on a field radio. 'Hello USS *Texas*, hello USS *Texas*,' he said in a perfect American accent. 'This is Captain Hills of C for Charlie 7. Fire mission. Immediate suppression. Grid 331802. High explosive. Enemy infantry massing for assault at treeline. Two minutes. At my command.'

Reece watched the German soldier impersonating an American officer; ordering a US warship to begin firing on land positions. And it became instantly clear why Berlin needed Parade to supply the army Order of Battle and the names of the Allied officers: the men before him would infiltrate the American command posts, cut those officers' throats and then impersonate them on the Allied communication networks to sow crippling confusion within the landing operation. The transmissions Reece had just witnessed were the practice runs.

Skorzeny had a record for high-risk infiltration raids. He would no doubt lead the op to kill the American officers and assume their identities.

But what was their precise strategy? It wasn't just general confusion, no. The warships' fire missions were key. If the cuckoo officers were to claim the Allied positions were under attack, they could order the huge offshore naval guns to fire on the Allies' own troop positions. It would decimate armour, artillery and infantry.

The deception would be uncovered at some point but it could take hours, with each warning from a genuine Allied officer countermanded by one of the infiltrators. And even then, it would leave the Allied command unable to trust any genuine signals from its own units; since they too could be deceptions. The units would be cut off from the senior field command. That would leave them exceptionally vulnerable to a conventional attack. With big holes smashed in the Allies' defensive lines by their own naval artillery barrage, and the surviving units unable to co-ordinate, a fast-moving conventional assault of the type Rommel favoured would devastate whatever was left. The second front, Reece realized, would be strangled at birth.

The deception ploy wasn't entirely new. The Germans had begun the war with an SS unit dressed as Polish soldiers pretending to attack a German border radio station, thus giving Hitler the thin excuse he wanted for the invasion of the neighbouring land. And in '42 Reece had been briefed on a British raid on the Libyan port of Tobruk. An SAS platoon of German-speaking Jews from Jerusalem had slipped through Rommel's lines disguised as Afrika Korps and armed with captured weapons, their mission being to open the harbour at night to a naval landing. To prepare for the op, they had used German POWs to check details of current slang and cultural references so that they could perfectly masquerade as Nazi soldiers.

But what set the plan he was viewing on a different level to its SAS precursor was its ambition: by crippling the bridgehead at its most vulnerable moment the Germans could entirely prevent the liberation of Europe.

Reece realized bitterly that when he had grinned at the tale in '42, he hadn't considered the possibility that it could be turned on its head. This was the legacy of Parade's treachery.

The American major approached the five or six men who were familiarizing themselves with the weapons. 'Over there,' he said, pointing to a corner of the room. 'We don't have all day.'

'Yes, sir,' an NCO responded.

Reece shifted very slightly and was able to make out a makeshift firing range marked with chalk on the floor and three paper targets stuck to a bare brick wall. The tank crew, sitting a few metres away, got up off their vehicle and sauntered moodily to the other side of the room. The gunmen lined up in threes and dutifully fired the small arms – pistols first, then the rifles and sub-machine guns. Judging by their insouciance, they were all used to the feel of the guns and how they shot. In the enclosed space, each shot exploded and echoed over the last, resulting in a strange wave-like orchestra of percussion.

From time to time the tank crew would clap a fine performance or grumble that they were sitting about doing nothing.

The soldiers were too far away for Reece to see the insignia on their uniforms. Instead, he tried to look for mistakes they made – signs that would give them away. But they seemed perfectly versed in the duties and behaviour of the men they were impersonating. The major noted actions on a clipboard. After the best part of an hour he called a halt to the exercise. 'Good work, men. I'll see Franks and Weber back at the barracks. The rest of you are dismissed.'

They shuffled away without saluting. The major finished his paperwork and followed them out of the room, shutting down the lights. In the full dark once more, Reece listened to his own breath. It seemed so loud now. He waited to see if anyone would return then stretched out his arms to get rid of cramp.

The blood seeped back into his numb legs and he climbed down. The torch's thin beam played on the tank at the end of the room then back towards the command post, which looked far less real in the torchlight, far more like a child's game.

Reece walked quickly towards the door through which he had entered. He couldn't let the SS know someone had been there and discovered the plan, so he crept up the stairs once again to the store room.

Inside the office he dragged the heavy body of the dead rifleman from where he had stowed it, tugged the man's jacket on to his body and poured some schnapps into the soldier's mouth. He lifted the man upright and then, with all his strength, wrenched the man's head to the side and back, snapping the neck. Checking there was no one outside the door, he pulled the corpse out to the stairwell, where he splashed some schnapps on the top step before hauling the body to the bottom of the stairs. He left the bottle a couple of paces away and slipped out the back. This time there was no guard in the courtyard. He descended into the foul drain, wound his way through and emerged at the other end. He tossed the lock picks and small microphone into the river. The camera would be unremarkable to a German patrol; the picks and microphone would not. He found Charlotte waiting two streets away. She threw a cigarette to the ground.

'Success?' she asked.

'Complete. We'll RV with Thomas and Hélène immediately.' Hélène could have a message transmitted to London to warn them about the German plan. Then the Lysander would come for him and Charlotte to take them back and he could hand over the film of the documents he had photographed. The detail of Parade's access to the naval Order of Battle would set 5 on his scent.

They strode away, Reece feeling the flush of success but mixed with trepidation over what he had seen. In every street they paced through he knew there were people huddled in houses bare of heat or food, desperate for the war to be over.

He had been in London for months, but Paris felt more like home and he wanted so much for the city to be free that he would have knowingly given his life for it. Would the contents of his notebook or exposing Parade be enough to win out over the Boche? No, no, it wouldn't. It would take hundreds of thousands of men and tens of thousands of lives. But it would be his contribution. The steps he would take alone towards the German lines.

By 9 a.m. the sky above Paris was black with clouds dropping a sea-like deluge on to the city. The streets ran with muddy water as people dashed from cover to cover. The wind was knocking down young trees and driving the rain sideways. Those caught in it feared the clammy onset of pneumatic fever and stayed in their homes, craving the shelter, even though they were hardly warmer than the town outside.

In the midst of it all Thomas struck a match and lit his pipe as he hurried down a small, soaking passage in the working-class east of Paris towards his flat.

'Hello, Thomas,' Reece said, greeting him warmly from the end of the lane. 'How are you?'

'Fine, fine,' Thomas replied, betraying only a hint of surprise. 'You?'

'The same. Anyway, I've got the drinks for later.' He reached his former comrade and shook his hand. 'It's safe,' he said under his breath, nodding towards the door. It felt so good to see Thomas again, to see him alive and well after the hell of the prison they had both lived through.

'Come in. No time like the present,' Thomas replied. Once they were inside, he threw his arms around Reece. 'Mother of God!' he said. 'I didn't even know if you had got out of the prison.'

'I did.'

'Yes, you did,' he said. 'Yes, you did! My God, when the bombs hit, I . . . Well, I don't have any wine, but I do have some utterly foul schnapps I bought from a sweaty German at the town hall.' He opened a cabinet. The door opened and Charlotte stepped in. Thomas wrenched out the drawer beside the cabinet and spun back. Reece saw the barrel of a Mauser extrude from his hand. They all held their breath. 'Is she with you?' Thomas demanded.

Reece lifted his hands away from his pockets. 'She's with me. We're not armed.'

'Take a step forward.' Thomas carefully patted down Reece's clothes then nodded to Charlotte. 'Now you.' He checked her clothes, then the bag she was carrying. 'Sit down. There.' He pointed to a half-collapsed sofa. 'Keep your hands up.' They did what he said. 'What is this?'

'No different to what you were expecting.'

'Are you crazy? You turn up with her in tow.' He paused. 'Someone betrayed us in Amiens. You must know how it looks.'

It must have looked like Reece had been the traitor all along. 'I had myself arrested and beaten?' he suggested.

'That can be staged.'

'Not so easily.'

'Easily enough,' Thomas retorted.

'No, you're right. Of course the Gestapo could do something like that. But look, I can show you the scars, if you like. Where they whipped me in Amiens.'

Thomas pursed his lips. 'All right, do that. Stand up.' Reece did so. 'Take off your jacket. Slowly. Don't go near the pockets.' Very hesitantly, Reece peeled away his blue workman's jacket. It fell to the floor with a soft sound. He unbuttoned his shirt, peeled it sopping from his skin, tossed it to the side, placed his hands on his head and twisted around. The long white weals through his flesh stood out like lightning. Thomas winced in empathetic pain. 'All right. Yes. But what about her?'

'You were right,' Charlotte said. 'I was working for the Abwehr.' Thomas's finger tightened on the trigger. 'Many of them hate the Nazis and want to wash their filth away. There's a network inside the service. I was one of them.'

'It's true,' Reece added. He outlined what Delaney had told him of Canaris's Janus-like dealing. 'The SD have an agent in London. He has a source in SOE, or 6, or somewhere else. He's been keeping track of us. He was the one who led the Gestapo to us. Not her.'

'How do you know?'

'No one in the circuit knew about the planned op against the prison or where the safe house was. Not her, not you, not Hélène. The SD's spy could only have got it from a source in London. Everything we were planning we told London in advance. That's how it got to Berlin.' Reece could see Thomas's resolve wavering. 'London sent us both. They checked her story from every angle. We're here to reactivate the circuit. You know how close it is.'

Thomas stayed still for a while, his eyes flicking between them. Eventually he seemed to come to a decision. 'All right, all right,' he said. He put the safety back on the gun. 'Jesus.' He seemed tired. Reece knew that feeling.

'It's exhausting, isn't it? Being constantly on edge.'

'You're right there.' Thomas glanced at a cheap clock on the table. 'Radio Londres will be on now. I need to listen for any more coded messages.'

He turned on the radiogram in the corner and it began to burble out strange sentences that would make sense only to the intended recipients in the *réseaux* and SOE circuits:

Angélique has new shoes. Angélique has new shoes. Five and five make ten. Five and five make ten. To dance . . .

Thomas sat back down. 'What do you need from me?'

'We're going out tonight by Lysander, then you need to keep a location under obbo. It's a warehouse in Billancourt, 2, rue de l'Église. The Waffen-SS are using it as a training base. Keep London updated as often as it's safe – at least twice a day. Send a message through Hélène. Can you contact her now?' Reece asked.

I want to see the spring. I want to . . .

'Yes.'

'We need to RV. Where do you suggest?'

'A friend runs a café bar in the fourteenth arrondissement. Café Reine in rue du Moulin Vert.'

'Fine. Can . . .'

. . . with a monotonous languor.

'Wait!' Thomas held up his hand and stared at the radiogram. They all fixed on the words drawled out from London. 'That one!'

Wound my heart with a monotonous languor.

Thomas jumped up and swept his hands over his head. Reece didn't know the meaning of the code, but from Thomas's reaction, he could guess. All across France, men and women were listening to those words and looking to their hidden guns and magazines wrapped in rags.

'It's the ready signal,' Reece said. Thomas could only nod.

'For an op?' Charlotte asked.

Reece's eyes met hers. 'For D-Day. We have twenty-four hours.'

CHAPTER 29

Security is essential for the existence of a clandestine organization, and all responsible members of the organization should constantly be on the look-out for breaches.

After eating some bread and a little porridge the three of them walked to the Métro. Once on the network, they changed direction and lines four times. A search patrol made up of collaborating French police and undercover Gestapo men checked their documents, but they were probably looking for low-level insurgents, such as couriers of the underground newspapers – *Guerrilla, L'Humanité* – or young men avoiding Obligatory Work Service in Germany.

They found the café bar Thomas had named. It was a large place in a busy street: workers on their way to the office or couples to friends' houses. A pair of French policemen sauntered past.

Reece, Thomas and Charlotte entered and took a table near the front. An ageing man with a shock of very blond hair was reading a newspaper behind the bar while four students laughed together in a tight, leather-padded booth in the rear corner. Reece noted a doorway at the back, presumably leading to the toilet, and one behind the counter that must have been to the kitchen. Chipped marble-topped tables and a black-and-white chequered floor said the bar had once been upmarket but had fallen on hard times.

A radio in the corner was playing jazz, violins jumping all around a double bass, a mad snare drum in the background.

Thomas greeted the barman. 'Hello, Jean. How are you?'

'My knees have gone, since you ask. No point going to war against age, though, is there?'

'True enough. You know, I was thinking about Astride the other day. Haven't seen her for ages. Want to see if she's around?'

'Could do. Hang on, I've got something under the grill. Back in a tick.' He went back to the kitchen.

They started chatting about food shortages until the barman returned and nodded that it had been done. 'Thanks,' Thomas said. 'A few glasses of your best red, then.'

'It's my only red,' the man replied, pouring three large glasses of real – if watered-down – wine from a bottle under the counter. Reece was happy to clink them together. He took a long draught of the wine. It really wasn't bad. In fact, if he closed his eyes, he could almost have been back before the war, enjoying a bottle of Merlot with friends and a girl he liked, listening to music before heading out to one of the clubs.

'Let's eat. Who knows if we'll get the chance again?' Thomas said. Reece was hungry; the black bread and porridge earlier had hardly filled his stomach. They checked the menu chalked on a board. It took no time to read: vegetable soup or rabbit stew.

'Rabbit stew?' Thomas asked the barman.

'It's good. My son raised the rabbits himself.'

'All right, I'll have it.' The other two asked for the same, and a glass of beer each. The man took their coupons and went out the back to prepare the food, clanging pots and pans. Charlotte seemed distracted, staring out the window. 'So we're back on active duty?' Thomas asked under his breath.

'We are.'

Charlotte walked over to the front of the café, still staring through the glass.

'Will more be joining us?'

'I can't say right now.'

'Maxime,' Charlotte said. There was a note of caution in her voice.

'Do you think –' Thomas began.

'Maxime!' She was pointing out on to the street. He stood and walked over to her.

'What is it?'

'There's no one out there.'

Thomas stood and stretched his legs. 'I'm going to the toilet,' he said.

The street was, indeed, completely dead. Where just a few minutes earlier there had been couples, a bus and cyclists going past, now it was silent as the grave. And Reece realized that there was no sound from the kitchen. The barman seemed to have left.

Charlotte pointed to her handbag, hanging on the back of her chair. 'In my bag!' she said urgently.

He tore it open and drew the Mauser she must have stolen from Thomas's kitchen. Reece covered the pistol with a newspaper from the bar so that the students in the booth wouldn't see.

'Thomas,' he called over as his friend was about to leave the room. 'Please don't.' He levelled the barrel.

He and Reece stared at each other for seconds that felt like hours, before Thomas's feet began to move, taking him towards the doorway to the kitchen. He must have known he could never make it. And yet he ran.

Reece threw aside the newspaper and pulled the trigger. He tensed his arm for the recoil.

It never came. No bullet cut through the air to tear into flesh. Nothing but a dull metallic click. Reece looked at the weapon. A small sliver of metal was poking from the ejection port – Thomas must have inserted it when he had had the gun earlier, to jam it in case it was taken from him. One of the students, a girl aged twenty wearing a blue jumper, screamed.

Reece dropped the weapon and threw himself at the other man, managing to grab hold of Thomas's jacket and pivot to swing him around. The students held each other and cowered into the booth, yelling pleas not to shoot them. Reece and Thomas slammed into the bar and fell to the ground, struggling, each attempting to free a hand to strike the other.

But then Thomas froze. Out of the corner of his eye, Reece saw Charlotte holding the gun, recocked and ready. He remembered the last time he had been on the ground and she had been pointing a gun.

'Don't, Thomas,' she said. 'I will do it if you make me.' Reece knew that she would.

But Thomas didn't know her so well. With a single motion he somehow twisted out of Reece's grip and jumped upright, springing for the gun. Reece saw its muzzle flash. Then he heard the explosion. And then Thomas was folding up in the middle. A hole had opened in his shirt, a tear of blackened flesh mixing with the fibres.

For a moment, he stayed like that, struggling to remain upright, before his knees gave way and he sank straight down like a dropped marionette.

Reece scrambled over, lifting Thomas's face, searching for signs of life. There was a patch of sticky blood soaking through his shirt. His breathing was laboured. The four youngsters were still shouting pleas not to hurt them.

Charlotte went to the door, the gun still in her hand, checking outside to see if anyone was coming. 'Troops!' she warned. He leaped to where she was. At both ends of the street big black cars now blocked the road and men with sub-machine guns were sprinting towards the café through sheets of rain. She fired twice in their direction and the men dropped into deep rivers of rainwater flowing across the ground.

Beside one of the cars Reece saw a man in a wheelchair wearing grey SS uniform. For a brief second his eyes met those of Siegfried Klaussmann.

'Take him!' Reece heard Klaussmann shout. 'Take him!'

'Out the back,' Reece said. They charged towards the kitchen. Charlotte scrambled over the bar but, as Reece was about to follow her, he felt something grab hold of his leg. He saw Thomas's eyes open and staring up to him.

'Maxime,' he rasped. 'Wait.' His hand fell and Reece saw his lips trembling, as if attempting more words. But any sound was muffled as bullets thudded into the wood beside them. By reflex, Reece fell to his side and he caught sight of a German soldier in front of the window firing a sub-machine gun. He felt another round slam into the wood, centimetres from his cheek. 'I . . .' Thomas groaned, his air fading. Then there was another sound: a pistol much closer than the sub-machine gun outside. The German dropped to the ground. Charlotte was behind the bar, her hot gun trained on the shattered void where the window had once been. The storm was now blowing through that space.

'Maxime.' Thomas was struggling to speak again, lifting his voice to fight the storm. 'I'm sorry. I didn't want to . . .' His head rolled to the side, but his chest rose and fell in short, panting breaths. Reece saw the German outside crawling away to a safer position.

'Come on!' Charlotte screamed.

Reece shouted down to Thomas. He grabbed Thomas's face and turned it up. 'I don't want your apology. Who were you informing? Who is Parade?' He felt the weight of his friend's betrayal.

'I . . .' His chest began to shake. Reece tried to hold it still.

'Maxime!' Charlotte cried again. She shot once more through the window.

'Who is he?' The other man's eyes fluttered in pain.

'Evans.'

'Evans.' The name echoed on Reece's lips as a whisper. He had been so close to Evans, had rightly suspected him and then had let him go. If only he had held on for longer, had challenged him . . . But there was no time for self-recrimination. Not now. The infection had to be cauterized. For that, they needed to know how deep it went. 'Does he know the army Order of Battle?' The only answer was hard, laboured breathing. He twisted his finger around, screwing the flesh. 'Has he given it to them?' He shook Thomas brutally, as if to shake the ebbing life back into him.

'Oh God, Maxime,' Thomas whispered. And his body seemed to fall into itself.

Then there was a rush of noise like the ocean. It crashed over them, throwing them to the floor, sending chairs and tables tumbling. It was as if the very ground had erupted.

When Reece opened his eyes again, and vision and sound returned, he saw Charlotte firing her gun and a German officer rushing towards the smashed window. And he saw the scorched hole in the floor where the grenade had fallen. Thomas lay with his neck torn open.

'I'm empty!' Charlotte screamed at him, casting her gun aside. He scrambled across the bar, barely feeling the shattered glass under his palms, and they ran out through the kitchen, across a rear courtyard and between dark buildings. They heard jackboots sprinting toward them, but a narrow alleyway strewn with rubble afforded an escape into the backstreets, and soon the only sound came from their own steps.

CHAPTER 30

6 June 1944

The Lysander dropped into an L-shaped flare path in a field west of Paris, fighting the night's storm. As its wheels thudded down Reece and Charlotte kicked sopping mud over the flares to douse them. The pilot taxied to the end of the pasture, turned around, ready to take off as soon as possible, and they scrambled into the rear seat. Charlotte had to sit on Reece's knee. It was the closest they had been since they spent their last night together six months previously. They were soaked to the skin.

The invasion was imminent. Thomas may well have told the Gestapo about Hélène, so they couldn't go to her to transmit. But they had to get back before Evans handed over the army Order of Battle and Parade One turned the Allied firestorm on their own troops.

'Hold on. It's rough up there,' the pilot called back as he revved the engine and started moving forward. The sound of the motor blotted out any more words as they pulled up into the swirling air.

'Why did Thomas do it?' Charlotte shouted above the rain rattling against the duralumin fuselage.

'I don't know. I just don't know.' He wanted to know why Thomas had done it. He could have been paid; he could have secretly favoured Hitler. Reece would probably never know. Evans could only have known about the two attempts to free Luc from a source in London, but it was Thomas who had, that morning, handed Reece over to the Gestapo – albeit on Evans's orders. And then he remembered the moments in Thomas's safe house months earlier when he had taken Reece in and given him the last of his food. Real friendship in the field was so difficult it was almost unknown. But Thomas was dead and that was an end to it. Yet Reece felt he had lost something. 'You took his gun.'

'I didn't trust him. I know what it is to betray those around you. I saw something in him that I've felt.'

The pilot kept them low to avoid the German radar and fighter patrols. They drifted over treetops and an isolated farm until the French coast appeared. The airman's voice came through the intercom. 'We'll keep on –' he began, but he was cut off by a sudden shaking of the plane, as if it had been kicked. Reece and Charlotte braced themselves against the sides and stared through the canopy. The rain blurred the night, and yet the light from the moon was enough to make out tiny black clouds exploding in the sky. Reece felt the radial engine whine and the fuselage vibrate as the pilot increased their speed. 'It's flak. They've seen us.'

'How bad?' Reece asked.

'We'll get there.' The nose of the aircraft lifted and they left the puffing flak behind. The English Channel rippled below as they sped on. After a while the pilot's voice came again. 'We're about an hour out.' Reece checked his watch. It was 2.19 a.m. British time.

But as he calculated how long it would take to get to London he caught sight of something new through the grimy canopy: two rapidly growing black spectres crossing the face of the moon. 'On your seven. High,' he barked through the intercom.

The pilot's head jerked to the left. 'Christ,' he muttered. 'They're 190s.'

They were coming in fast. The pilot increased speed again and climbed quickly – the unarmed Lysander had no defence but to attempt to lose itself in the clouds. If there had been no light that night, there would have been a chance, but it was only two days past the full moon and the pale beams picked them out like a searchlight.

The airman pushed the engine to its screaming limit, but the Germans were in full chase now – if there was ever a hope that the Lizzie hadn't been seen, it was gone. The 190s were climbing too, ready to fire.

'Go faster!' Reece shouted.

'We'll break apart!' the pilot shouted back at him. And then they had to brace themselves as the pilot banked sharply. Black explosive cannon shells were winding around them in the night. A distant bolt of lightning lit their two pursuers and the swarm of shells like a flashbulb.

Now they dived, feeling weightless as the aircraft powered towards the sea faster than gravity would take it. Reece tracked the two black beasts behind them. They were staying high, positioning to shoot from above. The shots were masked by the roar of the Lizzie's engine as it strained, until one of the little metal spears tore through the rear canopy and through the air between Charlotte's neck and Reece's eyes, before blasting out the side of the aircraft.

We have to get there, Reece thought to himself. *Just let us warn them.*

If he got there in time, he could alert them and they would be ready for Skorzeny's commando assault and the disguised Parade One units. If they had new recognition codes, they could identify and neutralize the German infiltrators and the commanders could ignore any false signals. The momentum of surprise would be turned on the Germans. But every ticking second sounded like another death.

'What if we don't make it?' Charlotte said to him.

'A slaughter,' he replied.

As he said it a series of tears opened up in the starboard wing, along the edge towards the tip. Then the tip sheered away, grabbed by the wind and tossed into the dark sea surging ten metres below them. The aircraft began to shudder unsteadily as the moonlight picked out the debris sinking under the waves.

Reece twisted around. The two fighters were directly behind and perhaps twenty metres above. The Lizzie could never outrun them and there was nowhere to hide. It seemed clear now that they would never make it back to the English coast. Another shell exploded in the fuselage.

'Hold on!' the pilot shouted through the intercom. 'I'm going to try –'

And then Reece felt his muscles drawn into his spine as the nose of the plane turned upwards. The sea fell away and was replaced by the stars in the veiled sky. And still they swept upwards, the force pushing him back into the seat. His arms wrapped around Charlotte to stop her falling through the shattered glass canopy and down to the sea. The plane's undercarriage touched the sky as the aircraft inverted perfectly, flying on its back, heading straight into the propeller blades of the two Luftwaffe fighters.

The German pilots broke, left and right, banking sharply to evade collision. They came so close that the canopy of the lead fighter grazed the broken tip of the Lysander's port wing.

Evans watched as the Morse key tapped up and down, sending short electronic pulses into the night air: *Invasion begins. Large force at sea ex Portsmouth and Southampton docks. Destination unknown. 109,000 troops first wave. Includes battleships USS Texas;*

Nevada; Arkansas. HMS Warspite; Rodney; Nelson one other. Twenty cruisers. Seven frigates. Eighteen destroyers. USS North Carolina delayed mechanical malfunction. Standby for full army Order of Battle.'

'Is that it?' the woman asked, placing her headset on the table.

'For now. We'll send more before dawn,' he replied. He lit a gasper. 'Have you ever stopped to think how much these little messages of ours are going to change it all? I mean . . .' His mind strayed to the hundreds of men he had drowned within sight of Hemsall Sands on the Dorset coast. Men weighed down by their packs and slipping to the seabed as the Kriegsmarine E-boats sped away. *And this is war, a necessity of man*, he thought to himself. *When it is over, then I can consider my penance.* 'We're actually going to change the course of history. You and me.'

She placed her headphones over her ears to listen for a reply.

Bursting between the two 190s, the RAF pilot rolled the Lysander so it was upright again.

'Now what?' Reece shouted through the intercom as he watched the two German nightfighters regroup. They had seconds before the Luftwaffe planes were back in attack position. 'Can we get back to France?'

'Not a chance.' He jerked the plane around again, turning towards the English coast. 'We can try to shake them off.'

We won't, Reece thought to himself. The pilot climbed again, once more trying for the clouds, as if they would offer some kind of protection. But Reece knew that the two German fighters could outfly the Lizzie, and as they lifted through the streaming rain he saw the two stalking forms move into firing position behind them, ready to turn on the guns. He braced himself for the rounds.

A second. Three, five seconds. No shots. Reece twisted around to see. The two fighters were still there, but suddenly they split apart, turning in opposite directions, curving away to speed back in the direction of France.

'What are they doing?' he shouted.

'I don't –' the pilot began. But then something in the air ahead of him, something coming from the English coast, made him stop and swear in surprise.

Charlotte, spotting the same sight, cried out too.

'What the hell is that?' the pilot said.

For a moment there was nothing but the roar of the engine and the sight of scores upon scores of black shadows blotting out the stars.

'Maxime,' Charlotte said. She was pointing to the sea below. Hulking dark forms silently flowed across the surface, a hundred ships and fast boats sprinting alongside them, the waves breaking on their side. And he knew it was something the like of which no one had ever seen before.

'It's the armada!' Reece shouted into the intercom. 'It's the invasion!'

'Are you sure?'

'Yes! That many crates in the air – and look, those at the back are tugs and gliders. They're troop transport. It's the invasion force.'

'Christ, yes, it is!' The pilot laughed into the intercom.

The emotions shook in them like boats in a storm: the joy of the moment that they had prayed for having finally come; hope of liberty for France and Europe; naked fury at the enemy; fear that they were too late to save the men in the waves below them. Each thought lasted a single heartbeat before another took its place. Reece saw Charlotte's arm lift across her eyes, and she shook. He placed his hand on her back.

But even as the moonlight fell on the mass of aircraft, boats and men on their way to drive a stake into the heart of the Reich, there was something strange, something he couldn't understand. 'Which direction are they heading?' he asked, watching their black journey.

The pilot checked his compass. 'Normandy. They're going to Normandy! Good hunting, boys.'

Reece felt his breath freeze in his throat. It couldn't be true.

'No,' he whispered. Then he shouted through the intercom in anger and fear. 'No, it can't be. It's not right!'

'What are you talking about?'

'It's wrong!'

'Why?'

'Calais! They're supposed to be going to Calais. It's where —' and in a moment, as the silhouettes swarmed past the moon and through the waves, Marc Reece finally understood what he had been caught in: Thomas's betrayal. Klaussmann's face in front of his as Reece told of his recce mission to the Calais harbour. MI5. The gliders full of men reciting their instructions. And, most of all, that meeting with Churchill and Delaney and the generals, where a map of the Pas de Calais had been fastened to the wall and he had circled landing points. The men in that room had sat and smoked cigars and silently watched him do it, knowing that the troopships would never land there. Now he saw it in its true, mirror-image form. After that, Parade, the Reich's prize source, had devoted so much effort to having Reece captured. And now he grasped the reason why. The writing was spread across the night and picked out in iron and steel.

And so at 2.23 a.m. on 6 June 1944, he and Charlotte looked ahead at the sight of hundreds of planes breaking through the night to blot out the moon, destined for drop zones on occupied French soil. Bombers, fighters and gliders carrying airborne troops flitted in the darkness. Below them powered an armada of warships, landing craft, minesweepers and motor gunboats carrying a hundred thousand men, the largest assault force ever assembled.

'What's wrong?' Charlotte asked, staring into his face.

'I understand now,' he said, looking out into the stars pricking the black sheet enveloping them. 'What they've done.' The aircraft around them could have dissolved in the rain and fallen to the waves below and he wouldn't have cared. For two years he had presented the world with one face while hiding another below it. As the world had caught fire he had clung to the few certainties he could reach – friendship, comradeship, duty – and a single compass bearing had shown them all to be built on shifting sands. 'Take us there faster,' he said.

'Are you hit?'

'No.'

'Can you see any damage to the crate?'

'Some shell holes. The canopy is smashed.' The rain was pouring in, running into his mouth. He cared no more about the canopy than he did about the fate of the waves below.

'We can handle that. Have any of the rounds hit anything vital?'

Reece looked at the hole in the metal fuselage. 'I don't know. Maybe. I can't see.'

'Right. Well, cross your fingers.' It was even colder in the rear seat without the canopy; the wind tore at their wet skin and the rain ran down their faces.

The pilot increased the throttle. 'Won't be long now.' As he said it the horizon seemed to lift up from the sea and gain a solid grey form. They passed over strident sea defences and within minutes saw the lights of RAF

Tangmere a few kilometres from the south coast, one of the two homes for the RAF's Special Duties squadrons. But as they approached the airfield Reece noticed a change in the engine: it wasn't just slowing, it was spluttering, on the verge of stalling.

'What's happening?' he said.

'They must have hit the header tank.'

'Will we make it?'

'We might. But the landing will be hard. Very hard. Be ready.' And as he said the words the whine of the motor suddenly became silence, leaving only the rush of the rain. The sky above the airfield was heavy with aircraft, large and small, taking off or waiting to land. Through them all, the Lizzie began to glide, moving only with the momentum it had built up. 'Hold on!' the pilot said, then he turned off the intercom. Reece knew that he was radioing a mayday to Tangmere, requesting a clear path down, a runway that they might be able to career along. The glide became a rush towards the ground.

A hundred, fifty, thirty metres from the earth. Reece began to pick out buildings, vehicles, and then men and women scurrying back and forth. He felt his stomach lift as they dropped faster, the pilot fighting to keep the craft trim, to touch the ground with the wheels, not the propellers. 'Just let us get there,' Reece whispered. And then they were falling towards the landing lights. Another aircraft, a hulking Hudson, was taxiing along the strip, in the direct path of the Lysander's descent. 'Move!' Reece screamed. But its widespread wings seemed to trundle along, inviting a collision. And then the Hudson's pilot must have seen or been alerted to the plane speeding to the earth, because he accelerated and turned away, bouncing off the landing strip into the rough ground along its side.

Reece saw the grass of the landing strip rise up to them. They were coming in far too fast, he knew. The Lysander seemed to shake as it reached ten metres above the ground, but it was level, he could feel it level. And then, at the last moment, a few metres from the ground, perhaps there was a blast of wind, or he had never realized how unstable they were, but the plane tipped on to its starboard side. They turned over, and the last thing Reece knew was the sight of the shredded wing gouging a deep rut in the ground and the metal cage around him tearing apart. Charlotte twisted and, just as he saw her face lit by flares around them, the world turned black.

Klaussmann writhed in pain. His back was the lower limit of feeling in his body; below it his legs had neither movement nor sensation, but his back necessitated morphine every few hours and it had been too long since the last dose. Now his spine burned as if he had been strapped to a table and cut apart.

'Go faster! What's wrong with you?' he demanded of his driver.

'Yes, sir.'

The hedgerows of night-time France flashed past him. He turned on the overhead light and stared again at the photograph of Marc Reece, taken in Amiens before they started work on him. The man who had killed Schmidt, who had left him unable to stand by himself, unable to wash himself.

Klaussmann had been so close to him in Paris, but Reece had disappeared. Since then, however, there had been a piece of luck. Earlier in the day, a fisherman had walked into the police station in Caen and said he had been on a boat that had picked up a couple of British spies the previous morning and delivered them to the Brittany coast. The man was now awaiting the Gestapo's arrival and asking for his brother to be released from a prison camp in return. Klaussmann switched the light off and looked out the window. 'How long before –' He broke off. 'My God!' he exclaimed.

'Sir?'

'What, are you blind? Look!' And the driver looked into the night sky to see scores of white silk parachutes fluttering to the earth.

'What is it?' he said, pressing the brake pedal hard.

'Paratroopers,' Klaussmann replied. And for a moment he was as dumbfounded by his words as his driver. 'Get us to a telephone. We have to call it in. Warn them.'

The driver accelerated again, speeding to the closest village. From his wheelchair, Klaussmann watched the man break the windows in the local café to wake up the owners and demand use of their telephone.

'This is Sturmbannführer Siegfried Klaussmann,' he barked into the handset. 'My men and I have seen paratroopers landing ten kilometres north-east of Caen in Normandy. It's the invasion.'

'It's a feint,' a Wehrmacht captain replied. 'What you saw were dummies being dropped. It's a puerile trick. They'll really come in Calais. We know that.'

'Send a brigade right now!'

'I'll do no such thing,' the captain snapped back. 'The only men we have available are reserves and they're exhausted from building defences. I'm not going to send them out because you've been taken in.'

'I know what I saw!' Klaussmann shouted at him.

'And I know better!' The receiver was slammed down.

CHAPTER 31

Where does the organizer fit into all these schemes? The organizer is the key man in all of them, and it is on his work and organization that the smooth carrying out of all the plans depends. You will have seen enough from what I have told you to realize that any one organizer has only a very small part – although an important one – in a vast organization, and that any work he carries out is only a minute part of a big general plan. You will therefore appreciate the absolute necessity of team work. Too much individualism on the part of any one organizer might go far to wreck the plan.

Never relax your precautions, and never fool yourself by thinking that the enemy are asleep. They may be watching you all the time, so watch your step.

Reece woke to the vision of stars in the sky. A sharp intake of breath, his lungs filling, cold rain running between his lips.

'Can you hear me? Son, can you hear me?' It was a woman's face. Charlotte? No, a fleshy face, older than hers. Someone wearing a green-brown uniform. A cap holding her hair down. 'Son, you're all right. You'll be all right, do you hear me?'

'I . . .' he mumbled. 'I've got to . . .'

'You're all right. You're going to the hospital as soon as we can get a car. You crashed.'

He looked around. There was salty blood on his tongue. 'Charlotte.'

'Is that who was in the plane with you? She's all right. Nothing broken,' she said.

Reece moved his neck. It hurt like fire, but he found he could sit up. He was on a stretcher but it was on the ground. He felt a surge of heat, then it all began to chill. His head filtered away a mist. 'You're going to the hospital.'

He looked around. 'What . . .' The aircraft lay beside them, its wheels and one wing smashed off. 'The pilot?'

'Unconscious. He'll live. We hope.' And then another face was in front of his. Charlotte had a gash on her cheek and was holding a white pad to it. He struggled to his feet. 'I said, you're going to –'

'No,' he said, his eyes on Charlotte's. 'I have to go somewhere else.' He looked at the woman in the WAAF uniform. 'I need a telephone. Urgently.'

She looked him up and down but recognized the seriousness. It was a day of need. 'Officers' mess over there.' She pointed.

He stumbled, stopped and retched, then he walked, followed by Charlotte. Miraculously, the telephone in the corner of the room wasn't in use and he got a line through to London.

'Yes?'

'It's Maxime. I need to speak to Delaney. Now.'

There was a pause as Delaney's assistant apparently wrestled with the decision whether to break protocol. 'I'm sorry, Maxime, he's not here. I can't say where he is.'

'Yes, you bloody can. I don't cry wolf, I need to know where he is.'

There was more silence. 'Portsmouth. Southwick House.'

'Tell him I'm coming. You got that? I'm coming.'

He hung up.

'Where?' asked Charlotte.

'Portsmouth. A few miles from here.'

Half an hour later the rain was still falling, running across the saturated earth in waves.

He no longer felt the urgency of a mission. He felt cold fury. Because somewhere between France and England the information that he bore had turned to dust in his hands.

They were standing in front of a huge Georgian manor with neoclassical columns fronted by a wide colonnade, but it was hours before sunrise and, despite the windows blazing with light and people hurrying in and out, the house looked somehow gloomy. They had been driven by a WAAF who had left them without a word before turning the car straight around and returning at speed to her station. There was a guard post at the edge of the driveway, wire and barriers preventing entry, and through dense trees Reece glimpsed long huts made of corrugated iron.

'May I see your identification, sir?' asked a Blue Cap military policeman.

'I'm Captain Reece. Here to see Major Delaney. He knows I'm coming.' Reece propped himself up against the white wood of the guard post. He could feel the very last of his energy and the Benzedrine seeping from his limbs, replaced by the pain of a bruise enveloping his chest, where he knew ribs had cracked. He saw Charlotte, exhausted by what they had come through, ready to fall into the ground.

'I need to see some identification, sir.' The Blue Cap peered at the pair in strange, torn civilian clothes, cuts on their faces.

'It's all right, Corporal,' a voice called over. They both turned to see Major Daniel Delaney walking quickly from the front of the house wearing his regimental uniform. Reece tried to see what was in his face. Did it betray anything? Anything about what was happening? Anything of what he expected Reece to say? 'Hello, Maxime, Charlotte,' he said, taking them away from the guard post. 'I was told you were coming. I didn't realize it would be so soon.' They walked a way down the path. 'My car's over there.' The driver, a young ATS woman with curling red hair, saluted. 'The garrison church, Richards,' he told her. 'Take us through the harbourside.'

The car started with a whine and they wound their way through an endless stream of tanks, tankers, half-tracks and troop vehicles. Soon they approached a checkpoint thrown across the street, through which military vehicles were slowly filtering. A private came to the driver's window and asked for their identification. Reece couldn't help but think of the many checkpoints he had been through in France. The soldier carefully checked the cards offered by Delaney and his driver, before waving them through.

'Cordon all around the town,' Delaney explained as they drove past men and women in many types of uniform, all heading towards the docks. The driver had to use the horn and shout out the window numerous times in order to get through. They came to a stop near the waterfront. All the buildings and open areas were covered with camouflage netting and arc lights gave everything a strange sheen. Fighters were on constant patrol overhead.

They parked outside a church set thirty metres from the seafront. It looked out on a sea teeming with troopships and gunboats. Hundreds of soldiers were trudging down the road in a long, heavy queue towards the seafront and a pier, where small tenders were ready to take them to larger vessels.

'The Royal Garrison church,' Delaney said, nodding towards a building of grey mediaeval stone set on ground raised slightly from the level of the street. 'Monty himself was its governor when he was a brigadier.' But the building was incomplete. A large square chancel still stood intact, but the roof of the nave had been bombed down, leaving the disembodied walls standing like mute mourners at a wake. 'Incendiaries, '41,' Delaney said. 'Charlotte, would you mind giving us a minute alone?' She glanced at Reece and stepped through the stream of young men, to the side of the road. 'We'll go in. It's a makeshift field post today and I have to see some people there soon.'

Reece and Delaney walked up the short path, between lichen-covered gravestones and a memorial to a soldier who had fallen in the Peninsular War, to the door of the church, which was guarded by a young Blue Cap. And this, Reece told himself, was where the truth would finally be dragged into the light. Some of the truth. A side of the truth.

Delaney showed his identification card and saluted as he passed through a porchway, with Reece slow in his wake.

In the old chancel, tables had been set between the dark oak choir pews. Maps were pinned to cheap boards and a wooden screen had been built to shut the nave off from the chancel – but it wasn't wide enough and there was a gap between it and one of the walls, wide enough for a man to walk through into the roofless nave.

Standing by one of the map boards, a lean commander was speaking hurriedly to a Wren as she made notes on a pad. The officer looked up as Delaney and Reece entered. Reece wiped his face on his sleeve and saw the bright smear of blood. He wouldn't be able to stand much longer. Delaney locked his eyes on the commander's and waited.

'Major, do you need the room?' the naval officer barked.

'Yes, sir.'

The commander immediately lifted a bundle of papers from the wooden lectern and led the Wren out without another word, shutting the church's door behind them with a heavy thud. The sound echoed around, resounding off the stone walls and high-vaulted ceiling until it died away like a sigh. Delaney took a step further into the room. 'You need to speak to me, Maxime,' he said as he turned around. He never saw the fist that cracked into his jaw. His feet stumbled and he fell backwards against the wooden screen that closed off the nave. And then he was on his back, pinned to the tiled floor, with Reece's bloody and bruised hands on his chest. His lapels were in Reece's fingers. The wooden lectern overturned and broke on the floor.

'Are you running him?' Reece shouted. He felt every stroke of the whip and beat of the cosh that he had suffered at the hands of Klaussmann in Amiens.

'Take your hands off –'

'Parade. Are you running him!'

Delaney twisted and put his hand under Reece's chin, forcing his head up.

'Stand down!'

Reece planted his knee into Delaney's rib, but the other man was strong too, and tipped Reece's body over. They stayed locked.

'Tell me or –'

'Look around you, Maxime. What do you see?' Delaney demanded through gritted teeth. Reece's eyes flickered to the walls. Faded and torn regimental colours hung above marble tombs and brass plaques, memorials to regiments long disbanded and men long dead. 'All for the greater good.' Reece stared at the names. All those other men who had been sacrificed.

He felt Delaney's strength beat him away and he couldn't stop himself being pushed off. He grabbed at his OC but Delaney scrambled to his feet and out through the gap to the broken nave, where the rain was falling between the blank, fire-blackened walls.

Reece sprinted after and threw all his body against his commander's back, knocking him against a pillar and tumbling with him so that they both fell to the broken floor. An empty doorway opened on to the road, showing the young men tramping towards their transports to France.

'What do you want me to tell you?' Delaney mumbled, the back of his head swimming in a puddle of filthy water.

'I want you to tell me if you're running Parade!'

Delaney lifted his face so that it almost touched Reece's. He seemed to summon up fire Reece had never seen. 'Yes!' he shouted back, his voice full of fury. 'Yes, I'm damn well running him. And I'd do it again and again and again! I'd do it a thousand times.' Reece stopped, hollowed out by the knowledge. Delaney's eyes met Reece's, looking into his dark irises and, for a moment, everything was still. It seemed to Reece that the very air had disappeared and there was nothing between them. Then Delaney spoke again, his voice cold and measured against the soft rain. 'You have no understanding of what is at stake, Maxime.'

Reece's fingers tightened on the fabric. 'He's –'

'He's a soldier! And so am I. And so are they.' Delaney pointed through the empty doorway towards the rivers of young men in green-brown uniforms shuffling towards the waterfront, to their boarding craft, to their gun boats. 'And succeeding today is more important than any of us.'

Reece formed his hand into a fist, ready to strike it down. Delaney grabbed for Reece's throat, but Reece was faster.

His fist thudded down on to Delaney's wrist, breaking a bone.

A noise made him turn – the Blue Cap sentry barely out of his teens was standing in the opening between the nave and the chancel staring at the two men, frozen by the sight. Then his fingers grabbed for his side-arm, wrenching the gun from its white holster. Reece leaped to his feet and ran for him.

The sentry hesitated as he lifted the pistol, giving Reece time to reach him and grab his forearm. A small explosion rent the air as a bullet burst from the barrel. It passed within a hand's breadth of Delaney's cheek, into an ancient stone pillar, ricocheting away in another direction. A wisp of heat and smoke from the gun was all that Reece could see of it.

He kicked away the Blue Cap's leg and, as the boy fell to the sopping floor, Reece snatched the gun, twisting it out of his hand. He trained the barrel on Delaney and placed his finger on the trigger. He could still hear the echo of the bullet's report, coming back to him again and again.

Delaney's eye met his. They stayed still for what seemed like a minute. 'Decide,' Delaney growled.

To his side, Reece saw movement. Another military policeman was charging through the doorway with his gun raised, pointing it at Reece. 'You, stop!' the soldier ordered.

Delaney was dead centre in his aim. He could fire any second and he wouldn't miss.

Delaney spoke calmly. 'Stand down,' he told the policeman.

'Sir?' the man replied, aiming at Reece.

'I said, stand down!' Delaney shouted before sinking back, his chest rising and falling in rapid bursts. 'Get the hell out of here.' Reece could see the man hesitate and lower his gun. The other policeman was looking up at him from the broken floor. 'Maxime,' Delaney sighed. His hands lifted in the air and they gazed at each other, both knowing that the ground under them could fall away at any second. 'Wait outside, both of you, say nothing to anyone,' he ordered the two Blue Caps. 'You understand?'

'Y-yes, sir.' The young man scrambled to his feet and the two left the broken body of the church.

For a long time the two SOE officers' eyes were chained together. Outside, there was the sound of men on the road, of vehicles moving and turning. Reece felt all the betrayals he had lived through: Charlotte, Thomas, the betrayal of France by so many of her own sons.

And Delaney. His betrayal was so wide and deep it would bury all the others like a sea of mud.

'Are you going to holster that weapon, Maxime?' Delaney asked quietly. Reece looked down at the pistol. It was a Colt like his own. It was pointed now at the floor, where weeds were growing through the tiles. His hand tilted it up, levelling the barrel. He felt the steel trigger moving back, closer to the trigger guard. He left it there, feeling the tension in the spring. For a long time Reece searched Delaney's eyes for recognition of what he had done, what he was guilty of, what it had cost. Then his finger relaxed. The trigger eased back into its cold position. He let the gun fall to his side. Then he turned his back on his OC. In the thin light and air, the rain drifting down to form a film on his hair and skin, he looked up to watch a wing of bombers slip overhead. 'Was it always Normandy?' he asked.

'Yes.' Delaney pushed himself to his feet and looked to the same sky and the squadrons heading for France. His uniform was muddied and wet, dripping to the ground. He brushed dirt from his face. 'We've found a way to create artificial harbours. We can use the beaches there.'

There was a pause. The engines overhead whined like wasps. 'So they've died for nothing.' Richard, Thomas, Sebastien.

'It isn't nothing. It's the mission. It's how the mission succeeds.' Delaney stopped and his voice fell. 'We had to make the Germans think we were going for the Pas de Calais. The best way of doing that was to let them beat it out of you. We ran Parade so he could give you to them.'

'Thomas?'

'He was under the highest orders to hand you to Klaussmann when you went back. He hated the instruction. Don't blame him,' Delaney said.

'The meeting with Churchill. That was all to reinforce the impression?' Reece had felt such a sense of duty that day, of a shared commitment to ending tyranny. Now he knew he had been their pawn sacrifice, a dupe first and last, for a plan he had no idea had wrapped him up. He knew it was just, but he had had no part in the bargain. He despised it with all the hate that he could clutch and he wanted to see Richard's blood and Thomas's blood on Delaney's hands.

'Yes.' Delaney paused and stared at Reece's back. 'I'm sorry you went through what you did.'

Sorry. Reece believed him. He didn't care. 'Did they believe it?' asked Reece, searching for something at the bottom of it all. 'Calais.'

'Yes, they believed it.'

'You're sure?'

'Klaussmann told Berlin as soon as you talked.'

Reece wiped his face. 'So why did you send me back?' He wanted to know it was worth Thomas's death too. In the end, Thomas had been as loyal as he had. Reece felt guilty that he was the one who had survived, that Thomas had lain there, his body ripped by the grenade.

Delaney walked to the doorway and stood beside Reece, staring at the shuffling troops. 'That was hard. Yes, that was hard. One or two in the German high command were growing suspicious that Parade could provide such high-level intelligence. Sending you there told them we were worried and desperate to know who he was. He's about to send them plans suggesting Normandy is just a feint and the real invasion is still to come in Calais. We need them to believe him and keep their forces away from the action.'

A blue darkness seemed to mist over Reece's vision. 'You sent me back to be caught.'

'I sent you back to be caught. And to talk. And to mislead them. And to save it all. Wouldn't you?' He turned and lifted his hands, palms up, asking for reason and understanding. 'We estimate that every extra day Rommel's Fifteenth Army waits for us in Calais, waits for a force that will never come, we save ten thousand soldiers and God knows how many tanks and guns. You were a part of the operation. It was the operation above all. And it's worked.'

'Parade One's a plan to impersonate American officers. But you know it all, don't you?'

Delaney nodded. 'They won't get within a hundred miles of those posts.'

A small brown bird soared down through the open roof, alighted on a broken pillar then flitted through to the sanctuary.

All that he had been told, all he had been led to believe, by Churchill's subtle questions, by Delaney's insinuations, by the desperation of the mission to free him from Amiens, had been a deception that he was to pass on to the Germans like a virus.

Would he have done the same as his commander? He didn't know. He had never had to make the decision. He could picture himself behind Delaney's desk, the papers laid out in front of him, the choice burning through in black ink, but he would never truly know the heat of that calculation.

'You created Parade.'

'Someone had to. I did it.'

'Behind the mask. There you are.'

'If you want to see it that way.' They turned towards the sea, where the fleet lay, the greatest air, sea and land armada ever assembled. The boats and ships seemed so still, even though the beating waves were high. 'Pity the poor Germans,' Delaney said under his breath. 'They don't even know the storm that's coming to them.'

A platoon of Pioneers shuffled towards their embarkation point. A staff car appeared from the same direction and a senior American officer emerged, surrounded by other officers.

'What was it called?' Reece asked, turning to look Delaney in the eye.

'What?'

'Its name. The operation. The one I was part of.'

Delaney wiped the rain from his face with his sleeve. 'It's had a few names. We called it Jael, then Torrent. Then we called it Appendix Y.'

'And now?'

'Maxime . . .'

'What is it now?'

'Fortitude. It's called Operation Fortitude.'

Reece turned the word over in his mind. Fortitude. What so many saints had placed their trust in. But it was another moral pillar that cracked and splintered as he tried to grasp it. All the roofs were falling in and the foundations cracking under their feet. 'Was there ever a real Parade?'

'There was, briefly,' Delaney replied. 'He was a desk officer in 5's American Liaison section. Fascist leanings.'

'But you caught him?'

'At the start of the war a Dutch SD agent, a pianist, walked into a police station in Liverpool and offered to work as a double for us. She led us straight to our little traitor. Evans has been impersonating him from the beginning, pointing them towards Calais. He knows the Nazi mindset. He's seen it first hand – even flirted with it a bit when he was a student, truth be told – so he's a good mimic. But we had to feed them some genuine information along the way to make them trust him. Good men have died for it.' He looked at Reece. There was silence between them, and noise from the troops all around. 'What are you going to do now, Maxime?' he asked. 'You could probably break my neck before anyone could stop you. You know how to do it.'

Reece looked him up and down. He saw the uniform and the small ribbons on the left breast designating service or bravery. And he turned and walked away, standing in the doorway to the churchyard, the pain in his limbs and his fingers beating with the blood through his veins.

'We could do with you back out there.'

Reece stopped. The words were unavoidable.

'This is just the beginning. It will take months just to break out of Normandy. We need Paris to rise up. We need someone there to take charge. Weapons. Barricades, when the day comes. Will it be you?'

Reece felt air enter his lungs, lifting his chest. When it sank again he walked on, along the path through the headstones to the street. The Blue Caps were standing guard at the entrance to the chancel with their pistol holsters unclipped. Reece saw them glance towards Delaney.

Somehow, until he was in the middle of it, Reece hadn't realized the chaos of that street. Hundreds of bodies were swarming, men and women shouting. Someone barged into him and said something, but he didn't hear the words – an oath, an apology or a warning. He walked a few paces and, when he lifted his eyes from his feet, he found he was in the line of young men laughing and joking, pushing towards the quayside and the boats that would take them across the Channel. It was a stream that led to a sea that led to a beach that led to a battleground, and he had seen it before and he would see it again.

'Move yourself, mate,' muttered one of the figures shoving past. Reece gazed at him. An infantryman, twenty years old, perhaps. 'Blokes trying to come through. Don't want to miss it all, do we?' His mates chuckled.

'It'll still be there,' Reece muttered. He wanted to tell them what it meant to be on the front line, to dive for cover and lose friends to shrapnel. He couldn't tell them.

'Sure of that? Still a few Jerries to share around. Well, that's nice to know.' As they laughed again, Reece saw Charlotte's face flash between their shambling bodies. She watched him come closer as someone began playing a mouth organ, a jaunty tune that contrasted with the slow pace of the men it was for. He reached her in a thin alleyway between two buildings. The ground was muddy with tramped dirt.

He told her.

She gazed at him, into his eyes. Then she tossed her cigarette to the pavement, where it lay burning in the dust. 'What now?'

He lifted his face to her. 'Delaney needs people back there,' he said. A young sailor squeezing past them tripped and dropped a metal canister at their feet. He apologized, hefted it over his shoulder and continued on his way. Reece saw him rejoin the line of men, then his vision swept over the heads of the moving mass to the dull sky peppered with fighters and soaring gulls, and to where Delaney stood watching him, from ground raised above the level of the street.

'In Paris?'

'Yes.'

A staff car stopped beside the church. Its door opened and Huw Evans got out, carrying a sheaf of papers. He approached Delaney, who took them without moving his gaze from Reece. Evans followed the OC's line of sight until he met Reece's eyes. Soldiers tramped past but the three of them remained still.

'You don't have to go,' she said.

Reece watched his OC and the man who had brought all the brutality of the Reich down upon him. 'I'm going.'

She pulled her coat tighter. 'Yes. I know.'

'Will you come?'

'I'll come,' she said.

'It will be harder this time. The Germans will be desperate.'

'What's our mission?'

'The Resistance will be open soon, an uprising. They need people to direct it.' The men crowding the road began a song, led by the mouth organ. Reece recognized the melody but didn't know where it was from. A show tune, he thought. It had been popular some years ago.

'What are you thinking of?' she asked.

'Paris.' He looked out at the boats on the sea. 'The Germans running. Their barracks burning down. Our people taking the streets.' He placed his foot on the still-smouldering cigarette butt and screwed it into the ground. Its ash spread out. 'I'm thinking of that.'

Historical Notes

The book is inspired by the tragic story of the Physician circuit, which operated in Paris and northern France. The network was built by Major Francis Suttill, service name Prosper, an immensely brave man. Brought up in France by an English father and a French mother, he was recruited to SOE in 1940 and parachuted into France in 1942.

Physician – widely known as Prosper, after its organizer – was a very large and successful network until 1943, when it was betrayed to the SD and began to unravel. The traitor was Henri Déricourt, a French air force officer who had joined SOE and been assigned to the circuit to identify drop zones for the RAF. In France, he was observed by SOE agents to meet SD officers. This may have been part of a plan to infiltrate the SD, but at least one SOE agent informed London that he suspected Déricourt of being a double agent.

Suttill himself was captured in June 1943 and tortured for information. One of the German interrogators later claimed he gave up intelligence in return for the lives of his fellow agents being spared, although this is uncertain. He was later taken to the Sachsenhausen concentration camp and executed in 1945.

After the war, Déricourt was investigated for the crime of betraying Prosper. His defence was that he had been secretly recruited by MI6 and had acted under orders. Evidence emerged – certainly not conclusive, but substantial – that he was telling the truth. Why MI6 would do such a thing is uncertain, but in May 1943 Suttill made a trip to England, possibly for a meeting with Churchill. It is believed by some that Prosper was fed disinformation regarding the time and place of D-Day – that it would come in northern France in 1943 – and the disinformation was to be extracted from him by the Gestapo, thus tying up many German troops in the wrong place at the wrong time.

We will probably never know the truth. Many of the relevant SOE files were destroyed in a fire in 1945. Some of the MI6 files will be opened in the 2040s, under the Hundred-year Rule. Perhaps they will contain a clue.

Francis Suttill was posthumously awarded the DSO. His name appears on the SOE memorial at Valençay in France.

M. R. D. Foot's *SOE: An Outline History of the Special Operations Executive* is the official history of the organization and still the most important, although it does tend to go for breadth over depth of analysis. For a very personal analysis of what lies behind Prosper's death, *Prosper: Major Suttill's French Resistance Network* is written by Suttill's son, also called Francis.

If Prosper really was betrayed as part of an Allied deception, it was part of Operation Fortitude, a huge, ambitious and ultimately astonishingly successful plan to misdirect Germany as to the location of the invasion, pointing them towards Calais (and, to a lesser extent, Norway). The most important part of the operation rested on the Double Cross system – German agents in Britain who were really working for MI5 and subtly disinforming Berlin. Germany sent a number of agents into Britain by parachute or via neutral third countries, but Britain found them all and they were given the choice of turning double or trial and execution as spies. A number of those who were part of Double Cross had volunteered to the German intelligence services specifically to betray them to the Allies.

The other main plan was the creation of a fake army, the First United States Army Group. It consisted entirely of a small number of men deemed medically unfit for combat, blow-up tanks and plywood aeroplanes. Radio chatter to and from it was faked. And when D-Day eventually came, dummies were dropped by the RAF and USAF to send the German defenders to the wrong beaches.

Ben Macintyre's *Double Cross* is a fine, very accessible narrative of the use of the double agents.

Wilhelm Canaris is a difficult figure. An early supporter of Hitler as a man who could rebuild Germany's nation and military, he later refused to let the Abwehr be used for the Holocaust – in fact recruiting a number of Jewish agents in order that they could escape using Abwehr papers. He was deposed after the Gestapo became aware of his connection to anti-Hitler plots and was later taken to a concentration camp, where he was executed by strangulation. But let us not whitewash his early support for Nazism, when it was clear where the movement was heading.

Biographies of Canaris are few and far between. *Hitler's Spy Chief* by Richard Bassett is as good as any but is unable to give many insights into the man, rather than his work.

Otto Skorzeny was in charge of Operation Griffin, a pet plan of Hitler's to defend against the Allied invasion using English-speaking troops in American uniforms. It was deployed during the Battle of the Bulge, the last German counter-offensive against the invasion, but failed largely because the Germans could find too few men who could speak good English and too little captured materiel. The operation was soon detected by the Allied command and its main effect was to slow some of the Allied advance, as extra security was introduced, such as asking unrecognized soldiers about their favourite baseball teams.

*

Operation Jericho was a daring RAF raid against Amiens prison. Extraordinary footage of the raid can be watched online, as can the 1941 film *Target for To-Night*, which focuses on 'Pick' Pickard. The rallying speech Pickard gives in this book before Jericho is the one he gave that morning.

Amiens prison was a strange target. Quite why the RAF would hit it is open to question. It is possible that the plan was part of Fortitude, to make the Germans believe that a high-value agent or Resistance leader – 'terrorists', as the Gestapo usually referred to them – was in the prison, again making them focus on the nearby Pas de Calais as the invasion point, or it may have been to boost Resistance morale.

The Jail Busters by Robert Lyman is a strong narration of the story, with discussion of the motivation behind the raid.

The assault on British and Canadian troops practising beach landings is based on Exercise Tiger, a disastrous April 1944 training exercise for American troops designed to introduce them to amphibious assault. Many were killed by friendly fire on the first day, after confusion about the start time of the exercise. Hundreds more perished the following day, when nine German E-boats attacked the exercise convoy. Overall, more than seven hundred men lost their lives. The affair was covered up in order to save the morale of the other troops who were destined for D-Day.

The Finishing School is back to being Beaulieu, a fine country house with an excellent museum about the SOE agents who trained there.

The London Cage is now the Russian embassy.

Acknowledgements

Thanks, as ever, to my agents, Simon Trewin and Jon Wood, and editor Joel Richardson. Advice was sought and freely given by Juliette Pattinson at the University of Kent; Thomas Weber at the University of Aberdeen; and James Daly at the D-Day Museum, Portsmouth. Ed Latham's feedback on the story was invaluable, and Katharina Neureiter made sure my German language made sense.